With a shout of triumph, the first Kubrati leaped off the gangway and onto the stone of the wall. That shout turned to a scream of agony moments later; beset by three imperials, he went down under spear and sword. So did the next Kubrati, and the next.

After that, even the nomads' fierce courage faltered. A Videssian, caught up in the same unthinking battle fury as his foes, jumped up onto the gangway and ran at the Kubratoi, slashing as he went.

"No!" Maniakes shouted. "Come back! Don't throw yourself away!"

The soldier paid no heed. He cut down the first nomad he faced but was pierced by an arrow a moment later. Leaping over the Kubrati he'd just slain, he seized the fellow behind that one by the waist and then leaped off the narrow plank, taking his foe down with him . . .

D0042428

By Harry Turtledove
Published by Ballantine Books:

VIDESSOS
BESIEGED

Book Four of
The Time of Troubles

Harry Turtledove

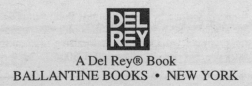

A Del Rey® Book
BALLANTINE BOOKS • NEW YORK

A Del Rey ® Book
Published by The Ballantine Publishing Group
Copyright © 1998 by Harry Turtledove

All rights reserved under International and Pan-American Copyright Conventions. Published in the United States by The Ballantine Publishing Group, a division of Random House, Inc., New York, and simultaneously in Canada by Random House of Canada Limited, Toronto.

http://www.randomhouse.com

Library of Congress Catalog Card Number: 98-96319

ISBN 0-345-40299-5

Manufactured in the United States of America

First Edition: November 1998

10 9 8 7 6 5 4 3

VIDESSOS BESIEGED

I

Outside the imperial residence in Videssos the city, the cherry trees were in bloom. Soon their pink and white petals would drift the ground and walks around the residence in much the same way as the snow had done till a few weeks earlier.

Maniakes threw wide the shutters and peered out at the grove that made the residence the only place in the palace quarter where the Avtokrator of the Videssians could find even a semblance of privacy. One of the many bees buzzing by made as if to land on him. He drew back in a hurry. When spring came, the bees were a nuisance: they were, in fact, almost the only thing he disliked about spring.

"Phos be praised," he said, sketching the good god's sun-circle above his heart, "now that good sailing weather is here again, we can get out of the city and fight another round with the men of Makuran." He made a sour face. "I *know* the Makuraners are my enemies. Here in the capital, foes come disguised, so they're harder to spot."

"Once we've beaten the Makuraners, things will go better here," said his wife, Lysia. She came over and took his hand and also looked at the flowering cherry trees. When another bee tried to fly into the chamber, she snatched up a sheet of parchment from Maniakes' desk and used it to chivvy the bee back outside. Then she smiled at him. "There. That's more use than we usually get out of tax registers."

"How right you are," he said fondly. Lysia had a gift for not taking the ponderous Videssian bureaucratic machine too seriously, while to the army of tax collectors and clerks and scribes and account reckoners it was not only as important as life itself but was in fact life itself. Better yet, she helped Maniakes not take the

1

bureaucracy too seriously, either, a gift he often thought beyond price.

He hugged her. The two of them were not very far apart in height. They were a little stockier, a little swarthier than the Videssian norm, being of Vaspurakaner blood even if almost completely Videssian in the way they thought. Both had lustrous, almost blue-black hair, bushy eyebrows—though Lysia plucked hers to conform to imperial standards of beauty—and high-arched, prominent noses. Maniakes' thick, heavy beard covered his cheeks and chin, but under the beard that chin, he suspected, was a match for Lysia's strong one.

Their resemblance was no mere accident of having sprung from the same homeland, nor was it a case of husband and wife coming to look like each other over the course of living together—such cases being more often joked about than seen. They were not just husband and wife; they were also first cousins—Lysia's father, Symvatios, was younger brother to Maniakes' father, with whom the Avtokrator shared his name.

Lysia said, "When we sail for the west to fight the Makuraners, have you decided whether to use the northern or southern route?"

"The southern, I think," Maniakes answered. "If we land in the north, we have to thread our way through all the valleys and passes of the Erzerum Mountains. That's the longer way to have to go to aim for Mashiz, too. I want Sharbaraz—" He pronounced it *Sarbaraz*; like most who spoke Videssian, he had trouble with the *sh* sound, though he could sometimes bring it out. "—King of Kings to be sweating in his capital the way I've sweated here in the city."

"He's had to worry more than we have, the past couple of years," Lysia said. "The Cattle Crossing holds the Makuraners away from Videssos the city, but the Tutub and the Tib are only rivers. If we can beat the soldiers the Makuraners put up against us, we *will* sack Mashiz."

She sounded confident. Maniakes felt confident. "We should have done it last year," he said. "I never expected them to be able to hold us when we were moving down the Tib." He shrugged. "That's why you have to fight the war, though: to see which of the things you don't expect come true."

"We hurt them even so," Lysia said.

She spoke consolingly, but what she said was true. Maniakes nodded. "I'd say the Thousand Cities between the Tutub and the

Tib are down to about eight hundred, thanks to us." He knew he was exaggerating the destruction the Videssians had wrought, but he didn't think there really were a thousand cities on the flood-plain, either. "Not only do we hurt the Makuraners doing that, but we loosen their hold on the westlands of Videssos, too."

"This is a strange war," Lysia observed.

Maniakes nodded again. Makuran held virtually all of the Vid-essian westlands, the great peninsula on the far side of the Cattle Crossing. All his efforts to drive them out of the westlands by go-ing straight at them had failed. But Makuran, a landlocked power till its invasion of Videssos, had no ships to speak of. Controlling the sea had let Maniakes strike at the enemy's heartland even if he couldn't free his own.

He slipped an arm around Lysia's waist. "You're falling down on the job, you know." She raised an eyebrow in a silent question. He explained: "The last two years, you've had a baby while we were on campaign in the Land of the Thousand Cities."

She laughed so hard, she pulled free of him. He stared at her in some surprise; he hadn't thought the small joke anywhere near that funny. Then she said, "I was going to tell you in a few more days, when I was surer, but . . . I think I'm expecting again."

"Do you?" he said. Now Lysia nodded. He hugged her, shaking his head all the while. "I think we're going to have to make the imperial residence bigger, with all the children it will be holding."

"I think you may be right," Lysia answered. Maniakes had a young daughter and son, Evtropia and Likarios, by his first wife, Niphone, who had died giving birth to Likarios. Lysia had borne him two boys, Symvatios and Tatoules. The one, a toddler now, was named for her father—Maniakes' uncle—the other for Mani-akes' younger brother, who had been missing for years in the chaos that surrounded the Makuraner conquest of the westlands. Mani-akes knew Tatoules almost had to be dead, and had chosen the name to remember him.

Maniakes also had a bastard son, Atalarikhos, back on the east-ern island of Kalavria. His father had governed there before their clan rose up against the vicious and inept rule of the previous Av-tokrator, Genesios, who had murdered his way to the throne and tried to stay on it with even more wholesale slaughter. Now Mani-akes prudently mentioned neither Atalarikhos nor his mother, a yellow-haired Haloga woman named Rotrude, to Lysia.

Instead of bringing up such a sticky topic, he said, "Shall we hold a feast to celebrate the good news?"

To his surprise and disappointment, Lysia shook her head. "What would be the point? The clan stands by us, and your soldiers do, because you've managed to make the Makuraners thoughtful about fighting Videssians, but most of the nobles would find polite reasons to be someplace else."

He scowled, his eyebrows coming down in a thick black line above his eyes. She was right, and he knew it, and he hated it. "The patriarch gave us a dispensation," he growled.

"So he did," Lysia agreed, "after you almost sailed back to Kalavria three years ago. That frightened Agathios into it. But only about half the priests acknowledge it, and far fewer than half the nobles."

"I know what will make everyone acknowledge it," Maniakes said grimly. Lysia half turned away from him, as if to say nothing would make people acknowledge the legitimacy of their union. But he found a magic word, one as potent as if spoken by a chorus of the most powerful mages from the Sorcerers' Collegium: "Victory."

Maniakes rode through the streets of Videssos the city toward the harbor of Kontoskalion on the southern side of the capital. Before him marched a dozen parasol-bearers, their bright silk canopies announcing to all who saw that the Emperor was moving through his capital. Because that thought might not fill everyone with transports of delight, around him tramped a good-sized bodyguard.

About half the men in the detachment were Videssians, the other half Halogai—mercenaries from out of the cold north. The native Videssians were little and dark and lithe, armed with swords. The Halogai, big, fair men, some of whom wore their long, pale hair in braids, carried long-handled axes that could take a head with one blow.

At the front of the procession marched a herald who shouted, "Way! Make way for the Avtokrator of the Videssians!" People on foot scrambled out of the street. People riding horses or leading donkeys either sped up or found side streets. One teamster driving a heavy wagon neither sped up nor turned. A Haloga suggested, "Let's kill him," to Maniakes.

He made no effort to lower his voice. Maniakes did not think he was joking: the Halogai had a very direct way of looking at the world. Evidently, the teamster didn't think he was joking, either. All of a sudden, the wagon not only sped up but also moved onto a side street. No longer impeded, the procession moved on toward the harbor of Kontoskalion.

Maniakes rode past one of the hundreds of temples in Videssos the city dedicated to the worship of Phos. Perhaps drawn by the herald's cries, the priest who served the temple came out to look at the Avtokrator and his companions. Like other clerics, he shaved his pate and let his beard grow full and bushy. He wore a plain wool robe, dyed blue, with a cloth-of-gold circle representing Phos' sun sewn above his left breast.

Maniakes waved to him. Instead of waving back, the priest spat on the ground, as if rejecting Phos' evil rival, Skotos. Some of the Videssian guardsmen snarled at him. He glared back toward them, armored in his faith and therefore unafraid. After a moment, he deliberately turned his back and went into the temple once more.

"Bastard," one of the Videssian guards snarled. "Anybody who insults you like that, your Majesty—"

"We kill him." Three Halogai said it together. They cared nothing for Videssian priests; they did not follow Phos, but still cleaved to the bloodthirsty gods of Halogaland. If ever a priest needed killing, they were the men to do the job.

But Maniakes said, "No, no. I can't afford trouble with the priesthood now. Just let it go. One of these days, maybe—"

That satisfied the Halogai, whose waits for revenge could span years, even generations. Inside, though, Maniakes ached at the priest's gesture. The half of the clergy who accepted his marriage to Lysia did so grudgingly, as if against their better judgment. The ones who rejected it as incestuous, though, did so ferociously and altogether without hesitation.

"One more reason to get to Makuran," Maniakes muttered. Makuraner custom saw nothing out of the ordinary about two first cousins marrying, or even uncles marrying nieces. And the Makuraners worshiped the God, not Phos; the only Videssian priests anywhere near Maniakes would be the ones he brought along for their gift of the healing art and for enspiriting the army. All of those would be men who tolerated his family arrangements, at least nominally.

Reaching the harbor was a relief. The sailors greeted him with genuine affection; they, like his soldiers, cared more that he led them to victory than that he'd married his first cousin. He had hoped the whole Empire of Videssos would come to see things the same way. It hadn't happened yet. He was beginning to wonder if it ever would.

Most of the ships tied up to the wharfs at the harbor of Kontoskalion were beamy merchantmen that would carry his men and horses and gear to the harbor of Lyssaion, where they would disembark and begin their campaign. Almost all the war galleys that would protect the fleet of merchant vessels were moored in the Neorhesian harbor, on the northern shore of Videssos the city.

Maniakes' flagship, the *Renewal*, was an exception to the rule. The *Renewal* was neither the biggest nor the swiftest nor the newest galley in the fleet. It was, however, the galley in which Maniakes had sailed from the island of Kalavria to Videssos the city when he rebelled against Genesios, and so had sentimental value for him. It stayed in the harbor of Kontoskalion because that was where it had first landed at the capital: sentiment again.

Thrax, the drungarios of the fleet, sprang from the deck of the *Renewal* to the wharf to which it was tied and hurried toward Maniakes. "Phos bless you, your Majesty," he said. "It's good to see you."

"And you," Maniakes said, wondering for what was far from the first time whether he also kept Thrax around for sentimental reasons. The drungarios looked like a sailor: he was lean and lithe, with the sun-dark skin and carved features of a man who'd lived his whole life outdoors. He was not old, but his hair and beard had gone shining silver, which gave him a truly striking aspect.

He'd captained the *Renewal* on the journey from Kalavria to the capital. Now he headed the whole Videssian navy. He'd never done anything to make Maniakes think giving him that post was a dreadful mistake. On the other hand, he'd never done anything to make Maniakes delighted he'd given him the post. *Competent but uninspired* summed him up.

As now: he said, "Your Majesty, we'll be ready to sail on the day you appointed." When he told you something like that, you could rely on it.

"Can we be ready five days earlier than that?" Maniakes asked. "The sooner we sail, the sooner we take the war back to Makuran." *And,* he added to himself, *the sooner Lysia and I can get out of Videssos the city.*

Thrax frowned. "I'm not so sure about that, your Majesty. I've set everything up to meet the day you first asked of me. To change it would be hard, and probably not worth doing." He hadn't thought about speeding up, then, and didn't want to think about it.

"See what you can do," Maniakes told him. When Thrax knew in advance what he was supposed to do, he did it with unruffled ease. When he had to improvise, he didn't come off so well. One thing that seemed to be missing from his makeup was any capacity for original thought.

"I'll try, your Majesty," he said after a moment.

"It's not that hard," Maniakes said encouragingly. He was used to improvising; both his campaigns in the Land of the Thousand Cities had been nothing but improvisation from beginning to end, as, for that matter, had been the campaign against Genesios that had won him the throne. He'd seen, though, that not everyone had the knack for seizing what the moment presented.

A cart rattled up the wharf to one of the merchantmen. The driver scrambled down, gave his mule a handful of raisins, and started tossing sacks of grain—or possibly beans—to the sailors, who stowed them below the deck and, with luck, out of the bilgewater.

Maniakes pointed to the carter. "You need to find out where he and all the people like him are coming from, how long they travel, how long they take to unload here, and how long to get back again. Then you need to sit down with the heads of the storehouses and see if there's anything they can do to make things move faster. If they can load more carts at once than we're sending, for instance—"

He broke off there, because Thrax was clutching both hands to his head as if it were about to explode like a tightly stoppered jar left too long in a cook fire. "Have mercy on my poor wits, your Majesty!" the drungarios cried. "How am I supposed to remember all that?"

"It's not that hard," Maniakes repeated, but, by Thrax's tormented expression, it was indeed that hard, or maybe harder. He felt as if he were the ecumenical patriarch, trying to explain some abstruse theological point to a drunken peasant who didn't care about theology in the first place and was more interested in pissing on his shoes.

"Everything *will* be ready on the day you first set me," Thrax promised, and Maniakes believed that. Thrax heaved a martyred sigh, as the holy Kveldoulphios might have done when he discovered his fellow Halogai weren't going to join him in converting to the worship of Phos, but were going to slay him to stop him from preaching at them. Sighing again, the drungarios went on, "And I'll *try* to have things ready as far before then as I can, even if I have to turn this whole harbor all cattywumpus to do it."

"That's the spirit!" Maniakes slapped him on the back. "I know you'll do what needs doing, and I know you'll do it well."

What a liar I've come to be since I donned the red boots, Maniakes thought. But a Thrax who was trying to meet the demands he'd put on him was far preferable to a Thrax who was merely . . . trying.

As Thrax and Maniakes walked from one wharf to the next, the drungarios did his best to be helpful. He knew what was supposed to be happening by the original schedule, and talked knowledgeably about that. He also began thinking about what he'd have to do to make that schedule move faster. Having once rejected changes out of hand, he now took the view that any cooperation he showed afterward was bound to be reckoned an improvement. He was right, too, though Maniakes did his best not to let on about that.

Once Maniakes had done everything he could to encourage the drungarios, he remounted and rode off: Thrax wasn't the only man under whom he had to light a fire. He made a point of returning to the palace quarter by a route different from the one he'd used to go out to the harbor of Kontoskalion, not wanting to meet again the priest who had spurned him.

But it was difficult to travel more than a couple of blocks in Videssos the city without passing a temple, whether a magnificent one like the High Temple or the one dedicated to the memory of the holy Phravitas where Avtokrators and their close kin were entombed or a little building distinguishable from a house only by the spire topped by a gilded globe springing from its roof.

And so, passing by one of those temples, Maniakes found himself watched and measured by another priest, watched and measured and rejected. For a copper or two, he would have set his Haloga guards on the blue-robe this time. But, however tempting he found the notion of taking a bloody revenge, he set it aside once more. It would embroil him with the ecumenical patriarch, and he could not afford that. Being at odds with the temples would put a crimp, maybe a fatal crimp, into the war against Makuran.

And so Maniakes endured the insult. It sometimes looked as if, even if he captured Mashiz, the capital of Makuran, and brought back the head of Sharbaraz King of Kings to hang on the Milestone in the plaza of Palamas like that of a common criminal or a rebel, a good many clerics would keep on thinking him a sinner shielded from Phos' light.

He sighed. No matter what they thought of him while he was winning wars, they'd think ten times worse if he lost—to say nothing of what would happen to the Empire if he lost. He had to go on winning, then, to give the clergy the chance to go on despising him.

Kameas the vestiarios said, "Your Majesty, supper is ready." The eunuch's voice lay in that nameless range between tenor and contralto. His plump cheeks were smooth; they gleamed in the lamplight. When he turned to lead Maniakes and Lysia to the dining room, he glided along like a ship running before the wind, the little quick mincing steps he took invisible under his robes.

Maniakes looked forward to meals with his kin, who were, inevitably, Lysia's kin, as well. They didn't condemn him for what he'd done. The only one of his close kin who had condemned him, his younger brother Parsmanios, had joined with the traitorous general Tzikas to try to slay him by magic. Parsmanios, these days, was exiled to a monastery in distant Prista, the Videssian outpost on the edge of the Pardrayan steppe that ran north from the northern shore of the Videssian Sea.

Tzikas, these days, was in Makuran. As far as Maniakes was concerned, the Makuraners were welcome to him. Maniakes presumed Tzikas was doing his best to betray Abivard, the Makuraner commander. Wherever Tzikas was, he would try to betray someone. Treason seemed in his blood.

Kameas said, "Your family will be pleased to see you, your Majesty."

"Of course, they will," Lysia said. "He's the Avtokrator. They can't start eating till he gets there."

The vestiarios gave her a sidelong look. "You are, of course, correct, Empress, but that was not the subject of my allusion."

"I know," Lysia said cheerfully. "So what? A little irrelevance never hurt anyone, now did it?"

Kameas coughed and didn't answer. His life was altogether

regular—without the distraction of desire, how could it be otherwise?—and his duties required him to impose regular functioning on the Avtokrator. To him, irrelevance was a distraction at best, a nuisance at worst.

Maniakes suppressed a snort, so as not to annoy the vestiarios. He was by nature a methodical sort himself. He used to have a habit of charging ahead without fully examining consequences. Defeats at the hands of the Kubratoi and Makuraners had taught him to be more cautious. Now he relied on Lysia to keep him from getting too stodgy.

Kameas strode out ahead of him and Lysia, to announce their arrival to their relatives. Somebody in the dining room loudy clapped his hands. Maniakes turned to Lysia and said, "I'm going to give your brother a good, swift kick in the fundament, in the hope that he keeps his brains there."

"With Rhegorios?" Lysia shook her head. "You'd probably just stir up another prank." Maniakes sighed and nodded. Even more than Lysia—or perhaps just more openly—her brother delighted in raising ruckuses.

Rhegorios flung a roll at Maniakes as the Avtokrator walked through the doorway. Maniakes snatched it out of the air; his cousin had played such games before. "Lese majesty," he said, and threw it back, hitting Rhegorios on the shoulder. "Send for the headsman."

Some Avtokrators, not least among them Maniakes' predecessor, the late, unlamented Genesios, would have meant that literally. Maniakes was joking, and obviously joking at that. Rhegorios had no hesitation in shooting back, with words this time rather than bread: "Anyone who keeps us waiting and hungry deserves whatever happens to him."

"He's right," the elder Maniakes declared, glaring at his son and namesake with a scowl too ferocious to be convincing. "I'm about to waste away to a shadow."

"A noisy, grumbling shadow," the Avtokrator replied. His father chuckled. He was twice Maniakes Avtokrator's age, shorter, heavier, grayer, more wrinkled: when Maniakes looked at his father; he saw himself as he would look if he managed to stay on the throne and stay alive till he was seventy or so. The elder Maniakes, a veteran cavalry commander, also carried a mind well stocked in treacheries and deviousness of all sorts.

"It could be worse," said Symvatios, Lysia's father and the elder Maniakes' younger brother. "We could all be in the Hall of the Nineteen Couches, lying on those silly things propped up on one elbow while from the elbow up our arms go numb." He chuckled; he was both handsomer and jollier than the elder Maniakes, just as his son Rhegorios was handsomer and jollier than Maniakes Avtokrator.

"Eating reclining is a dying ceremony," Maniakes said. "The sooner they wrap it in a shroud and bury it, the happier I'll be."

Kameas' beardless face was eloquent with distress. Reproachfully, he said, "Your Majesty, you promised early in your reign to suffer long-standing usages to continue, even if they were not in all ways to your taste."

"Suffer is just what we do when we eat in the Hall of the Nineteen Couches," Rhegorios said. He was not shy about laughing at his own wit.

"Your Majesty, will you be gracious enough to tell your brother-in-law the Sevastos that his jests are in questionable taste?"

Using the word *taste* in a context that included dining was asking for trouble. The gleam in Rhegorios' eye said he was casting about for the way to cause the most trouble he could. Before he could cause any, Maniakes forestalled him, saying to Kameas, "Esteemed sir—" Eunuchs had special honorifics reserved for them alone. "—I did indeed say that. You will—occasionally—be able to get my family and me to eat in the antique style. Whether you'll be able to get us to enjoy it is probably another matter."

Kameas shrugged. As far as he was concerned, that old customs were old was reason aplenty to continue them. That made some sense to Maniakes—how could you keep track of who you were if you didn't know who your grandparents had been?—but not enough. Ritual for ritual's sake was to him as blind in everyday life as it was in the temples.

"This evening," Kameas said, "we have a thoroughly modern supper for you, never fear."

He bustled out of the dining room, returning shortly with a soup full of crabmeat and octopus tentacles. The elder Maniakes lifted one of the tentacles in his spoon, examined the rows of suckers on it, and said, "I wonder what my great-grandparents, who never set foot outside Vaspurakan their whole lives long, would have said if they saw me eating a chunk of sea monster like this. Something you'd remember a long time, I'll wager."

"Probably so," his brother Symvatios agreed. He devoured a length of octopus with every sign of enjoyment. "But then, I wouldn't want to feast on some of the bits of goat innards they'd call delicacies. I could, mind you, but I wouldn't want to."

Rhegorios leaned toward Maniakes and whispered, "When our ancestors first left Makuran and came to Videssos the city, they probably thought you got crab soup at a whorehouse." Maniakes snorted and kicked him under the table.

Kameas carried away the soup bowls and returned with a boiled mullet doused with fat and chopped garlic and served on a bed of leeks, parsnips, and golden carrots. When he sliced the mullet open, his cuts revealed roasted songbirds, themselves stuffed with figs, hidden in its body cavity.

A salad of lettuces and radishes followed, made piquant with crumbly white cheese, lemon juice, and olive oil. "Eat hearty, to revive your appetites," Kameas advised.

Maniakes glanced over at Lysia. "It's a good thing you're not feeling any morning sickness yet."

She gave him a dark look. "Don't mention it. My stomach may be listening." Actually, she'd gone through her first two pregnancies with remarkable equanimity, which, considering that she'd been on campaign through a good part of each of them, was just as well.

Mutton chops followed the salad, accompanied by a casserole of cauliflower, broccoli, cabbage, and more cheese. Candied fruit finished off the meal, along with a wine sweeter than any of those that had accompanied the earlier courses. Maniakes raised his silver goblet. "To renewal!" he said. His whole clan drank to the toast. It wasn't merely the name he'd given his flagship, but what he hoped to accomplish for the Empire of Videssos after Genesios' horrific misrule.

It would have been ever so much easier had the Makuraners not taken advantage of that misrule to steal most of the westlands and had the Kubratoi not come within inches of capturing and killing Maniakes a few years before. He'd since paid the Kubratoi back. Avenging himself on Makuran, though, was proving a harder fight.

The commander of the garrison on the wall of Videssos the city was a solid, careful, middle-aged fellow named Zosimos. You wanted a steady man in that job; a flighty soul subject to the vapors could do untold harm there. Zosimos filled the bill.

And so, when he came seeking an audience with the Avtokrator, Maniakes not only granted it at once but prepared himself to listen carefully to whatever the officer had to say. Nor did Zosimos waste any time in saying it: "Your Majesty, my men have spotted Kubratoi spies from the wall."

"You're sure of that, excellent sir?" Maniakes asked him. "They've been quiet since we beat them going on three years ago now. For that matter, they're still quiet; I haven't had any reports of raids over the border."

Zosimos shrugged. "I don't know anything about raids, your Majesty. What I do know is that my men have seen nomads keeping an eye on the city. They gave chase a couple of times, but the Kubratoi got away."

Maniakes scratched his head. "That's—peculiar, excellent sir. When the Kubratoi come down into Videssos, they come to raid." He spoke as if setting forth a law of nature. "If they're coming to spy and nothing more . . . Etzilios is up to something. But what?"

He made a sour face. The khagan of Kubrat was an unwashed barbarian. He was also a clever, treacherous, and dangerous foe. If hc was up to something, it would not be something that benefited Videssos. If Etzilios was making his horsemen forgo their usual looting and robbery, he definitely had something large in mind.

"I'd better have a look at this for myself." Maniakes nodded to Zosimos. "Take me to where the Kubratoi have been seen."

Even a journey out to the walls of Videssos the city was inextricably intertwined with ceremony. Not only guardsmen accompanied the Avtokrator, but also the twelve parasol-bearers suitable to his rank. He had to argue with them to keep them from going up onto the wall with him and announcing his presence to whoever might be watching. Reluctantly, they admitted secrecy might serve some useful purpose.

Zosimos had taken Maniakes further south than he'd expected, most of the way down to the meadow outside the southern end of the wall that gave Videssian horse and foot a practice ground. "Are they spying on our exercises or on the city?" Maniakes asked.

"I cannot say," Zosimos answered. "If I could see into a barbarian's mind, I would be well on the way to barbarism myself."

"If you don't look into your enemy's mind, you'll spend a lot of time retreating from him," Maniakes said. Zosimos stared at him, not following that at all. Maniakes sighed and shrugged and ascended the stairs to the battlements of the inner wall.

Once up on that wall and looking out beyond Videssos the city, Maniakes felt what almost all his predecessors had felt before him: that the imperial capital was invulnerable to assault. The crenelated works on which he stood were strong and thick and eight or nine times as high as a man. Towers—some square, some round, some octagonal—added still more strength and height. Beyond the inner wall was the outer one. It was lower, so that arrows from the inner walls could not only clear it and strike the foe beyond but also could rake it if by some unimaginable mischance it should fall. It, too, boasted siege towers to make it still more commanding. Beyond it, hidden from the Avtokrator's view by its bulk, was a wide, deep ditch to hold engines away from the works.

A couple of soldiers pointed toward a stand of trees not far from the practice grounds. "That's where we spied 'em, your Majesty," one of them said. The other one nodded, as if to prove he hadn't been brought before his sovereign by mistake.

Maniakes looked out toward the trees. He hadn't expected to see anything for himself, but he did: a couple of riders in furs and leathers, mounted on horses smaller than Videssians usually rode. "We could cut them off," he said musingly, but then shook his head. "No—they haven't come down by themselves, surely. If we snag these two, the next bunch further north will know we have 'em, and that's liable to set off whatever Etzilios has in mind."

"Letting 'em find out whatever they're after is liable to do the same thing," one of the soldiers answered.

That, unfortunately, was true. But Maniakes said, "If Etzilios is willing to sneak around instead of coming right out and invading us, I'm willing to let him be sneaky for another year longer. The lesson we gave him three years ago has already lasted longer than I thought it would. After we settle with the Makuraners once and for all, which I hope to do this year, then I can try to show Etzilios that the lesson he got was only the smaller part of what he needs to learn."

He'd done some learning himself, in the years since he'd taken the throne. The hardest thing he'd had to figure out was the necessity of doing one thing at a time and not trying to do too much at once. By the time he had mastered that principle, he had very little empire left from which to apply it.

Now he reminded himself not to expect too much even if he was ever free to loose the Empire's full strength against Kubrat. No doubt, somewhere in one of the dusty archives of Videssos the city, maps a century and a half old showed the vanished roads and even more thoroughly vanished towns of the former imperial province that was presently Etzilios' domain. But Likinios Avtokrator *had* loosed Videssos' full strength against Kubrat, and all he'd got for it was the rebellion that had cost him his throne and his life.

Maniakes looked out toward the Kubratoi one last time. He wondered if any Videssian Avtokrator would ever again bring under imperial control the land the nomads had stolen. He hoped he would be the one, but had learned from painful experience that what you hoped and what you got too often differed.

"All right, they're out there," he said. "As long as they don't do anything to make me notice them, I'll pretend I don't. For the time being, I have more important things to worry about."

Videssos had the most talented sorcerers in the world and, in the Sorcerers' Collegium, the finest institution dedicated to training more of the same. Maniakes had used the services of those mages many times. More often, though, he preferred to work with a wizard he'd first met in the eastern town of Opsikion.

Alvinos was the name the wizard commonly used to deal with Videssians. With Maniakes, he went by the name his mother had given: Bagdasares. He was another of the talented men of Vaspurakan who had left the mountains and valleys of that narrow country to see what he could do in the wider world of Videssos.

Since he'd kept Maniakes alive through a couple of formidable sorcerous assaults, the Avtokrator had come to acquire a good deal of respect for his abilities. Coming up to the mage, he asked, "Can you tell me what the weather on the Sailors' Sea will be like when we travel to Lyssaion?"

"Your Majesty, I think I can," Bagdasares answered modestly, as he had the past two years when Maniakes had asked him similar questions. He spoke Videssian with a throaty Vaspurakaner accent. Maniakes could follow the speech of his ancestors, but only haltingly; he was, to his secret annoyance, far more fluent in the Makuraner tongue.

"Good," he said now. "When you warned of that storm last year, you might have saved the whole Empire."

"Storms are not hard to see," Bagdasares said, speaking with more confidence. "They are large and they are altogether natural—unless some mage with more pride than sense tries meddling with them. Weather magic is not like love magic or battle magic, where the passions of the people involved weaken the spells to uselessness. Come with me, Emperor."

He had a small sorcerous study next to his bedchamber in the imperial residence. One wall was full of scrolls and codices; along another were jars containing many of the oddments a wizard was liable to find useful in the pursuit of his craft. The table that filled up most of the floor space in the little room looked to have been through several wars and perhaps an uprising or two; sorcery could be hard on the furniture.

"Seawater," he muttered under his breath. "Seawater."

Maniakes looked around. He saw nothing answering that description. "Shall I order a servant to trot down to the little palace-quarter harbor with a bucket, eminent sir?"

"What? Oh." Alvinos Bagdasares laughed. "No, your Majesty, no need for that. I was thinking out loud. We have fresh water, and I have here—" He plucked a stoppered jar from its niche on the wall. "—sea salt, which, when mixed with that fresh water, gives an excellent simulacrum of the sea. And what is the business of magic, if not simulacra?"

Since Maniakes did not pretend to be a mage, he let Bagdasares do as he reckoned best. That, he had found, was a good recipe for successful administration of any sort: pick someone who knew what he was doing—and picking the right man was no small part of the art, either—then stand aside and let him do it.

Humming tunelessly, Bagdasares mixed up a batch of artificial seawater, then, praying as he did so, poured some of it into a low, broad silver bowl on the battered table. Then he used a sharp knife with a gold hilt to cut several roughly boat-shaped chips off an oak board. Twigs and bits of cloth gave them the semblance of rigging.

"We speak of the Sailors' Sea," he explained to Maniakes, "and so the ships must be shown as sailing ships, even if in literal truth they use oars, as well."

"However you find out what I need to know," the Avtokrator answered.

"Yes, yes." Bagdasares forgot about him in the continued intense concentration he would need for the spell itself. He prayed, first in Videssian and then in the Vaspurakaner tongue to Vaspur the Firstborn, the first man Phos ever created. To the ear of a Videssian steeped in orthodoxy, that would have been heretical. Maniakes, at the moment, worried more about results. In the course of his troubles with the temples, his concern for the finer points of orthodoxy had worn thin.

Bagdasares went on chanting. His right hand moved in swift passes above the bowl that held the little, toylike boats. Without his touching them, they moved into a formation such as a fleet might use traveling across the sea. A wind Maniakes could not feel filled their makeshift sails and sent them smoothly from one side of the bowl to the other.

"The lord with the great and good mind shall favor us with kindly weather," Bagdasares said.

Then, although he did not continue the incantation, the boats he had used in his magic reversed themselves and began to sail back toward the side of the bowl from which they had set out. "What does that mean?" Maniakes asked.

"Your Majesty, I do not know." Bagdasares' voice was low and troubled. "If I were to guess, I—"

Before he could say more, the calm water in the center of the bowl started rising, as if someone had grabbed the rim and were sloshing the artificial sea back and forth. But neither Bagdasares nor Maniakes had his hand anywhere near the polished silver bowl.

What looked like a spark that flew from two iron blades clashing together sprang into being above the little fleet, and then another. A faint mutter in the air—was that what thunder might sound like, almost infinitely attenuated?

One of the boats of the miniature fleet overturned and sank. The rest sailed on. Just before they reached the edge of the bowl, Maniakes had—or thought he had—a momentary vision of other ships, ships that looked different in a way he could not define, also on the water, though he did not think they were physically present. He blinked, and they vanished even from his perception.

"Phos!" Bagdasares exclaimed, and then, as if that did not satisfy him, he swung back to the Vaspurakaner tongue to add, "Vaspur the Firstborn!"

Maniakes sketched Phos' sun-circle above his left breast. "What," he asked carefully, "was that in aid of?"

"If I knew, I would tell you." Bagdasares sounded like a man shaken to the core. "Normally, the biggest challenge a mage faces is getting enough of an answer to his question to tell him and his client what they need to know. Getting so much more than that—"

"I take it we'll run into a storm sailing back to Videssos the city?" Maniakes said in what wasn't really a question.

"I would say that seems likely, your Majesty," Bagdasares agreed. "The lightning, the thunder, the waves—" He shook his head. "I wish I could tell you how to evade this fate, but I cannot."

"What were those other ships, there at the end of the conjuration?" Maniakes asked. With the interpretation less obvious, his curiosity increased.

But Bagdasares' bushy eyebrows came down and together in a frown. "What 'other ships,' your Majesty? I saw only those of my own creation." After Maniakes, pointing to the part of the bowl where the other ships had briefly appeared, explained what he had seen, the mage whistled softly.

"What does this mean?" Maniakes asked. Then he chuckled wryly. "I have a gift for the obvious, I fear."

"Were the answer as obvious as the question, I should be happier—and so, no doubt, would you," Alvinos Bagdasares said. "But questions about meaning, while easy to ask, have a way of being troublesome to wrestle with."

"*Everything* has a way of being troublesome," Maniakes said irritably. "Very well. I assume you can't tell me everything I would know. What *can* you tell me?"

"To meet your gift for the obvious, I would say it is obviously true my magic touched on something larger than I had intended," Bagdasares replied. "As I said, you will have good weather sailing to Lyssaion. I would also say it is likely you will have bad weather sailing back."

"I didn't ask you about sailing back."

"I know that," Bagdasares said. "It alarms me. Most times, magic does either what you want or less, as I told you a little while ago. When it does more than you charge it with, that is a token your spell has pulled back the curtain from great events, events with a power of their own blending with the power you bring to them."

"What can I do to keep out of this storm?" Maniakes asked.

Regretfully, Bagdasares spread his hands. "Nothing, your Majesty. It has been seen, and so it will come to pass. Phos grant that the fleet pass through it with losses as small as may be."

"Yes," Maniakes said in an abstracted voice. As Avtokrator of the Videssians, ruler of a great empire, he'd grown unused to the idea that some things were beyond his power. Not even the Avtokrator, though, could hope to bend wind and rain and sea to his will. Maniakes changed the subject, at least slightly: "What about those other ships I saw?"

Bagdasares looked no happier. "I do not know, so I cannot tell you. I do not know if they be friends or foes, whether they come to rescue the ships from your fleet that passed through the storm or to attack them. I do not know whether the rescue or the attack succeeds or fails."

"Can you try to find out more than you do know?" Maniakes said.

"Aye, I can try, your Majesty," Bagdasares said. "I *will* try. But I make no guarantees of success: indeed, I fear failure. I was not granted the vision, whatever it might have been. This suggests it might well have been meant for you alone, which in turn suggests reproducing, grasping, and interpreting it will be extraordinarily difficult for anyone but yourself."

"Do what you can," Maniakes said.

And, for the next several hours, Bagdasares did what he could. Some of his efforts were far more spectacular than the relatively uncomplicated spell Maniakes had first requested of him. Once, the chamber glowed with a pure white light for several minutes. Shadows appeared on the walls with nothing to cast them. Words in a language Maniakes did not understand came out of thin air.

"What does that mean?" he whispered to Bagdasares.

"I don't know," the wizard whispered back. A little while later, he gave up, saying, "Whatever lies ahead is beyond my ability to unravel now, your Majesty. Only the passing of time can reveal its fullness."

Maniakes clenched his fists. If he'd been willing to wait for the fullness of time, he wouldn't have asked Bagdasares to work magic. He sighed. "I know the army will get to Lyssaion without any great trouble," he declared. "For now, I'll cling to that. Once I get there, once I punish the Makuraners for all they've done to Videssos, then I'll worry about what happens next."

"That is the proper course, your Majesty," Bagdasares said. His large, dark eyes, though . . . his eyes were full of worry.

What looked at first glance like chaos filled the harbor of Kontoskalion. Soldiers filed aboard some merchantmen; grooms and cavalrymen led unhappy, suspicious horses up the gangplanks of others. Last-minute supplies went onto still others.

"The lord with the great and good mind bless you, your Majesty, as you go about your holy work," the ecumenical patriarch Agathios said to Maniakes, sketching Phos' sun-sign above his heart.

"I thank you, most holy sir," the Avtokrator answered, on the whole sincerely. Since granting the dispensation recognizing his marriage to Lysia as licit, Agathios had shown himself willing to be seen with them and to pray with them and for their success in public. A good many other clerics, including some who accepted the dispensation as within the patriarch's power, refused to offer such open recognition of it.

"Smite the Makuraners!" Agathios suddenly shouted in a great voice. One thing Maniakes had noted about him over the years was that, while usually calm, he could work himself up to rage or down to panic with alarming speed. "Smite them!" he cried again. "For they have tried to wipe out and to pervert Phos' holy faith in the lands they have stolen from the Empire of Videssos. Now let our vengeance against them continue."

A good many soldiers, hearing his words, made the sun-sign themselves. Maniakes had punished the Land of the Thousand Cities for the outrages the Makuraners had visited upon the Videssian westlands, for the temples pulled down or burned, for the Vaspurakaner doctrine forcibly imposed upon Videssians who reckoned it heretical, for the priests tormented when they would not preach the Vaspurakaner heresy.

Maniakes recognized the irony there, even if he did not go out of his way to advertise it. He himself inclined toward what the Videssians called orthodoxy, but his father stubbornly clung to the doctrines so loathed in the westlands.

He'd gone out of his way to wreck shrines dedicated to the God the Makuraners worshiped. Having begun a war of religion, they were now finding out what being on the receiving end of it was like.

Agathios, fortunately for Maniakes' peace of mind, calmed as quick as he inflamed himself. Moments after bellowing about the iniquities of the Makuraners, he said, in an ordinary tone of voice, "If the good god is kind, your Majesty, he will let you find a way to put an end to this long, hard war once and for all."

"From your lips to Phos' ear," Maniakes agreed. "Nothing would make me happier than peace—provided they restore to us what they've stolen. And nothing would make them happier than peace—provided they keep what they took when Videssos was weak. You do see the problem, most holy sir?"

"I do indeed." The ecumenical patriarch let out a long, sad sigh. "Would it were otherwise, your Majesty." He looked embarrassed. "You do understand, I hope, that I speak as I do in the interest of Videssos as a whole and in the interest of peace rather than that of the temples."

"Of course," Maniakes answered. He'd had so much practice at diplomacy—or perhaps hypocrisy was the better word—that Agathios didn't notice his sarcasm. Back when the fight against the Makuraners had looked as black as the gaping emptiness of the imperial treasury, he'd borrowed gold and silver vessels and candelabra, especially from the High Temple but also from the rest, and melted them down to make the gold and silver coins with which he could pay his soldiers—and with which he could also pay tribute to the Kubratoi so he could concentrate what few resources he had on fighting the Makuraners. With peace, the temples would—might—be repaid.

Thinking about the Kubratoi made him glance eastward. He was not up on the walls of Videssos the city now; he could not see the Kubrati scouts who had come down near the imperial city to see what he was doing. But he hadn't forgotten them, either. The nomads had never before sent out spies so openly. He wondered what they had in mind. Etzilios had been very quiet in the nearly three years since he'd been trounced . . . till now.

While Maniakes was musing thus, Agathios raised his hands toward the sun and spat down onto the planks of the wharf to show his rejection of Skotos. "We bless thee, Phos, lord with the great and good mind," he intoned, "by thy grace our protector, watchful beforehand that the great test of life may be decided in our favor."

Maniakes joined him in Phos' creed; so, again, did many of the sailors and soldiers. That creed linked worshipers of the good god in distant Kalavria, almost at the eastern edge of the world, with their coreligionists on the border with Makuran—or rather, on what had been the border with Makuran till the westerners began taking advantage of Videssos' weaknesses after Genesios killed Likinios and his sons.

Agathios bowed low. "May good fortune go with you, your Majesty, and may you come back wreathed with fragrant clouds of victory." Maniakes had been trained as a soldier, not as a rhetorician, but he knew a mixed metaphor when he heard one. Agathios seemed to notice nothing out of the ordinary, adding, "May the King of Kings cower like the whipped ox you have for your slaves." And, bowing again, he departed, sublimely unaware he had left meaning behind along with Maniakes.

Thrax waved from the *Renewal*. Maniakes waved back and hurried down the wharf toward his flagship. His red boots, footgear reserved for the Avtokrator alone, thudded on the gangplank. "Good to have you aboard, your Majesty," Thrax said, bowing. "Will the Empress be along soon? When everyone's here, we don't have anything left to hold us in the city."

"Lysia will be along shortly," Maniakes answered. "Do you mean to tell me Rhegorios is already aboard?"

"That he is." Thrax pointed aft, to the cabins behind the mast. On most dromons, only the captain enjoyed the luxury of a cabin, the rest of the crew slinging their hammocks or spreading blankets on the deck when they spent one of their occasional nights at sea. A ship that habitually carried the Avtokrator, his wife, and the Sevastos, though, carried them in as much comfort as was to be found in the cramped confines of a war galley.

Maniakes knocked at the door to the cabin his cousin was using. When Rhegorios opened it, Maniakes said, "I didn't expect you to be on board ahead of me and Lysia both."

"Well, life is full of surprises, isn't it, cousin your Majesty brother-in-law of mine?" Rhegorios said, stringing together with reckless abandon the titles by which he might address Maniakes. He had a habit of doing that, not least because it sometimes flustered Maniakes, which amused Rhegorios no end.

Today, though, the Avtokrator refused to rise to the bait. He said, "Lysia and I have our own reasons for wanting to be out of Videssos the city, but you're popular here. I'd think you'd want to stay as long as you could."

"Any fool with a big smile can be popular," Rhegorios said with an airy wave of his hand. "It's easy."

"I haven't found it so," Maniakes answered bitterly.

"Ah, but you're not a fool," Rhegorios said. "That makes it harder. When a fool goes wrong, people forgive him; he isn't doing anything they didn't expect. But if a man with a reputation for knowing what he's doing goes astray, they're on him like a pack of wolves, because he's let them down."

Lysia boarded the *Renewal* then, which should have distracted Maniakes but didn't. A great many people in Videssos the city reckoned he had gone wrong by falling in love with his cousin. The feeling would have been less powerful had it been more rational. Getting away from the capital, getting away from the priests who still resented the dispensation he'd haggled out of Agathios, was nothing but a relief.

Thrax shouted orders. Longshoremen ran out to cast off lines. Sailors nimbly coiled the ropes in snaky spirals. They stowed the gangplank behind the cabins; Maniakes felt the thud through the soles of his feet when it crashed down onto the deck planking.

A drum began to thud, setting the pace for the rowers. "Back oars!" the oarmaster shouted. The oars dug into the water. Little by little, the *Renewal* slid away from the wharf. Maniakes inhaled deeply, then let out a long, glad sigh. Wherever he went, and into whatever sort of battle, he would be happier than he was here.

Coming into Lyssaion was like entering another world. Here in the far southwest of the Videssian westlands, the calendar might still have said early spring, but by all other signs it was summer outside. The sun pounded down out of the sky with almost the relentless authority it held in the Land of the Thousand Cities. Only the Sailors' Sea kept the weather hot rather than intolerable.

But even the sea here was different from the way it looked in Videssos the city. Back by the capital, the seawater was green. Off Kalavria, in the distant east, it was nearer gray. You could ride out from Kastavala over to the eastern shore, and look across an endless expanse of gray, gray ocean toward the end of the world, or whatever lay beyond vision. No ship had ever come out of the east to Kalavria. Over the years, a few ships had sailed east from the island. None of them had come back, either.

Here, now . . . here the water was blue. It was not the blue of the sky, the blue enamel-makers kept trying and failing to imitate in

glass paste. The blue of the sea was darker, deeper, richer, till it almost approached the color of fine wine. But if, deluded, you dipped
it up, you found yourself with only a cup of warm seawater.

"I wonder why that is," Rhegorios said, having made the
experiment.

"To the ice with me if I know." Maniakes spat in rejection of
Skotos, whose icy hell held the souls of sinners in eternal torment.

"Phos is a better wizard than all the mages ever born put together," Rhegorios said, to which his cousin could only nod.

Against bright sky and rich blue sea, the walls of Lyssaion, and
the buildings that showed over them, might have been cast of shining gold. They weren't, of course; such a test of man's cupidity could
never have been built, nor survived long if by some miracle it had
been. But the yellow-brown sandstone shone and sparkled in the
fierce sunlight till the eye had to look away lest it be dazzled.

Till two years before, Lyssaion had been nothing but a sleepy
little town that baked in the summer, mostly stayed warm through
the winter, and, in times of peace, sent goods from the west and
occasional crops of dates to Videssos the city. The palm trees on
which the dates ripened grew both near and even within the city,
as they did in the Land of the Thousand Cities. Maniakes found
them absurd; they put him in mind more of outsized feather dust-
ers than proper trees.

Lyssaion had been so unimportant in the scheme of things that
the Makuraners, when they overran the Videssian westlands, hadn't
bothered giving it more than a token garrison. The thrust of their
invasion had been toward the northeast, toward Videssos the city.
Towns on the way to the capital lay firmly under their thumb. Other
towns . . .

"They didn't pay enough attention to other towns," Maniakes
said happily as his men and horses left their ships and filed into
Lyssaion.

"They certainly didn't," Rhegorios agreed, also happily. "And
now they're paying for it."

Looking at Lyssaion, though, Maniakes thought the Makuraners could have done little to keep him from seizing it as a base
no matter how much they wanted to do exactly that. It had a stout
wall to hold off enemies approaching by land, but none to keep
ships from drawing near. Without ships, the place had no reason to
exist. Fishing boats sailed out from it; in peacetime it enjoyed

modest prosperity from its dates and as a transshipment point between Makuran and Videssos. Wall off the harbor to hold out a fleet: the town would die, the people would flee, and who would feed a garrison then?

Maniakes settled Lysia in the hypasteos' residence, where the city governor's wife fussed over her: between an unexpected touch of morning sickness and a touch of seasickness, she was looking wan. "I'm glad it's only my stomach moving now," she said, "not everything around me, too."

Before long, she was going to be in a wagon, jouncing along toward the Land of the Thousand Cities and, Phos willing, toward Mashiz. Maniakes did not mention that. He knew Lysia knew it. How could he blame her for not wanting to think about it?

His horse, Antelope, was just as glad as his wife to get back on solid ground. The beast snorted and kicked up dirt once led off the wharf. "Can you smell where we are?" Maniakes asked, stroking the side of the horse's nose. The wind smelled hot and dusty to him, but he didn't have an animal's nose. "Do you know what these smells mean?"

By the way Antelope whickered, maybe he did. Maniakes had to use his eyes. Seeing those hills—almost mountains—against the northeastern and northwestern horizon, seeing the green thread of the Xeremos River flowing through the dry desert, by Lyssaion, and into the Sailors' Sea . . . all that made him remember the fights in the Land of the Thousand Cities that had forced Sharbaraz King of Kings to dance to his tune instead of the other way round. One more year of fighting there might even bring the victory that had seemed unimaginable when he took the throne from Genesios.

His army filled Lyssaion to the bursting point and even a little beyond: tents sprang up like toadstools, out beyond the city walls. He wanted to head northwest along the banks of the Xeremos straight toward enemy country, but had to wait until not just men and horses but also supplies came off his ships. Once in the Land of the Thousand Cities, they could live off the fertile countryside. On the way there, though, much of the countryside was anything but fertile.

"Phos bless you, your Majesty, on your journey against the foe," said the local prelate, an amiable little fellow named Boinos, at supper that night. Maniakes smiled back at him; he'd never heard

Please go someplace else and stop eating us out of house and home more elegantly expressed.

"I'll take all the blessings I can get, thank you," the Avtokrator answered. "I already think the good god is watching over us; the Makuraners could easily have tried coming down the Xeremos against Lyssaion. We'd have driven them out again, no doubt, but that might have delayed the start of the campaign, and it wouldn't have been good for your city." He beamed at Boinos, pleased with his own understatement.

The prelate sketched the sun-circle above his heart. So did Phakrases, the hypasteos, who looked like Boinos' unhappy cousin. And so did the garrison commander, Zaoutzes, who, from his years in the sunbaked place, was as brown and weathered as a sailor. He said, "You know, your Majesty, I looked for something like that from them, but it never came. I kept sending scouts up the river to see if they were up to something. I never found any sign they were heading this way, though, for which I thank the lord with the great and good mind." He signed himself again.

"Maybe they didn't bother, knowing we could always get to the Land of the Thousand Cities by way of Erzerum if word came Lyssaion had fallen," Rhegorios suggested.

"Forgive me, your highness, but I do not like to think of my city falling back into the hands of the misbelievers," Phakrases said stiffly. "I do not like to think what happens in Lyssaion is important in Videssos the city only in the way it might make you change your plans, either."

So there, Maniakes thought. Rhegorios, for once, had no quick comeback ready; perhaps he hadn't expected the city governor to be so blunt—even if politely blunt—with him.

Lysia said, "Lyssaion is important for its own sake, and also because it is the key in the lock that, when fully opened, will set the whole Empire of Videssos free. I said the same thing when we came here two years ago, and I say it again now that it has begun to come true."

"You are gracious, Empress," Phakrases answered, inclining his head to her. Almost everyone in Lyssaion maintained a polite silence about the irregularities in her relationship with Maniakes, for which both she and the Avtokrator were grateful. Maybe it was that Agathios' dispensation sufficed, out here away from the capital, in country where people were more stolid, less argumentative.

Or maybe, conversely, living so close to Makuran, where marriages between cousins and even between uncles and nieces were allowed, made the folk of Lyssaion take such unions in stride. Maniakes had no intention of asking which, if either, of those interpretations was true.

Instead, he followed Zaoutzes' thought: "What if the Makuraners *are* up to something, but it's not aimed at Lyssaion?"

The garrison commander shrugged. "I have no way to know about that, your Majesty. None of my men got deep enough into the Land of the Thousand Cities to tell for certain."

"All right," Maniakes said. "If Sharbaraz and Abivard are up to something else, I expect we'll find out when they turn it loose against us." He started to add something like, *We've stopped everything they've thrown at us so far,* but left that unspoken. If the Videssian westlands hadn't lain under Makuraner control, he wouldn't have had to sail to Lyssaion to put himself in a position of being able to carry the war to the foe.

Rhegorios said, "We've managed to stay alive this long," which came closer to summing up what the situation was really like. Rhegorios, as was his way, sounded cheerful. When mere survival was enough to make a man cheerful, though, the clouds overhead were dark and gloomy.

As Avtokrator of the Videssians, Maniakes could not afford to show that he was worried, lest by showing that he made his subjects worry, too, thus turning a bad situation worse. When he and Lysia were getting ready for bed, though, in the chamber Phakrases had given them, he said, "We've ducked so many arrows from the bows of the Makuraners, and been able to give back so few. How long can that go on?"

Lysia paused to think before she answered. As his cousin, she'd known him almost all his life. As his wife, she'd come to know him in a different, more thorough way than she had as cousin alone. At last, she said, "The Makuraners have done everything they can to Videssos, because they can't reach the imperial city. We're a long way from doing everything we can to them. The more we do, the sooner they'll come to their senses and make peace."

"Other people have said the same thing to me, ever since I got the idea of moving my army against them by sea," he answered. "The advantage you have is that you make me believe it."

"Good," she said. "I'm supposed to. Isn't that what they call wifely duty?"

He smiled. "No, that's something else."

She tossed her head, flipping her black curls back from her face. "*That's* not a duty. Duties you endure. That—"

It *was* enjoyable, not least because she didn't look on it as a duty; he thought sadly of Niphone, who had looked on it so. Afterward, he slept soundly. The next morning, the army left Lyssaion, heading northwest.

II

Where the waters of the Xeremos reached, its valley was green and fertile. Where canals and underground channels in the style of those on Makuran's western plateau could not reach, it was desert. Here and there, the locals had thrown up walls of mud brick and stone, not against human foes but to hold encroaching sand dunes at bay. Here and there, the remains of such walls sticking up through sand told of fights that had failed.

This was the second time the farmers in the valley had seen the Videssian army sally forth to attack Makuran. The first time, two years before, they'd wavered between panic and astonishment; no Avtokrator had been seen in that out-of-the-way part of the Empire for centuries, if ever. They hadn't known whether the soldiers would plunder them of their few belongings. True, they and the soldiers owed allegiance to the same sovereign, but how often did that matter to soldiers?

Maniakes had kept his men from plundering back then, and also during the fall just past, when they'd withdrawn from the Thousand Cities by way of the Xeremos. Now the peasants waved from the fields instead of running from them.

When Maniakes remarked on that, Rhegorios said, "The farmers between the Tutub and the Tib won't be so glad to see us."

"The peasants in the westlands—farmers and herders alike—haven't been glad to see the Makuraners, or to have their substance stolen, or to have to pay ruinous taxes to the King of Kings, or to have the way they worship deliberately disturbed to fuel feuds among them," Maniakes returned.

"That's so, every word of it, cousin your Majesty brother-in-law of mine," Rhegorios agreed, grinning one of his impudent grins. "But it won't make the peasants in the Land of the Thousand Cities glad to see us, no matter how true it is."

"I don't want them to be glad to see us," Maniakes said. "I want them to hate us so much—I want all of Makuran to hate us so much, aye, and to fear us so much, too—that they give over their war, give back our land, and settle down inside their own proper borders. If Sharbaraz offers to do that, as far as I'm concerned he's bloody well welcome to however many of the Thousand Cities that are left standing by then."

He looked back over his shoulder. A good many of the wagons in the baggage train carried not fodder for the beasts or food for the men but stout ropes, fittings of iron and brass, and a large number of timbers sawn to specific lengths. The paraphernalia looked innocuous—till the engineers assembled the catapults from their component parts, which they could do much faster than most Makuraner garrison commanders realized.

The timbers that went into the siege engines were also useful in another way. Canals crisscrossed the flat floodplain between the Tutub and the Tib. To slow the Videssians, the Makuraners were not averse to opening the banks of the canals in their path and letting water flow out to turn roads and fields alike to mud. Plopped down into that mud, the timbers could make a passable way out of one that was not.

In a thoughtful voice, Rhegorios said, "I wonder what Abivard will try to do against us this year, now that he has some of the Makuraner boiler boys—" Videssian slang so named the fearsome Makuraner heavy cavalry, whose members did indeed swelter to the boiling point in the full armor that encased not only them but their horses, as well. "—to go with the infantry levies from the city garrisons."

"I don't know." Maniakes suspected he looked unhappy. He was certain he felt unhappy. "We would have done better the past two years if Sharbaraz had sent a worse general against us. I first got to know Abivard more than ten years ago now, and he was good then—maybe better than he knew, since he was just starting to lead campaigns. He's got better since." His chuckle had a wry edge to it. "I hardly need say that, do I, since he's the one who conquered the westlands from us?"

"This army isn't so good as the one he used to do that," Rhegorios said. "He hasn't got all the heavy horse with him, only a chunk of it, with the rest in the westlands or up in Vaspurakan. And do you know what? I don't miss the ones I won't see, not one bit I don't."

"Nor I," Maniakes agreed. They rode on in silence for a little while. Then he went on, "I wonder what Abivard thinks of me—how he plans his campaigns against me, I mean."

"What you do—what you do that most people don't, I mean—is that you learn from your mistakes," his cousin answered.

"Is that so?" Maniakes said. "Then why do I keep putting up with you?"

Rhegorios mimed being wounded to the quick, so well that his horse snorted and sidestepped under him. He brought it back under control, then said, "No doubt because you recognize quality when you see it." That wasn't bragging, as it might have been from another man; Rhegorios, in fact, did not sound altogether serious. But the Sevastos continued in a more sober vein: "You do learn. Things that worked against you two years ago won't work now, because you've seen them before."

"I hope so," Maniakes said. "I know I used to rush ahead too eagerly, without looking to see what was waiting for me. The Kubratoi almost killed me on account of that, not long after I took the throne."

"But you don't do that anymore," Rhegorios said. "A lot of people keep on making the same mistakes over and over again. Take me, for instance: whenever I see a pretty girl, I fall in love."

"No, you don't," Maniakes said. "You just want to get your hands, or something, up under her tunic. It's not the same thing."

"Without a doubt, you're right, O paragon of wisdom," Rhegorios said with a comical leer. "And how many men *ever* learn that?"

He was laughing as he asked the question, which did not mean it wasn't a good one. "Eventually you get too old to care, or else your eyes get too bad to tell the pretty ones from the rest," Maniakes replied.

"Ha! I'm going to tell my sister you said that."

"Threatening your sovereign, are you?" Maniakes said. "That's lese majesty, you know. I could have your tongue clapped in irons." This time, he leered at his cousin. "And if I do, the girls won't like you so well."

Rhegorios stuck out the organ in question. It was easy to laugh now. The campaign was young, and nothing had yet gone wrong.

* * *

The Xeremos sprang from hilly country north and west of Lyssaion. Those same hills gave rise to the Tutub, which, with the Tib, framed the Land of the Thousand Cities. Instead of flowing southeast to the Sailors' Sea, the Tutub ran north through the floodplain till it emptied itself in the landlocked Mylasa Sea.

Having traveled quickly up the length of the Xeremos, Maniakes' army slowed in the rougher country that gave birth to the river. The soldiers had to string themselves out in long files to make their way along the narrow trails running through the hill country. A small force of Makuraner troops could have made life very difficult for the advancing imperials.

No such force, though, tried to block their advance. That roused Rhegorios' suspicions. "They might have held us up here for weeks if they really set their minds to it," he said.

"Yes, but they might have had to wait for weeks to see if we were coming," Maniakes replied. He waved to the poor, rock-ribbed country all around. "What would they eat while they were waiting?"

Rhegorios grunted. As far as he was concerned, war meant fighting, nothing else but. He cared little for logistics. Maniakes could not make himself get excited about the details of keeping an army fed and otherwise supplied. But, whether those details were exciting or not, tending to them made the difference between campaigns that failed and those that won.

Maniakes went on, "You'd have to carry provisions not to starve in this country." He exaggerated, but not by much. A handful of farmers plowed fields that often seemed to run nearly as much up and down as from side to side. A few herders pastured sheep on the hills. Again, because of the steepness of those hills, the black-faced animals often looked to be grazing on a slant. A few of the trees bore nuts. That was enough to keep the small local population going. An army that didn't carry its own supplies would have eaten the countryside empty in short order.

A couple of days into the badlands, a scout came riding back toward the Avtokrator from up the track by which the army would be moving. He shouted, "Your Majesty, I've found the headwaters of the Tutub!"

"Good news!" Maniakes dug in the pouch he wore on his belt, pulled out a goldpiece, and tossed it to the soldier. Grinning, the man tucked away the coin. Maniakes wondered what the soldier would have done had he known the goldpiece was minted to a standard slightly less pure than the Videssian norm. So far as Mani-akes knew, nobody outside the mint suspected that; it was one way of making his scanty resources stretch further. If he ever got the chance, he intended to return to the old standard as soon as he could. Cheapening the currency was a dangerous game.

By the look on the scout's face, he wouldn't have minded too much. It was still one goldpiece more—well, actually, almost one goldpiece more—than he would have had otherwise.

"All downhill from now on, boys!" Maniakes called, which got a cheer from the soldiers who heard him. If that proved true of the campaign as well as the line of march, he would be well pleased. The next easy campaign he had as Avtokrator would be his first. The Makuraners, now, they'd had easy campaigns, seizing the west-lands while Videssos, under the vicious and inept rule of Genesios, writhed in the throes of civil war like a snake with a broken back instead of coming together to resist them.

As the army made its way through the hill country toward the Land of the Thousand Cities, it found more and larger villages. It did not find more people in them. It found hardly any people in them at all. Scouts or herders must have brought word the Vid-essians were coming. If he'd had that word in good time, Mani-akes would have fled before his army, too.

He ordered the villages burned. He sent cavalry squadrons out to either side of his line of march, with orders to burn the more dis-tant villages, too. Since he'd begun campaigning in Makuran, he'd done his best to make the enemy feel the war as sharply as he could. Sooner or later, he reasoned, either Sharbaraz would get sick of seeing his land destroyed or his subjects would get sick of it and revolt against the King of Kings.

The only trouble was, it hadn't happened yet.

Almost imperceptibly, the hills leveled out toward the flat, canal-pierced, muddy soil of the floodplain between the Tutub and the Tib. Peering north and west, Maniakes could see a long, long way. The nearest of the Thousand Cities, Qostabash, lay ahead.

He'd bypassed Qostabash the autumn before. He'd been retreat-ing then, with Abivard's army harrying him as he went. He hadn't enjoyed the luxury of a few days' time in which to stop and sack the place. He promised himself it would be different now.

Qostabash, like a lot of the Thousand Cities, stuck up from the smooth land all around it like a pimple sticking up from the smooth skin of a woman's cheek. It hadn't been built where it was for the sake of the hillock on which it perched. When it was first built, that hillock hadn't been there. But the Thousand Cities were old, old. They'd sprung up between the Tutub and the Tib before Videssos the city was a city, perhaps before it was even a village. Over the long stretch of years, their own rubble—collapsed walls and houses and buildings of mud brick, along with centuries of slops and garbage—had made a hill where none had been before.

Their walls were still brick, though now mostly of fired brick, the better to resist siege engines. Better resistance was not the same as good resistance. Maniakes looked toward Qostabash the way a hungry hound was liable to look toward a butcher's shop.

But, as he approached, he discovered the town was not so defenseless as he had hoped. Its walls had not improved since the year before. But having an army between it and the Videssians did make it harder to seize.

"Well, well," Maniakes said. "Isn't that interesting?" *Interesting* was not the word he had in mind, but it was a word he could bring out without blistering everyone within earshot.

"They are getting better at reacting to us, aren't they?" Rhegorios said. "Year before last, they let us get halfway across the floodplain to Mashiz before they did anything much against us, and last year we got to have some fun when we came down from Erzerum, too. Not this time, though."

"No." Maniakes squinted, trying to sharpen his eyesight. The Makuraners were still too far away for him to be sure, but— "That's a good-sized force they have there."

"So it is," Rhegorios agreed. "They can afford to feed a good-sized force here a lot more easily than they could in the hill country." Maybe he'd been paying attention to logistics after all. He glanced toward Maniakes. "Do we try to go through them or around them?"

"I don't know yet," Maniakes answered. Hearing those words pass his lips was a sign of how far he'd come since the ecumenical patriarch had proclaimed him Avtokrator of the Videssians. He didn't charge ahead without weighing consequences, as he had only a few years before. "Let's see what the scouts have to say. When I know what's in front of me, I'll have a better chance of making the right choice."

Off rode the scouts, down toward the waiting Makuraner army. The rest of the Videssian force followed the outriders.

Maniakes wished he had some better way than eyes alone of looking at the enemy army. His eyes didn't tell him so much as he would have wished, and he didn't altogether trust what they did tell him. But magic and war did not mix; the passions war engendered made sorcery unreliable. And so he waited for the scouts. He knew more than a little relief when one of them came riding back and said, "Your Majesty, it looks to be mostly an infantry army. They have some horsemen—a few rode out to skirmish with us and hold us away from the foot soldiers—but no sign of the boiler boys from the field army."

"I thought I saw the same thing from here," Maniakes said. "I wasn't sure I believed it. No boiler boys, eh? Isn't that interesting?" Now he'd used it twice when he meant something else. "Where is the heavy cavalry, then? Abivard's gone and done something sneaky with it. I don't like that." He didn't like it at all. Not knowing where your enemy's best troops were made you look over your shoulder all the time.

He looked over his shoulder now. No force of heavy Makuraner cavalry came thundering out of the hills behind him. Had they been there, he would have discovered them.

Rhegorios rode up to hear what the scout had to say. He tossed his head. "Well, cousin your Majesty brother-in-law of mine, I'll ask you the same question again: what do we do now?"

"If you were Abivard, what would you do with the field army?" Maniakes replied, answering question with question.

"If I were Abivard," Rhegorios said slowly, thinking as he spoke, "I wouldn't know whether we were coming up from Lyssaion or down from Erzerum. I would know I could move a cavalry force faster than I could a bunch of foot soldiers. I could use infantry to slow down those cursed Videssians—" He grinned at Maniakes. "—as soon as they got into the Land of the Thousand Cities, while I stayed back somewhere in the middle of the country so I could get to wherever I was going in a hurry."

"Yes, that makes good sense," Maniakes said, and then, after a moment's reflection, "in fact, it makes better sense than anything I'd thought of myself. It tells me what needs doing, too."

"That's good," his cousin said. "What does need doing?"

Maniakes spoke with decision, pointing ahead toward the drawn-up Makuraner army. "I don't want to get bogged down fighting foot soldiers. If I do, I won't be able to maneuver the way I'd want to when Abivard comes after me. I want to beat the real Makuraner army, break past it, and strike for Mashiz. Abivard kept me from doing that last year. I don't aim to let him keep me from doing it again."

"Been a good many years since an Avtokrator of the Videssians sacked Mashiz," Rhegorios agreed in dreamy tones. Then he turned practical once more: "So you won't want to engage these fellows or to attack Qostabash, then? We'll get around them and look for more rewarding targets?"

"That's the idea," Maniakes said. "Foot soldiers have trouble engaging us unless we choose to let 'em. I don't choose that here. Let them chase us. If they get out of line doing it, we double back and punish them. If they don't, we leave them eating our dust."

Horns relayed his commands to the Videssian horsemen. In line of battle, they rode past the Makuraner army at a distance of about half a mile. That was plenty close to let his men hear the enemy shouting at them and probably calling them a pack of cowards for not coming closer and fighting.

To give the Makuraners something to yell about, he sent a few squadrons of scouts close enough to ply the mostly unarmored infantry with arrows. The enemy shot back. They put a lot more arrows in the air than had his scouts, but to less effect: they were aiming at small, armored moving targets. A couple of horses went down and one scout pitched from the saddle with an arrow in the face, but the Videssians gave better than they got.

The Makuraners also tried to use their small force of cavalry to slow down the Videssians so their infantry could move forward and come to close quarters with them. Had the force been larger, that might have worked. As things were, the Videssians used horse archers and javelin men to send their foes reeling back in retreat.

"Keep moving!" Maniakes called to his men after the Makuraner horse recoiled back onto their foot for protection. "We'll pick the field. They can't make us do it against our will."

He'd grown used to raising a cheer from the army on going into battle. Raising a cheer on escaping battle was something else again, and almost a harking back to the bad old days when the Videssians had fled the Makuraners for no better reason than that they *were* Makuraners. But the resemblance to those bad old days was only superficial. His men could have attacked the Makuraners had he given them the order. He thought they would have beaten the foe.

But an army of foot soldiers was not the foe he wanted to beat, not the foe he needed to beat. He wanted Abivard's men, the best the King of Kings could throw against him. No lesser force deserved his notice.

He and his horsemen rode wide around Qostabash. On the walls of the city, more Makuraners watched. Maybe they, too, were foot soldiers. Maybe they were ordinary townsfolk imitating foot soldiers. The men of the Thousand Cities used all sorts of tricks to try to keep him from testing their inadequate walls. If this was a trick, it would work. He couldn't afford to assail Qostabash, not with that infantry army close on his heels.

On and on the Videssians went, now walking their horses, now trotting them. Maniakes dropped back to the rear guard and peered behind them. Their pursuers had dropped out of sight. He nodded to himself, well enough pleased.

When evening came, the army camped on irrigated land not far from the Tutub. The only enemies close by were mosquitoes and gnats, and they were impartial foes to all mankind. Maniakes looked east, back toward Videssos. No help would reach him from that direction, not with the Makuraners controlling the westlands. Messengers might be able to come up from Lyssaion in case of need, but the need would have to be urgent for them to risk capture by the men of Makuran. He had trouble imagining a need so urgent.

He walked over to the wagon in which Lysia had ridden. "Here we are, altogether surrounded by the foe," he said with a melodramatic wave and an even more melodramatic pause. The pause over, he added, "Isn't it wonderful?"

Lysia laughed, understanding him perfectly. "It certainly is," she said.

The Makuraners wasted no time in trying to make his life difficult. When the army began to move the next morning, it soon encountered flooded fields that came from broken canals. He faced the problem with equanimity: they'd done the same thing each of the past two years. He had enough timbers along to corduroy a road to drier ground, at which point his engineers picked up the timbers and stowed them again. Sooner or later, those infantrymen would try to follow in his footsteps. They'd have a slow, wet, muddy time of it.

Up ahead, seemingly secure on its hillock, squatted one of the

Thousand Cities. No large Makuraner army lurked nearby now. Maniakes pointed to the town, whose name he did not know. "We'll take it," he said.

With practiced efficiency, engineers and soldiers went to work. The muddy timbers that had let the Videssian army make its way through muck now were reassembled as frames for catapults and rams. The catapults began lobbing big pots filled with pitch and other inflammable substances into the town. The engineers used oil-soaked rags as wicks for the pots. Before long, columns of smoke rose from burning roofs and awnings and boards inside the city.

Anywhere else, the catapults would also have flung heavy stones at the wall. In the land between the Tutub and the Tib, heavy stones were hard to come by. Forcing breaches, then, was the work of the rams. Under leather-covered wooden frames, they inched up the slope of the artificial hillock toward the city. The defenders on the wall shouted defiance at them and shot at the men who carried the frames and would swing the rams.

Anywhere else, the defenders would have dropped heavy stones down onto the frames, trying to break them and either render the rams useless or at least tear openings through which the boiling water and red-hot sand they poured down onto the attackers could find their way. Again, though, heavy stones were few and far between in the Land of the Thousand Cities.

Videssian archers filled the air with shafts, doing their best to keep the men of the city garrison from interfering with the rams. *Thud!* The pointed iron tip of one of them slammed into the wall. Maniakes was standing just out of bowshot from the foes. The ground quivered beneath his feet, as if at a small earthquake. *Thud!* Another blow, another little tremor transmitted up through the soles of his shoes.

Thud! That one was smaller still. Off on the other side of the city, halfway round the circuit of the walls, another ram had gone into action. Now the defenders would have two things to worry about at the same time. Maniakes wondered which ram would first make the wall give way.

It proved to be the closer one. With a rumble that seemed almost like a tired sigh, some of the brick masonry came tumbling down. Through it, the screams of the defenders who came tumbling down with the wall rang high and shrill. Videssians rushed into the breach.

Surviving city garrison men met them and, for some little while, fought fiercely enough to hold them in check. But the city garrison was small, and its men neither well trained nor well armed. When a couple of its officers fell, the men began to lose heart. A few of them fell back from the breach, and then a few more. That could not go on long, not if they intended to hold back their enemies. And then, with cries of "Phos with us!" the Videssians began jumping down into the city. The defense was over. The sack had begun.

A captain asked Maniakes, "The usual rules, your Majesty?"

"Aye, the usual, Immodios," he answered. "Wreck the town, men may plunder and burn as they like, but no attacks against anyone who doesn't attack first, no murdering women and children for the sport of it. Any shrine to the Makuraner God you find, tear it down."

"As you say, your Majesty." Immodios saluted, right fist over his heart, then hurried off to spread the news.

As methodically as they had breached the wall, the Videssians went about the business of knocking down the city. A couple of the blue-robed priests who had accompanied the army urged them on, shouting, "Phos will bless you for the vengeance you inflict on his foes and the false god they worship."

Maniakes listened to that fiery talk with some regret, but made no effort to stop it. The Makuraners had turned the war into a religious struggle, not only by wrecking Phos' temples all over the westlands but also by forcing the people in the lands they occupied to follow Vaspurakaner usages rather than Videssian orthodoxy. Calling the counterattack a holy war made his men fight harder than they would have otherwise.

Eventually, the Avtokrator supposed, peace might come to Videssos and Makuran. The bitterness of the war they were fighting now would not make that peace any easier to find. Maniakes knew that. But he also knew he did not want peace to come to Videssos if it was dictated by Sharbaraz King of Kings.

With the garrison overcome, the Videssians threw open the gates and let people stream out of the city and down toward the floodplain. After a while, they would probably come back and start rebuilding. By then, of course, the rubble left from the sack would raise the artificial hillock on which the city stood another palm's breadth or so, making it that much harder for the next Videssian

Avtokrator who campaigned here, ten years from now, or fifty, or five hundred, to take the place.

Well, Maniakes thought, *that will be for my successor to worry about, not me. My job is to make sure I have a successor who one day will be in a position to worry about it.*

Lysia came up to him when the sack was nearly over. Much as he loved her, he would sooner not have seen her at that moment. He knew what she was going to say. Sure enough, she said it: "I pray the lord with the great and good mind will forgive our soldiers for what they're doing to the women here. War is a filthy business."

"War is a filthy business," Maniakes agreed. "This one was forced upon us."

"I know," Lysia said; they had this argument whenever one of the Thousand Cities fell. "That doesn't mean we have to make it filthier."

Maniakes shrugged. "If they'd surrendered instead of trying to fight, they could have all left undisturbed; you know I would have let them do that. But they chose to make a fight of it. Once they did, that changed the rules and what the soldiers expected. Next time—"

"Phos forbid a next time," Lysia broke in, sketching the sun-circle above her left breast. "I've heard too many stories about all the horrid things the Makuraners did when they took our cities in the westlands; I don't want them telling horrid stories about us."

"I wish there were no need for them to tell horrid stories about us," Maniakes answered. "That's not quite the same thing, though. They've made themselves frightful to us. If we make ourselves frightful to them in return, sooner or later they'll get the idea that they can't afford to fight us anymore. That's what I'm after."

"I know that's what you're after." Lysia's face stayed troubled. "The good god grant you find it, that's all."

"What I really want to find," Maniakes said, "is Abivard's army. Once I beat him, the whole of this country falls into my hands and I can push straight for Mashiz. Taking his capital, by Phos—that would be a revenge worth having."

Now Lysia did smile, ruefully. "I don't think you've heard a word I've said. I can understand that, I suppose. I can even see that Videssos may be better off on account of what you're doing. But that doesn't mean I have to like it." She walked off, leaving him scratching his head.

* * *

From the hillock where yet another of the Thousand Cities went up in flames behind him, Maniakes peered out over the floodplain. He could see a long way from here, but seeing far was not the same as seeing clearly. Turning to Rhegorios, he said, "Drop me into the ice—" He spat in rejection of Skotos. "—if I know where Abivard and the cursed Makuraner field army are. With what we've been doing hereabouts, I thought they'd surely have come to pay us a visit by now."

"So would I," his cousin agreed. "But no sign of them so far. Outside of these worthless little city garrisons, the only Makuraner army we've seen is the one that's been following in our footsteps ever since Qostabash."

"And they're foot soldiers." Maniakes stated the obvious. "What they are, in fact, is the same kind of force Abivard used to fight us year before last. They're probably garrison troops themselves, though they've had so much action the past couple of years, they might as well be regular infantry."

"They're not the worst fighters around," Rhegorios allowed. "When they were working alongside the boiler boys, they made pretty good fighters." Now he looked around, too. "Where *are* the boiler boys?"

"If I could find them, I'd tell you," Maniakes said. "Since I can't find them, I'm going to talk with someone who can, or at least who may be able to: I'm going to see what Bagdasares can do."

"Can't hurt," Rhegorios said. "It may even do some good. Why not?"

"That's why you go see wizards," Maniakes answered, "to find out why not."

Dubious recommendations notwithstanding, he did go to consult the mage from Vaspurakan. "You have been in close contact with Abivard for years," Bagdasares said. "That will help." He looked thoughtful. "Have you got anything of his we might use as a magical source to find him?"

"I don't think so." Maniakes suddenly barked laughter. "It almost makes me wish Tzikas were in camp. He's been back and forth between me and Abivard so many times, each of us could use him as a magical source against the other."

"Contact and affinity are not necessarily one and the same," Bagdasares observed.

"The only person Tzikas has an affinity for is Tzikas," Maniakes said. "I should have taken the traitor's head when Abivard gave him back to me. Even if I did get some use out of him, I never slept easy with him around. That's why I said I almost wish he were back, not that I wish he really was. He's with Abivard again, and Abivard is welcome to worry about him or kill him, whichever he pleases."

"Aye, your Majesty." Bagdasares ran a hand through his thick, curly beard as he contemplated ways and means. "You have clasped his hand, not so?" Maniakes nodded. The wizard produced a small knife. "Let me have a bit of nail from a finger of your right hand, then. And you have spoken to him, so I shall ask for a few drops of your spittle." He quickly sketched the sun-sign over his heart. "By the lord with the great and good mind, I shall destroy these by fire when my magic is completed."

"I'll watch you do it," Maniakes said. "You I trust with my life, Bagdasares, but you're one of the few. Tzikas came too close to slaying me with sorcery for me to be easy about letting parts of myself, so to speak, get loose where other wizards might lay their hands on them."

"And right you are to be cautious," Alvinos Bagdasares agreed. "Now, if I may—"

Maniakes let him cut a bit of fingernail from his right index finger. The Avtokrator spat into a little bowl while Bagdasares bound the nail clipping to one end of a small stick with crimson thread. The mage filled the bowl into which Maniakes had spat with water from a silver ewer. He lifted the little stick with a pair of tongs and let it float in the water.

"Think about Abivard, about wanting to learn in which direction from this place he is," Bagdasares said.

Obediently, Maniakes held the image of the Makuraner marshal in his mind. Bagdasares, meanwhile, chanted first in Videssian, then in the Vaspurakaner tongue Maniakes spoke only in snatches. Maniakes hoped the Makuraner mages weren't deliberately trying to keep him from learning his opponent's whereabouts. They probably were, just as Bagdasares and the other mages accompanying the Videssian army were doing their best to keep its location from their Makuraner counterparts.

Of its own accord, the small stick began to twist in the water, sending small ripples out toward the edge of the bowl. Maniakes kept his eye on the thread tied to the nail clipping. That end of the little stick swung to the east and stayed there. Maniakes scratched his head. "I won't believe Abivard's left the Land of the Thousand Cities."

"That is what the magic suggests," Bagdasares said.

"Could the Makuraners have twisted it so that, say, the stick points in exactly the opposite direction to the proper one?" Maniakes asked.

"I suppose it is possible, so I shall investigate," the wizard replied. "I sensed no such deception, however."

"If it were done well, you wouldn't, though," Maniakes said. "The Makuraners needed quite a while to figure out how you twisted that canal back on itself last year, for instance."

"That is so," Bagdasares admitted. "And Abivard would like nothing better than to make us think he is in one place when in fact he is somewhere else."

"Somewhere else probably being a place from which he can breathe right down our necks," Maniakes said.

"No point in using such a magic unless you gain some advantage from it, now is there?" Bagdasares plucked at his beard as he thought. "Opposites, eh? Well, we shall see what we shall see."

He pulled the stick out of the water, removed Maniakes' fingernail clipping from it, and tossed the clipping into a brazier. He smeared the end of the stick with pitch, getting his fingers stuck together in the process. Then he took a silver Makuraner arket from his beltpouch and used an iron blade to scrape several slivers of bright metal from the coin. He affixed the slivers to the pitch-smeared stick and put it back into the water.

"We shall use the bits of silver from the arket to represent Makuran's marshal in a somewhat different version of the spell," he told Maniakes.

"You know your business best," the Avtokrator answered. "I don't much care how you do what you do, as long as you get the answers I need."

"Your Majesty's forbearance is beyond price," Bagdasares said. The Vaspurakaner wizard once more began to chant and make passes over the bowl in which the stick floated. The incantations this time, especially the ones in the Vaspurakaner tongue, were different from those he'd used before, though Maniakes would have been hard-pressed to say how.

As it had during the previous incantation, the stick began to quiver in the water. And, as it had during the previous incantation, the end with the magical focus affixed swung toward the east.

Bagdasares looked from it to Maniakes and back again. "Unless I am utterly deceived, Abivard is indeed east of here."

"But that's mad," Maniakes exclaimed. "It's utterly useless. Why on earth would Abivard—and the Makuraner field army with him, no doubt—go into the Videssian westlands? Makuran holds the westlands, except for a port here and there and some holdouts in the hills of the southeast. What can he possibly do there that he didn't do years ago? He's not about to take Videssos the city—not without ships he's not, and I don't care how many soldiers he has. And for anything less important than that, he'd have been wiser to stay here and fight me instead."

"Your Majesty, my magic can tell you what is so—or what I believe to be so, at any rate," Bagdasares said. "Finding out why it is so—looking into the heart of a man that way—is beyond the scope of my art, or of any wizard's art. Often a man does not fully understand himself why he acts as he does—or have you not seen that?"

"I have," Maniakes said. "But this still perplexes me. Abivard is a great many things, but no one has ever called him stupid. He must have known we were coming back to the Land of the Thousand Cities this year. He didn't try to stop us by seizing Lyssaion. He couldn't stop us from landing up in Erzerum and heading south. If he knew we were coming, why isn't he here to meet us? That's what I want to know."

"It is a proper question, an important question, your Majesty," Bagdasares agreed gravely. "It is also a question to which my magic can give you no good answer. May I ask a question of my own in return?"

"Ask," Maniakes told him. "Anything you can do to let Phos' light into what looks like Skotos' darkness would be welcome." He drew the good god's sun-circle above his heart.

Bagdasares also sketched the sun-circle, saying, "I have no great and wise thoughts to offer, merely this: if, for whatever reason, Abivard chose to absent himself from the land between the Tutub and the Tib, should we not punish him for his error by doing all the harm we can in these parts?"

"That's what we've been doing," Maniakes said. "That's what I aim to go on doing. If Abivard wants to go haring off on some business of his own, let him. Makuran will suffer on account of it."

"Well said, your Majesty."

Maniakes did not bother answering that. Everything he'd said made perfect sense—and not just to him, if Bagdasares had seized on it so readily. He'd told himself as much a good many times before he'd come seeking Bagdasares' sorcerous counsel. But if Abivard wasn't stupid, why had he left the almost certain scene of this year's action? What reason had he found good enough for him to do such a thing?

"No way to tell," Maniakes murmured. Alvinos Bagdasares' eyebrows rose; no doubt he hoped to learn what was in Maniakes' mind. Not likely, not when Maniakes was far from sure himself. But whatever Abivard was up to, Maniakes had the feeling he'd find out, and that he wouldn't be overjoyed when he did.

As the Videssians did with temples to Phos, the Makuraners built shrines to the God not only in cities for the benefit of merchants and artisans but also out by the roadside in the country so peasants could pray and worship and then go back to work. Maniakes had been destroying those roadside shrines ever since he first entered the Land of the Thousand Cities. If nothing else, that inconvenienced the farmers, which in a small way would help the Videssian cause.

The God was usually housed in quarters less elaborate than Phos' temples. Some of the shrines were in the open air, with the four sides of the square altar facing in the cardinal directions, each one symbolizing one of the Makuraners' Four Prophets. As the Videssians came closer to Mashiz, the shrines grew more elaborate, as Maniakes had known to be the case from previous incursions into the land between the Tutub and the Tib.

And then, as the Videssian army approached the Tib, the soldiers came upon a shrine so extraordinary, they summoned the Avtokrator to see it. "We don't know what to do with it, your Majesty," said Komentiolos, the captain of the company that had overrun the shrine. "You have to tell us, and before you can do that, you have to see it."

"All right, I'll have a look," Maniakes said agreeably, and dug his heels into Antelope's sides.

The shrine had walls and a roof. The walls were baked brick rather than plain mud brick, but that did not greatly surprise Maniakes: the Makuraners gave the God and the Four Prophets the best they had, as the Videssians did with Phos. The entranceway stood open. Maniakes looked a question to Komentiolos. The captain nodded. Maniakes went inside, Komentiolos following.

Maniakes' eyes needed a bit to adjust to the gloom within. There at the center of the shrine stood the usual foursquare Makuraner altar. Komentiolos ignored that, having seen its like many times before. He waved to the far wall, the one toward which the side of the altar honoring Fraortish, the eldest prophet, pointed.

Standing against that smoothly plastered wall was a statue of the God, the first such Maniakes had ever seen. The God was portrayed in the regalia of a Makuraner King of Kings. The sun and the moon were painted on the wall beside him in gold and silver. He held a thunderbolt in one hand and was posed as if about to hurl it against some miscreant. His plump face, mouth twisted into a rather nasty smile, said he would enjoy hurling it.

As far as Maniakes was concerned, Videssian craftsmen depicted Phos in a far more artistic and awe-inspiring way. Phos, now, Phos was portrayed as a god worth worshiping, very much unlike this petulant—

Abruptly, Maniakes realized the face the Makuraner sculptor had given the statue was not intended to be an idealized portrait of the God, as images of the lord with the great and good mind were rightly idealized. This portrait was intended to show the features of a man, and of a man the Avtokrator knew, even if he had not seen him for ten years and more.

Maniakes turned his head away from the statue. He did not want to look at it; even thinking of it gave him the feeling of having just taken a big bite of rotten meat.

"Isn't that the most peculiar excuse for a shrine you ever saw, your Majesty?" Komentiolos said. "There's a chamber back there with a lot of metal drums and stones, to make it sound like the statue of the God is thundering at whatever he's taken a mind to disliking."

"It's not a statue of the God, or not exactly a statue of the God,"

Maniakes answered. "What it is, exactly, is a statue of Sharbaraz King of Kings."

For a moment, Komentiolos didn't understand. Then he did, and looked as sickened as Maniakes felt. "It's a statue of Sharbaraz King of Kings *as* the God," he said, as if hoping Maniakes would tell him he was wrong.

However much Maniakes wished he could do that, he couldn't. "That's just what it is," he said.

"But don't the Makuraners—" Komentiolos spread his hands in helpless disbelief. "—don't they think this is blasphemy, too?"

"I don't know. I hope so," Maniakes told him. "But I do know one thing: Sharbaraz doesn't think it's blasphemy."

Back when he'd known Sharbaraz, more than a decade before, the King of Kings—or, as he was then, the claimant to the title of King of Kings—would never have had such a building erected. But Sharbaraz-then was not Sharbaraz-now. Through all the intervening years, he'd been unchallenged sovereign of Makuran. Everyone had sought his favor. No one had disagreed with him. The result was . . . this.

Sketching the sun-circle over his heart, Maniakes murmured, "It could have been me." The sycophancy in the court of Videssos was hardly less than that in the court of Makuran. Thanks to his father, Maniakes had taken with a grain of salt all the flattery he'd heard. Sharbaraz, evidently, had lapped it up and gone looking for more.

Komentiolos said, "Now that we've got this place, your Majesty, what do we do with it?"

"I wish I'd never seen it in the first place," Maniakes said. But that was not an answer. He found something that was: "We bring some Makuraner prisoners in here, so they can see it with their own eyes. Then we let them go, to spread the tale as they will. After that, we let some of our soldiers see it, too, to give them the idea of what sort of enemy we're fighting. Then we let them wreck the statue. Then we let them wreck the building. Then we burn it. Fire purifies."

"Aye, your Majesty. I'll see to all of that," Komentiolos said. "It sounds good to me."

"None of it sounds good to me," Maniakes said. "I wish we weren't doing it. I wish we didn't have to do it. By the good god, I wish this shrine had never been built."

He wondered how Abivard, who had always fought him as one soldier against another, no more, no less, could bear to serve under a man who was coming to believe himself on a par with his god. He wondered whether Abivard knew this place existed and, if so, what he thought of it. He filed that last question away, as possibly worth exploring later.

First things first. "Gather up the prisoners and send them through here, quick as you can. Then turn our men loose on this place. The longer it stands, the greater the abomination."

"You're right about that, your Majesty," Komentiolos said. "I'll see to it, I promise you."

"Good." Maniakes tried to imagine portraying himself as Phos incarnate on earth. Absurd. If the good god didn't strike him down, his outraged subjects would. He hurried out of the shrine, feeling a sudden need for fresh, clean air.

Maniakes looked back toward the southeast, toward Lyssaion. He couldn't see the Videssian port now, of course. He couldn't even see the hills that were the watershed between the Xeremos and the Tutub. The only hillocks making the horizon anything but flat were the artificial ones upon which perched the Thousand Cities.

His chuckle was sheepish. Turning to Lysia, he said, "When I'm back in Videssos the city, I can't wait to get away. Once I am away, I wish I had news of what's going on there."

"*I* don't miss the city," Lysia said. "We haven't heard much from it the past couple of summers, and what news they did bring us here wasn't worth having."

She spoke with great certainty, and with more than a little anger in her voice. The mockery and disapproval she'd taken in the capital for becoming her cousin's consort wore more heavily on her than they did on Maniakes. He'd already seen that, as Avtokrator, nothing he did was going to make everybody happy. That let him take scorn philosophically . . . most of the time.

"Not easy to get messengers through, anyway," he said, as if consoling himself. "Not hearing doesn't have to mean anything. They wouldn't send out dispatches unless the news was important enough to risk losing men to make sure it got to me."

"To the ice with news, except what we cause," Lysia said positively. "To the ice with Videssos the city, too. I'd give it to the Makuraners in a minute if doing that wouldn't wreck the Empire."

Yes, she'd let her resentment fester where Maniakes had shrugged—most of—his off.

He stopped worrying about news from home and looked west instead. The horizon was jagged there, with the peaks of the Dilbat Mountains shouldering themselves up into view above the nearer flatlands. In the foothills of those mountains lay Mashiz. He'd been there once, years before, helping to install Sharbaraz on his throne. If he reached Mashiz again, he'd cast Sharbaraz down from that throne . . . and from his assumption of divinity. Destroying that shrine was something Maniakes had been delighted to do.

Closer than the Dilbats, closer than Mashiz, was the Tib. Canals stretched its waters out to the west. Where the canals failed, as at the eastern margins of the Tutub, irrigation failed. Irrigation, though, was only marginally in his mind now. He concentrated on getting over the river. It wasn't so wide as the Tutub, but ran swifter, and was no doubt still in spring spate. Crossing it wouldn't be easy; the Makuraners would do everything they could to keep him from gaining the western bank.

He didn't expect to capture a bridge of boats intact; that would be luck beyond any calculation. Whatever soldiers the foe had on the far side would mass against him. If they delayed him long enough, as they might well, the Makuraner infantry army he'd left behind would catch up to him. With so many soldiers mustered against his men, with the river limiting the directions in which he could move, all that might prove unpleasant.

When he grumbled about the difficulties of getting over the Tib, Rhegorios said, "If we have to, you know, we can always turn south toward the source of the river and either ford it where it's young and narrow or go round it altogether and come up along the west bank."

"I don't want to do anything like that," Maniakes said. "It would take too long. I want to go straight at Mashiz."

His cousin looked at him without saying anything. Maniakes felt his cheeks grow hot. In the early days of his reign, his most besetting fault had been moving too soon, committing himself to action without adequate preparation or resources. Rhegorios thought he was doing it again.

On reflection, though, he decided he wasn't. "Think it through," he said. "If we turn south, what will the fellow in charge of the foot soldiers from Qostabash do? Is he likely to chase us? Can he hope to catch us, foot pursuing horse? If he has any sense, what he'll do is cross the Tib himself and wait for us at the approaches to Mashiz. If you were in his sandals, isn't that what you'd do?"

Rhegorios did think it through, quite visibly. Maniakes gave him credit for that, the more so as his young cousin was inclined to be headstrong, too. "Cousin your Majesty brother-in-law of mine, I think you're likely to be right," the Sevastos said at last. "Revolting how doing something simple will spill the chamber pot into the soup of a complicated plan."

"We have to find a way to get across ourselves, once we do reach the river," Maniakes said. "The trouble is, if the defenders are even half awake, that's almost as hard a job as getting over the Cattle Crossing has been for the Makuraners. They've been trying to figure out how to manage that for years, and they haven't come close yet, Phos be praised."

"I know what you need to do," Rhegorios said suddenly. "Have Bagdasares turn the whole Tib into a Voimios strap and flip it about so that all at once we're on the west side and the cursed Makuraners are on the east."

Maniakes laughed out loud. "You don't think small, do you, cousin of mine? Except for the detail that that sounds like a magic big enough to burn out the brain of every wizard in Videssos, it's a splendid notion."

"I thought you'd like it," Rhegorios said. Now both men laughed. Rhegorios went on, "If you've got a better idea, I'd like to hear it."

"What I'd like to do," Maniakes said, "is play a trick on them like the one my father used against Smerdis' men when we were fighting alongside Sharbaraz. My father made a big, fancy, obvious move to cross a waterway—pinned the enemy's attention to it nice as you please. Then he put a force across downstream from his feint, just far enough that nobody noticed them till they were too well established to be checked."

"That sounds good," Rhegorios agreed. "How do we bring it off?"

"We're short of rafts, and this country doesn't have enough trees to make building them easy," Maniakes said. "Maybe we can try using the hide boats the locals make."

"You mean the round ones that look like soup bowls?" Rhegorios rolled his eyes. "To the ice with me if I'd be happy getting into one of those. I can't see how the people who use them keep them from spinning round and round and round. Or were you talking about the rafts that float on top of blown-up hides so they'll carry more? If those are the kinds of ideas the Makuraners get when they think of boats, it's no wonder they never tried coming over the Cattle Crossing."

"The locals *aren't* Makuraners," Maniakes reminded him. "And take a look around, cousin of mine. They do what they can with what they have: not much wood, not much of anything but mud. You can't make a boat out of mud, but you can raise beasts on what grows out of the mud and then use their hides to go up and down the rivers and canals."

"Do you really want to try putting our men into those crazy things to get to the west bank of the Tib?" Rhegorios said. "Even more to the point, do you think you can get horses into them? Men are stupid; if you order them to go and do something, they'll go and do it, even if they can see it's going to get a raft of them—" He used the term with obvious relish. "—killed. Horses, now, horses have better sense than that."

Like his cousin, Maniakes knew horses all too often showed lamentably little sense of any sort. That, however, wasn't relevant. Rhegorios' objection was. Maniakes said, "Maybe you're right. But if you are, how do you propose getting over the river?"

"Who, me? You're the Avtokrator; you're supposed to be the one with all the answers," Rhegorios said, which was highly annoying and true at the same time.

"One of the answers the Avtokrator is allowed to use is picking someone who knows more about a particular bit of business than he does and then listening to what he has to say," Maniakes returned.

"If you want to talk about the business of chasing pretty girls, I know more than you do," Rhegorios said. "If you want to talk about the business of guzzling neat wine, I know more than you do. If you want to talk about the business of leading a cavalry column, I know at least as much as you do. If you want to talk about the business of crossing a river without bridging or proper boats, neither one of us knows a bloody thing."

"You certainly made noises as if you knew," Maniakes said.

"If you want to talk about the business of making noises, I know more than you do," Rhegorios said, impudent as usual.

"I know what I'll do." Maniakes thumped himself in the forehead with the heel of the hand to show he'd been stupid. "I'd have had to do it when we got to the Tib any which way. I'll talk with Ypsilantes."

For the first time in their conversation, he discovered he had Rhegorios' complete and ungrudging approval. "That's a *good* idea," Rhegorios said. "If the chief engineer can't figure out a way to do it, it can't be done. If you want to talk about the business of having good ideas, you may know more than I do."

Being praised for an idea as obvious as it was good did not make Maniakes feel much better; the thought that it hadn't occurred to Rhegorios, either, consoled him to some degree. He wasted no time in summoning Ypsilantes. The chief engineer was nearer his father's age than his own; he had commanded the engineering detachment accompanying the Videssian army the elder Maniakes had led in alliance with Sharbaraz and against Smerdis.

"How do we get across the river?" he repeated when Maniakes put the question to him. His handsome, fleshy features did not show much of the amusement he obviously felt. "Your Majesty, you leave that to me. Tell me when and where you want to go across and I'll take care of it for you."

He sounded as confident as if he were discussing his faith in Phos. That made Maniakes feel better; he'd seen Ypsilantes was a man who delivered on his promises. Nonetheless, he persisted: "Tell me one way in which you might accomplish that."

"Here's one—first one that pops into my head," Ypsilantes said. "Suppose you want to cross somewhere near the place where a good-sized canal flows off to the northeast from the Tib—flows off behind where we already are, in other words. If we divert water from the river to the canal, what's left of the river will be easy enough to manage. Like I say, you leave all that sort of thing to me, your Majesty."

Maniakes remembered his thoughts back in Videssos the city on how best to run affairs. Here was a man who plainly knew how to do what needed doing. "When the time comes, Ypsilantes, I will," the Avtokrator said.

The engineer saluted, clenched right fist over his heart, then hurried off to ready what might need readying. Some officers of his ability would have had their eye on the throne. All he wanted was the chance to play with his toys. Maniakes was more than willing to give him that, and so could give him free rein as well. He wondered if Sharbaraz would have been so trusting, and had his doubts.

* * *

When the army was only a couple of days' ride from the Tib, a scout came galloping back to Maniakes. "Your Majesty," he called, "the King of Kings has sent you an ambassador. He's on his way here now."

"Has he?" Maniakes said, and then, a moment later, "Is he?" The scout looked confused. Maniakes knew it was his own fault. He went on, "Sharbaraz has never done that before. How can he send me an ambassador when he doesn't recognize me as rightful Avtokrator of the Videssians?"

"I don't know, your Majesty," the scout said, which had the virtue of being an altogether honest answer.

"Go back and tell this ambassador I'll listen to him," Maniakes said without any great warmth. The scout hurried off as fast as he had come. Maniakes watched his back. The most likely reason he could find for Sharbaraz to send him an envoy was to try to delay him so the Makuraners on the west bank of the Tib could shore up their defenses. But he couldn't refuse to see the fellow, because the likely reason might not be the true one.

The ambassador reached him less than half an hour later. The fellow rode a fine gray mare and wore a striped caftan shot through with silver threads. He was about fifty, with a full gray beard and the long face, swarthy skin, and deep-set eyes that marked the Makuraners. Bowing in the saddle, he asked in fair Videssian, "You are Maniakes son of Maniakes?"

"Yes," Maniakes answered. "And you?"

"I am Rafsanj son of Shidjam," the ambassador said, "and I bring you greetings from Sharbaraz son of Peroz, King of Kings, may his years be many and his realm increase, mighty, powerful, awesome to behold, a man whom the God delights to honor—"

Maniakes held up a hand. Sharbaraz bore more titles and attributes than a stray dog had ticks; Maniakes wasn't interested in having them all trotted out. "Sharbaraz hasn't been interested in treating with me before," he remarked. "After all, he recognizes the fraud he calls Hosios son of Likinios as Avtokrator of the Videssians, not me. What has made him change his mind?" He thought he knew the answer to that: an invasion that looked like succeeding was a good way to get anyone's attention.

Rafsanj coughed delicately. "I was not bidden to treat with Avtokrator of the Videssians, but with Maniakes son of Maniakes, commander of the forces currently disturbing the realm of Maku-ran, who, I presume, is yourself."

"I told you yes already," Maniakes said, and then, to himself, "Presumption." Sharbaraz had a good deal of gall if he thought he could keep his own puppet Avtokrator around and treat with Mani-akes at the same time. But then, any man who made a shrine where he was worshiped as a god had gall and to spare.

That he was willing to talk to Maniakes at all was a step for-ward. And maybe, having created the false Hosios, Sharbaraz felt he could not abandon him without losing face among his own courtiers. Rafsanj asked, "Will you hear what I have to say, Mani-akes son of Maniakes?"

"Why should I?" Maniakes asked. "Why shouldn't I find some mean prison and throw you into it, the way Sharbaraz did to the eminent Triphylles, the envoy I sent to him asking for peace?"

"Because—" Rafsanj hesitated. *Because he was winning then and he's not so sure now,* was what went through Maniakes' mind. *He never thought I'd have the chance to collect the debt he owes me.* But that would have been Sharbaraz's thinking, not what was going through the mind of this Rafsanj now. The ambassador said, "Because if you imprison me, you will not hear what the King of Kings offers."

"That's not necessarily so," Maniakes answered, smiling. "I could hear the offer and then jail you, as Sharbaraz did with Triphylles."

"You are pleased to jest, Maniakes son of Maniakes," Rafsanj said. He made a good envoy; if he was nervous, he didn't let on. But he did not, would not, call Maniakes *your Majesty.*

"Let's find out if I am joking, shall we?" the Avtokrator said. "Give me Sharbaraz's terms and then we'll see how long you stay free. How does that sound to you?"

"Not good," Rafsanj answered, no doubt truthfully. "Sharbaraz King of Kings, may his years be many and his realm increase, bids you give over the devastation you are working in the Land of the Thousand Cities."

Maniakes displayed his teeth in what was not really a smile. "I'm sure he does. I wanted him to stop devastating the westlands. I was even willing to pay him to stop devastating the westlands. Did he listen to me?" That question answered itself, and suggested the next one: "Why should I listen to him?"

"He bids you bide here, that we may discuss the composition of differences between Videssos and Makuran," Rafsanj said.

"And he will, of course, hold all his armies in place while I'm doing that," Maniakes said.

"Of course," Rafsanj answered. Maniakes watched him narrowly. He was good, but not quite good enough. He went on in fulsome tones: "And once agreement has been reached, will there not be rejoicing on both sides of the border? Will voices not be raised in joy and gladness?"

"The border? Which border? The one before Sharbaraz began his war against us?" Maniakes asked. Rafsanj did not answer that question; maybe Sharbaraz had not given him an answer for it. "I don't think I'm ready to talk peace quite yet, thanks," the Avtokrator said. Strange how things had changed—a few years before, he would have fallen on such an offer with a glad cry. But not now. "I don't want to talk here, either. Tell Sharbaraz that if he still wants to discuss these things with me when I get to Mashiz, we may be able to do it there."

"Beware lest your arrogance bring you down," Rafsanj said. "Overweening pride has laid many a man low."

"I'm not the one who built a statue of the God in my own image," Maniakes retorted, raising a scowl from Sharbaraz's envoy. "I'm not the one who plans to move armies around after pledging I wouldn't, either. When is the King of Kings going to pull Abivard and his horsemen out of the sleeve of his caftan and hurl them at me? They must be around here somewhere." He still had trouble giving credence to Bagdasares' magic.

And his probe struck a nerve, too; Rafsanj jerked, as if Maniakes had jabbed a pin into his legs. But the envoy answered, "I have no obligation to speak to you of the manner in which your doom will fall and all your hopes be swallowed by the Void."

"And I have no obligation to stay here while Sharbaraz moves his pieces around the board," Maniakes returned. "I have no obligation to let myself be cozened, either. Tell Sharbaraz I'll see him in Mashiz."

"That shall never be," Rafsanj told him.

"I know better," Maniakes jeered. "Videssos has taken Mashiz before; we can do that. What will never happen is Makuran taking Videssos the city."

Again, Rafsanj started. This time, he mastered himself without saying anything. He sawed at the reins, roughly pulling his horse's head around. He rode away from Maniakes faster than he had approached him.

Maniakes watched him go. He waved to his own men, calling, "Onward!" Onward they went, toward the Tib. They did not go so fast as Maniakes would have liked. The Makuraners in front of them opened canal after canal. The harvest in this part of the Land of the Thousand Cities was liable to be scanty. The Makuraners, plainly, did not care. One of their armies would have bogged down, and might have become easy meat for raiders. The Videssians did not bog down. But corduroying a road and then recovering the timber that let them do it again was slow, hard work.

Even so, they had come within a day's—a normal day's—march of the river when a courier caught up with them from behind. That was no mean feat in and of itself. Maniakes congratulated the fellow and plied him with rough, sour army wine before asking, "What brought you here through all the Makuraners? It can't be anything small, that's certain."

"I'm the first to reach you, your Majesty?" The courier sounded dismayed but not surprised. "I'm not the first who was sent, that's certain."

"What's toward?" Maniakes demanded, worry in his voice now.

The courier took a deep breath. "Your Majesty, the Kubratoi have swarmed down over the border, heading straight for Videssos the city. For all I know, they're sitting outside the walls by now."

III

"Phos curse Etzilios to an eternity in Skotos' ice!" Maniakes exclaimed, spitting on the muddy ground. At the same time as he cursed the Kubrati khagan, though, he knew a grudging admiration for him. Etzilios' spies had seen the Videssians set sail for the west. He knew, then, that the Empire's best troops were gone. And, knowing that, he had decided to take his revenge for the beating Maniakes had given him three years before.

"He's hit us hard, your Majesty," the messenger said, confirming the thought in Maniakes' mind. "This isn't just a raid, or it doesn't look like one, anyhow. The way Etzilios was storming for the city, you'd think he aimed to take it." He grinned to show how unlikely that was.

Maniakes grinned, too. "If that's what's in his mind, he'd better think again," he said. "The nomads have no siege engines. He can come up to the walls. He can do all manner of horrible things outside them. But he can't break in." That no one unwelcome could break into Videssos the city from outside had been an article of faith, and deservedly so, for centuries. "What are we doing against him?" he asked the courier. "Have we used our ships to land men behind his force?"

The man took another swig of wine, then shook his head. "Hadn't done that by the time I set out, your Majesty. Matter of fact, the Kubratoi were using those single-log boats of theirs, those monoxyla, to move their own men down the coast against us."

"Yes, to the ice with Etzilios, all right," Maniakes said. "He learns his lessons too bloody well." The Avtokrator had landed troops in the rear of the Kubratoi before. Now they looked to be returning the favor.

Videssians being the sort of people they were, the courier's arrival seemed a signal for officers of all ranks to converge on Maniakes, trying to learn what news the fellow had brought. "Cheeky as sparrows, the lot of them," Rhegorios complained after he finally made it to Maniakes' side. "Haven't they got any patience?"

"Almost as much as you," the Avtokrator said, earning himself a glare from his first cousin. He turned to the courier. "Give his highness the Sevastos your message, the same as you gave it to me."

"Aye, your Majesty," the man said, and repeated himself for Rhegorios.

Rhegorios listened intently, then nodded. "Isn't that interesting?" he said when the courier was done. He raised an eyebrow and asked Maniakes, "What do you intend to do about it?"

"By the good god, not one thing," Maniakes answered. "Having the Kubratoi overrun the countryside, even if they do it all the way down to the walls of Videssos the city, isn't essential, because the city won't fall to them. What we're doing here *is* essential. If we take Mashiz, the Makuraners will have to pull troops out of the westlands to deal with that. So we'll go on doing exactly what we have been doing, and worry about Etzilios later."

"Cousin, that is an excellent plan," Rhegorios said. "For that matter, it's not only getting the Makuraners to commit troops from our westlands. Getting them to commit Abivard's force, wherever that is, has been hard enough."

"If crossing the Tib won't do it, nothing will," Maniakes predicted. He looked thoughtful. "I wonder if Abivard is hanging back on purpose, hoping we'll take out Sharbaraz and leave him a clear path to the throne. His sister is married to the King of Kings, after all, which gives him a claim of sorts."

"My sister is married to the Avtokrator of the Videssians," Rhegorios pointed out. "And I, I assure you, have no interest in claiming our throne."

Maniakes nodded. As a courtier, Rhegorios had to say that. In his case, Maniakes was convinced it was true. How true it was for Abivard, though, was liable to be a different question. "From things I've heard, I don't think Sharbaraz trusts his brother-in-law as far as I trust mine."

"Your Majesty is gracious."

"My Majesty is stinking tired of distractions, is what my Majesty is," Maniakes said, his scorn for his own title bringing a smile to Rhegorios' lips. "I am not going to let myself be distracted, not here, not now. I know where I need to go, I think I know how to get there from where I am, and I think I know what happens when I do. Stacked against all that, Etzilios is a small loaf of bread."

"No doubt you're right," Rhegorios said. "We're *that* close—" He held up thumb and forefinger, each almost touching the other. "—to paying back a decade of debt and more."

"*That* close," Maniakes echoed. He imitated his cousin's gesture and then, slowly and deliberately, brought thumb and forefinger together till they touched. Rhegorios smiled a hungry smile.

Maniakes stared across the Tib, a discontented expression on his face. The river ran strongly toward the north, blocking his way across it, blocking his way toward Mashiz. Beside him, Ypsilantes also looked unhappy. The engineer's earlier confidence now seemed misplaced. "The spring floods are strong and long this year," he remarked.

"So they are," Maniakes said. "It is as Phos wills." Even as he spoke the words, he wondered why the good god would prevent Makuran from being chastised for all its people had done to Videssos and to Phos himself. Maybe the Makuraner God held some sway here, after all. Or maybe the God was in league with Skotos against the lord with the great and good mind.

Across the Tib, parties of Makuraner foot soldiers looked to be readying a warm reception for the Videssians. Back out of sight, back behind the imperial army, that infantry force Maniakes had evaded was still dogging his heels. Their general didn't have all the resources Abivard had enjoyed the year before, but he was making the most of what he did have.

He was on Ypsilantes' mind, too. The chief engineer said, "We haven't the time to sit down in one place and work out what all it will take to cross the river with it running the way it is. If we do sit down, we'll have a battle on our hands sooner than we'd like."

"Yes." Maniakes fixed him with a sour stare. "I thought you said you could come up with any number of expedients for getting over the Tib."

"For one thing, your Majesty, like I say, I didn't figure it'd be running so high," Ypsilantes replied with some dignity. "And, for another, I did expect more time to work. An army that's digging a canal to divert the Tib can't leave off and start fighting again at a moment's notice."

"If you spoke so plain to Sharbaraz, he'd probably thank you by tearing out your tongue," Maniakes said. "Sometimes what's true matters more than what sounds good at the moment, though. I try to remember that."

"I know you do, your Majesty," Ypsilantes answered. "That's why the only people who need fear you are the ones who have done wrong."

"You're kinder than I deserve," Maniakes said, "and, if you want to see how kindly I can be, find us a way to get over the Tib no matter how it's running."

"I'll do everything I can," the engineer said. "Right now, though, I haven't got any good ideas."

"They have the bridges of boats that usually run across the river." Maniakes pointed to the far bank of the Tib. "We won't see any of them. How do we substitute without using those palm trees you hate so much? How do we make sure we don't have to use the natives' horrible boats made of skins?"

"Common sense is plenty to make sure we don't want those boats," Ypsilantes said. He looked unhappy again, now at the world rather than at Maniakes in particular.

"What's left, then?" the Avtokrator asked.

"We need boats of some sort or another, your Majesty," Ypsilantes replied. "If we can't get anything better, those hide monstrosities will have to do. We need timber. If we can't get anything better, that will have to come from date palms. And if we have to use all those things I wish we didn't, we'll also need more time to get a bridge ready than we would otherwise."

"What about using the timbers from the stone-throwers and dart-throwers as pieces of the bridge?" Maniakes said.

Ypsilantes shook his head. "We'll need at least some of those engines. When we get within a bowshot of the western bank of the Tib, we'll have to drive back the Makuraner archers so we can extend the bridge all the way out to the end."

"You know best." Maniakes took on some of the engineer's jaundiced approach to the topic. "I wish you hadn't told me we'll need more time than we might if we had better materials around here." He held up a hasty hand. "No, I'm not blaming you. But I don't want to fight those Makuraner foot soldiers slogging after us somewhere back there, not if I can help it." He turned back toward the east.

"I understand that, your Majesty," Ypsilantes said. "I'll do everything I can to push the work ahead." He rubbed his chin. "What I really worry about is Abivard coming out of whatever bushes he's using to hide himself and hitting us a lick when it hurts the most."

"I'd be lying if I said that thought hadn't also occurred to me." Maniakes looked east again. "I wish I knew where he was. Even if he were someplace where I couldn't do anything about him— the same way I can't do anything about the Kubratoi—knowing what he might be able to do to me would take a good-sized weight off my mind."

"That's it, your Majesty," Ypsilantes agreed. "You can't fight a campaign looking over your shoulder every hour of the day and night, waiting for him to pop up like a hand puppet in a show. Or rather, you can, but you'd be a lot better off if you didn't have to."

"We'd be better off if a lot of things were different," Maniakes said. "But they're not, so we're going to have to deal with them as they are."

"That's so, too, your Majesty," Ypsilantes said, sounding as if he wished he could engineer the unfortunate condition right out of existence.

Maniakes sent men up and down the length of the Tib and the major canals nearby. They came back with a few boats of various sorts—fewer than he and Ypsilantes had hoped. The Avtokrator also set men to work chopping down date palms so they could use the rather stringy timber they got from them.

That outraged the inhabitants of the Land of the Thousand Cities more than anything else he had done up till then: more even than his having burned a good many of those cities. The farmers fought the lumbering parties as best they could, and began ambushing Videssian soldiers whenever they caught a few away from the main mass of men.

In the pavilion she shared with Maniakes, Lysia held up a jar of date wine, saying, "You'd think the local peasants would thank us for getting rid of the trees that let them make thick, sweet slop like this."

"Yes, I know," Maniakes said. "I first drank date wine when I was helping my father put Sharbaraz back on the throne. As far as I can see, the only people who like it are those who know no better."

"That's what I think of it, too," Lysia said. "But—"

"Yes, but," Maniakes agreed. "The locals are bushwhacking us, and some of my men have taken to massacring them whenever they get the chance." He sighed. "They do something, we pay them back, they do something worse—where does it end?"

Lysia didn't answer, perhaps because the answer was obvious: it ended with the two of them close by the Tib, with their gazes set on Mashiz beyond the river. Eventually, one side hit the other such a blow that it could not respond. That put an end to the fighting— for a generation, sometimes even two.

"Once we break into Mashiz," Maniakes said, "the Makuraners won't be able to stay in the field against us." He'd been saying that ever since he'd first conceived of the notion of bypassing the Videssian westlands and taking the war straight to the heart of the realm of the King of Kings. He still believed it. Before long, he hoped to find out whether he was right.

Thinking along with him as she often did, Lysia asked, "How soon can we cross the Tib and make for the capital?"

"A few more days, Ypsilantes tells me," Maniakes answered. "The squabbles with the peasants have slowed things up, but we finally have enough boats and almost enough timber. Get a little more wood, cut it to the right lengths, and then over the river we go."

Lysia looked westward. "And then it will be over." She did not speak in tones of blithe confidence. *One way or the other,* her words suggested. Maniakes did not try to reprove or correct her. After all the misfortunes he had watched as they befell Videssos, how could he? *One way or the other* was what he felt, too. Nothing was certain till it happened.

As if to prove that, one of his guards called from outside the tent: "Your Majesty, a scout is here with news."

"I'll come," he said, and did.

The scout had already dismounted. He started to perform a proskynesis, but Maniakes, impatient to hear what he had to say, waved for him not to bother prostrating himself. The scout did salute, then said, "Your Majesty, I hate to tell you this, but all those foot soldiers we bypassed back near Qostabash are about to catch up with us again."

"Oh, a pestilence!" Maniakes burst out, and spent the next couple of minutes swearing with an inventiveness that left the scout pop-eyed. The Avtokrator did not care. He'd spent more time as soldier than as sovereign and had learned how to vent his spleen.

Gradually, he calmed. He and Ypsilantes had known this might happen. Now it had. They would have to make the best of it. The scout watched him. After a moment, the fellow nodded and chuckled once or twice. "Your Majesty, I think there's going to be some Makuraner infantry out there—" He pointed east. "—sorry they were ever born."

"By the good god, I hope so." Maniakes stared east, off toward that approaching force of infantry. "You saw only foot soldiers there?" he demanded of the scout. "None of the Makuraners' boiler boys?"

"No, your Majesty, none to speak of," the scout answered. "They have a few horsemen with 'em, scouts and messengers and such, but I didn't see a sign of their heavy cavalry. If they'd been there, I'd have spotted 'em, too. You'd best believe that—those bastards can really fight, and I want to know when they're around."

"So do I," Maniakes said in abstracted tones, and then, more to himself than to the man who'd brought the unwelcome news, "To the ice with you, Abivard; where have you gone and hidden?" But even that was not the relevant question: when would Abivard emerge from hiding, and how much trouble would he cause once he did?

The Avtokrator nodded to the scout, dismissing him, then sent one of his guards after Ypsilantes. When the chief engineer arrived, Maniakes told him in a few words what had happened. Ypsilantes heard him out before loosing a long sigh. "Well, your Majesty, they never told us this business was going to be easy, now did they?"

"I'm afraid they didn't—whoever *they* are," Maniakes agreed. "Can we protect all the timber we've cut and the boats we've collected while we're fighting these cursed foot soldiers?"

"We'd better," Ypsilantes said bluntly, which made the Avtokrator glad to have him along. He continued, "Aye, I expect we can.

The Makuraner infantry moving on us won't come close to that stuff, not unless somebody really pisses in the stew pot. And if those odds and sods across the river have the nerve to try to sneak over here to this side and tear things up while most of us are busy, I'll be the most surprised man in the Land of the Thousand Cities."

Maniakes corrected him: "The second most surprised man."

Ypsilantes thought that one through, blinked like a frog swallowing a fly, and barked out a couple of syllables' worth of laughter. "I'll make sure it doesn't happen, your Majesty. Count on me."

"I will," Maniakes said. "I do." He waved Ypsilantes away, then started shouting orders, preparing his force to meet the Makuraners. He had more respect for the foe's foot than he'd brought to their first clashes a couple of years before; they had rapidly turned into real soldiers. He looked around the camp, where his own men were starting to stir. He smiled. They were better warriors than they had been a couple of years before, too.

The red-lion banner of Makuran flapped lazily in a light breeze. The enemy standard-bearer was an enormous man with shoulders like a bull's. Maniakes was glad to see him used for ornamental purposes rather than as a true fighter. Every little edge helped.

The Avtokrator looked out over the battle line advancing behind the standard-bearer. The Makuraner general disposed of more men than he did. Since the fight was infantry against cavalry, that mattered less than it would have had he been facing Abivard and the field army. It did not leave him delighted with the world, even so.

Most of the foot soldiers in the enemy army were not, strictly speaking, Makuraners, but rather men from the Thousand Cities. They were shorter and stockier and a little swarthier than the boiler boys from the high plateau to the west, with hair so black it shone with blue highlights, often worn in a neat bun resting on the nape of the neck. Their chief weapon was the bow; they carried knives and clubs for fighting at close quarters. Some of them wore helmets: businesslike iron pots, or sometimes leather caps strengthened with iron bands. Past that, the only armor they bore was their wicker shields.

They could fight. Maniakes had seen that. They hadn't done much fighting in the years before the Videssians had plunged into the Land of the Thousand Cities, but, as he'd thought a little while before, they'd learned their trade since. That was partly Abivard's fault—or to his credit, if you looked at things from the Makuraner point of view. It was also partly Maniakes' fault. By fighting a series of battles against the local infantry, he'd given them a course in how to go about fighting Videssians. Some of them had learned better than he would have wished.

He nodded to Rhegorios, who sat his horse beside Maniakes and Antelope, and pointed out toward the enemy infantry. "See— they're laying down some sort of barricade to keep us from charging home against them. Thornbushes, maybe, or something like that."

"We aren't planning on charging in among them right away anyhow, though," his cousin answered. "That kind of barrier would do more against Makuraner heavy cavalry, the kind that closes on you with the lance, than it does against our horse-archers."

"It'll be a nuisance for our men, too," Maniakes said, "and they're liable to pull the barricade away if they see a good place to come charging right out at us. In the fights last fall, as we were pulling back toward Lyssaion, their infantry was as aggressive as any general could want."

"Of course, they were working alongside cavalry of their own then," Rhegorios said. "They won't be so tough without the boiler boys here."

Mention of the Makuraner heavy cavalry was plenty to make Maniakes look north and then south, wondering still where Abivard was and how and when he might appear. When the Videssian army was locked in combat with the local infantry seemed a good bet.

"You'll get the right wing," Maniakes told his cousin when Abivard once more failed to materialize. "I won't give you any detailed orders about what to do with it, but you can move faster than foot soldiers. If you can flank them out of their position, that would be a good thing to do."

"Easier if they weren't cutting more canals," Rhegorios observed. "But I will try—you know that."

"Everything would be easier if they didn't make it harder," Maniakes said, which drew a nod and a laugh from his cousin. He went on, "Keep scouts out wide on your flank, too. Abivard's lurking out there somewhere."

"Maybe he's fallen into that Void where the Makuraners are always consigning people they don't like," Rhegorios said. "But that would be too much to hope for, wouldn't it? Aye, I'll watch for him. And you, cousin, you keep a good watch on your other flank, too."

"I'll watch as carefully as a Makuraner noble checking his women's quarters to make sure nobody sneaks in." The Avtokrator slapped Rhegorios on his mailed back. "Now, let's see what kind of dance we'll have with all these lovely people, shall we?"

"They've come a long way. We wouldn't want to disappoint them." Rhegorios looked thoughtful. "We've come a long way, too."

"So we have," Maniakes said. "We wouldn't want to disappoint us, either."

Rhegorios rode off to take charge of his wing of the army. The Makuraners were leaving the choice of when and how to begin the battle to the imperials. Under most circumstances, Maniakes would also have had the option of whether to begin the battle at all, as his horsemen were more mobile than the infantry opposing them. But, having almost completed his preparations for fording the Tib, he could not abandon the timber and boats without losing them and abandoning his plans as well. Unwilling to do that, Maniakes knew he had to fight here.

He watched Rhegorios and his division ride out for the flanking maneuver they might or might not prove able to bring off. Wanting to keep his center strong, he sent a smaller force off to the left. He warned Immodios, who was commanding it, to keep an eye out for Abivard.

"I'll do that, your Majesty," the officer answered. "If he does show up, we'll stop him cold, I promise you."

"Good man," Maniakes said. If Abivard showed up with a good-sized force of boiler boys, Immodios wasn't going to stop him. The Avtokrator knew that. He hoped Immodios did, too. With luck, though, the horsemen on the left would slow down a cavalry attack from the flank enough to give the center some hope of dealing with it.

Horns brayed out orders for the advance. As the Videssians drew near, their opponents shouted curses at them in the Makuraner tongue and in the harsher, more guttural language of the Thousand

Cities. "Ignore those vicious calumnies, whatever they may mean," a blue-robed priest of Phos declared. "Go forth to victory and glory, defending the true and holy faith of Phos with all the weapons of war. Go forth, and may the lord with the great and good mind shine down upon you and light your way forward."

A few men cheered. More—those who had already heard a lot of priests' homilies and seen a lot of battles won or lost or drawn— savored the rhetoric without letting it carry them away. Phos would do as he pleased, they would do as they pleased, and eventually the fight would have a winner.

The first arrows began flying soon thereafter. Whoever commanded the Makuraner army had a fine grasp of logistics, because the foot soldiers from the Land of the Thousand Cities shot and shot and shot, showing not the slightest sign that they were likely to run out of the shafts anytime soon. Such a barrage bespoke endless slow-trundling wagons filled with endless bundles of arrows. Seeing their flight was like watching a great swarm of locusts taking off from one field to descend in another.

The Videssians shot back. They were less well supplied with missiles than their foes. On the other hand, when one of their shafts struck a soldier from the Makuraner army, it usually wounded. The reverse was not true, their chain mail holding many arrows at bay.

"Get in among them and they're ours!" Maniakes shouted, urging his men forward despite the swarm of enemy arrows.

But getting in among the soldiers from the Makuraner army was anything but easy. The soldiers they had stationed immediately behind their thornbush barricades sent arrows flying out as far as they could. The second line of men from the Thousand Cities lobbed shafts high over the heads of the first line, so that those arrows came down on anyone who had reached the barricade and was trying to tear it away. All in all, it was like going forward in a rain of iron-tipped wood.

Seeing the difficulties his men were having in closing with the Makuraner force, Maniakes summoned Ypsilantes. Engineers were made for situations ordinary soldiers found impossible. Over the cries of men, the shrieks of wounded horses, through the constant whistling hiss of arrows, Maniakes pointed to the barricade and said, "What can we do about that, excellent sir?"

"They're not fools, worse luck, your Majesty," Ypsilantes

answered. "They soaked the bushes well, so they won't be easy to set afire." Only after Maniakes had nodded did he think to be surprised the chief engineer had already checked about such a tiny detail—but then, that sort of attention to detail was what made Ypsilantes chief engineer. He went on, "When you look at it, it's almost like storming a city wall. Some of the same tools should answer."

Maniakes had not thought of a fight on flat, open ground as being like the climax of a siege. Once the comparison was pointed out to him, it seemed obvious enough. He shook his head. A lot of things seemed obvious—once they were pointed out. "Your detachment is ready to do what needs doing?" he asked.

"Aye, your Majesty," Ypsilantes told him. "Shouldn't be that hard to bring off." He sounded like a man studying an interesting position in the Videssian board game, not one speaking in the midst of a real war's chaos. Maniakes didn't know whether to admire him for that detachment or to be appalled by it.

Whether his detachment was admirable or appalling, Ypsilantes rapidly proved to know what he was talking about. Under the cover of portable sheds of the sort usually used to bring a battering ram up close to a wall so it could pound away, parties of engineers approached the barricades and began clearing it. For them, the work was relatively easy. No one on this field was dropping great stones or boiling oil or melted lead down onto their shelter, which, having been designed to ward against such things, all but laughed at mere arrows raining down on it.

The Makuraners also tried to shoot straight into the sheds. Soldiers standing with big, stout shields at the exposed end made that difficult. Before long, some of the enemy foot soldiers tried a more direct approach, rushing at the engineers to cut them down.

But when they did that, their comrades, of necessity, had to leave off shooting at the shed. That let the Videssian cavalry dash forward through gaps already cleared to fight the foot soldiers. It was an uneven battle. The foot soldiers were brave enough and to spare, but against armored horsemen they went down in dreadful numbers.

"You see, your Majesty," Ypsilantes said.

"Yes, I do," Maniakes answered. "You've set the enemy commander a choice of the sort I'm glad I don't have to make. Either he can send his men out to try to keep the barricade from going down—and have them slaughtered; or he can hold his men back and let the barricade be cleared—and have them slaughtered."

"If you get into a fight like this, that's the chance you take," Ypsilantes agreed. "The best answer is not to get into a fight like this."

"It would have been different if Abivard—" Maniakes made himself stop. He'd seen no sign of the Makuraner marshal, nor of the heavy cavalry Abivard had led in the last campaigning season. He didn't know where they were, but they weren't here. If Abivard hadn't shown up to support the foot soldiers, he couldn't be anywhere close by. That thought tried to touch off an echo in Maniakes' mind, but shouts from the front drowned it.

The gaps in the thornbush barricade had grown wide enough for the Videssian horsemen to begin pouring through them and attacking the Makuraner army with sword and javelin as well as with arrows. Even now, though, the enemy foot soldiers continued to show spirit. Those from the farthest ranks rushed forward to the aid of their beset comrades. They used their clubs and shortswords as much against the Videssians' horses as against the imperials themselves. The more confusion they could create, the better for them.

"Have we got enough men?" Maniakes asked the question more of Phos or of himself than of Ypsilantes, though the chief engineer sat his horse beside him.

Ypsilantes did not hesitate over replying, regardless of whether the question had been meant for him: "Your Majesty, I think we do."

He proved a good prophet; little by little, the Videssians drove their foes back from what had been the line of the thornbush barricade. By then, the sun was sinking down toward the Dilbat Mountains. The fight had gone on most of the day.

Maniakes sent messengers to the soldiers fighting at the front: "Press them with everything you have and they'll break."

He could not fault the way in which his men obeyed the order. They pressed the Makuraners, and pressed them hard. At last, after tough fighting—tougher than that at the center—Rhegorios broke through the obstacles in his path and delivered the flank attack Maniakes had awaited all day long.

But the enemy did not break. He'd hoped for a slaughter, with the Makuraners fleeing every which way and his own men gleefully hunting them down like partridges. That was, perhaps, unsporting. He didn't care. Battle was not sport; if you went into it for any other reason than smashing the foe, you were a fool.

Sullenly, the foot soldiers drew back toward the east, yielding the field to the Videssians. But they retreated in good order, holding their formation as best they could, and did not scatter and let Maniakes' army destroy them one piece at a time. Having made more fighting retreats than he cared to remember, the Avtokrator knew how hard they were to bring off.

He did not pursue so vigorously as he might have. For one thing, daylight was leaking out of the sky. For another, he thought he'd beaten the foot soldiers from the Land of the Thousand Cities so badly, they would not try to renew the struggle anytime soon. That was what he'd hoped to accomplish. With that army of foot soldiers out of the picture, he could return to the business they'd interrupted: crossing the Tib and advancing on Mashiz.

"We'll camp," he said. "We'll tend to our wounded and then we'll get back to doing what we were doing before we had to turn around and fight: taking the war to Sharbaraz so he knows what a bad idea starting it was."

Ypsilantes nodded approval. So did Rhegorios, when he came into the camp with his soldiers as twilight was giving way to night. "They're good, that they are," he told Maniakes. "A little more discipline, a little more flexibility in the way they shift from one line to the other, and they'll be quite good. If we can grab Mashiz, fine. That should end the war, so we don't have to go on teaching them how to be soldiers."

Maniakes said, "Aye." He knew he sounded as if he'd been listening to his cousin with but half an ear. Unfortunately, that happened to be true. The noise on a battlefield just after the battle was done was apt to be more dreadful than what you heard while the fighting raged. All the triumph melted away with the battle itself, leaving behind only the pain.

Men groaned and shrieked and shouted and cursed. Horses made worse noises still. Maniakes often thought on how unfair war was for horses. The men who had been hurt on the field that day had at least some idea of why they were fighting and how they had come to be injured. It was all a mystery to the horses. One moment they were fine, the next in torment. No wonder their screams tore at the soul.

Horseleeches and troopers went over the field, doing what they could for the animals. All too often, *what they could* was nothing more than a dagger slashed quickly and mercifully across a throat.

By their cries, more than a few men would have welcomed such attention. Some of them got it: most of the enemy's wounded were left behind on the battlefield. That was hard, but it was the way wars were fought. A few Videssians, too, no doubt, those horribly wounded, were granted the release of a quick slide out of this life and toward eternal judgment.

For the rest, surgeons whose skills were about on a level with those of the horse doctors aided men not desperately hurt, drawing arrows, setting broken bones, and sewing up gashed flesh with quick stitches any tailor would have looked upon with distaste. Their attentions, especially in the short run, seemed to bring as much pain as they relieved.

And a band of healer-priests wandered over the field, looking for men badly wounded who might yet be saved if something like a miracle reached them. All healers were not only priests but magicians, but not all magicians could heal—far from it. The gift had to be there from the beginning. If it was, it could be nurtured. If it wasn't, all the nurturing in the world would not bring it forth.

Heading the healers was a blue-robe named Philetos, who in times of peace—in Maniakes' recent experience, a purely theoretical conception—taught experimental thaumaturgy at the Sorcerers' Collegium in Videssos the city. He had also, not quite coincidentally, performed the marriage ceremony uniting Maniakes and Lysia, ignoring the ecumenical patriarch's prohibition against the clergy's doing any such thing. Despite the later dispensation from Agathios, some rigorist priests still condemned Philetos for that.

Maniakes found Philetos crouched beside a soldier who had a wound in his chest and bloody froth bubbling from his mouth and nose. The Avtokrator knew the surgeons would have been powerless to save the fellow; if that wound did not prove rapidly fatal, fever would take the man in short order.

"Is there any hope?" Maniakes asked.

"I think so, your Majesty," the healer-priest answered. He had already stripped off the soldier's mail shirt and hiked up the linen tunic he wore under it to expose the wound itself. As Maniakes watched, Philetos set both hands on the injury, so that the soldier's blood ran out between his fingers.

"You must know, your Majesty, that direct contact is necessary for this healing to succeed," he said.

"Yes, of course," Maniakes said.

He was not sure whether Philetos heard him or not. "We bless thee, Phos, lord with the great and good mind," the healer-priest intoned, "by thy grace our protector, watchful beforehand that the great test of life may be decided in our favor." Philetos repeated the formula again and again, partly as a prayer, partly as a tool to lift himself out of his usual state of consciousness and onto the higher plane where healing might take place.

The moment when he reached that other plane was easy enough to sense. He seemed to quiver and then grow very firmly planted on the ground, as if fixed there by a power stronger than any merely mortal. Maniakes, standing a few feet away, felt the current of healing pass from Philetos to the wounded soldier, though he could not have said with which of his senses he felt it. He sketched the sun-circle and murmured Phos' creed himself, filled with awe at the power for which Philetos was the conduit.

The healer-priest grunted. All at once, his eyes focused on the merely mundane world once more. He took his hands away from the arrow wound and wiped them on the soldier's tunic, then used the tunic to scrub away the rest of the blood on the man's chest. Instead of a hole through which more blood came, only a white, puckered scar remained there, as if the fellow had suffered the injury years before.

He opened his eyes and looked up at Philetos. "Holy sir?" he said in tones of surprise. His voice might have been that of any young man, certainly not that of a young man who had just taken an arrow in the lung. Memory filled his face with pain, or rather with the recollection of pain. "I was shot. I fell. I couldn't breathe." His eyes widened as he realized what must have happened. "You healed me, holy sir?"

"Through me, the good god healed you." Philetos' voice came out as a harsh croak. His face was haggard, the skin stretched tight across his cheekbones. "Phos was kind to you, lad." He managed a weary chuckle. "Try not to stop any more arrows with your chest, eh?"

"Yes, holy sir." The soldier, at the point of death a few minutes earlier, scrambled to his feet. "Phos bless you." He hurried away;

but for the blood still round his mouth and nose, no one would have known he'd been hurt.

Philetos, by contrast, looked about to fall over. Maniakes had seen that reaction in healer-priests before; using their talent drained them dry. The Avtokrator shouted for food and wine. Philetos gobbled and gulped, downing enough for two ordinary men. Maniakes had seen that before, too.

"Where is the next one?" the healer-priest said, still wearily but with some restored vigor. A healer-priest of extraordinary talent, such as he was, could heal two, three, sometimes even four men who would have died without his attentions. After that, the effort grew too great, and the would-be healer collapsed before being able to establish the conduit with the force that flowed through him.

"You don't want to kill yourself, you know," Maniakes told him. "I've heard that can happen if you push yourself too hard."

"Where is the next one?" Philetos repeated, taking no notice of him. But when no answer was immediately forthcoming, the healer-priest went on, "Because we can do so little, your Majesty, honor demands we do all we can. The healing art is a growing thing; healers of my generation can do more at less cost to themselves than was so in my great-grandfather's day, as surviving chronicles and texts on the art make plain. In days to come, as research continues, those who follow us will accomplish still more."

"Which is all very well," Maniakes said, "but which doesn't keep you from killing yourself if you do too much."

"I shall do all I can. If I die, it is as Phos wills," Philetos answered. He suddenly looked not just exhausted but thoroughly grim. "As is also true of those whom we try but fail to heal."

That made Maniakes' mouth twist, too. Philetos had tried to heal his first wife, Niphone, after she'd had to be cut open to allow Likarios to be born. She'd been on the point of death when the surgery was attempted, but Philetos still blamed himself for failing to bring her back.

"You don't work miracles," the Avtokrator said.

Philetos dismissed that with a wave of his hand, as if it weren't worth refuting. "What I do, your Majesty, is I work, with no qualifiers tacked onto the end of it." His head went this way and that, taking in as much of the field as he could, looking for one more man he might restore to vigor before his own strength failed him.

"Healer!" Faint in the distance, the cry rose. Someone—maybe a surgeon, maybe just a soldier out for loot—had come across a wounded man the special power of the healer-priests might save.

"By your leave, your Majesty," Philetos said. But he wasn't really asking leave; he was telling Maniakes he was leaving. And leave he did, at a dogged trot. He might have been tired unto death, he might have been courting it himself—perhaps to make amends for Niphone and the rest of his failures—but he would fight it in others as long as he had breath in him.

Maniakes watched him go. He could have ordered the healer-priest to stop and rest. One thing he had learned, though: the most useless order was one given without any hope of its being obeyed.

"Let's see," Ypsilantes said, peering across the Tib at the foot soldiers on the western bank, "weren't we here a few days ago?"

"I think we might have been," Maniakes said. "Something or other interrupted us, though, or we'd have been busy trying to cross by now."

Both men laughed. Their humor had a touch of the macabre to it; the air was thick with the stench of corruption from the battle Maniakes had offhandedly called *something or other*, as if he couldn't remember why the attempted crossing had been delayed. He suspected Makuraners and Kubratoi cracked those same jokes. If you wanted to stay in your right mind, you had to.

Ypsilantes made a clucking noise that put Maniakes in mind of a chicken examining a caterpillar trying to decide whether it was one that tasted good or one of the horrid kind. "I don't quite like the way the river looks," the chief engineer said. "It might have one more flood surge left in it."

"So late in the year?" Maniakes said. "I can't believe that."

"It would be more likely if we were talking about the Tutub," Ypsilantes admitted. "You can't trust the Tutub. But I think the Tib here is fuller in its banks and has bigger ripples than a couple of days ago."

Maniakes examined the Tib. "Looks remarkably like a river to me," he said, thereby showing the extent of his professional knowledge.

"It's a river, all right, and any river can be trouble," Ypsilantes said. "I'd hate to try to cross and have our bridge and such swept away with half the army on this side of the river and the other half on that one."

"Could be embarrassing," Maniakes agreed, again with that dry lack of emphasis: he might not have been a professional engineer, but he was a professional soldier, and, like a lot of men in that calling, used language that minimized the sorts of things that might happen to him.

"Maybe we should wait a few days before we go looking to cross," Ypsilantes said. "Hate to say that—"

"I hate to hear it, too," Maniakes broke in. "We've already had to wait longer than I would have liked, what with having to forage for timber and boats, and what with the attack the Makuraners brought home on us."

Ypsilantes' jaw tightened. "I own, your Majesty, I don't know for certain the river is going to rise. If you want to say I'm being a foolish old woman and order me to go ahead, no one can tell you you're wrong. You're the Avtokrator. Tell me to move and I'll obey."

"And we'll both be looking over our shoulders every minute, even if no trouble comes," Maniakes said unhappily. "You can't know what's going to happen, I can't know what's going to happen . . ." He paused. "But Bagdasares might be able to know what's going to happen."

"Who?"

"Alvinos, you might know him as," the Avtokrator answered. "He knows I've got Vaspurakaner blood in me, so when we talk he usually goes by the name he was born with, not the one he uses with ordinary Videssians."

"Oh, one of those," Ypsilantes said, nodding. "Puts me in mind of that rebel a hundred and fifty years ago, the Vaspurakaner chap who would have ruled as Kalekas if he'd won. What was his real name? Do you know?"

"Andzeratsik," Maniakes told him, adding with a wry grin, "hardly a fitting name for an Avtokrator of the Videssians, is it? My clan has some sort of distant marriage connection to his. Since he didn't win the civil war, it's not anything we talk about much."

"I can see that," Ypsilantes agreed gravely. "Good enough, then—check with the wizard. See what he has to say."

"Bagdasares?" Maniakes rolled his eyes. "He always has a good deal to say. How much of it will have to do with the question I first ask him—that's liable to be another matter." The crack was unfair if taken literally, but, like most unfair cracks, held a grain of truth.

"What can I do for you, your Majesty?" Bagdasares asked after Maniakes had ridden Antelope over to his tent. The Avtokrator explained. Bagdasares plucked at his beard. "A spell much like the one we used to examine the passage of the fleet from the city to Lyssaion should serve here, I believe."

"Good enough," Maniakes said, "but can you guarantee me that it won't show more than we want to know, as that one did?"

"Could I guarantee what magic would reveal and what it would not, your Majesty, I should be Phos, or at the least Vaspur, the good god's sole perfect creation. The principal reason for casting a spell is to see what will happen, and by that I mean not only in the outer world but with the magic itself."

Having thus been put in his place, the Avtokrator spread his hands, conceding defeat. "Have it your way, then, excellent sir. Whatever your magecraft can show me, I shall be glad to view it."

Bagdasares proceeded briskly to work. He filled a bowl with dirt he dug up from close by where he was standing—"What better symbol for the local land than the local land?" He made a channel in it, and poured in water from the pitcher that rested by his bedroll—"How else to represent the water of the Tib than by the water of the Tib?"

The landscape created, he used little twigs and chips of wood to symbolize the bridge of boats that would soon stretch across the river. "You want to know whether some flood is impending, not so?"

"That's right," Maniakes said.

"Very well, then," the wizard answered, more than a little absently: he was already gathering himself for the spell proper. He began to chant and make passes over the bowl. "Reveal!" he cried in Videssian, and then again in the Vaspurakaner tongue Maniakes had trouble following.

The Avtokrator wondered if Makuraner mages were trying to interfere with Bagdasares' conjuration. He would not have been surprised to learn they were; knowing whether he could cross the Tib in safety was obviously important to him, and the magical method for determining the truth not too complex.

But Alvinos Bagdasares gave him a straight answer. The Avtokrator watched the bridge extend itself toward the western bank of the model of the Tib, then saw little ghostly, glowing specks spring into being and cross the symbolic river from east to west.

"Weather shall not hamper us, your Majesty," Bagdasares murmured.

"I see that," Maniakes answered, still looking down into the bowl. And, as he had at his friend's earlier attempt to learn what lay ahead, he saw more than he had bargained for. Those ghostly specks suddenly recrossed the Tib, this time from west to east. "What does that mean?" he asked Bagdasares.

This time, the mage had seen for himself what had happened, instead of needing to rely on his sovereign's description. "At a guess—and a guess is all it is—we are not destined to stay long in Mashiz, if indeed we succeed in reaching the seat of the King of Kings."

"That was my guess, too," Maniakes said. "I was hoping yours would be more palatable."

"I'm sorry, your Majesty," Bagdasares said. "I do not know for a fact that what I say here is true, mind you, but all other interpretations strike me as less probable than the one I offered."

"They strike me the same way," Maniakes said. "As I say, I'm just wishing they didn't." He brightened. "Maybe the magic means Sharbaraz will be so frightened after we cross the Tib, he'll make peace on our terms. If he does that, we won't have to stay west of the river long."

"It could be so," Bagdasares answered. "Trying by magic to learn what the King of Kings might do is hopeless, or as near as makes no difference, he being warded against such snoopery as you are. But nothing in the spell I have cast contradicts the meaning you offer."

Nothing in the spell contradicted it, perhaps, but Maniakes had trouble believing it even though it came from his own mouth. The trouble was, however much he wanted to think it likely, it went dead against everything he knew, or thought he knew, of Sharbaraz's character. The next sign of flexibility the Makuraner King of Kings displayed would be the first. The envoy he had sent to negotiate with Maniakes had been sent not to make peace but to delay the Videssians till that army of foot soldiers could fall on them. Which meant . . .

"Something's going to go wrong," Maniakes said. "I have no idea what, I have no idea why, but something is going to go wrong."

He watched Bagdasares. The Vaspurakaner mage had been a courtier for a good many years now, and plainly wanted to tell him nothing could possibly go wrong with the plans of the ever-victorious Videssian army. The only trouble was, Bagdasares couldn't do that. Both he and Maniakes had seen plans go wrong before, had seen that the Videssian army was a long way from ever-victorious. Flattery worked a lot better when both sides were willing to ignore small details like truth.

"Perhaps it won't go totally wrong," Bagdasares said.

"Aye, perhaps it won't," Maniakes said. In an unsafe, imperfect world, sometimes that was as much as you could reasonably expect. He held up one finger. "No one save the two of us need know of this conjuration." Bagdasares nodded. Maniakes figured he would tell Lysia, who could be relied upon not to blab. But if the army didn't know, maybe what the magic foretold would somehow fail to come true for them.

Maniakes let out a silent sigh. He had trouble believing that, too.

Engineers ran planks and chains from one boat to the next. One piece at a time, the bridge they were building advanced across the Tib. Ypsilantes glanced over at Maniakes and remarked, "It's all going very well."

"So it is," the Avtokrator answered. He hadn't told Ypsilantes anything about the conjuration except that it showed the bridge could advance without fear of flooding. Too late, it occurred to him that too much silence might well have made the chief engineer draw his own conclusions, and that the conclusions were liable to be right. Whether Ypsilantes had his own conclusions or not, he carried out the orders Maniakes gave him.

Foot soldiers were drawn up on the west bank of the Tib to harass the engineers and, Maniakes supposed, to resist the Videssians if that harassment failed. Thanks to magic, Maniakes knew it would. The Makuraners, being more ignorant, kept trying to make nuisances of themselves.

They did a fair job of it, too, wounding several Videssian engineers once the end of the bridge moved into archery range. Not too troubled, Ypsilantes sent forward men with big, heavy shields:

the same shields, in fact, that had protected the barricade-clearing engineers in the sheds in the recent battle with the Makuraners. Behind those shields, the bridge builders kept working. Surgeons tended the injured men, none of whom was hurt badly enough to need a healer-priest.

Maniakes remembered Abivard's story about the Makuraners' building a bridge across the Degird River so they could cross it and attack the Khamorth out on the Pardrayan steppe. The Makuraner expedition had come to grief: indeed, to disaster, with Peroz King of Kings dying there on the plains. The Avtokrator hoped his own luck would be better than that. He had no way of knowing whether he would become one of the little points of light Bagdasares' magic had shown recrossing the Tib.

After a while, Ypsilantes also sent archers out to the end of the bridge to shoot back at the Makuraners. The enemy, though, had more men on the bank than the chief engineer could place at the end of the bridge. Seeing that, he sent out boatloads of archers, too, and a couple of rafts with dart-throwers mounted on them. They pumped enough missiles into the unarmored Makuraner infantry, those from the dart-throwers beyond the range at which it could respond, to sow a good deal of confusion in the foot soldiers' ranks.

"Here, let's do this," Maniakes said, calling Ypsilantes over to him. The chief engineer grinned a nasty grin after they were done speaking together.

Those boats with archers in them began going rather farther up and down the Tib, and making as if to land. That got the Makuraners running this way and that. A couple of boats did land Videssian bowmen, who stayed on the west bank of the Tib long enough to shoot a volley or two at the Makuraners, then reembarked and rowed back out onto the river.

Meanwhile, the engineers kept extending the bridge of boats till it got quite close to the western bank of the Tib. Watching their progress, Maniakes said to Rhegorios, "This is when I wouldn't mind having some Makuraner-style heavy cavalry of my own. I could send them charging over the bridge and scatter that infantry like this." He snapped his fingers.

Rhegorios said, "I think the horsemen we have will be plenty to do the job."

"I think you're right," Maniakes said. Bagdasares' magic went a long way toward persuading him his cousin was right. How much good his being right would do in the end was a different question, one Maniakes didn't want to think about. Sometimes acting was easier than thinking. He assembled a force of horsemen with javelins near the eastern edge of the bridge, ready to move when the time came.

It came that afternoon: one of the engineers reported, "Your Majesty, the water under the bridge is only three or four feet deep now."

"Then we're going to go." Maniakes shouted orders to the trumpeters. Their horn calls sent the horsemen thundering down the bridge toward the Makuraner foot soldiers. It also sent the Videssian engineers and shieldmen leaping off the bridge into the warm, muddy waters of the Tib.

He'd succeeded in surprising the Makuraners and their commander. The horses splashed down into the water, then, urged on by their riders, hurried toward the foe. Some of the cavalrymen flung their javelins at the infantry awaiting them, while others imitated the Makuraner boiler boys and used the light spears as if they were lances.

The Videssians gained the riverbank and began to push the foremost Makuraners back. That threw the ranks of the Makuraner infantry into worse disorder than they had already known, and let the Videssians gain more ground still. At Maniakes' orders, more imperials rode over the almost-completed bridge to aid their comrades.

"You're a sneaky one," Rhegorios shouted. "They figured the bridge would have to be finished for us to use it."

"You don't want to do the thing they expect," Maniakes answered. "If they know what's coming, they're most of the way to knowing how to stop it. If they haven't seen it before, though—"

He watched avidly as his men carved out a bridgehead on the western bank of the Tib. The riders who had used up their javelins slashed at the Makuraners with swords. Whoever was commanding this enemy army lacked the presence of mind of the infantry general who'd given battle against the Videssians a few days before. When he saw his troops wavering, he pulled them away from their opponents. That made them waver even more. The Videssians, sensing victory, pushed all the harder.

Little by little, Makuraner foot soldiers began to flee, some to the north, some to the south, some to the west. Once serious resistance had ended, the Videssians did not pursue as hard as they might have. Instead, they formed a perimeter behind which the engineers finished the bridge of boats. Maniakes rode across to the west bank of the Tib without having himself or Antelope get wet.

"Mashiz!" the soldiers shouted. "On to Mashiz!" They knew what they had done, and knew also what they wanted to do. Had Mashiz been only an hour's gallop distant, it might have fallen. But it was a couple of days away, and the sun was sliding down behind the Dilbat Mountains. Maniakes judged he had taken enough risks, or maybe more than enough. He ordered the army to halt for the night.

Having done that, he wondered whether he should dispense with leaving a garrison behind to protect the bridge of boats. He was tempted not to bother: after all, the magic had shown his army would come back safe over the Tib. After some thought, though, he decided idiocy might be stronger than sorcery, and so warded what obviously needed warding.

"On the far bank at last," he told Lysia once his pavilion had been set up. "Didn't come close two years ago, came close but didn't make it last year. Now—we see what we can do."

She nodded, then said, "I wish you hadn't had Bagdasares cast that spell. I'd be more hopeful than I am. Can we take Mashiz so quickly? If we do, why would we turn back so soon? What could go wrong?"

"I don't know the answers to any of those questions," he said. "That's why we're going ahead and moving on Mashiz: to find out what can go wrong, I mean."

Lysia made a face at him. "What if nothing goes wrong? What if we go in, seize the city, and capture Sharbaraz or kill him or make him run away?"

"For one thing, Bagdasares will be very embarrassed," Maniakes answered, which made Lysia look for something to throw at him. He caught a hard roll out of the air and went on, "I don't know what then, except that I'd be delighted. I've been trying to go ahead as if I thought that was what would happen, but it's not easy. I keep wondering if something I do will make whatever is going to go wrong, go wrong."

"Better in that case not to have had the magic," Lysia said.

"I know," Maniakes answered. "I've had that thought before, every now and then. Knowing the future, or thinking you know the future, can be more of a curse than a blessing." He gave a wry shrug. "I didn't want to know as much as the spell showed me; it did more than I asked. And, of course, *not* knowing the future can be more a curse than a blessing, too."

"Life isn't simple," Lysia said. "I wonder why that isn't a text for the ecumenical patriarch to preach on at the High Temple. It doesn't work out the way you think it will. No matter how much you know, you never understand as much as you think you do."

"That's true," Maniakes said. He glanced over at her. She was glancing over at him, too. For most of their lives, they'd never expected to be married to each other. Many things would have been a good deal simpler had they not ended up married to each other. The only problem was, life wouldn't have been worth living. "How do you feel?" he asked her.

She knew what he meant when he asked that question; of itself, her left hand went to her belly. "Pretty well," she answered. "I'm still sleepy more than I would be if I weren't going to have a baby, but I haven't been sick very much this time, for which I thank the lord with the great and good mind."

Maniakes let his fancy run away with him. He knew he was doing it; it wasn't, he thought, as if he were deluding himself. "Wouldn't it be fine if we did run Sharbaraz King of Kings out of Mashiz and if Bagdasares did turn out wrong? We could spend the rest of the campaigning season there, and maybe even the winter, too. We could have a prince—or a princess—of the Videssian imperial house born in the capital of Makuran."

"No, thank you," Lysia said at once, her voice sharp. "I know that sounds very grand, but I don't care. I want to go home to have this baby. If we go home after we've beaten the Makuraners, that's wonderful—better than wonderful, in fact. But beating the Makuraners isn't reason enough for me to want to stay here. If you decide to do that, well and good. Send me back to Videssos the city."

In marriage as in war, knowing when to retreat was not the least of virtues. "I'll do that," Maniakes promised. He scratched at his beard while he thought. "Meanwhile, though, I have to figure out

how to arrange the triumph after which I get to send you home."
He snapped his fingers. "Should be easy, shouldn't it?"

Lysia laughed. So did he.

For the next few days, Maniakes wondered whether he had magical powers to put those of Bagdasares to shame. One snap of the fingers seemed to have been plenty to rout all the opposition the Makuraners had mustered against his men. The foot soldiers, who had put up such a persistent fight for so long, now began melting away rather than resisting as they had.

Every now and then, some of them would try to hold back the Videssians, while others broke canals open. But these men seldom stood in place as the other, larger, force west of the Tib had done so often over the past couple of years; it was as if his crossing the river had taken the spirit out of them.

And opening the canals was less effective west of the Tib than it had been in the heart of the Land of the Thousand Cities. As was true east of the Tutub, there was land beyond that which the network of canals irrigated. Instead of having to slog through fields made all but impassable by water and mud, the Videssians simply went around them, and once or twice scooped up good-sized bands of foes in the process.

Far more easily than Maniakes had imagined possible, his men neared the approaches to Mashiz. There their advance slowed. The usurper Smerdis had fortified those approaches against Sharbaraz. Once Sharbaraz won the civil war between them and became King of Kings himself, he'd rebuilt and improved the fortification, though no obvious enemy threatened his capital.

"We helped break these works once," Maniakes said to Ypsilantes, "but they look a good deal stronger than they did then."

"Aye, that's so, your Majesty," the chief engineer said, nodding. "Still, I expect we'll manage. Smerdis, now, he had horsemen who would fight for him, and that made life hard for us, if you'll recall. The walls and such are better now, I'll not deny, but so what? The troops in and around 'em count for more; men are more important than things."

"Do you know," Maniakes said, "I've had a bard tell me just that. He said that as long as the people in his songs were interesting, the settings mattered little—and if the people were dull, the finest settings in the world wouldn't help."

"That makes sense, your Majesty—more sense than I'd expect from a bard, I must say. When you get down to the bottom of anything you can think of, near enough, it's about people, isn't it?" Ypsilantes looked at the fortifications ahead. "People who huddle behind thick stone are more difficult, worse luck."

"If they're trying to keep us from doing what we need to do, I should say so."

"We'll manage, never fear," Ypsilantes repeated. "With no cavalry, they'll have trouble sallying against us, too, the way Smerdis' men did."

"That's so," Maniakes said. "I'd forgotten that sally till you reminded me of it. Makuraners popping out everywhere—I won't be sorry not to see *that*, thank you very much."

The Makuraners did not sally. They did fling large stones from catapults in their fortresses. One luckless Videssian scout drew too close to one of those forts at exactly the wrong moment; he and his mount were both smashed to bloody pulps. That made Maniakes thoughtful. Even with his own stone- and dart-throwers set up to shoot back at the ones the Makuraners had in place, his army would have to run the gauntlet before breaking into Mashiz. It would be expensive, and he did not have all that many men he could spare; that he had any army that could stand against the Makuraners he took as something close to direct intervention from Phos, considering how many years of defeat Videssos had suffered.

He cast about for ways other than the most direct one to break into Mashiz. The riders he sent forth to spy out those others ways returned to him unmashed but less than optimistic: Sharbaraz had made sure getting into his capital would not be an easy business. He lacked the Cattle Crossing to hold foes away, but had done all he could with what he had.

"Straight on, then," Maniakes said reluctantly. Ypsilantes nodded, now less enthusiastic than he had been. Even Rhegorios looked worried about the likely size of the butcher's bill. Maniakes also kept worrying about what Bagdasares' magic had meant. Should he go ahead, knowing—or thinking he knew—he could not stay west of the Tib for long?

With his usual unassuming competence, Ypsilantes readied the Videssian catapults to oppose those of the Makuraners. Maniakes mustered the army for what he hoped would be a quick, fierce descent on Mashiz. He was about to give the order for the attack to begin when a courier galloped up from out of the northeast, holding up a message tube and shouting, "Your Majesty! Your Majesty! The Makuraners are in Across, the whole great army of them, and they and the cursed Kubratoi have made common cause against Videssos the city. The city might fall, your Majesty."

IV

For a long moment, Maniakes simply stared at the messenger as if he'd been spouting some incomprehensible gibberish. Then, all at once, the pieces seemed to make a new and altogether dreadful pattern. Keeping his voice under tight control, he asked, "When you say the Makuraners are back at Across, do you mean the main army under Abivard son of Godarz?"

"Aye, your Majesty, that's who I mean—who else?" the fellow answered. "Abivard and Romezan and stinking Tzikas the traitor, too. And all the boiler boys. And all the siege gear, too." He pointed toward Ypsilantes' catapults to show what he meant.

Rhegorios said, "All right, the Makuraners are back at Across again. So what? They've been there before, for years at a stretch. They can't cross over to Videssos the city."

But the messenger said, "This time, maybe they can, your highness, your Majesty. The Kubratoi have a whole great swarm of those one-trunk boats of theirs out on the water, and they've been going back and forth to the westlands. We can't stop all of that, as much as we wish we could."

"By the good god," Maniakes whispered in horror. "If they can get their stone-throwers and towers and such up against the walls of the city—"

"The walls are strong, your Majesty," Rhegorios said, for once not bothering to ring playful changes on his cousin's title. "They've stood a long time, and nobody yet has found a way through them."

"That's so," Maniakes answered. "I can think of two drawbacks to it, though. For one, the Makuraners really know how to attack fortifications; they're at least as good at it as we are. We've seen that in the westlands, more times than I care to think about. And for the other, walls aren't what keep attackers out. Soldiers are. Where are the best soldiers in the Empire? No, to the ice with that. Where are the only soldiers in the Empire who've proved they can stand up to the Makuraners in battle?"

Rhegorios didn't say anything. Maniakes would have been astonished had his cousin said anything. The answer to the rhetorical question was only too obvious: he led the sole Videssian army that had proved itself against the foe. The rest of the Empire's forces, he feared, were still all too much like the armies that had lost to the boiler boys again and again and again. That would not be true in another two or three years—which, unfortunately, did him no good whatever now.

And then, to his astonishment, Rhegorios started laughing. Both Maniakes and the messenger looked at the Sevastos as if he'd lost his mind. "Beg your pardon, your Majesty," Rhegorios said after a moment, "but we've been making jokes about what might happen if we took the Makuraners' capital at the same time as they took ours. Now the jokes have turned real. If that isn't funny, what is?"

"Nothing," Maniakes said. Nothing struck him funny at the moment, that was certain. He felt like getting off his horse so he could kick himself. He'd been too headstrong again. With no sign of Abivard, he'd just charged ahead, worrying about what he himself was doing but not paying enough attention to what the enemy might be up to at the same time.

Videssos had been known to incite the steppe nomads against Makuran from time to time. He'd never expected the Makuraners to turn the tables so neatly. Etzilios, no doubt, had thirsted for revenge ever since the Videssians beat him three years before. And if Sharbaraz had somehow gotten an embassy to him . . . Maniakes hadn't thought the King of Kings possessed of such duplicity. How expensive would correcting that mistaken opinion prove?

Rhegorios said, "What happens if we *do* take Mashiz while they're sacking Videssos the city?"

Maniakes weighed that. The idea appalled him at first consideration. After he'd thought on it a little while, he liked it even less. "If we take Mashiz," he said, "the Makuraners fall back to their plateau, and we have no hope of going after them there. But if they take the city, what's to stop them and the Kubratoi from flooding across all the land we have left? No mountains like the Dilbat chain, no great rivers—nothing."

His cousin nodded. "I think you have the right of it. If we make that trade, we're ruined. The thing to do, then, is to keep from making it."

"Yes." Maniakes took a long look west toward Mashiz. He wondered when or if he would ever see the Makuraner capital again. Seeing his own again, though, suddenly counted for more. "We go back."

Seeing the bridge the engineers had forced across the Tib still intact filled Maniakes with relief. He had thought it survived; consideration of what Bagdasares' magic had shown him made it seem likely the bridge survived. But Maniakes had long since received a forceful education on the difference between what seemed likely and what turned out to be true. Seeing the makeshift ugliness of that bridge with his own eyes was like his first sight of Lysia after returning to Videssos the city from beating the Kubratoi. Now he could breathe easier and get on with the rest of the things that needed doing.

Rhegorios must have been thinking along similar lines, for he said, "I guess this means the Makuraners didn't capture any couriers who tried to bring us news out of the east. If they'd known how much harm they could do us by burning this bridge, they would have tried it."

"Can't argue with you there," Maniakes said. How much time would he have lost had the foe tried trapping him on the west bank of the Tib? It wasn't a question with a precise answer, but *too much* tolled through his head like a bell with two mournful notes.

Once the army had passed over the bridge, Ypsilantes pointed back to the structure his engineers had bled to build. "What do we do with it now?"

"Collect whatever timbers you need and burn the rest," Maniakes snapped. "That won't matter much—the Makuraners have their own bridges of boats—but it may slow them some. And why should we make life easy for them?"

Flames crackled. Smoke rose into the sky, thick and black. When the Makuraners had gone over the Degird under Peroz King of Kings to attack the Khamorth nomads, they'd thrown a bridge across that river: Maniakes remembered Abivard speaking of it. And once their survivors, the handful of them, had returned to Makuran, they'd burned that bridge. Now he understood how their engineers must have felt then.

Back on the west bank of the Tib, a few Makuraner soldiers stood watching the Videssians wreck the bridge. He wondered what they thought of his retreat. They hadn't beaten him. They hadn't come close to beating him. In the end, though, what did that matter? Regardless of the reason, he was quitting their land. If that didn't mean they had won and he had lost, he had no idea what it did mean.

"We want to move fast," he told his warriors. "We don't want to give the Makuraners the chance to delay us with skirmishes or anything of the sort. We're faster than they are; that means we mostly get to choose when to engage and whether to engage—and the answer is going to be no unless we can't possibly help it. If they offer battle, we'll go around them if we find any way to do it. If we don't—" He shrugged. "—we go through 'em."

For the first couple of days on the move through the Land of the Thousand Cities, they saw only scouts and the peasants who worked the land. One of those looked up from the garden plot he was weeding and shouted, "Thought you thieves had gone on to afflict somebody else!"

After riding past the irate farmer, Rhegorios snapped his fingers in annoyance. "Oh, a pestilence!" he burst out. "I should have told him it was his turn again. It would have been worth it, just to see the look on his face."

"Nice to know you don't always think of the right thing to say when you need to say it," Maniakes told him. "But I tell you this— you're not going to turn around and go back for the sake of watching his jaw drop. Nobody goes back for anything, not now."

Sooner than Maniakes had hoped, the Makuraner forces in the Land of the Thousand Cities realized the Videssian army was withdrawing. The enemy began trying to obstruct the withdrawal, too. That irked him; he had hoped they would be content to see him go and not seek to delay him and let him do more damage to the floodplain.

His captains took renewed skirmishing and floods ahead of them almost as a personal affront. "If they so badly want us to stay, we ought to go back to thrashing them, the way we have the past couple of years," Immodios said angrily.

"I don't think anyone in the Land of the Thousand Cities wants us to stay," Maniakes answered. "I think the King of Kings is the one who wants us stuck here. If we're fighting here between the Tutub and the Tib, even if we're beating everything they throw at us, we aren't heading back to Videssos the city and defending it against Abivard. Delaying us here helps the enemy there."

Immodios considered that, then nodded. "Sharbaraz has a long reach and a sure one, if he can keep his mind on what he does here and far away at the Cattle Crossing, both at the same time."

"This year, Sharbaraz has shown me more than in all the time before this I've had on the throne," Maniakes replied, genuine regret in his voice. "Making an alliance with Kubrat against us—no King of Kings ever thought of anything like that before. He's a good deal more clever than I dreamed he could be. But he's not so clever as he thinks he is, not if you think back to that shrine we found, the one where he was made out to be the Makuraner God. He doesn't live at the very center of the world and have it all spin round him, no matter what he thinks."

"Ah, that shrine. I'd forgotten that." Immodios sketched Phos' sun-circle above his heart. "You're right, your Majesty. Anyone who's foolish enough to think of himself as a god, well, it doesn't matter how smart he is other ways. Sooner or later, he's going to make a bad mistake. Another bad mistake, I should say."

"Sooner or later," Maniakes echoed. "I think you're right. No, I know you're right. It would be nice, though, with things as they are, to have the mistake come sooner. We could use it."

His army crossed the major north-south canal between the Tutub and the Tib. Getting over it made him smile; Bagdasares' magic had done a good job of delaying the Makuraners there the year before. Then Maniakes' smile congealed on his face. Abivard was supposed to have a Videssian wizard with him, someone he'd scooped up as he conquered the westlands. Absent that, the magic of the Voimios strap might have held the Makuraners at bay even longer than it had done.

When he'd left Videssos the city, Maniakes had been content— had been more than content, if less eager than Lysia—to leave behind reports of and from the imperial capital. Now that he moved toward the city once more, he hungered for news about it. Was he rushing back toward a town already fallen to the foe? What would he do if that turned out to be so? He did not want such macabre imaginings loose in his mind, but felt reluctant to dismiss them. If they stayed, he might come up with answers for them.

He'd been concentrating on how to go about attacking Mashiz when the messengers brought word first of the Kubratoi invasion of Videssos and then of Abivard's joining forces with the nomads. He'd seen no messengers since. Had the Makuraners captured them before they ever got to him? If they had, they would know more than he about what was going on at the heart of the Empire. Or had his own people—Phos! his own family—not sent out more men, either because they were too pressed or because they could not? Anxiety on account of his ignorance ate at him.

One day when the army was a little more than halfway across the Land of the Thousand Cities, Rhegorios rode up next to him and asked, "If you were the Makuraner commander and you knew we were leaving this country, what would you do to make things hard for us?"

"What the enemy is doing, more or less," the Avtokrator answered, "skirmishes and floods and anything else that would slow us up."

Rhegorios nodded, but then went on, "That's true, but it's not what I meant, or not all of what I meant, anyhow. What's he going to do with the men he doesn't have skirmishing with us now?"

"Ah, I see what you're saying." Maniakes' thick eyebrows came down together in a frown. When you asked the question as Rhegorios had, you also indicated the answer: "He's going to put them where they'll do the best job of blocking us: down by Qostabash and maybe in the hill country where the Tutub rises."

His cousin nodded. "That's what I thought, too. I was hoping you would tell me this heat has melted the brains right out of my head. How are we going to get through them if they do that?"

"As long as we and they are on the floodplain, it won't matter so much, because we'll be able to outmaneuver them. Up in those hills, though—" Maniakes broke off. "I'm going to have to think about that."

"Always happy to hand you something to take your mind off your worries," Rhegorios said, so blithely that Maniakes had only a little trouble fighting down the urge to punch him in the face.

* * *

Maniakes did think about what Rhegorios had suggested. The more he thought, the less he liked it. He went to check with Ypsilantes, who had such maps of the Land of the Thousand Cities as the Videssians had been able to put together, along with others dating back to an invasion several centuries before. After studying the maps for a while, he took counsel with Rhegorios, Ypsilantes, and Immodios.

He pointed to his cousin. "This is your fault, you know. It's what you get for complicating my life—no, not my life, all our lives."

"Thank you," Rhegorios said, which was not the answer Maniakes had been looking for but not one to surprise him, either.

To Ypsilantes and Immodios, Maniakes said, "His Highness the Sevastos there—the one with the tongue hinged at both ends—made me realize we ought to get to the hill country between the headwaters of the Tutub and those of the Xeremos as fast as we can." He explained why, then went on, "Unless I'm dead wrong, going back by way of Qostabash isn't the best route, either."

"Then why have we been doing it?" Immodios asked. "Going back by way of Qostabash, I mean."

Maniakes tapped two parchment maps, one new, one old. "As near as I can tell, the answer is, force of habit. Here, look: the trade route down to Lyssaion runs through Qostabash nowadays." He ran his finger along the red squiggle of ink showing the route. Then he traced it on the other map, the old one. "It's been running through Qostabash for a *long* time. But just because the trade route runs through Qostabash, that doesn't mean we have to go that way ourselves."

He traced another path with his finger, this one running well east of the town that was the southern gate to the Land of the Thousand Cities. "If we take this route, we save ourselves a day or two of travel—and, with luck, we don't have so many enemies waiting for us at the other end of it."

Immodios frowned. He had a face made for frowning, with tight, almost cramped features. "I don't follow all of that, your Majesty. Yes, we reach the hill country faster by your route, which is to the good. But what's to keep the Makuraners from shifting forces from Qostabash—if they have them there—to the east to try to block us? That would eat up the time we save."

"What's to keep them from doing it?" The smile Maniakes wore was broad but felt a little unnatural, as if he were trying too hard to be Rhegorios. "You are."

"Me?" Immodios looked splendidly surprised; no wonder, Maniakes thought, his cousin had so much fun in life.

"You," the Avtokrator said. "You're going to take a regiment, maybe a regiment and a half, of soldiers and you're going to ride to Qostabash as if you had the whole Videssian army with you. Burn the fields as you go, set out lots of fires at night, make as big a nuisance of yourself as you can."

"If you want a nuisance, you should send me," Rhegorios said.

"Hush," Maniakes told him. "You're a nuisance by yourself; for this job, I want someone who takes a little more professional approach." He turned back to Immodios. "Your task is to keep the Makuraners too busy noticing you to pay any attention to the rest of us as we slide south. Have you got that?"

"I think I have, your Majesty." Immodios pointed to one of the imperial banners, gold sunburst on sky blue, that floated not far away. "Let me have my fair share and more of those, so anyone who sees my detachment will think you're with it."

"All right," Maniakes said, fighting down misgivings. He wondered whether he shouldn't have given Rhegorios the assignment after all. If Immodios failed and the banners were captured, Videssos would be embarrassed. And if Immodios decided that bearing imperial banners gave him the right to other imperial pretensions, Videssos would be worse than embarrassed: the Empire would have a new civil war on its hands.

But Immodios was right to ask for the banners, given the role the Avtokrator had set him to play. And if Maniakes had said no, he might well have set resentment afire in a heart free of it till then. The business of ruling was never simple, and got more complicated the harder you looked at it.

Brave with banners, Immodios' detachment rode off, intent on convincing the Makuraner infantry commanders that it was the whole Videssian army. The large majority of that army, meanwhile, abandoned their journey toward Qostabash and swung south, into a region of the Land of the Thousand Cities they had never visited before.

That the region was new did not mean it was remarkable. Cities still squatted on hillocks made from millennia of rubble. Canals still crisscrossed fields of wheat and barley and beans and garden patches green with growing onions and lettuces and melons. Those absurd little boats still plied the canals. Mosquitoes and gnats still swarmed, thick as heavy rain.

Maniakes had hoped to glide through all but unnoticed. Since he was leading an army of several thousand mounted men, that hope, he admitted to himself if to no one else, was unrealistic. Getting through the untouched country cleanly and with as little fighting as he could—that he had a better chance of doing.

Scouts reported messengers pelting off to the east. Some they caught, some they could not. Those who escaped were no doubt taking word of his arrival to those in the best position to do something about it. He wondered if they would be believed. He hoped they wouldn't, not when Immodios was ostentatiously pretending to be what his army really was.

One calculation of his came true: in a land not much touched by war, the locals hesitated to open canals to slow him down. "They'd have done just that, nearer Qostabash," he said to Rhegorios.

His cousin nodded. "So they would. We'd have done some more sacking and wrecking ourselves, too. This feels as if we're traveling through their country, not fighting a war in it."

"We're here to travel," Maniakes said, and Rhegorios nodded again.

Travel they did, at a good pace. Once, not long after Immodios had separated himself from them, a delegation came out from one of the cities in the southern part of the floodplain: officials of some sort, along with yellow-robed servants of the God. Maniakes supposed they wanted to ask him not to sack their town, or perhaps not to plunder its fields. He never found out for certain, because he did not wait around for them to catch up to him. He wondered what they ended up doing. Going back into their city, he supposed, and thanking the God he'd passed it by.

He had no trouble keeping the army fed. With plenty of water, good soil, and heat the year around, the Land of the Thousand Cities bore even more abundantly than the coastal lowlands of the Empire of Videssos. Something was always ripe enough for men and horses to enjoy.

Messengers rode back and forth between Maniakes' army and

Immodios' division impersonating that army. A couple of days after Maniakes didn't stop to listen to the local delegation, one of Immodios' riders brought in not only the officer's report of his position but also a message tube whose leather was stamped with the lion of Makuran. "Well, well," Maniakes said. "Where did you come by this?"

"Fellow who was using it won't need it anymore." The messenger grinned at him.

Maniakes spoke and understood the Makuraner language fairly well. In its written form, though, it used different characters from Videssian, and he'd never learned them. He found that Philetos could make sense of it. "Some interesting magical texts come out of Makuran," the healer-priest remarked, "which are well worth reading in the original."

"I don't think there's anything magical about this," Maniakes said, handing him the parchment.

Philetos unrolled it and went through it with a speed and confidence that said he was indeed fluent in the written Makuraner language. "Your Majesty, this is from the commander of the army near Qostabash—Turan is his name—to the city governors in the region through which we are passing."

"Ah," Maniakes said. "That sounds interesting. I'll wager we've caught one copy of several, then. What does he say?"

"He warns them to be alert for Videssian brigands—his phrase, I assure you—who may be operating in this area. He says their depredations are a snare and a ruse, as the main Videssian force is advancing against him, and he expects to do battle against it soon."

Maniakes smiled at Philetos. The healer-priest smiled back at him. "Isn't that nice?" the Avtokrator said. "This Turan doesn't know which end is up, sounds like." He sobered. "He doesn't, that is, unless he manages to pick off one of our messengers. That would give the game away."

"So it would," Philetos agreed. "Here as elsewhere in life, secrets are never so secret as we might like."

"That's truer than I wish it were," Maniakes said. "And, speaking of wishes, I wish I'd thought of having a code for Immodios and me to use when we write back and forth to each other. Too late now, I'm afraid: if I send him one, I'll have to worry about the Makuraners capturing it and reading things I think they can't. Best leave it alone."

Surprisingly soon, the hills from which the Tutub rose came into sight ahead of the Videssian army. Maniakes sent several messengers to Immodios, ordering him to leave off his imposture and join the main force. A rider from his division came back to Maniakes, confirming that he'd got the command. Of the division itself, though, there was for the moment no sign.

For the first couple of days, Maniakes did not worry over that. Indeed, he took advantage of it, sending scouts deep into the hill country to make sure the ways south and east remained open. And those ways *were* open; Turan had not set traps along them to slow his progress. He supposed that, whatever orders the Makuraner general might be getting from Sharbaraz, he was just as well pleased to see the Avtokrator of the Videssians abandoning the Thousand Cities.

But, when Immodios did not arrive after those couple of days, Maniakes began to fret and fume. "Curse him," the Avtokrator grumbled, "doesn't he realize this country isn't so rich as the Land of the Thousand Cities? We're going to start eating it empty pretty soon."

"He has only a division of men," Rhegorios said. "As near as I can see, this whole countryside breeds foot soldiers the way a dead dog breeds flies."

He didn't say any more. As far as Maniakes was concerned, he'd said too much already. The Avtokrator had sent out Immodios' force as a distraction. He hadn't intended to have the Makuraners swallow it up. The Makuraners could afford the losses doing that would take, but he couldn't afford those they'd inflict on him.

No messengers came from Immodios. The scouts Maniakes sent north, in the direction of Qostabash, could not find a way past Turan's infantry, which was, as Rhegorios had said, abundant, and also very alert. Maniakes found himself facing a most unpleasant choice: either abandoning Immodios' division to its fate or going north to rescue it, delaying his return to Videssos the city on account of that, and possibly losing the capital to the Kubratoi and Makuraners.

To any Avtokrator of the Videssians, the capital had to come first. Maniakes told himself that, but still could not make himself leave Immodios in the lurch. Nor could he make himself order his army to head north, away from the route to Videssos the city. For two or three days, he simply dithered.

When at last he nerved himself to order the army to forget about Immodios, he found himself saved from the consequences of his own decision, for outriders from the missing division joined up with his own scouts. Immodios' main body came into his camp half a day later.

The dour officer prostrated himself before Maniakes. Most of the time, the Avtokrator would have waved for him not to bother. Today, he let Immodios go through with the proskynesis as a sign of his displeasure. When he did signal for the captain to rise, Immodios said, "Your Majesty, you can do as you like with me. By the good god, the Makuraners had me so plugged up along a river and canal line, I thought I'd never break out and get past them."

Much of Maniakes' anger vanished. "Abivard did the same thing to us a couple of years ago—do you remember? He defied us to get onto his side of the water, but we beat him once we managed it."

"So we did, your Majesty, but we had the whole army then, and I had only a piece of it," Immodios replied. "I'm afraid I did too good a job of convincing him you were with us—he pulled out everyone under the sun to carry shield and bow and hold us away from Qostabash."

"I can see how that would have been a problem, yes," Maniakes said. "How did you finally get over the waterline?"

"The same way we did two years ago," Immodios answered. "I used part of my force to look as if I was going to force a crossing at one spot, then crossed someplace else where my scouts reported he was thinning out his garrison to cover the feint. Horses are faster than foot soldiers, so I managed to pull everyone across without too much trouble. I didn't do any more fighting afterward that I didn't have to: hurried down here to you."

"All right," Maniakes said. The dressing-down he'd planned to give Immodios died unspoken. The commander seemed to have given a good part of it to himself. "We'll head back toward Lyssaion, then."

The farmers and herders who lived in the hills from which the Tutub sprang fled into the roughest country they could find when the Videssian army made its way through their land for the second time in a relatively short interval. No doubt they stared down at the imperials with helpless resentment from their craggy refuges, wondering what had prompted Maniakes to revisit them on such short notice.

They might have been surprised to hear he was at least as unhappy about the necessity as were they. He would much sooner have been fighting outside their capital than rushing back to try to save his own.

"Next interesting question," Rhegorios observed as the army came out of the hills and into the valley of the Xeremos, "is whether any ships will be waiting for us once we get to Lyssaion."

Maniakes had entertained that same worry—had entertained it and now rejected it. "There will be ships," he said, as if he had seen them himself: and so, in a manner of speaking, he had. "Bagdasares showed them to me." Of the tempest Bagdasares had also shown him, he said nothing.

"I'd hate to have him wrong, that's all," the Sevastos murmured.

"He's not wrong," Maniakes said. "Think it through—do you think my father would send word the city was in trouble without giving us a way to get back there? I don't need magic to see that."

"Uncle Maniakes?" Rhegorios shook his head, visibly taking the point. "No, he'd never make that kind of mistake. My father calls him the most careful man he ever heard of." He pointed at the Avtokrator. "How did he ever get a son like you?"

"He was born luckier than I was, into a time where you didn't need to take so many chances," Maniakes answered. "By the time I got the crown, I had to do all sorts of desperate things to make sure I kept having an empire to rule. The trouble with desperate things is, a lot of them don't work." He sighed. "We've found out more than we ever wanted to know about *that*, haven't we?"

"So we have," Rhegorios said, adding, "Well, now we and the Makuraners are even." When Maniakes looked puzzled, his cousin condescended to explain: "Wouldn't you say throwing everything they have into an attack on Videssos the city is about as desperate as our throwing everything we have into an attack on Mashiz? Maybe they're more desperate still, because the city is harder to take than Mashiz."

"Ah, now I understand," Maniakes said. "Put that way, you're right, of course." Some of the desperate things he'd done had been disasters. Some of them, against the Kubratoi and Makuraners both, had succeeded better than he'd dared hope. Now he had to do everything he could to ensure that Abivard and Sharbaraz's desperate attack—if that was what it was—didn't fall into the second category.

One of the things he did, as soon as he was sure no substantial Makuraner force lurked ahead of him, was to send riders through the hill country and down the valley of the Xeremos to make sure that the fleet he confidently expected to find waiting for him was in fact there. He got less confident by the day till the first rider returned. If the fleet wasn't there, he didn't know what he'd do. Travel through the westlands by land? Go up to Erzerum and hope to find a fleet there? Leap off a tall promontory into the sea? With the third choice, at least, the agony would be over in a hurry.

But, by the way the returning horseman was waving at him, he didn't have to worry about that—one down, hundreds left. "They're there, your Majesty," the fellow shouted when he got close enough for the Avtokrator to hear him. "A whole great forest of masts in the harbor, waiting for us to come aboard."

"The lord with the great and good mind be praised," Maniakes breathed. He turned to the trumpeters who were usually nearby. "Blow the quick trot. The sooner we get to Lyssaion, the sooner we sail."

The sooner the storm strikes us, he thought. He wondered if he should hold back his pace in the hope the bad weather would go by before the fleet did. He didn't think that would help. If he held back, somehow or other the storm would manage to do the same. And, if he held back, who could say what might happen in Videssos the city while he was delaying?

His soldiers rode down the valley of the Xeremos as fast as they could without foundering their horses. Blue banners with gold sunbursts on them snapped in the breeze. Brisk as ever, the horns called out the commands that held the army together. As the horsemen rode by, the peasants who farmed the valley looked up from their endless labor. Did they know the soldiers were coming back too soon, too soon?

What they knew mattered little, not here, not now. Maniakes knew. Knowledge gnawed at him like a toothache.

Then, faster than he'd expected, more slowly than he would have liked, Lyssaion lay before him, baked golden under the sun.

Beyond the town splashed the water. He saw, at first, only a narrow strip of that deep, implausible blue. But where there was a strip, there was a sea.

It would take him where he wanted to go. Like a mad and jealous lover, it would try to kill him. It might succeed. Bagdasares' magic hadn't shown him anything about that, not one way or the other. He rushed forward to embrace the sea just the same.

In Lyssaion waited the hypasteos and the garrison commander. They knew what was happening in Videssos the city. They had known longer than he; messengers who reached him went past them first.

In Lyssaion also waited Thrax. The drungarios' silver hair seemed out of place amidst all the golden stonework. Maniakes realized he should not have been surprised to see the commander of the fleet there, but somehow he was. The idea of Thrax's doing anything unexpected was itself unexpected.

"Aye, your father sent me and the *Renewal* here," Thrax said, which made Maniakes feel better: the drungarios hadn't done anything so strange as thinking on his own, then. "You're needed back home, that you are."

"I was needed where I was, too," Maniakes answered. But saying that gained nothing. The past two campaigning seasons, he'd moved according to his own plan. This year, the will directing him belonged to Abivard and Sharbaraz. They'd outwitted him. It was that revoltingly simple. He asked the question that had to be asked: "How bad is it back there?"

"Well, Videssos the city's still standing, or was when I left," Thrax said. Maniakes wished he hadn't added that qualifier. Thrax went on, "We've spied a Makuraner or two on the eastern side of the Cattle Crossing, looking at the city the way a cat looks at a bird in a cage: it looks tasty, but they have to figure out how to get inside."

"Makuraner soldiers on our side of the Cattle Crossing," Maniakes murmured, and hung his head. A series of humiliations from Makuran and Kubrat had punctuated his reign, but this was the worst of all. For all the centuries of Videssian history, the strait had shielded the capital—till now.

"No siege gear on our side," Thrax said, as if in consolation— and it was consolation of a sort. "Those monoxyla the Kubratoi use, they can sneak men across easily enough, but only a few at a time, on account of our dromons still catch and sink a good many. Some of the tackle is right bulky, though."

"Less than you'd think," Maniakes said worriedly. The more he thought about it, the more worried he got, too. Ropes and metal fittings and a few special pieces of gear were all the Makuraners needed to bring over with them. They could make the rest out of green timbers, using the Kubratoi for labor ... "Aye, we have to get back to the city as fast as we can."

"That's what I'm here for, your Majesty," Thrax said. The elder Maniakes had told him why he was here. Maniakes had a well-founded suspicion the drungarios would have had trouble figuring it out without advance instruction.

With advance instruction, he was capable enough. Wanting to use him to best advantage, Maniakes said, "You should know to expect stormy weather on the way back to Videssos the city. Bagdasares' magic warned me of it when he cast a spell to make sure we would come safe from the city to Lyssaion."

When Thrax's sun- and wind-leathered skin wrinkled into a frown, he seemed to age ten years in a moment. "I'll do all I can to make the ships ready in advance," he said. And then, anxiously, "That is the reason you're telling me this, isn't it?"

"Yes, that's the reason," Maniakes answered in a resigned voice. He and Thrax had been together for a long time. The drungarios was steady enough; that was why Maniakes had named him to his post. In most circumstances, steadiness was plenty. Every once in a while, Maniakes would have liked to see a bit of flash along with it.

As Thrax had been waiting in the harbor of Lyssaion for some time while the army returned from the Land of the Thousand Cities, he did have the fleet ready to reembark the men and horses. The men grumbled a bit filing onto the wharves to board the ships that would take them away: after hard campaigning, they'd finally returned to a Videssian city, but they weren't going to have the chance to sample such fleshpots as it held.

"Cheer up," Maniakes told a few of them. "This is just a little backwoods town. The sooner we get back to Videssos the city, the sooner you'll *really* be able to enjoy yourselves." *And the sooner you'll start fighting the Makuraners and the Kubratoi,* he added to himself—but not to them.

The horses didn't like boarding ship, either, but then horses never did. Their potential for trouble was much smaller than that of the men. In all of Videssian history, not one mutiny had ever been started by a horse.

"Phos go with you and bring you victory," Phakrases said. The hypasteos sounded worried, and well he might. If by some mischance Videssos the city fell, he would be city governor for a regime that, in effect, no longer existed. If Videssos the city fell, Lyssaion would, too, and then he would no longer be city governor at all.

If Videssos the city fell, Maniakes would hardly be Avtokrator at all, either. The key, then, was making certain the city did not fall. So he reasoned as the fleet left the harbor and set out across the Sailors' Sea.

As ships usually did, the fleet carrying Maniakes and his army back toward Videssos the city stayed within sight of land, even if, to give the ships room to maneuver when and if a storm struck them, Thrax had them sail out till the land was no more than a blur on the northern horizon. The prevailing westerlies drove them along, faster than they had gone heading out to Lyssaion.

When night came, they anchored not far offshore. Had the shore been under their control, they would have beached the ships. As things were, no telling whether a Makuraner force might try to make trouble for them if they did. No telling, for that matter, whether some of the locals might have tried to make trouble for them. The southern coast of the westlands had been a pirate haven till the imperial fleet crushed the raiders. If the Empire of Videssos collapsed, Maniakes was sure piracy would again start flourishing in these waters in a few years' time.

He paced the deck of the *Renewal* during the day. "I hate this," he said to Lysia not long after they began sailing east. "I can't do anything to change the way things are while I'm here. I can't do anything about Videssos the city because I'm far away, and I can't even do anything about how we get there because Thrax is the one in charge of the fleet."

"You've already done everything that needed doing about the fleet—you and your father, I should say," she replied. "He made sure it was there to bring you back to the city if that was what you wanted, and you decided it was and sent the men back to Lyssaion. Past that, everything else is unimportant."

He sent her a grateful look. "You're right, of course. But I want to do things, and I can't. Waiting's not easy."

She set both hands on her belly. Her pregnancy didn't show yet, but would soon. She'd had practice waiting, nine months at a time.

Maniakes suspected the folk who lived by the Sailors' Sea had practice waiting, too. Whenever the fleet drew near the limestone cliffs common there, whenever he spotted one of the inlets not big enough to support any kind of proper harbor but more than adequate as a base for a swift galley or two, he concluded that a lot of the locals were biding their time, as they had for generations. If ever Videssos grew weak, they would grow strong, and they had to know it.

He also watched the weather with a careful and dubious eye. Every speck of cloud, no matter how small, no matter how fluffy, appeared to his worried gaze as a thunderhead loaded with rain and pushed along by winds that would whip the sea to fury. But the days went by, the little puffy clouds remained little puffy clouds, and the gentle swells under the keel of the *Renewal* were not enough to make even Lysia's sensitive stomach complain.

They rounded the southeastern corner of the westlands and started the journey north toward Videssos the city. Now Maniakes stood in the bow of the *Renewal*, peering forward even though he knew the capital was still days away. He wondered if Bagdasares really was as good a wizard as he thought.

"We'll find out," Rhegorios replied when Maniakes asked that question out loud. The Sevastos was also looking north. "Nothing out there now but ocean. Plenty of time for a storm to blow up, if one has a mind to."

"Thank you, cousin of mine," Maniakes said. "No one knows how to build my spirits the way you do."

Rhegorios bowed. "Your servant," he said. Maniakes snorted, then laughed out loud. In a perverse way, his cousin's rampant pessimism had built his spirits, after all.

The coastal lowlands were the most fertile section of the Empire of Videssos, rivaling even the Land of the Thousand Cities for abundance. This far from Videssos the city, they were not heavily garrisoned by the Makuraners. Indeed, Videssian dominance at sea had maintained a stronger imperial presence along the coasts than almost anywhere else in the westlands. All the same, the fleet did not enter any harbors or beach itself on any inviting stretches of sand. A Makuraner force might have been prowling through the countryside, looking for trouble. Wrecking the fleet carrying Videssos' best army certainly counted as trouble in Maniakes' mind.

The next day, a lookout shouted, "The Key! The Key off the starboard bow!"

Maniakes turned to see the island for himself. The Key had got its name because its position, south and east of Videssos the city, made it crucial for holding the capital in any naval campaign—any naval campaign fought by Videssian ships, anyhow. The Makuraners and Kubratoi seemed to have come up with a different idea.

Though it was merely a smudge on the horizon, seeing it also reassured him because of its two excellent harbors, Gavdos in the south and Sykeota in the north. If the storm did come, they would give the fleet more places to shelter.

They had other uses, too. Thrax came up to Maniakes and said, "By your leave, your Majesty, I'd like to put in at Gavdos, draw food there, and refill the water casks, too. We've spent more time at sea all at once than I think I've ever done, and we're lower on supplies than I'd like."

Maniakes frowned. Having come so far, he grudged any delay. But good food and water and keeping the ships and their sails in top condition counted, too. "Go ahead," he told Thrax, and did his best not to show the stop bothered him.

"We'll pick up news of the capital there," Lysia said after he'd confessed he was going to grant Thrax's request. One corner of her mouth twitched up in a wry smile. "You don't need to tell me in the tone of voice you'd use to let me know you were unfaithful."

"Oh, yes, I've had a lot of chances for *that* during this campaign," he said, holding up his hand. " 'Stop the battle, please, and bring me the latest wench.' "

The cabin they shared was cramped for two; the cabin they shared would have been cramped for one. Maniakes couldn't escape when Lysia reached out to poke him in the ribs. "Who is this latest wench?" she asked darkly.

"Right now, she's carrying my child," he answered, and took her in his arms. The cabin did have a door, and shutters over the windows, but sailors still walked past it every minute or so. That meant, for dignity's sake, they had to be very quiet. To his surprise, Maniakes had found that sometimes added something. So did the gentle motion of the *Renewal* on the sea—for him, at least. Lysia could have done without it.

"Get off me," she whispered when they had finished. She looked slightly green, which made Maniakes obey her faster than he might have otherwise. She gulped a couple of times, but things stayed down. She started to dress. As she pulled her undertunic on over her head, she said in reflective tones, "It's just as well my belly will stop you from getting on top after a while. My breasts are sore, too, and you squashed them."

"I'm sorry," he answered. He'd said that during each of her pregnancies. She believed it each time—believed it enough to stay friendly, and more than friendly, at any rate. *A good thing, too,* he thought. Without her, he would have felt altogether alone against the world, as opposed to merely overmatched.

Behind Gavdos rose the mountains in the center of the Key. Thrax let out a small laugh. "I remember the first time I brought the *Renewal* into this port, your Majesty."

"So do I. I'm not likely to forget," Maniakes answered. He'd been a rebel then and had managed to bring part of the fleet that sailed from the Key over to his side. Had the rest of that fleet not gone over to him after he sailed into Gavdos . . . had that not happened, Genesios would still be Avtokrator of the Videssians.

Maniakes' mouth twisted into a thin, bitter line. Everything Genesios did had been a catastrophe—but when Maniakes overthrew him, Videssos had still held a good chunk of the westlands, and the lord with the great and good mind knew no Makuraners had come over the Cattle Crossing to stare up close at the walls of Videssos the city with hungry, clever eyes.

He cursed Genesios. He'd spent a lot of time cursing Genesios, these past half-dozen years. The incompetent butcher had left him nothing—less than nothing—with which to work.

And yet . . . Just before he'd taken Genesios' head, the wretch had asked him a question that had haunted him ever since: "Will you do any better?" So far, he could not say with certainty the answer was yes.

Oarsmen guided the *Renewal* alongside a quay. Sailors leapt up onto it and made the dromon fast. More sailors set the gangplank in place, to let people go back and forth more readily. When Maniakes set foot on the wharf, he wondered if he'd arrived in the middle of an earthquake: the planks were swaying under his feet, weren't they? After a moment, he realized they weren't. He'd never spent so long at sea before, and found himself without his land legs.

Waiting to greet him was the drungarios of the fleet of the Key, a plump, fussy-looking fellow named Skitzas who had a reputation for aggressive seamanship that belied his appearance. "Hello, your Majesty," he said, saluting. "Good to see you're here and not there." He pointed west.

"I wish I were there and not here, and my army, too," Maniakes answered. "But, from the messages that got through to me, Sharbaraz and Etzilios have made that a bad idea."

"I'm afraid you're right," Skitzas said. "The Kubratoi are playing it smart, may Skotos drag them down to the eternal ice. Their monoxyla aren't a match for dromons: they've learned that the hard way. So they aren't even trying to fight us. They just keep sneaking across to the westlands, mostly at night, and carrying Makuraners back toward Videssos the city. After a while, they'll have a good many of them on the side where they don't belong."

"Makuraners don't belong on either side of the Cattle Crossing," Maniakes said, and Skitzas nodded. The Avtokrator went on, "What are you doing about it?"

"What we can," the officer answered. "Every so often, we'll meet up with a one-trunk boat in the water and put paid to it. We've been scouring the coast north and east of Videssos the city, too, doing everything we can to catch the monoxyla beached. We've burned a good many." He made a sour face. "Trouble is, the cursed things are easy to drag up well out of the water and hide. Once the masts are off them, they're only tree trunks, after all. We aren't having all the luck we ought to, I own that."

"All right," Maniakes said, and then held up a hand. "All right that you've given me a straight answer, I mean; I needed one. What's going on by the city isn't all right, not even a little bit."

"I know that, your Majesty," Skitzas said. "The one thing we and the fleet in Videssos the city have done is, we've managed to keep the Kubratoi from getting a big flotilla of monoxyla over to the westlands and ferrying the whole Makuraner army over the

Cattle Crossing in one swoop. To the ice with me if I ever thought I'd be happy about delaying the enemy instead of beating him, but that's how it is right now."

"They caught us with our drawers down," Maniakes said, which wrung a grunt of startled laughter out of Skitzas. "Delaying them counts; I was wondering if I'd come back only to find the city fallen."

"The good god forbid it." Skitzas sketched the sun-circle. "Anything I can do to help you along—"

"I think Thrax has that well in hand," Maniakes said. The drungarios of the fleet was bellowing instructions at the officers who had advanced to see what he required. He told them in alarming detail. When he had a chance to prepare in advance, he was a nonpareil.

Before long, laborers started carrying sacks of flour, sacks of beans, barrels of salted beef, and jars of wine aboard the ships of his fleet. Others brought coils of rope, canvas, casks of pitch, and other nautical supplies. By the time the sun went down, the fleet was in better shape than it had been since the day after it sailed out of Lyssaion.

Sunset turned clouds in the west the color of blood. Maniakes noted that, at first made nothing of it, and then turned back to look at the sunset again. He hadn't seen clouds in the west for a good long while now. Were they harbingers of the storm Bagdasares had predicted?

If they were, could he wait out the storm here at Gavdos and then sail on to Videssos the city undisturbed? He wished he thought the answer to that were yes. But he had the strong feeling that, if this was a coming storm and he waited it out, another would catch him as soon as he put to sea. He'd gain nothing that way, and lose precious time.

"We'll go on," he said aloud. "Whatever my fate is, I'll go to meet it; I won't wait for it to come to me."

The *Renewal* bounced and shook in the waves as if it were a toy boat in a washbasin inhabited by a two-year-old intent on splashing all the water in the basin onto the floor before his mother could finish washing him. Rain drummed against Maniakes' face. The wind howled like a whole pack of hungry wolves.

Thrax screamed something at him. The drungarios of the fleet stood close by Maniakes, but he had no idea what his naval commander was saying. The rain plastered Thrax's thick pelt of white hair against his skull, giving him something of the look of an elderly otter.

Whatever my fate is, I'll go to meet it. Maniakes savored the stupidity of the words. He'd been overeager again. That was easy enough to see, in retrospect. There were storms, and then there were storms. In his haste to get back to Videssos the city, he'd put the fleet in the way of a bad one.

Thrax tried again, but whatever he'd bellowed got buried in a thunderclap that made Maniakes' ears ring. The *Renewal* nosed down into a trough between two waves. It nosed down steeply, for the waves were running very high. Maniakes staggered, but managed to keep his feet. Thrax stayed upright without apparent effort. Whatever his shortcomings, he was a seaman.

Well off the starboard bow, another dromon fought its way northward. The rowers were keeping the bow into the wind and making what progress they could, as were those of the *Renewal*. At the moment, Maniakes worried little about progress. All he wanted to do was stay on top of the water till the storm decided to blow past and churn up some other part of the Sailors' Sea. Somewhere beyond the weeping gray clouds floated Phos' sun, chiefest symbol of the good god's light. He hoped he'd live to see that symbol again.

Suddenly, without warning, the other galley broke its back. One of those surging waves must have struck it exactly wrong. It went from a ship almost identical to the *Renewal* to floating wreckage in the space of half a minute. The two halves of the hull filled with water almost at once. Here and there, scattered across the ocean, men clung to planks, to oars, to anything that would bear even part of their weight for a little while.

Maniakes pointed toward the survivors. "Can we save them?" he yelled to Thrax. At first, he thought the drungarios hadn't heard him. Thrax made his way back to the stern of the *Renewal* and bawled in the ears of the men at the steering oars, pointing in the direction of the wrecked galley as he did so. The *Renewal* swung toward the struggling men.

Sailors tied themselves to the rail before throwing lines out into the heaving sea in hope some of the men who floundered there might catch hold of them. And some of those men did catch hold of them, and were pulled half-drowned from the water that had tried to take their lives.

And some of the crew from the smashed dromon could not be saved in spite of all that the men from the *Renewal* did. One luckless sailor let go of the spar to which he had been clinging to grab for a rope. A wave slapped him in the head before his hand closed on the line. He went under.

"Come up!" Maniakes shouted to him. "Curse you, come up!" But he did not come up.

Other men lost hold of whatever they were using to keep their heads above water before the *Renewal* got close enough to pluck them from the sea. Maniakes groaned every time he saw that happen. And he knew other sailors—too many other sailors—had already drowned.

A wave broke over the *Renewal*'s bow. For a hideous moment, he thought the dromon was going to imitate the one that had broken up. The ship's timbers groaned under his feet. Another, bigger wave hit her—and hit him, too. The wall of water knocked him off his feet. He skidded across the deck, fetched up hard against the rail—and started to go over, out into the foaming, roaring sea.

He grabbed at the rail. One hand seized it. He hung on with everything he had, knowing he would not live above a minute if his grip failed.

A hand closed on his wrist. A sailor with a silver hoop in one ear hauled him back aboard the *Renewal*. The fellow shouted something at him. Wind and storm blew the words away. Then the sailor offered him a length of line. He tied one end around the rail, the other around his waist. That done, he shook a fist at the sky, as if defying it to do its worst.

It seemed to take up his challenge. The wind blew harder than ever. Rain came down in sheets. Only by tasting whether the water on his lips was sweet or salt could Maniakes be sure whether storm or sea buffeted him.

A sailor pointed off to port. More wreckage drifted there, along with human forms. Maniakes started to bellow for more lines to be cast, but stopped with the words unspoken. Those luckless fellows would be walking the bridge of the separator now, to see whether their souls tumbled down into Skotos' icy hell or spent eternity bathed in Phos' light.

Maniakes turned and looked southeast, back toward the Key.

They'd cleared Sykeota some while before, and he could not see very far in any case. He didn't think they would be dashed against the shore, and realized he wouldn't find out for certain till too late to stay disaster if it came.

Lysia staggered out of the cabin the two of them shared. Maniakes ran toward her, signaling with his hands for her to go back inside. He pointed to the rope around his own midsection. Lysia nodded, thrust a pot in which she'd been copiously sick into his hands, and retreated.

He poured the pot into the sea. Like everything else, its contents were scattered and swept away. He was so soaked, he hardly felt wet: it was almost as if he were immersed in a swimming bath. In the middle of summer, both sea and rain were warm, the sole blessing Maniakes could find in the present situation.

One of the broad-beamed merchantmen carrying soldiers wallowed past. It rode lower in the water than it should have; sailors and soldiers both were bailing with might and main. Maniakes murmured a prayer that the ship would survive.

Thrax came back up toward the *Renewal*'s bow. The drungarios disdained an anchoring rope. Maniakes thought that disdain a foolish display of bravado, but held his tongue; he was not Thrax's nursemaid. At the top of his lungs, Maniakes bellowed, "How long will this storm last?"

He had to repeat himself three or four times before Thrax understood. "Don't know, your Majesty," the drungarios screamed back. He, too, did not make Maniakes hear him at the first try. When he was sure the Avtokrator had gotten his first sentence, he tried another: "Maybe it'll blow itself out by nightfall."

"That would be good," Maniakes said—and said, and said. "How long till nightfall?"

"To the ice with me if I know." Thrax pointed up to the sky. One part of it was as gray and ugly and full of driving rain as the next. The only way they would be able to tell when the sun went down was by its getting dark—or rather, darker.

Nor had Thrax promised the storm would end when night came. Maniakes, then, was faced with waiting an indefinite length of time for something that might not happen. He wished he saw a better alternative. The only alternative that came to mind, though, was drowning immediately. Compared to that, waiting was better.

Not far away, a bolt of lightning lanced down out of the sky.

Purple streaks dimmed Maniakes' vision. The lightning could as easily have struck the *Renewal* as not: one more thing about which the Avtokrator tried not to think.

He tried not to think at all. In the storm, thinking did him no good. He was just another frightened animal here, trying to ride out the forces of nature. On dry land, in among his soldiers or in a sturdy fortress, he could fancy himself the lord of all he surveyed. Here he surveyed little, and could control none of it.

A little while later, Rhegorios emerged from his cabin. A sailor gave him a safety line, which he accepted with some reluctance. "I thought you'd have been here on deck for the whole storm," Maniakes said. "You're always wild for adventures like this."

His cousin grimaced. "I've been puking my guts up, is what I've been doing, if you really want to know. I always thought I was a decent sailor, but I've never been in anything like—" Instead of finishing the sentence, Rhegorios leaned over the rail. When the spasm passed, he said, "I wish they hadn't given me this cursed rope. Now it's harder for me to throw myself into the sea."

"It's not that bad," Maniakes said, but all that meant was, it wasn't that bad for him. Rhegorios laughed at him—till he started retching again. Maniakes tried to hold the hair out of his face while he heaved.

"Is it getting darker?" Rhegorios asked when he could speak again. "Or am I starting to die?"

Maniakes hadn't paid much attention to the sky for a while, most likely because he'd come to assume the day would never end. Now he looked up. It *was* darker. "Thrax said the storm might blow itself out when night fell," he shouted hopefully, over the roar of the wind.

"Here's hoping Thrax is right." Rhegorios' abused stomach rebelled again. Nothing came forth this time, but he looked as miserable as if something had. "I hate the dry heaves," he said, adding, "Bloody shame they're the only thing about me I can call dry." Water dripped from his beard, from the tip of his nose, from his hair, from his sleeves, and from his elbows when he bent his arms. Maniakes, who had stayed on deck through most of the storm, was wetter still, but the distinction would be meaningless in moments.

Darkness, having once made an appearance, quickly descended on the sea. The rain dropped from torrent to trickle; the wind ebbed. "Praise the good god, lads," Thrax shouted to the crew. "I think we've come though the worst."

A couple of sailors took him literally, either reciting Phos' creed or sending their own prayers of thanks to the lord with the great and good mind. Maniakes murmured a prayer of his own, part thanks but more a fervent hope the storm really was over and would not resume with the dawn.

"Break out a torch, boys!" Thrax yelled. "Let's find out if we have any friends left on the ocean."

Maniakes would have bet a dry torch or, for that matter, any means of setting it alight, could not be found anywhere aboard the *Renewal*. He would have lost that bet, and in short order, too. Even in darkness, more than one sailor hurried for the torches wrapped in layer on layer of oiled canvas. And the cook had a firesafe, a good-sized pot in which embers were always smoldering. Thrax took the blazing torch and waved it back and forth.

One by one, other torches came to life on the Sailors' Sea, some close by, others so far off they were hard to tell from stars near the horizon. But there were no stars, the sky still being full of clouds. The ships that had survived the storm crawled across the water toward one another. When they got within hailing range, captains shouted back and forth, setting forth the toll of those known lost and, by silences, of those missing.

"It's not so bad as it looks, your Majesty," Thrax said, somewhere getting on toward midnight. "More will join us tomorrow morning, and more still, blown so far off course that they can't see any torches at all, will make straight for the imperial city. Not everybody who isn't here is gone for good."

"Yes, I understand that," Maniakes answered. "And some, like that one transport out there somewhere—" He pointed vaguely past the bow of the *Renewal*. "—can't show torches because they haven't got any fire left. I think it's Phos' own miracle so many of our ships have been able to make lights. But still—"

But still. In any context, those words were ominous, implying lost gold, lost chances, lost hopes. Here they meant lost ships, lost men, lost animals—so many lost without any possibility of rescue, as when the dromon had broken up in the raging sea not far from the flagship.

Not all the survivors had stories like that to tell, but too many of them did. Maniakes did what he could to piece together his losses, bearing in mind what Thrax had said. They came to somewhere not far from a quarter of the force with which he'd set out from Lyssaion. He hoped not too many of the ships Thrax reckoned scattered were in fact lost.

"And speaking of scattered," he said around a yawn, "where are we, anyhow?" He yawned again; now that the storm and the crises were for the moment past, he felt with full—perhaps with double—measure how tired and worn he was.

"To the ice with me if I know exactly, your Majesty," Thrax answered. "We'll sail north when morning comes, and we'll sight land, and we'll figure out what land we've sighted. Then we'll know where we're at, and how far away from Videssos the city we are, too."

"All right," Maniakes said mildly. He was no sailor, but he'd spent enough time at sea to know that navigation was an art almost as arcane as magecraft, and less exact. Knowing how to find out where they were was nearly as good as knowing where.

He undid the rope that had been around his waist so long, he'd almost forgotten it was there. Nothing worse than gentle chop stirred the *Renewal*'s deck under his feet as he walked to the cabin. He opened the door as quietly as he could. Lysia's soft snores did not break their rhythm. He lay down in wet robes on wet bedding and fell asleep himself.

A sunbeam in his face woke him. For a moment, he simply accepted that, as he had clouds at sunset before. Then he sketched Phos' sun-circle over his heart, a sign of delight. He'd never known anything more welcome than a day of fair weather.

Still in those wet robes, he went out on deck. Sailors were busy repairing storm damage to the railing, to the rigging of the square sail, and to rips in its canvas. They'd taken it down fast when the storm struck, but not fast enough.

Thrax pointed north. "Land there, your Majesty. If I remember the shape of it aright, we're not so far from the imperial city as I would have guessed."

"Good," Maniakes said. "Aye, that's good." Spotting small sails on the sea between the fleet and shore, he pointed in his turn, off to the northwest. "Look. All the fishermen who weren't sunk yesterday are out after whatever they can get today."

"What's that, your Majesty?" Thrax hadn't noticed the sails. Now he did, and stiffened. "Those aren't fishermen, your Majesty. Those are cursed monoxyla, is what those are." His voice rose to a bellow: "Make ready for battle!"

V

THE FLEET COULD HARDLY HAVE BEEN LESS READY TO FIGHT, battered by the storm as it was. All Thrax had wanted to do, all Maniakes had wanted to do, was limp into Videssos the city, unload the warriors and animals, and take a little while to figure out what to do next. Once again, the Avtokrator wasn't going to get what he wanted. The Kubratoi in their single-trunk boats were making sure of that.

"Dart-thrower's going to be useless," Thrax grumbled, pointing to the engine at the *Renewal*'s bow. "Cords are sure to be too soaked to do any good."

Maniakes didn't answer at once. Till this moment, he'd never actually seen any of the vessels the Kubratoi had been using for years to raid his coast. They were, he discovered, more formidable than their name suggested. Each one might have been hewn from a single trunk, but the Kubratoi had taken forest giants from which to make their boats. Some of them looked to be almost as long as the *Renewal*, though of course they carried far fewer men. Along with their sails, which were made of leather, they were propelled by paddles—and propelled surprisingly fast, too.

They had spotted the Videssian ships, either before they were seen themselves or at about the same moment. Maniakes had expected that would be plenty to make them flee. Instead, they swung toward the Videssians. The paddles rose and fell, rose and fell, rose and fell. Yes, they could make a very good turn of speed.

"We'll smash them," Maniakes said.

Now Thrax didn't reply right away. He looked distinctly less happy than Maniakes would have liked to see him. At last, he said, "Your Majesty, I'm not worried about the dromons. The transports are a different game, though."

He started shouting orders across the water. Trumpeters echoed

115

his commands. The dromons slid toward the less mobile, less protected vessels they were shepherding to the imperial city. They were none too soon in doing so, either, for the Kubratoi had no more trouble figuring out the way the game needed to be played than did Thrax. Their monoxyla were also making for the slower, beamier ships in the Videssian fleet.

"Maybe we ought to let them try to board one of the troop transports," Thrax said. "I don't think they'd be glad they'd done it."

"Something to that," Maniakes agreed, but neither one of them meant it seriously, as they both knew. Maniakes put that into words: "Too many things could go wrong. They might get lucky, or they might manage to start a fire—"

"Wouldn't be easy, not today," Thrax said, "not with the timbers soaked from yesterday's storm. But you're right, your Majesty: it could happen."

One of the dromons, oars slashing the water, rushed at a monoxylon. The Kubratoi not only managed to avoid the bronze-shod ram at the dromon's bow, they sprayed the Videssian ship with arrows. A sailor fell *splash!* into the sea.

Another single-trunk vessel got up alongside a ship transporting horses. The Kubratoi didn't try swarming aboard the vessel, but, again, shot arrows at it as rapidly as if they were shooting at Videssian soldiers from horseback.

Thrax pointed to that monoxylon. "They're so busy doing what they're doing, they aren't paying any attention to us." He shouted to the oarmaster: "Build the stroke. Give us everything you have!"

"Aye, lord," the oarmaster replied. The drum that beat time for the rowers on the two-man sweeps speeded its rhythm. The rowers responded. The wake leaping out from under the *Renewal*'s hull got thicker and whiter. Thrax ran back to the dromon's stern to take charge of one of the steering oars and yell directions to the man at the other.

Maniakes, by contrast, hurried up toward the bow. He hadn't been in a sea fight since the one in the waters just off Videssos the city that let him enter the capital. This wasn't like fighting on land; ships carried a company's worth of men, but were themselves individual pieces, and valuable ones, on the game board.

The *Renewal* had closed to within fifty yards before the Kubratoi realized the dromon was there. They were close enough for Maniakes to hear their shouts of dismay when at last they spied her. They threw down their bows then and snatched up their paddles, doing their best to escape the pointed, sea-greened beak aimed square at their stern.

Their best was not good enough. They'd slowed to stay alongside the transport, and needed time to build up speed again—time they did not get. Thrax had a nice sense of aim and timing. He drove the ram home as the Kubratoi turned slightly broadside to his dromon.

The ram did not hole the monoxylon, as it would have done to a Videssian vessel. Instead, the *Renewal* rode up and over the smaller Kubratoi craft, rolling and crushing it. The collision staggered Maniakes, who almost went into the sea. What it did to the Kubratoi—

Heads bobbed in the sea, but surprisingly few of them. The Kubratoi were demons on horseback; Maniakes had never before had occasion to wonder how many of them could swim. The answer, it seemed, was *not many*. Some, who might or might not have known how to swim, clung to paddles or other floating bits of wreckage.

Videssian sailors shot arrows at the struggling Kubratoi. From what Maniakes could see, they scored few hits. It didn't matter. Either the Kubratoi would drown, or some Videssian ship would capture them once the sea fight was done. They might well have preferred to drown.

"Well done!" Thrax bellowed. "Now let's get another one." He steered the *Renewal* in the direction of the next closest monoxylon. "Keep us going there, oarmaster!" he added. The thudding drum that pounded out the strokes never faltered.

Unlike the Videssian fleet, the Kubratoi must have stayed ashore during the storm. That meant they had no trouble getting fires started. Several single-log craft bobbed in the waves near another transport. Smoke trails through the air showed they were shooting fire arrows at it.

Maniakes wished he could have seen more of how that came out, but the *Renewal* was bearing down on the monoxylon Thrax had chosen as his new target. This one, unlike the first, was not taken unawares, and the Kubrati commanding it was doing everything he could to get away. The little leather sail was raised and full of air; the paddles beat the water to froth as the nomads worked for all they were worth.

"Prepare to ram!" This time, Thrax had the courtesy to shout the warning a couple of seconds before his dromon crunched into the single-log boat. Again, Maniakes staggered at the impact. Again, the *Renewal* went right over the monoxylon. This time, though, that was a slower, more grinding business, because the difference in speed between the two vessels was much smaller than it had been before.

Again, Kubratoi spilled into the water. Again, many of them quickly sank to their deaths. But a few managed to catch hold of the *Renewal*'s planking and scramble up onto the deck.

They were dripping. By the look in their eyes, they were half-stunned and more. But none of them seemed in any mood to surrender. They wore swords on their belts. Drawing them, they rushed at the Videssian sailors—and one of them came straight for Maniakes.

He was so startled, he almost left his own sword in its scabbard till too late. He yanked it out just in time to turn aside a fierce cut at his head. The Kubrati then chose a low line, slashing at his shins. He parried again, and hopped back. The fellow might not have been an outrageously good swordsman, but enough grim energy for at least three men filled him.

One sailor was down and screaming. Others, though, fought the Kubrati with swords and bows and clubs. Once the first surprise at being boarded began to fade, they realized how greatly they outnumbered their assailants. The fight on deck did not last long after that.

Somebody clubbed the Kubrati who was fighting Maniakes. The fellow groaned and staggered. Maniakes' sword ripped his belly open. The Avtokrator twisted his wrist to make sure it was a killing stroke. The Kubratoi did not scream or clutch at himself; the blow to the side of his head must have dazed him and given him an easy death.

He had been almost the last of his people still upright. Maniakes pulled his sword free, grabbed the Kubrati by the heels, and said, "Let's throw this carrion overboard," to the sailor with the bludgeon. The Kubrati's body splashed into the Sailors' Sea.

Thrax pointed. "Ahh, the filthy bastards, they did manage to burn one," he shouted. In spite of wet timbers, flames were spreading on one of the transports. Videssian soldiers and sailors leapt into the water. Like the Kubratoi from sunken and capsized monoxyla, they grabbed for anything they could reach to keep themselves afloat a little longer.

"Shall we pick them up or pursue the foe, your Majesty?" Thrax asked. The monoxyla still unsunk had clearly had enough of the unequal fight with the Videssian dromons. Under sail and paddle, they were heading off to the east as fast as they could go.

Maniakes hesitated not even a heartbeat. "We make pickup," he said. "Then we head on to the imperial city. To the ice with the Kubratoi; let 'em go."

"Aye, your Majesty," Thrax said. He bawled the needed orders, then turned back to the Avtokrator with a puzzled look on his face. "You usually want to finish the foe when you find the chance."

"Yes, usually." Maniakes fought hard to hold in his exasperation. Thrax sometimes had trouble seeing past the end of his nose. "Now, though, the most important thing we can do is get back to Videssos the city and make sure it doesn't fall. Those single-trunk boats were sailing straight away from it. We're not going to waste time going after them."

"Ah," Thrax said. "When you put it that way, it does make sense, doesn't it?"

To give him his due, he handled the rescue of the men who had abandoned the burning transport about as well as anyone could have done. A good many soldiers were lost, drowned before any rescuers could reach them, but a good many were pulled from the sea, too. It could have been worse. How many times had Maniakes thought that after some new misfortune?

Bagdasares' magic had shown no further trouble facing the Videssian fleet after the storm and the attack by those other ships. Maybe that meant they would reach Videssos the city with ease once they'd surmounted that attack—in the case of the *Renewal*, literally, as it rode over the Kubratoi monoxyla. Then again, maybe it meant Bagdasares had metaphorically had his elbow joggled before the sorcery showed everything it could. One way or the other, Maniakes expected he would learn soon.

Close by the imperial city, no single-log boats dared show themselves by day. The fleet based in the capital made sure of that. But, from the *Renewal*, Maniakes saw the nomads' encampments outside the double wall of the capital. That ate at him, as did knowing

Makuraner engineers were teaching the Kubratoi the art of building siege engines. From now on, no Videssian city would be safe.

From the walls, Videssian defenders cheered when they saw the imperial standard flying from the *Renewal*. Maniakes did not flatter himself that all those cheers were for him. He had taken to Makuran the best soldiers the Empire of Videssos had. Getting those soldiers back made Videssos the city likelier to hold. Had he been a defender hopefully awaiting them, he would have cheered their return, too.

"We'll land as many ships as we can in the little harbor for the palace quarter," he told Thrax. "That will include the *Renewal*."

"Aye, your Majesty," the drungarios said, nodding in obedience. "You'll want to send the rest around to the Neorhesian harbor in the north?"

"That's right," Maniakes agreed.

"When we tie up at that little harbor, you'll be able to get a good look at what's going on in Across," Thrax said, as if the idea had only just occurred to him. It probably *had* only just occurred to him; that saddened Maniakes, who was used to looking further ahead. Thrax could, of course, have been the sort of man who did not look ahead at all; too many men were like that. But in that case he would not have been drungarios of the fleet.

Across looked to be buzzing. The red-lion banner of Makuran flew from a silk pavilion situated barely out of range of dart-throwers mounted on dromons. Yes, Abivard would know exactly how far that was, having spent so much time on the wrong—or, from the Videssian perspective, the right—side of the Cattle Crossing from Videssos the city.

Maniakes wondered whether the Makuraner marshal remained on the western side of the Cattle Crossing, or whether the Kubratoi had sneaked him over the narrow strait so he could gauge the land walls of the imperial city with his own eyes. Suddenly and rather sharply, the Avtokrator wondered which side of the Cattle Crossing Tzikas was on these days. Before he began his treacheries, Tzikas had been a Videssian general, and a formidably good one. If anyone knew of weaknesses in the walls—if there were any weaknesses to know—he was likely to be the man.

The Makuraners saw the imperial standard, too, when the *Renewal* drew near Across to give Maniakes a closer look at them.

The curses they sent his way warred with the cheers from Videssos the city. Their whole camp was much closer to the Cattle Crossing than had been their way during earlier stays in Across. Then they had seemed content merely to have come so close to Videssos' capital. Now they had the notion they could cross, could reach the goal so long denied them.

"They're wrong," Maniakes murmured. Saying that and ensuring it was true, though, were two different things. Maniakes turned back to Thrax. "Take us to the harbor. I've seen enough here."

With his father, and with Rhegorios and Symvatios, Maniakes passed through the Silver Gate's opening in the inner wall of Videssos the city and strode out toward the lower outer wall. "By the lord with the great and good mind, the parasol-bearers are still fuming because I wouldn't let them come out here with me," he said, fuming himself. "That would be all I needed, wouldn't it? Showing the Kubratoi exactly whom to shoot, I mean."

"That's the kind of nonsense you don't have to put up with in the field," the elder Maniakes agreed. "I don't blame you for getting out of Videssos the city whenever you can, son. You don't have idiots getting in the way of what needs doing."

"No," the Avtokrator said. Escaping the stifling ceremonial of the imperial court *was* one reason he was glad to get out of Videssos the city. He noticed his father did not mention the other one. The elder Maniakes did not approve of his marriage to Lysia, either, but, unlike so many in the city, was at least willing to keep quiet about it.

The massive portals of the Silver Gate's entryway through the outer wall were shut. The even more massive bars that held those portals closed were in place in their great iron brackets. Behind the gate, the iron-faced portcullis was lowered into its place in the gateway. Up above it, murder holes let defenders pour boiling water and heated sand down on the heads of warriors who might try to break down the defenses. Maniakes would not have cared to assault the Silver Gate, were he besieger rather than besieged.

But, if the Makuraners taught the Kubratoi how to build and use siege engines, they would not have to attack the gate. They might choose instead to try to break down some less heavily defended stretch of wall. If they had any sense, that was what they would do. But who could say for certain what lay in Etzilios' mind? Maniakes wondered whether the Kubrati khagan himself knew.

The Avtokrator climbed the stone stairway to the walk atop the outer wall. His father, cousin, and uncle followed. He tried to make himself climb slowly out of consideration for the elder Maniakes and Symvatios, but they were both breathing hard by the time they gained the walkway.

Maniakes peered out toward the Kubratoi camp nearby. Etzilios had chosen to set his own tent opposite the Silver Gate, the chief way into Videssos the city. The horsetail standards that marked his tent were unmistakable. Also as near unmistakable as made no difference was the banner fluttering next to that standard. White and red . . . Maniakes could not make out the lion of Makuran on the flag, but had no doubt it was there.

Kubratoi rode back and forth, out beyond the ditch in front of the wall. They weren't doing much: he didn't see any of them shooting arrows at the Videssians defending the city, for instance. But they were alert enough to make a sally look like a bad idea.

"How are we fixed for grain?" Maniakes asked. He looked back over his shoulder. The bulk of the inner wall hid Videssos the city from his view. He could feel the weight of its populace pressing out at him all the same. How many people did the city hold? A hundred thousand? A quarter of a million? Twice that? He didn't know, not even within such a broad range. What he did know was that, however many of them there were, they all needed to eat and to keep on eating.

"We're not too bad off," Symvatios answered. "The granaries were fairly full when the siege started, and we've been bringing in more from further south and east, where the Kubratoi haven't reached. We can last . . . a while."

"Other question is, how long can the Kubratoi last out there?" The elder Maniakes pointed toward Etzilios' encampment. "What do they do for food once they've eaten the countryside empty?"

"Starve or go home," Rhegorios said. "Those are the choices they have."

"Those are two of the choices they have," Maniakes said, which made his cousin look puzzled. Wishing he didn't have to, the Avtokrator explained: "They can also try breaking into the city. If they do that, it doesn't matter how much grain we have left or how little food they have. If they break in, they win."

Rhegorios nodded, now unwontedly serious. "Do you know, cousin of mine—" He didn't string titles together now, either. "—that never crossed my mind. In spite of everything they've gathered out there, I have trouble making myself believe they might break in."

"We all have trouble believing it," the elder Maniakes said. "That may be good or bad. It's good if the Kubratoi have doubts in the same proportion as we have confidence. But if we're slack because we know Videssos the city has never fallen and they're all eager and zealous to make a first time, we're in trouble."

"That's so," Maniakes said. "They haven't tried storming the walls?"

His father shook his head. "No. Some days they aren't quiet like this, though. They'll come up into archery range and shoot at our people on the walls. They haven't done that so much lately. It's as if they're—waiting."

"And we know what they're waiting for, too," the Avtokrator said unhappily. "They're waiting to see what the Makuraners can show them and how much help it will be. The boiler boys are good at what they do, too. I wish they weren't, but they know as much about siege warfare as any Videssian."

"Abivard will probably want to get more of his people over to this side of the Cattle Crossing before any serious attack on the walls," Symvatios said. "He won't fancy the Kubratoi taking all the spoils if we fall."

"And they won't want him taking any—Etzilios sucked in treachery at his mother's breast." Maniakes grew thoughtful. "I wonder if we can make the allies distrust each other more than they hate us."

"That *is* an interesting notion," the elder Maniakes said. He, too, stared out toward the Kubrati camp. "I have to say I'd guess the odds are against it. We might as well try, though. The worst they can tell us is no."

"The world doesn't end if you get your face slapped," Rhegorios remarked. "You just ask another girl the same question. Or sometimes you ask the same girl the same question a little later on, and you get a different answer."

"Hear the voice of experience," Maniakes said dryly. His cousin coughed and spluttered. His father and uncle both laughed. The world looked a little brighter, giving him three, maybe even four, heartbeats' worth of relief—till he thought about the Kubratoi again.

A postern gate swung open. Despite all the grease the soldiers had poured onto the hinges, they still squeaked. Maniakes wondered when anyone had last oiled them. Had it been a year ago, or five, or ten? Till this year, no one had expected Videssos the city to be besieged, and a siege was the only time when a postern gate was useful.

"Curse it, we don't want to let all the Kubratoi and Makuraners know we're doing this," the Avtokrator hissed. "The idea is to keep it secret—otherwise we wouldn't have chosen midnight."

"Sorry, your Majesty," the officer in charge of the gate answered, also in a low voice. "That's as quiet as we could manage." He peered out into the darkness. "Here comes the fellow, so he is on time. I wouldn't have thought it, not with a barbarian."

No shouts from the wall above warned of any other Kubratoi moving forward with the single emissary Maniakes had suggested to Etzilios. The khagan was keeping his end of the bargain, most likely because he didn't think he could wring any great advantage from betraying it now. At Maniakes' command, the soldiers at the postern gate ran a long plank out over the far side of the ditch.

"Mind you don't fall off," one of the men called softly to the newcomer. "It's a goodish way down."

"I shall beens very carefuls, thank youse," the Kubrati answered in Videssian fractured but fluent. His footfalls thudded confidently on the gangway. When he came into Videssos the city, the guardsmen pulled back the plank and shut the postern gate once more.

"Moundioukh, isn't it?" Maniakes said. No torches burned nearby—that would have given away the parley. But the Avtokrator had heard only one man capable of mangling Videssian as this fellow did.

And, sure enough, the Kubrati nodded in the darkness and said, "Whose else would the magnifolent Etzilios sends to treat against youse?" Maniakes wondered whether that *against* was more slipshod grammar or a slip of the tongue. He'd find out.

With the gate closed, a couple of torchbearers came hurrying up. Yes, that was Moundioukh, in the flesh as well as in the voice. His scraggly beard had more gray in it than Maniakes remembered. "Your master is a treacherous man," the Avtokrator said severely.

To his surprise, Moundioukh burst out laughing. "Of courses him are," the Kubrati answered. "Otherwisely him never talkings at youse."

"I daresay," Maniakes said. "All right—what does he want from me for him to give over his alliance with the Makuraners? I presume there must be something I can give him, or he wouldn't have sent you to me."

Moundioukh's large, square teeth flashed in the torchlight as he laughed again. "The magnifolent Etzilios tell me, 'Go to this Mani-akes. See him crawl. See him slithither'—is word, yes, slithith-ering? 'Then youse tells he what me tells youse.' "

"And what did the magnifolent Etzilios tell you?" Maniakes knew a certain amount of pride at bringing the epithet out with a straight face.

"Not seen enough of slithitherings yettish times," the Kubratoi replied pointedly.

Maniakes exhaled through his nose in exasperation. "To the ice with him, and to the ice with you, too. I don't know what else I can do but tell you I'll do whatever you and the khagan want." He couldn't say *magnifolent* again, no matter how hard he tried.

"You prostitute yourselves for I, like youse always having I prostitute myselves to youse?" Moundioukh said.

The guards growled. "He means 'prostrate,' " Maniakes said quickly. He wondered if that made the demand any more bearable. He was vicegerent of Phos on earth; who was this nasty barbarian envoy to demand that he go down on his belly before him? *The man with the whip hand*—the answer was painfully plain. "I said *anything*, and I was not lying." Maniakes did the deed. He'd seen it performed before him countless times, but hadn't done it him-self since Likinios Avtokrator sat on the Videssian throne. His body, he discovered, still remembered how.

"Youse really doing this things." Moundioukh sounded amazed.

"Yes, I really did it. Have I slithithered enough for you now?" After performing a proskynesis, desecrating the Videssian lan-guage came easy.

"Is enoughly, yeses," Moundioukh admitted. "Now we tells youse what the magnifolent khagan tell we. He tell, nothing in all these world youse does—" He made it sound like *yooz dooz*. "—am enoughs to make he go buggering Makuraners. Us, theys see chance to slaughterize you, and usses takes it."

"You and the Makuraners would quarrel afterward, even if you won," Maniakes said. "We have a saying—'thieves fall out.' "

"We quarrels?" Moundioukh shrugged. "Then we quarrels. Not having mores of quarrels with Videssians, not nevers again. Magnifolent Etzilios sezzing, that worths any sizes of quarrelings with Makuran."

The khagan was probably right, too, when you looked at things from the Kubrati point of view. If Videssos the city fell, it would be a frontier province to the Makuraners, far from their center. But Videssos the city was the very heart of the Empire of Videssos. Cut it out and the Empire had no heart left. Free rein hereabouts, near enough—that was the stake for which Etzilios was playing.

"And beside," Moundioukh added, "you beat Etzilios. He pay youse back how youse am deservings."

For a barbarian, the khagan was a rational man. But a hunger for revenge, coupled with sound reasons of policy, could make him unreasonable—and apparently had made him so. "If I hadn't beaten him, he would have been down here by the city years before," Maniakes pointed out.

"Should has beed," Moundioukh said. "Should has killed you in trick making treaty. Save Kubrat shitpot full troubles, that beed happening."

"I'm so sorry," Maniakes said dryly. "I should have killed Etzilios, that last fight where I landed troops behind your raiders. That would have saved me a lot of trouble."

"Now youse gots troubles, Etzilios gots troubles, all gots troubles," Moundioukh said, apparently in agreement. "Am time of troubles."

"No agreement from the khagan, then?" Maniakes said unhappily.

"Nones," Moundioukh said. "He says I says no. Youse pushing, I says no and futter yourself, youse pushings hard and I tells youse something really with lots of juices in it. You wants I should?" He sounded delighted to oblige.

"Never mind," Maniakes told him. He didn't bother waving the torchbearers away from the postern gate now—if any Makuraners saw Moundioukh coming back, maybe they'd think the Kubratoi were betraying them even when they weren't. "Let him out," he said to the men in charge of the gate. "We're not going to be able to come to terms."

Having opened once, the gate proved more willing to do so quietly the second time—when Maniakes would have preferred it noisy. The Videssian soldiers slid the gangway out across the ditch. Moundioukh walked across it. This time, no one urged him to be careful. If he fell down and broke his neck in the ditch now, what difference would it make? None Maniakes could see.

"I think that was worth a try, your Majesty," the officer in charge of the gate said. "We're no worse off now than we were before."

"That's true." Maniakes remembered throwing away his crown and the rest of the imperial regalia to escape the Kubratoi when they'd ambushed him in that treaty ceremony. "Aye," he said, half to himself, "I've had worse from the nomads. This time, Moundioukh didn't cost me anything but my dignity."

"I kept hoping it wasn't true," Maniakes said, looking out from a tower thrusting up from the inner wall.

"Well, it bloody well *is* true," Rhegorios answered. He was looking in the same direction. "You're not going to try and tell me the Kubratoi could build those all on their lonesome, are you?"

Those were siege engines, some of them stone- and dart-throwers, other the skeletal beginnings of towers to overtop the outer wall. On the timber frames, the Kubratoi would soon add raw hides to make the towers harder to burn. If they could bring them up to the wall, they'd be able to put men on the walkway. If they did that, anything could happen.

"You're right, of course—they couldn't," Maniakes said unhappily. "Abivard, Skotos curse him to the ice—" He turned his head and performed the ritual expectoration. "—did sneak one of his engineers, or maybe more than one, over the Cattle Crossing. Those are Makuraner-style engines, or else I'm a wolf with a purple pelt."

"Nothing would surprise me, not anymore," his cousin said. "The only worse thing would be having to try handstrokes with all those heavy-armored Makuraners."

"That mail is better for horseback," Maniakes said.

"I know," Rhegorios replied. "But it's not so heavy they can't use it afoot, either, and I wouldn't want to be in their way if they tried."

"Well, neither would I," the Avtokrator admitted. "The key to making sure that doesn't happen is keeping them on . . . the far side of the Cattle Crossing." He scowled, angry at himself. "I almost said, keeping them on their own side of the Cattle Crossing. It's not theirs. It's ours. I aim to get it back, too."

"Sounds fine to me," Rhegorios said. "How do you propose to do that?"

"Which? Keep them on that side of the Cattle Crossing or get the westlands back?"

"Whichever you'd rather tell me about. You're the Avtokrator, after all." Rhegorios gave him a saucy grin.

"And you're incorrigible," Maniakes retorted. "We've got dromons prowling up and down the coast, north and east from the city. Whenever they find any of the Kubrati monoxyla, they burn them or sink them. The trouble is, they don't find that many. The cursed things are too fornicating easy to hide. We're doing what we can. I console myself with that."

"Something," his cousin agreed. "Maybe not much, but something. How about getting the westlands back?"

"How about that?" Maniakes said, deadpan, and then made as if not to go on. When Rhegorios was somewhere between lese majesty and physical assault, the Avtokrator, chuckling, deigned to continue: "Once this siege fails, I don't think they'll be able to mount another one for a long time. That gives the choice of what to do next back to me. How does another trip to the Land of the Thousand Cities sound? Better that Sharbaraz should worry about his capital than that we worry about ours."

"That's the truth." Rhegorios sent him a respectful look. "You really do have it figured out, don't you?"

Maniakes coughed, spluttered, and finally laughed out loud. "I know what I'd *like* to do, yes. How much I'm going to be *able* to do is another question, and a harder one, worse luck."

Rhegorios looked thoughtful. "Maybe we ought to use our ships against the Kubratoi the way we did three years ago: land troops behind their army and catch 'em between hammer and anvil."

"Maybe," Maniakes said. "I've thought about it. The trouble is, Etzilios is looking for it this time. The dromon captains report that he's got squads posted along the coast every mile or so, to bring him word if we do land. We wouldn't catch him by surprise, the way we did then. And the likeliest thing for him to do would be trying to storm the city as soon as he heard we'd pulled out some of the garrison."

"That makes unfortunately too much sense," Rhegorios said. "You're quite sharp when you get logical, you know. You should have been a theologian."

"No, thank you," Maniakes said at once. "I've had so much trouble from the theologians, I wouldn't want to inflict another one on the world. Besides, I'd be an indifferent theologian at best, and I'm vain enough to think I make something better than an indifferent Avtokrator."

"I'd say so," Rhegorios agreed. "Of course, if I said anything else, I'd get to find out how the weather is up at Prista this time of year." He was joking; he didn't expect to be sent into exile across the Videssian Sea. The joke, though, illustrated the problem Maniakes had in getting straight answers from his subjects, no matter how much he needed them.

And some of the answers he got from his subjects he didn't like for other reasons. As he was riding back to the palace quarter from the walls, a fellow in a dirty tunic shouted to him, "This is your fault, curse you! If you hadn't married your cousin, Phos wouldn't be punishing all of Videssos and letting Skotos loose here for your sins!"

Some of the Avtokrator's guardsmen tried to seize the heckler, but he escaped them. Once away from Middle Street, he lost himself in the maze of lanes and alleys that made up most of the city's roads. The guards came back looking angry and disappointed.

"Don't worry about it," Maniakes said resignedly. "Skotos will have his way with that fellow. I hope he enjoys ice, because he's going to see an eternity of it."

He hoped that, by making light of the incident, he would persuade the guards it wasn't worth mentioning. Otherwise, they would gossip about it with the serving women, and from them it would get back to Lysia. He was also glad Rhegorios had stayed back at the wall and hadn't heard the heckler. Predicting that such troubles would be long-lasting, his cousin had proved himself a better prophet than Maniakes.

The Avtokrator didn't stay at the imperial residence long. Likarios, his son by Niphone and the heir to the throne, asked him seriously, "Papa, when they're bigger, will my little brothers throw me out of the palaces?"

"By the good god, no!" Maniakes exclaimed, sketching the sun-circle over his heart. "Who's been filling your head with nonsense?"

Likarios didn't give a direct answer; he'd very quickly learned to be circumspect. "It was just something I heard."

"Well, it's something you can forget," Maniakes told him. His son nodded, apparently satisfied. Maniakes wished he were satisfied himself. Though Likarios was his heir, the temptation remained to disinherit the boy and place the succession in the line of his sons by Lysia.

She had never urged that course on him. Had she done so, he would have worried she was out for her own advantage first and the Empire's only afterward. But that did not keep the idea from cropping up on its own.

He went out to the seawall to escape it. A dromon glided over the water of the Cattle Crossing. The sight, though, was far less reassuring than it had been when the Makuraners were encamped in Across before. Monoxyla crept out at night and made nuisances of themselves, just as mice did even in homes where cats prowled.

Then a different image occurred to him. Two or three times, in barns and stables, he'd seen snakes with their coils wrapped around rats or other smaller animals. The rats would wiggle and kick and sometimes even work a limb free for a little while, but in the end that wouldn't matter. They'd be squeezed from so many directions, they ended up dead in spite of all their thrashing.

He wished that picture hadn't come to mind. In it, the Empire of Videssos was rat, not snake.

What did Abivard plan, over there in Across? He couldn't smuggle his whole army to this side of the Cattle Crossing ten and twenty men at a time, not if he aimed to take Videssos the city before winter came. Maniakes' guess was that he wanted to take the city as fast as he thought he could. The Kubratoi couldn't indefinitely maintain the siege on their own. They'd eat the countryside empty, and then they'd have to leave.

That meant . . . what? Probably an effort on Abivard's part to get a good-sized chunk of the Makuraner field force over here to the eastern side of the Cattle Crossing fairly soon now. If the fleet managed to stop him, the siege would probably collapse of its own weight. If the fleet didn't stop him, Videssos the city was liable to fall, all past history of invincibility notwithstanding. For the Makuraners to teach the Kubratoi siegecraft was bad enough—

worse than bad enough. For the Makuraners to conduct the siege would be worse still. Unlike the nomads, they really knew what they were doing.

"I wish I had a better drungarios of the fleet," Maniakes murmured. Erinakios, the prickly former commander of the fleet of the Key, would have been ideal . . . had Genesios' chief wizard not slain him by sorcery while the tyrant was trying to hold off Maniakes.

A guardsman came trotting toward him. "Your Majesty, there's a messenger from the land wall waiting for you in the imperial residence," the fellow called.

"I'll come," Maniakes said at once. "Has the attack begun?" The Kubrati siege towers weren't finished yet, but that might not figure. If the attack had begun, all Maniakes' worries about what might be would vanish, subsumed into worries over what was. Those, at least, would be immediate, and—with luck—susceptible to immediate repair.

But the guardsman shook his head. "I don't think so, your Majesty—we'd hear the racket from here, wouldn't we? The fellow acts like it's important even so."

"You're probably right about the racket," Maniakes admitted. He followed the soldier at a pace halfway between fast walk and trot. As he hurried along, he scratched his head. He'd been at the wall only a little while before the guard arrived. What had changed of such importance, he had to find out about it right away? He forced a shrug, and forced relaxation on himself as well. He was only moments from learning.

The messenger started to prostrate himself. Maniakes, losing the patience he'd cultivated, waved for him not to bother. The man came straight to the point: "Your Majesty, Immodios, who knows him well, has spotted Tzikas out beyond the wall."

Maniakes stiffened and twitched, as if lightning had struck close by. Well, maybe that wasn't so far wrong. "Spotted him, has he?" he said. "Well, has he tried killing him yet?"

"Uh, no, your Majesty," the messenger said.

"By the good god, why not?" Maniakes demanded. He shouted for Antelope—or, if his warhorse wasn't ready, any other animal that could be saddled in a hurry. The gelding he ended up riding lacked Antelope's spark, but got him out to the wall fast enough to keep him from losing all of his temper.

The messenger led him up to the outer wall, close by one of the siege towers. Immodios stood there. He pointed outward. "There he is, your Majesty. Do you see him? The tall, lean one prowling around with the Kubratoi?"

"I see him," Maniakes answered. Tzikas stalked out beyond archery range. He wore a Makuraner caftan that billowed in the breeze, and had let his beard grow fuller than the neatly trimmed Videssian norm, but was unmistakable nonetheless. His build, as Immodios had said, set him apart from the stocky nomads who kept him company, but Maniakes thought he would have recognized him even among Makuraners, whose angular height came closer to matching his. All you had to do was wait till you saw him point at something, at anything. *I want it* radiated from every pore of his body.

A dart-thrower stood a few paces away, ready to fling its missiles at the Kubratoi when they attacked in earnest. Darts waited ready beside it, in wicker baskets that did duty for outsized quivers. It would hurl those darts farther than the strongest man could shoot a bow.

Maniakes' father had made sure Maniakes knew how to operate every sort of engine the Videssian army used. The Avtokrator could almost hear the elder Maniakes saying, "Learning doesn't do you any lasting harm, and every once in a while some piece of it—and you never know which one beforehand—will come in handy."

After sketching a salute to his father, Maniakes remarked, "I make the range out to the son of a whore to be about a furlong and a half. Does that seem about right to you, Immodios?"

"Uh, aye, your Majesty," Immodios replied. Though the question had caught him by surprise, he'd considered before he spoke. Maniakes approved of that.

He seized a dart, set it in the catapult's groove, and said, "Then perhaps you'll do me the honor of serving on the other windlass there. I don't know if we can hit him, but to the ice with me if I don't intend to try."

Immodios blinked again, then worked the windlass with a will. For a range of a furlong and a half, you wanted fifteen revolutions of the wheel; more would wind the ropes too tight and send the dart too far, while fewer and it would fall short. The wooden frame of the catapult creaked under the building tension of the rope skeins.

The dart-thrower didn't point in quite the right direction. Maniakes used a handspike to muscle it toward Tzikas. He checked his aim with two pins driven into the frame parallel to the groove. Still not quite right. He levered the engine around a little further with the handspike, then grunted in satisfaction.

Tzikas paid no attention to the activity of the wall. He was pointing to something at ground level, something to which the Kubratoi were paying rapt attention. Maniakes hoped they would go right on paying rapt attention to it. He looked over to Immodios. "Are we ready?"

"Aye, your Majesty, I believe we are," the somber officer answered.

Maniakes picked up a wooden mallet and gave the trigger a sharp whack. That released the casting arms, which jerked forward, sending the dart on its way. The engine that had propelled it bucked like a wild ass. Half the frame jounced up in the air. It crashed back down to the walkway a moment later.

The dart flew straight toward Tzikas, faster and on a flatter trajectory than any archer could have propelled a shaft. "I think we're going to—" Maniakes' voice rose in excitement.

A Kubrati strode in front of the Videssian renegade. The nomad must have spied the dart, for he flung his arms wide an instant before it struck him. Before he had a chance to do anything more, he himself was flung aside by the terrible impact.

"Stupid fool," Maniakes snarled. "To the ice with him—it was Tzikas I wanted." He seized another dart and thrust it into the catapult's trough.

Too late. Even as he and Immodios worked the windlasses on either side of the engine, he knew it was too late. Tzikas and the Kubratoi were scattering, all except the luckless fellow the dart had slaughtered. He lay where he had fallen, as a cockroach will after a shoe lands on it.

Maniakes sent that second dart whizzing through the air. It nearly nailed another nomad, and missed Tzikas by no more than ten or twelve feet. The traitor kept right on going till he was out of range of the engines on the wall. He knew to the foot how far they could throw. *He ought to,* Maniakes thought bitterly.

"Close," Immodios said.

"Close, aye," Maniakes answered. "Close isn't good enough. I wanted him dead. I thought I had him. A little bit of luck—" He shook his head. He hadn't seen much of that during his reign, and whatever he had, he'd had to make for himself. A timely error by the enemy, a truly important Makuraner message falling into his hands ... the next time he saw anything like that would be the first.

"I wonder what the traitor was showing the Kubratoi," Immodios remarked.

"I have no idea," Maniakes said. "I don't much care, either. The trouble is, he can still show it to them whenever he wants, whatever it may be. He wouldn't be showing them anything if it hadn't been for that one miserable nomad, may Skotos clutch him forever." That the Kubrati had paid with his life for moving into the wrong place at the wrong time seemed to Maniakes not nearly punishment enough.

Immodios persisted: "What does Tzikas know about the way the city walls are built?"

"Quite a lot, worse luck for us," Maniakes answered. "He's not going to get close enough to use whatever he knows, though, not if I have anything to say about it."

But how much would he have to say about it? Immodios, being alert, sharp-eyed, and a former colleague of Tzikas', had recognized the traitor at long range. How many other officers were likely to do the same tomorrow, or the day after, or in a week? The longer Maniakes thought about that, the less he liked the answer he came up with.

Whatever Tzikas knew, he'd probably have the chance to show it to the men he now called his friends ... unless he decided to betray them again. If Tzikas did that, Maniakes decided, he would welcome him with open arms. And if that wasn't a measure of his own desperation, he didn't know what was.

Watching the Kubrati siege towers grow and get bedecked with hides and with shields on top of those was almost like watching saplings shoot up and put out leaves as spring gave way to summer. Maniakes found only two differences: the towers grew faster than any saplings, and they got uglier as they came closer to completion, where leaves made trees more beautiful.

The Kubratoi were being more methodical about the entire siege than Maniakes would have thought possible before it began. He credited that to—or rather, blamed it on—the Makuraners the nomads' monoxyla had smuggled over from the westlands. Abivard and his officers knew patience and its uses.

Well out of range of Videssian arrows or darts or flung stones, the Kubratoi practiced climbing up into their siege towers and rushing up the wooden stairs they'd made. They also practiced moving the ungainly erections, with horses and mules on ropes and then by men inside the towers.

"They're going to find out that's not so easy as they think," the elder Maniakes remarked one day as he and his son watched a siege tower crawl along at a pace just about fast enough to catch and mash a snail—always provided you didn't give the snail a running start.

"I think you're right, Father," the Avtokrator agreed. "Nobody's shooting at them now. No matter what they do, they won't be able to keep all our darts and stones from doing them damage when the fighting starts."

"That does make a bit of a difference, doesn't it?" the elder Maniakes said with a rheumy chuckle. "You know it, and I know it, and Etzilios has been too good a bandit over the years not to know it, but does your ordinary, everyday Kubrati know it? If he doesn't, he'll learn quick, the poor sod."

"What do we do if the nomads manage to get men on the wall in spite of everything we've done to stop 'em?" Maniakes asked.

"Kill the bastards," his father answered at once. "Until Etzilios rides into the palace quarter or the Mobedhan-Mobhed chases the patriarch out of the High Temple, I'm too stubborn to think I'm beat. Even then, I think I'm going to take some convincing."

Maniakes smiled. He only wished things were as simple as his father, a man of the old school, still reckoned them to be. "I admire the spirit," he said, "but how do we go on if that happens?"

"*I* don't know," his father answered, a little testily. "Best thing I can think of is to make sure it doesn't."

"Sounds easy, when you put it that way," Maniakes said, and the elder Maniakes let out a grunt undoubtedly intended for laughter. The Avtokrator went on, "I wish they weren't guarding all their siege engines so closely. I told Rhegorios I wouldn't, but now I think I would sally against them and see how much damage we could do."

His father shook his head. "You were right the first time. Biggest advantage we have is fighting from the inside of the city and

the top of the wall. If we sally, we throw all that out the window."
He held up a hand. "I'm not saying, never do it. I am saying that
the advantage of surprise had better outweigh the disadvantage of
giving up your position."

Weighing that, Maniakes rather regretfully decided it made good
sense. "So long as they stay alert, then, a sally's not worthwhile."

"That's what I'm telling you," the elder Maniakes agreed.

"Well, people on the wall will just have to keep their eyes open,
that's all," Maniakes said. "If the chance comes, I want to take it."

"Different matter altogether," his father said.

"It all depends on how you look at things," Maniakes said, "same
as anything else." He made a face that suggested he'd been sucking on a lemon. "I must say, I am tired of people screaming at me
that the siege is my fault because I married Lysia."

"Aye, I can see how you might be," the elder Maniakes said
steadily. "But that's not surprising, either, is it? You knew as soon
as you decided to marry her that people would be yelling that sort
of thing at you. If you didn't know it, it's not because I didn't tell
you. The question you've had to ask yourself all along, same as if
we were talking about sallying against the Kubratoi, is, does the
trouble outweigh everything else you get from the marriage?"

"Cold-blooded way of looking at things," Maniakes remarked.

"I'm a cold-blooded sort of fellow," his father replied. "So are
you, come to that. If you don't know what the odds are, how can
you bet?"

"It's been worth the trouble. It's been more than worth the
trouble." The Avtokrator sighed. "I had hoped, though, that things
would die down over the years. That hasn't happened. That hasn't
come close to happening. Every time anything goes wrong, the
city mob throws my marriage in my face."

"They'll be doing the same thing twenty years from now, too,"
the elder Maniakes said. "I thought you understood that by now."

"Oh, I do," Maniakes said. "The only way I know to make all
of them—well, to make most of them—shut up is to drive away
the Makuraners and the Kubratoi both." He pointed out toward the
siege towers. "You can see what a fine job I've done of that."

"Not your fault." The elder Maniakes held up a forefinger. "Oh,
one piece of it is—you beat Etzilios so badly, you made him wild
for revenge. But that's nothing to blame yourself about. We were

trying to hit Sharbaraz where he lives, and now he's trying to return the favor. That makes him clever. It doesn't make you stupid."

"I should have worried more about why Abivard and the boiler boys had disappeared," Maniakes said. Self-reproach came easy; he had been practicing all the way from the outskirts of Mashiz.

"And what would you have done if you'd *known* he'd left the Land of the Thousand Cities?" his father asked. "My guess is, you'd have headed straight for Mashiz and tried to take it because you knew he couldn't stop you. Since that's what you did anyway, why are you still beating yourself because of it?"

Maniakes stared at him. He'd found no way to forgive himself for failing to grasp at once what Abivard and Sharbaraz had plotted. Now, in three sentences, his father had shown him how.

As if sensing his relief, the elder Maniakes slapped him on the back. "You couldn't have counted on this, son. That's what I'm saying. But now that it's here, you still have to beat it. That hasn't changed, not one single, solitary, miserable bit it hasn't."

Off in the distance, the Kubratoi were still hauling their siege towers back and forth, trying to learn how to use them and what to do with them. On another tower, one that wasn't moving, a crew of workmen nailed hides ever higher on the frame. Before long, that tower would be finished, too.

"I know, Father," Maniakes said. "Believe me, I know."

Splendid—*perhaps even magnifolent,* Maniakes thought wryly—in his silk vestments shot through with gold and silver thread and encrusted with pearls and other gems, Agathios the ecumenical patriarch paraded up Middle Street from the procession's starting point close by the Silver Gate and the embattled land walls of Videssos the city. Behind him marched lesser priests, some swinging censers so the sweet-smelling smoke would waft the prayers of the people up to the heavens and to the awareness of the lord with the great and good mind, others lifting trained voices in songs of praise to Phos.

Behind the priests came Maniakes, riding Antelope. Almost everyone cheered Agathios. Everyone without exception cheered the more junior priests. Though all of them had been chosen at least in part because they vigorously supported the dispensation Agathios had granted Maniakes for his marriage to Lysia, that was not obvious to the city mob. Priests who entertained them—anyone who entertained them—deserved praise, and got it.

The parade would not have come off at all had Maniakes not instigated it. The city mob paid no attention to that. Some people booed and heckled him because the Kubratoi and Makuraners had laid siege to Videssos the city. Those were the ones who remembered nothing earlier than the day before yesterday. Others booed and heckled him because they reckoned his union with his cousin Lysia to be incestuous. They were the ones, almost as common as the other group, who remembered everything and forgave nothing.

And a few people cheered him. "You beat the Kubratoi," someone shouted as he rode by, "and you beat the Makuraners. Now you get to beat them both together." More cheers followed, at least a few.

Maniakes turned to Rhegorios, who rode behind him and to his left. "Now I get to beat them both together. Doesn't that make me a lucky fellow?"

"If you're a lucky fellow, you *will* beat them both together," his cousin returned. "It's what happens if you aren't lucky that worries me."

"You're always reassuring," Maniakes said, to which Rhegorios laughed.

When the chorus wasn't chanting hymns to the crowd, Agathios called an invitation to the people on the colonnaded sidewalks who stood and stared at the procession as they would have stood and stared at any entertainment: "Come join us in the plaza of Palamas! Come join us in praying for the Empire's salvation!"

"Maybe we should have done this at the High Temple, after all," Maniakes said. "It would have given the ceremony a more solemn air."

"You want solemn air, find a polecat," Rhegorios said, holding his nose. "Only the nobles and a handful of ordinary people can get into the High Temple. Everyone else has to find out secondhand what happened in there. This way, all the people will know."

"That's so," Maniakes said. "If everything goes well, I'll say you were right. But if things go wrong, all the people will know about that, too."

As far as he was concerned, the ecumenical patriarch was doing his best to make things go wrong. "Come pray for the salvation of the Empire!" Agathios cried again. "Come beg the good god to forgive our sins and make us pure again."

"I'll purify him," Maniakes muttered. "I'll bake him for two weeks, till all the grease runs out of him." When the patriarch spoke of forgiving sins, to what were the minds of the people likely to turn? To their own failings? Maniakes let out a snort of laughter. Not likely. They would think of him and Lysia. He would have suspected anyone else of deliberately inciting the people against him. He did suspect Agathios, in fact, but only briefly. He'd seen that the ecumenical patriarch was as a sucking babe when it came to matters political.

He wondered what sort of crowd they would draw to the plaza of Palamas, which was not commonly made the scene of religious gatherings. While wondering, he looked back over his shoulder. Behind the Imperial Guards, behind a couple of regiments that had distinguished themselves in the Land of the Thousand Cities, came a swelling tide of ordinary Videssians intent on hearing what the patriarch and the Avtokrator had to say. The plaza would be full.

The plaza, in fact, was packed. Agathios had trouble making his way to the platform that had been set up for him, a platform more often used by emperors to address the city mob. Maniakes looked back over his shoulder again. This time he waved. The guardsmen came trotting up through the ranks of the priests. Efficiently using elbows, spear shafts, and sheathed swords to clear a path, they got the patriarch to the platform in minimum time while also leaving people minimally angry—no small feat in Videssos the city, where everyone was touchy even when not under siege.

"We bless thee, Phos, lord with the great and good mind," Agathios intoned, "by thy grace our protector, watchful beforehand that the great test of life may be decided in our favor." Reciting the good god's creed was the blandest thing the patriarch could possibly have done. Picking the blandest thing to do was altogether in character for him.

As he must have known they would, the crowd joined him in the creed; many of them sketched Phos' sun-circle above their hearts as they prayed. Sometimes the blandest choice was also the wisest. Agathios had his audience as receptive as he could have hoped to get them for whatever else he planned to say.

"We need to come together, to remember we all follow Phos

and we are all Videssians," the ecumenical patriarch declared. Maniakes' lips moved along with Agathios'. He knew the sermon to come at least as well as the patriarch did: not surprising, since he'd written most of it. Agathios had not argued it was unsound doctrine. *A good thing, too,* Maniakes thought. *I wouldn't want to have to change patriarchs at a time like this.*

Agathios gestured out beyond the wall. "There, encircling us, lie the tents of the Makuraners, who revere their false God and who have forced Phos' temples in the lands they have stolen from Videssos to conform to the erroneous usages of the Vaspurakaners; and there, also encircling us, lie the tents of the Kubratoi, who worship only their swords and the murderous power of sharpened iron. May the good god keep our disunion from granting our foes victory against us, for such victory would surely extinguish the light of our true faith throughout the world."

Applause started close by the platform and rippled outward. Maniakes and Rhegorios exchanged an amused glance. At functions of this sort, you didn't want to leave anything to chance. A couple of dozen men with goldpieces in their belt pouches could create a good deal of enthusiasm and transmit it to the crowd.

Telling Agathios about such chicanery would have been— *pointless* was the word Maniakes found. If the ecumenical patriarch was gratified at the response he received, he would preach better. So the Avtokrator told himself, at any rate.

And so it proved. Voice all but oozing sincerity, Agathios went on: "And so, fellow seekers after truth and after Phos' holy light and the enlightenment springing therefrom, let us for the time being exercise the principle of economy and agree to disagree. Let us lay aside all issues now dividing us until such time as they may be considered without also considering the threat of imminent extermination under which we now lie."

Again, the paid claque began the applause. Again, it spread beyond the claque. As far as Maniakes was concerned, Agathios was only talking plain sense. How Videssos, on the edge of falling to its foes, could be exercised about whether he'd married within limits proscribed by the temple hierarchy was beyond him.

It was not, however, beyond some Videssians. "Traitor!" they shouted, safe in the anonymity of the crowd. "Capitulator!" "Better to die in the sack and go to Phos' light than to live in sin and pass eternity in Skotos' ice!" They shouted things at Maniakes, too, and at Lysia—who was not there—things for which he would have drawn sword had he known upon whom to draw it.

He took a couple of steps toward Agathios. Rhegorios set a hand on his arm. "Careful," the Sevastos warned. "Are you sure you know what you're doing?"

"I'm sure," the Avtokrator growled.

His tone made his cousin look more worried still. "Whatever it is, are you sure you won't be sorry about it this time tomorrow?"

"I'm fairly sure," Maniakes said, sounding more like his usual self. Rhegorios, still looking unhappy, had no choice save stepping aside and letting his sovereign do whatever he would do.

Agathios looked surprised to see the Avtokrator approaching; had things gone according to plan, Maniakes would not have spoken till after the patriarch had finished. *Well,* Maniakes thought, *things don't always go according to plan. If they did, I'd be in Mashiz right now, not here.*

As the Sevastos could not restrain him, so the ecumenical patriarch could not keep him from speaking now, since he had shown the desire to do so. "Your Majesty," Agathios said, and, bowing, withdrew.

Maniakes stood at the edge of the platform and looked west. The crowd packing the plaza of Palamas filled his vision, but there at the far side of the plaza was Middle Street, up which the procession had come from close to the land walls of the city. And out beyond the walls, apparently discounted by many city folk, remained the Kubratoi and the Makuraners.

For a couple of minutes, Maniakes simply stood in the place that had been Agathios'. A few taunts flew his way, but most of the throng waited to hear what he would say. That made the jeers seem thin and empty, isolated flotsam of sound on a sea of silence.

At last, the Avtokrator did speak, pitching his voice to carry as if on the battlefield. "I don't much care whether you love me or not." That was a thumping lie, but it was also armor against some of the things people had called him and Lysia. "What you think of me is your concern. When my soul walks the bridge of the separator and I face the lord with the great and good mind, I'll do it with a clear conscience.

"But that doesn't matter, as I say. When Midwinter's Day comes around, you can rail at me however you like. And you will. I know you, people of the city—you will. Go ahead. In the meanwhile, we have to make certain that we *can* celebrate Midwinter's Day in the Amphitheater. You need not love me for that to happen—soldiers need not love their captain, only do what he requires of them and keep from making things worse. After we've defended the city, we can attack one another to our hearts' content. Till then, we'd be wiser to wait."

Silence. From the whole crowd, silence. A few members of the paid claque applauded, but their clapping seemed as lost in emptiness as the earlier jeers had been. Maniakes thought he'd won abeyance, suspension of judgment, if not acceptance. He would gladly have settled for that. And then, out of the silence, a cry: "Phos will let the city fall, on account of *your* sin." And after that, more cries, hot, ferocious, deadly.

Were the worse enemies outside the walls, or within? He wanted to cry out himself, to scream for the soldiers to slaughter the hateful hecklers. But, having done that, what matter if he threw back the Makuraners and Kubratoi? Over what would he rule then, and how?

He held up a hand. Slowly, silence returned. "If the city does not fall, then, the holy ecumenical patriarch's dispensation must be valid. And the city shall not fall." Silence again, now lingering.

Challenge. Accepted.

VI

Out beyond the walls, a horn blew. Maybe, once upon a time, it had been a Videssian horn. The Kubrati who winded it, though, knew nothing of Videssian notions of music. What he wanted was to make noise with the horn, as much noise as he could, as a child will make noise to hearten his army of wooden soldiers when they march out to war.

But only in a child's imagination will wooden soldiers charge and fight and, of course, bravely sweep all before them. What the Kubrati called into being was real, so real and so frightening that he might almost have been sorcerer rather than mere horn player.

Yelling like demons, the Kubratoi burst from their encampments and rushed toward Videssos the city, some mounted, others afoot. They started shooting arrows at their foes atop the walls even before they were in range, so that the first shafts fell into the ditch at the base of the great stone pile and the ones coming just after smacked the stone and mostly shivered.

But, like raindrops at the start of a storm, those were only the first among many. Soon as could be, the arrows walked up the side of the outer wall and flew among the defenders at the top. One hummed past Maniakes' face and then down to strike the inner wall near its base.

Not all shafts flew *among* defenders. Not twenty feet from the Avtokrator, a man tumbled to the walkway, writhing, weeping, cursing, screaming. A couple of his comrades, braving more arrows themselves when they could have crouched behind crenelations, hustled him to a siege tower. Surgeons waited inside there to do what they could for the wounded. Healer-priests waited, too, to fling their own faith and strength against the wounds of war.

A catapult bucked and thudded. A dart flew out, flat and fast. It pinned a nomad's leg to his horse. The horse fell as if poleaxed, pinning the fellow's other leg between its kicking corpse and the ground. The Kubrati's cries, if he raised them—if he lived—were lost, buried, forgotten in the tumult.

Stone-throwers on the wall cast their fearful burdens at the attackers, too. A man hit by a stone weighing half as much as himself and traveling like an arrow ceased to be a man, becoming instead in the twinkling of an eye a red horror either lying still, smeared along the ground, or wailing like a broken baby bereft of breast, bereft of brother, bereft of hope.

And Maniakes, seeing what he would have mourned had it befallen one of his own subjects, even one who hated him as an incestuous tyrant, clapped his hands with glee and shouted to the crew that had launched the fatal stone: "Give 'em another one just like that, boys!"

And the crew did their best to obey, and cried out in fury and disappointment when their next missile fell harmlessly to earth. Maniakes moaned when that happened, too. Only later did he think on what a strange business war was.

He had no leisure for such thoughts in any case, for some of the Kubratoi, instead of pausing at the ditch in front of the outer wall, dropped down into it along with ladders tall enough to reach from that depression to the top of the wall. Not many of those ladders ever went up, though. A stone dropped straight down rather than flung from a catapult crushed a man as thoroughly, if not so spectacularly, as one actually discharged from a stone-thrower. The Videssian defenders also rained arrows and boiling water down on the heads of the Kubratoi directly below them.

Wearing an ordinary trooper's mail shirt and a much-battered helmet, the elder Maniakes came up beside his son. He peered down into the ditch for a moment, then nodded in somber satisfaction. "I don't think they'll try that again any time soon," he said. "Bit of a slaughter down there."

"This is the high ground," Maniakes agreed. "If they let us keep it, they'll pay the price." He frowned. "If they let us keep it high, they'll pay the price." He pointed to show what he meant.

Maybe Etzilios, in spite of the better advice the Makuraners undoubtedly must have given him, had thought Videssos the city would fall to direct assault, and never mind all the fancy engines he'd spent so much time and effort building. Maybe he'd believed that the imperials huddled inside their walls from fear alone and lacked the spirit to resist his ferocious warriors. If that was so, he'd received an expensive lesson to the contrary.

And now he was going about things as he should have done from the beginning. The ladders lay in the ditch; after a while, the Videssians set them afire, to be rid of them.

Meanwhile, though, Etzilios' warriors and teams of horses dragged his own stone-throwers, the ones the Makuraners had taught him to make, up to where they would bear on the walls. More men—Maniakes thought them Videssian prisoners, not Kubratoi—carried stones up and piled them beside the engines.

"Knock them down!" he shouted to his own catapult crews. But at long range, that was not so easy. The Kubratoi had only to hit the wall, a target they could hardly miss. Hitting specific stone-throwers, as the Videssians needed to do, was a different proposition.

Every once in a while, by the curious combination of good shooting and luck so necessary for success in war, a Videssian catapult crew would manage to land a stone square on an enemy engine, with results as disastrous for that engine as for a man unfortunately in the path of such a missile. The stricken stone-thrower would go from engine to kindling in the course of a heartbeat, and the Videssian catapult crew would caper and pound one another on the backs and brag to anyone who listened or, more often, to anyone nearby, listening or not.

And the Kubratoi would make their prisoners haul away the wreckage of the ruined stone-thrower, the said wreckage sometimes extending to the men who served the engine and were injured when a piece flying off it smote them. And they would drag up another stone-thrower and go back to pounding away at the walls of Videssos the city.

Up on the walkway of the outer wall, Maniakes felt caught in an unending medium-sized earthquake. Stones crashed against the stonework of the wall, which brought every impact straight to the soles of his boots. The roar of stone striking stone put him in mind of an earthquake's fearsome rumble, too.

But earthquakes, no matter how fearsome they were, stopped in a minute or two. This went on and on, the continuous motion underfoot almost making him seasick. Many of the stones the engines cast bounded away from the walls without effect; the masons who had built those works centuries before knew their business.

Every so often, though, the Kubratoi let fly with a particularly hard stone, or with one hurled particularly hard, or with one that hit in a better spot or at a better angle. Then stone on the face of the wall shattered, too.

"How much pounding can we stand?" Maniakes asked his father.

"Haven't the foggiest notion," the elder Maniakes replied. "Never had to worry about it quite this way before. Tell you what, though— knowing where to find the answers is nearly as good as knowing what they are. Anything Ypsilantes can't tell you about the walls isn't worth knowing."

"That's true, by the good god," Maniakes agreed, and summoned his chief engineer.

"We should be able to hold out against pounding like this a good long while, your Majesty," Ypsilantes said. "Only a few stretches of the wall have a rubble core; most of it is either solid stone all the way through or else double-thick stone over storerooms and kitchens and such."

"That's what I'd hoped," the Avtokrator said. "Nice to have hopes come true every now and again."

"I am pleased to have pleased you, your Majesty," Ypsilantes said. "And now, if you will please excuse me—" He hurried away on missions more vital than reassuring his sovereign.

After Ypsilantes had left, the elder Maniakes tapped his son on the arm. "Come back to the palaces," he said. "Get some rest. The city isn't going to fall to pieces while you go to bed, and you're liable to fall to pieces if you don't."

Maniakes shook his head. "As long as I'm here, the men on the wall will know I'm with them. They'll fight harder."

"Maybe a little, but not that much," his father replied. "And I tell you this: if you're the only prop holding the defenders up, then the city *will* fall. They're fighting for more reasons than just your being here. For one thing, they're good soldiers already, because you've made them into good soldiers over the past few years. And for another, believe me, they like staying alive as much as anyone else does. Now come on."

He put some roughness into his voice, as he had when Maniakes disobeyed him as a boy. The Avtokrator laughed. "You sound like you'll take a belt to my backside if I don't do what you tell me."

The elder Maniakes looked down at the belt he was wearing. As befitted the Avtokrator's father, he had on a gold one with a fancy jeweled buckle. He undid the buckle, took off the belt, and hefted it speculatively. "I could give you a pretty fair set of welts with this one, son," he remarked.

"So you could," Maniakes said. "Well, if that's not lese majesty, to the ice with me if I know what is." He and his father both laughed. When the elder Maniakes started down from the wall, the Avtokrator followed him. They rode back to the palaces together.

All the way there, though, Maniakes heard heavy stones thudding against the wall. He didn't think he'd get much rest.

"A sally, that's what we need," Rhegorios said. "A sally to scatter some of their archers and put paid to some of their engines. The stone-throwers would do, I suppose, but I'd really like to be rid of those siege towers. That would be something worth doing."

Maniakes eyed his cousin with amusement. "How did you manage to slide from *what we need* to *I suppose* in a couple of sentences there? What you mean is, you feel like going out and fighting Kubratoi and you want me to tell you it's all right."

Rhegorios gave him a glance respectful and resentful at the same time. "Anyone would think we'd grown up together, or something like that," he said. "How can I sneak anything past you? You know me too well. For that matter, how do you sneak anything past my sister? She knows you too well."

"How do I try to sneak anything past Lysia?" Maniakes said. "Mostly I don't. It doesn't work well, for some reason. But that has nothing to do with whether we ought to sally against the Kubratoi."

"I suppose not," his cousin agreed. "But are we just going to sit here and let them pound on us?"

"That was exactly what I had in mind, as a matter of fact," the Avtokrator said. "Whenever I've got in trouble, all through my reign, I've tried to do too much. I'm not going to do that this time. I'm going to do as little as I can, and let the Kubratoi and Makuraners wear themselves out, banging their heads on our walls. That's why the walls went up in the first place."

"What kind of battle plan is that?" Rhegorios said indignantly.

"A sensible one?" Maniakes suggested.

"Where's the glory?" Rhegorios demanded. "Where are the heroes parading down Middle Street singing songs of victory?"

"As for the heroes," Maniakes said, "more of them will be left alive if we play the game cautiously. As for the glory, the Kubratoi and the Makuraners are welcome to it, for all of me. Now wait." He held up a hand to check his cousin's expostulation. "Whoever wants glory for glory's sake can have it, as far as I'm concerned. If I can win the war by sitting here like a snail pulled back into its shell, I'll do that, and gladly."

"Cold-blooded way to look at things," Rhegorios said. Then, after a moment, he admitted, "Your father would tell me the same, though; I will say that much. Which leaves me with only one question: what does a snail do when somebody tries to smash in his shell?"

"That's simple," Maniakes said. "He twists around and bites him from the inside." Rhegorios went off, dissatisfied.

Maniakes' attitude toward warfare might well have been more typically Videssian than that of his cousin. Only the Imperial Guards, for instance, had a name and reputation stretching over generations. When the Avtokrator went out to the wall a few days later, then, he was surprised to find a stretch of it defended by a unit of stone-throwers decorated with graffiti proclaiming, THE BITING SNAILS! DON'T CRACK OUR SHELLS!

"Did my cousin put you up to this?" he demanded with mock severity.

"His highness the Sevastos might have mentioned it, your Majesty, but he didn't put us up to it, like," their commanding officer said. "The lads and I, we liked the name, so we decided to wear it."

"May your teeth be sharp, then," Maniakes said, and the soldiers cheered.

As he walked along the walls, he realized all the defenders, not just the Biting Snails, were going to need sharp teeth. The Kubratoi were dragging their siege towers, one after another, into position for an assault on the city. They stood just beyond the range of the engines the Videssians had mounted on the outer wall.

Immodios was studying the towers, too, and not looking very happy while he did it. Maniakes consoled himself by remembering how seldom Immodios looked happy about anything. The officer said, "Your Majesty, I fear we're going to have a hard time stopping them or even slowing them down much before they reach the wall."

"I think you're wrong," Maniakes answered. "I think the darts and the stones and the fire we'll hurl at them from the wall will make sure they never reach it. I think most of them will burn up or be smashed before they get within bowshot of the wall."

"If the Kubratoi had figured out siege towers on their own, your Majesty, I'd say you were likely to be right," Immodios said. "They wouldn't build them strong enough. But the Makuraners know what they're doing, same as we do."

"They just did the showing," Maniakes said. "The Kubratoi did the building. They've never tried anything like this before. My bet is, they haven't built strong enough."

"The lord with the great and good mind grant that you have the right of it," Immodios said. He didn't sound as if he believed it.

He had reason to worry, too, as the Avtokrator soon discovered. Maniakes had even dared hope that the Kubratoi would try to use beasts of burden to haul the siege towers up close to the wall. The Biting Snails, the other dart- and stone-thrower crews, and the archers would have enjoyed targets to dream of, even if massacring beasts of burden was a stomach-turning business in and of itself.

But Etzilios, perhaps having ignored one set of instructions from his Makuraner tutors, did not ignore two. No horses or mules ever came within range of the engines on the outer wall. The nomads led the animals away and disconnected the ropes with which they'd been harnessed. Then they herded ragged men—Videssian prisoners again—into the towers, treating them not much differently from the way they used any other beasts of burden. Kubrati warriors went into the towers, too, a few to make the prisoners propel them forward, most for the assault on Videssos the city.

Very slowly, the towers began to advance.

"Now we find out," Maniakes said. To his dismay, the closer the towers got, the sturdier they looked.

When he said as much, Immodios nodded. "That's so, your Majesty," he agreed. It wasn't quite *I told you so*, but it would do.

"Well, well," Maniakes murmured. "How stupid was I?" He held up a hand before Immodios could speak. "Never mind. You don't have to answer that. In fact, I'd be happier if you didn't answer that."

Whatever Immodios' opinions were, he dutifully kept them to himself. Foot by foot, the siege towers moved forward. When they came into range of the engines on the walls, the Videssians let fly with everything they had. Some of their darts did pierce the hide covering and shields on the front of the siege towers. Some, no doubt, pierced warriors and haulers in the towers. Such pinprick injuries, though, did little to make the Kubratoi give over their assault.

Stone-throwers hurled their missiles at the towers, too. They hit with loud crashes, but they bounced off without doing any visible damage. Maybe the Kubratoi had listened to the Makuraner engineers, after all. Instead of looking just somber, Immodios looked somber and vindicated. Maniakes did his best not to notice.

But the stone-throwers could throw more than stones. Their crews loaded them with jars full of a nasty mix of tallow and rock oil and naphtha and sulfur, then lighted the mix with torches before flinging it at the foe. Fire dripped down the fronts of the towers. The harsh smoke stank. When it got into Maniakes' eyes, it made them water and burn. Inhaling some, he coughed. "What vile stuff!" he said, coughing some more.

Fire the Kubratoi could not ignore, as they had the darts and stones. Some of them came up onto the tops of the towers and poured water down onto the flames. That did less good than they might have hoped. Instead of putting out the fires, the water only made them run faster down the fronts of the towers.

That sufficed, though, for the flames had trouble igniting the hides that faced the siege towers. Maybe the Kubratoi had soaked them to leave them wet and slimy and hard to burn. Whatever the reason, they did not catch fire. Inch by slow inch, the towers advanced.

Looking north and south, Maniakes spied seven or eight of them. Three moved on the Silver Gate, near which he stood. The others crawled singly toward the wall. Kubrati stone-throwers flung boulders at the outer wall and at the walkway atop it, making it hard and dangerous for the Videssians to concentrate their defenders where the attacks would come.

Maniakes bit his lip. Somewhere back at one of the Kubrati encampments, those Makuraner engineers had to be hugging themselves with glee. The towers were doing everything they wanted, which meant they were doing everything Maniakes didn't want them to do.

Off to the north, cheers rang out from the wall. The Avtokrator stared to see why his men were cheering in the middle of what looked like disaster. He needed a while, peering in that direction, before he understood: one of the towers wasn't moving forward any more. Maybe it had tried to go over damp ground and bogged down. Maybe a wheel or axle had broken under the strain of the weight the tower carried. Maybe the ground sloped ever so slightly, so it had to try to go uphill. Whatever the reason, it wasn't going anywhere now.

Maniakes felt like cheering himself. He didn't, though, not with only one threat gone and so many remaining. And then, right before his eyes, one of the siege towers bearing down on the Silver Gate began to burn at last. The flames and smoke rising from it were no longer solely from the incendiary liquid with which the Videssians had been bombarding it. The timbers of its frame had also caught fire.

So did the Kubratoi inside the tower. Enemies though they were, Maniakes pitied them then. Above the snap of catapults discharging, above the thud of stones and darts striking home against the wall and against the siege tower, rose the screams of the warriors in that inferno.

What was it like in there? Maniakes tried to imagine himself a nomad on the stairs between, say, the fourth and fifth floors. It would be packed and dark and frightening even without fire; every stone that slammed into the tower had to feel like the end of the world. The odor of smoke would have been in the air for some time already, what with jars of blazing grease striking the tower along with the stones.

But what happened when the odor changed, when the Kubratoi smelled unmistakable woodsmoke and saw flames above them? Worse, what happened when they smelled unmistakable woodsmoke and saw flames *below* them?

Warriors streamed out of the base of the siege tower and fled away from the walls of Videssos the city back toward their encampment. Stones and darts and ordinary arrows took a heavy toll among them. At that, though, they were the lucky ones: that was a quicker, cleaner way to die than they would have found had they remained in the tower.

At the very peak of the siege tower, a doorway opened and a gangway was thrust forth, as if a boy had stuck out his tongue.

With the tower more than half a bowshot from the wall, it was a gangplank to nowhere. But that did not mean no one used it.

Kubratoi desperate to escape the flames and smoke inside the siege tower dashed out onto the gangway. Maniakes got the feeling that a lot of them would have been content simply to stand there, to rest for a moment after getting away from the fire. But that was not to be, could not be. For one thing, smoke poured out of the doorway from which the long plank had emerged. And for another, more and more Kubratoi, men who could not use the stairs and ladders down to the ground, tried to get out on the gangway.

What happened after that was grimly inevitable. Some nomads, crowded off the plank by their comrades, fell to the ground nearly forty feet below. Others jumped, no doubt thinking it better to propel themselves off into space than to be forced off at a time and attitude not of their choosing.

A few of the nomads were lucky, getting up apparently uninjured from their falls. A few, as unlucky as they could be, lay unmoving. More dragged themselves away, hurt but alive. A couple of those, at least partly lucky at first, were unlucky later, when other Kubratoi, either forced off or springing from the gangway, landed on top of them or when a stone from a Videssian engine finished them where the fall had not.

And then fire reached the end of the gangway still inside the siege tower. Maniakes could hear the wood crack, and the board, burning, crashed to the ground along with the nomads left on it.

The siege tower collapsed in on itself a minute or two later, flames flaring brighter and higher in the breeze of the collapse for a little while and then beginning to subside once more.

"There's one we don't have to worry about any more," Maniakes said.

That, unfortunately, left all the siege towers about which the Videssians did still have to worry. Several of them were going to reach the wall: that seemed revoltingly obvious, despite the Avtokrator's earlier optimism. The places where they would reach the wall seemed obvious, too—they could hardly change their paths, twisting and dodging like rabbits chased by hounds.

"That means we'll just have to give them a nice, warm reception," Maniakes said, more than half to himself. But the stream of orders he sent forth after that was meant for the men on the wall.

Soldiers around the Silver Gate got those orders straight from his lips. Couriers dashed off to give his ideas to men on other stretches where the towers were advancing.

When one of the couriers returned, he said, "Begging your pardon, your Majesty, but the officers I talked to said they'd already thought of that for themselves."

"No need to beg my pardon," Maniakes answered. "I'm not angry if the soldiers who serve me think for themselves. The reverse, in fact."

Archers and stone- and dart-throwers from the inner wall rained missiles down on the siege towers as those drew near the lower outer wall. A few of the missiles they rained down fell short, wounding defenders instead of attackers.

An arrow from behind Maniakes shattered against a battlement only a couple of feet to his left. An assassin could slay him so easily, and then say it was an accident. He made himself shrug. He couldn't do anything about that.

Closer and closer to the Silver Gate crawled the two towers still unburnt. The bombardment they took from the Videssian catapults on the walls was harsher than any Maniakes had seen. The Avtokrator wished the Makuraner engineers who had taught the Kubratoi the art of making such towers into Skotos' coldest icepit.

Videssians in mail shirts crowded the walkway by the spots where the towers would send forth their gangplanks. The Kubratoi on the ground did everything they could to keep the imperials from concentrating against the towers, redoubling their own barrage of arrows and catapult-flung stones. Hale men hauled their wounded comrades to the siege towers on either side of the Silver Gate. More soldiers took the places of those hurt or slain.

"We have to beat them back," Maniakes called to his men. "No foreign foe has ever set foot inside Videssos the city. And besides," he added practically, "if we don't kill them, they'll kill us, and enjoy themselves doing it, too."

A few of the soldiers laughed. More, though, simply nodded. He'd phrased his words as a joke, but that didn't mean they weren't true.

Now the first tower almost touched the wall. Maniakes could see that a couple of the shields mounted on it had burned when his men hurled fire at it, but the hides below those shields had kept the fire from turning to conflagration. His nostrils twitched. Those hides weren't fresh. He hoped the Kubratoi inside the tower were good and sick. It would make them easier to beat.

The doorway in the upper story of the siege tower opened. Like the rest of the tower, it was armored with shields and hides. The Kubratoi waiting inside let out a cheer at seeing the light of day once more and shoved the gangway out toward the wall.

"Now!" Maniakes shouted, as loud as he could to make himself heard over the din of battle.

He wasn't sure afterward, but he didn't think the catapult crew waited for his command before letting fly. As soon as the doorway came open, they launched a great jar full of the Videssian incendiary mix straight at it. The jar smashed against the foremost couple of Kubratoi, knocking them over and drenching them and the inside of the tower with clinging flames.

The inside of the tower, of course, was made of wood. In moments, it began to burn. Smoke billowed out of the door. The gangway remained perhaps a third extended, several feet shy of the wall.

"They're not going to come at us that way, by the good god!" Maniakes said. The soldiers around him yelled themselves hoarse and him deaf. He didn't care. The Kubratoi had only one limited way of getting at the Videssians on the wall. Turn that way into a seething mass of fire, and the whole immense siege tower, on which they'd labored so long and hard, all at once became useless.

Not so many Kubratoi were trapped here as had been in the other tower that burned. With the fire at the top, the warriors packing this tower had the chance to flee out the bottom. The Videssians killed and wounded many of them with stones and darts and arrows, but many also fled back out of range of those missiles without taking any hurt.

Maniakes dismissed them from his mind even as they ran: if they were running away from Videssos the city, they were for the time being no threat. He also dismissed the burning siege tower, except insofar as the smoke now pouring from it made him cough and his eyes stream tears. The tower that had not yet opened its door posed the greater threat.

"Be ready!" he shouted to the crews of the catapults facing that second tower. "We'll treat this one the same way we did the other, and then we'll go and help our friends farther up along the wall."

"That's right, your Majesty!" the Biting Snails yelled. "We'll lick 'em, same as we'll lick anybody you turn us loose against."

"Good men!" he said, and a couple of the warriors turned their heads to grin at him. Even after returning to Videssos the city, they didn't care whom he'd married. That he'd led them to victory counted for more. He wished the same held true for people he hadn't led into battle.

The second siege tower assaulting the Silver Gate crawled forward slowly, ponderously. Maniakes thought it was taking a very long time to reach the wall. Maybe it had slowed when some of the men inside saw what had happened to its companion. Maybe, too, time simply seemed to have slowed down for him, as it often did in battle.

Whatever the truth there, at last it came close enough for the Kubratoi inside to open the door. "Now!" Maniakes shouted, as he had before.

And, as the other catapult had done, this one flung a jar full of the Videssians' incendiary liquid straight into the doorway. But the Kubratoi must have thought on what went wrong when the first tower tried extending its gangway toward the wall. All the men crowding forward thrust big shields up against the impact of the jar.

They were so tightly jammed into that little space up there, the impact did not, could not, tumble them backward, as it otherwise would have done. The jar shattered against the upthrust shields, and probably broke arms and ribs in so doing, but most of the burning stuff dripped down over the shields and hides and did not start a great, inextinguishable blaze inside the top of the tower.

Out came the gangway, snaking toward the wall. A Videssian with an axe he must have taken from a Haloga guardsman chopped at it, once, twice, before an arrow caught him in the face. He dropped the axe and reeled back with a groan.

Even before the gangway reached the stones of the outer wall, several Kubratoi charged out onto it. *Snap!* The crew at a dart-thrower smote the engine's trigger. Those darts could slay a man at a quarter of a mile. At such short range, this one drove through two Kubratoi and skewered a third behind them. All three tumbled to the ground, which they struck a second later with heavy, meaty thuds.

No one who had faced the Kubratoi, weapons in hand, had ever claimed they were anything less than brave. After having fire hurled at them, after a dart had hurled to their doom the first three bold enough to try the gangway, the warriors who came after could hardly have been blamed had they hesitated. They did nothing of the sort. Shouting fierce war cries, they shoved one another aside in their eagerness to rush at the Videssians.

Arrows thudded into the shields they held up to protect their vitals. An arrow caught one of them in the thigh. He stumbled and fell, screaming, to the ground below. Another one went down on the gangway, whereupon the Kubrati behind him tripped and also fell.

But the rest came on. The Videssians at the end of the gangway met them not with swords or even spears, but with long, stout poles. They swept a couple of Kubratoi off the narrow way and into that long, deadly drop. The nomads chopped at the poles with their swords. One of the poles split. A Kubrati grabbed another by the end and, instead of trying to fend it off, pulled with all his might. Caught by surprise, the Videssian wielding it did not let go before overbalancing. "Phooooos!" he shrieked all the way down. His cry cut off abruptly when he hit.

With a shout of triumph, the first Kubrati leapt off the gangway and onto the stone of the wall. That shout turned to a scream of agony moments later; beset by three imperials, he went down under spear and sword. So did the next Kubrati, and the next.

After that, even the nomads' fierce courage faltered. A Videssian, caught up in the same unthinking battle fury as his foes, jumped up onto the gangway and ran at the Kubratoi, slashing as he went.

"No!" Maniakes shouted. "Come back! Don't throw yourself away!"

The soldier paid no heed. He cut down the first nomad he faced, but was pierced by an arrow a moment later. Leaping over the Kubrati he'd just slain, he seized the fellow behind that one by the waist and then leapt off the narrow plank, taking his foe down with him.

Maniakes sketched the sun-circle above his heart. The Videssian hadn't thrown himself away; the Avtokrator silently admitted as much to himself. He'd made the Kubratoi pay two to get one—and, in the way he'd done it, he'd made them think, too.

They kept coming, but the moment's hesitation the soldier's self-sacrifice bought let more Videssians rush up toward the gangway. The Kubratoi did manage to put men on the wall every so often, but none of the men they put there lived more than moments. Maniakes' greatest fear was that they would be able to force the Videssians back and create a perimeter behind which more and more of their men would gain the wall.

It did not happen, not by the Silver Gate. "Phos be praised," Maniakes murmured, and anxiously looked up and down the wall to see if the Kubratoi had gained lodgments with any of their other towers. Seeing no signs of that, he said "Phos be praised" again and gave his attention back to the fighting close by him.

The stone-thrower crew had finally managed to load another jar of incendiary liquid into their engine. They could not shoot it at the Kubratoi, though, or at their tower, because too many Videssian soldiers crowded round the machine, which stood near the forefront of the fighting. At last, seeing their moment, they loosed the jar.

It smashed a Kubrati on the gangway near the tower. He fell spinning to the ground below, some of the burning sticky stuff clinging to him. More splashed onto Kubratoi directly behind him. Screaming, they tried to run back into the siege tower, but could make no progress against the stream of warriors trying to come forward. Indeed, those warriors fended them off weapons in hand, not wanting to burn along with the couple of unfortunates.

And some of the mixture of oil and fat and sulfur and naphtha dripped down on the gangway and set the wood afire. The burning Kubratoi kept the others from dousing it, not that it would have been easy to douse with water. The men closer to the wall than the two on fire were so intent on pressing ahead against the Videssians, they did not notice the flames till far too late to stamp them out.

The gangway burned, then, till it broke in two. Both halves, and all the men on them, tumbled down, down, down. Maniakes let out a cry of triumph when that happened. "Come ahead!" he shouted, shaking his fist at the Kubratoi staring out of the siege tower. "Come ahead and get what we just gave your friends!"

He'd hoped they had but a single gangway and would be stuck in the siege tower after losing it. But they, or more likely the Makuraner engineer from whom they'd learned how to build the tower, had planned better than that. Out snaked another plank toward the wall of Videssos the city.

"Here!" Maniakes bawled to his men. "To me!" He snapped orders. Videssian soldiers carried yet another jar of inflammable liquid up to the very edge of the wall. At his command, they poured some of the stuff onto the stone where the gangway would reach the wall, then thrust a torch into it.

Yellow flames sprang up. Thick clouds of black, choking smoke made the Videssians pull back from the fire they'd started. That might have worked to the advantage of the Kubratoi, had they been able to put men on the wall then. But the nomads in charge of the gangway halted with it half-extended, not daring to push it forward into the flames.

"Come on!" Maniakes shouted again. "Don't you want to see the rest of the welcome we have waiting?"

He didn't know whether they heard him or not. If they did hear, he didn't know whether they understood. What he did know was that the gangway advanced no farther. Through the blowing smoke, he saw the Kubratoi pull it back into the tower. And then, so slowly that at first he did not believe what his eyes told him, the tower drew back from the Silver Gate. The other surviving towers were also moving away from the wall.

Now, for the first time that whole mad, terrifying day, Maniakes spoke softly, in tones of wonder: "By the lord with the great and good mind, we've won."

And one of his veterans, a fellow with a scar on his forehead and a kink to his nose, shook his head and said, "No, your Majesty. They've just had enough for today, that's all."

"You're right, of course," the Avtokrator said, recognizing truth when he heard it. Also for the first time that day, he laughed. "And do you know what else? That will do nicely, thank you very much."

No one disagreed with him. He did not think the soldiers deferred to his views because he was their ruler. He thought they kept silent because they, like he, were glad to be alive and not driven from the outer wall.

"What will they do next?" That was the elder Maniakes, taking the question his son addressed to the council of war and doing his best to answer it: "Whatever it is, I hope it won't be as bad as what they threw at us today."

"I expect it will be worse," Maniakes answered. "In today's fight, they were seeing what they could do. Now, curse them to the ice, they have a pretty good notion."

Symvatios said, "The khagan will have a rare old time trying to get them to bring the towers forward again, after what we did to them this time. A warrior who's just watched a good many of his friends go up like so many joints of beef isn't going to be dead keen on heading up to the wall to cook himself afterwards."

"Something to that," Maniakes said. "A lot to it, I hope."

Rhegorios said, "What worries me most of all is that these were the Kubratoi. No sign that many Makuraners were in the fighting today." He pointed westward. "Best we know, they're still over on the other side of the Cattle Crossing. If they once reach this shore—"

"We have more troubles," the Avtokrator broke in. "That wouldn't be the worst move for Etzilios to make, either. It would make his own men happier, because their allies are helping them, and it would make the attack stronger, too, because—"

The elder Maniakes took a father's privilege of interrupting his sovereign: "Because the Makuraners really know what they're doing." That hadn't been what Maniakes intended to say, but it fit well enough. His father went on, "If we could, we really ought to find out what the Kubratoi and Makuraners are planning, not what we'd be doing in their sandals. It's not battle magic, not precisely . . ."

"They'll be warded," Maniakes said glumly. "I'd bet a goldpiece against a copper that their mages are trying to listen in on us right now. If they learn anything, some heads that are in the Sorcerers' Collegium ought to go up on the Milestone instead."

"If we don't try, it's sure we won't do it," the elder Maniakes said.

"That's so," Maniakes agreed. "Let it be as you say, Father. I'll summon Bagdasares."

Alvinos Bagdasares said something startled in the throaty Vaspurakaner tongue. Maniakes, though of the same Vaspurakaner blood as the mage, understood that language only haltingly. He did not think, though, that Bagdasares had thanked him for the sorcerous assignment.

"Your Majesty, this will be a difficult conjuration at best, and may well prove impossible," Bagdasares warned, returning to Videssian.

"If it were easy, I could pick a wizard off a street corner to do it for me," Maniakes returned. "I know you may not get the answers I want, but I want you to do everything you can to find out what Abivard and Etzilios are plotting against us now."

Bagdasares bowed. "It shall be as you command, of course, your Majesty." He tugged at his bushy black beard, muttering in both Videssian and Vaspurakaner. When Maniakes caught a word— *affinities*—he nodded to himself. Yes, the mage would do his best.

To symbolize Abivard, Bagdasares came up with a shiny silver arket. "I have nothing similar for the Kubrati khagan," he said unhappily.

"Why not just use one of our goldpieces, then?" Maniakes answered, sounding anything but gleeful himself. "We were going to pay Etzilios enough of them—but not enough to suit him."

"The analogy needs to be more exact." Bagdasares didn't notice that Maniakes was indulging in a wry joke—or else whipping himself for past failures. The mage finally chose a Kubrati saber. Its blade shone, too, though with a different sort of gleam from that of the Makuraner coin. Bagdasares looked almost pleased with the world after that. "Now I need but one thing more: you."

"Me?" Maniakes heard himself squeak, as if he were a youth whose voice broke every other word.

"Certainly, your Majesty," the wizard said. "You shall be the element transmuting the general to the specific. This is not Etzilios' sword, only a Kubrati weapon. The odds are long against this coin's ever having been in Abivard's beltpouch. But you have met both men. By the working of the law of contagion, you remain in touch with both of them. And that contact strengthens the action of the law of similarity here, linking these artifacts not only with their respective nations but also with the individuals whose plans we are trying to learn."

Maniakes had hoped to get back to the wall in case Etzilios, instead of conferring with Abivard, simply decided to attack again. If that happened, though, a messenger would no doubt bring him word of it. He could leave when that happened. The urgent needs of battle would give him a good excuse for interrupting Bagdasares' magic. Meanwhile, he resigned himself to wait.

"Take the arket in one hand, your Majesty, and the sword in the other," Bagdasares said. "Think on the two men whom the objects represent. Think on them talking with each other, and on what they might say in the situation in which they find themselves."

"I've been doing nothing but thinking on what they *might* say," Maniakes answered. "I want to find out what they *did* say or *will* say."

Bagdasares did not reply. Maniakes was not sure Bagdasares even heard. The mage had begun the chanting invocation he would use for the spell and the passes that would accompany it. If a wizard did not fix his mind on the essential, his magic would surely fail.

It might fail even if he did everything perfectly. Bagdasares' frown made him look older. "Wards," he said to Maniakes in a moment when his hands were busy but he did not need to incant orally. "I am resisted." His forehead corrugated in thought. When he began to chant again, the rhythm was subtly different from what it had been.

Different, perhaps, but not better. Frown darkened into scowl. "They have a Videssian mage with them," he said, releasing the words as if from a mouth full of rotting fish. "He has forereadied charms against many things I might try. Many, aye, but not all."

Once more, the rhythm of the chant shifted. This time, so did the language. From archaic Videssian, he turned to the Vaspurakaner tongue. Now his eyes brightened, his voice firmed—progress, Maniakes judged.

A moment later, he was able to judge progress for himself. He began to feel . . . something pass between silver coin and iron sword. He did not think he was feeling it with any of the five ordinary senses. It was more akin, or so he judged, to the current that passed from a healer-priest to the person he was helping: as indescribable as that, and as real.

"We have to do this together," a voice said from out of the air in front of him. "The delay hurts my men, too—half of them want to go north tomorrow."

"Get enough of my soldiers over the Cattle Crossing and we'll lead the way up the towers and onto the wall," another voice replied, apparently from that same empty place.

Maniakes started in surprise. It was not so much at hearing

Etzilios and Abivard: he'd required that Bagdasares make him able to hear them. Having the mage succeed though he'd doubted whether success was possible gratified the Avtokrator without astonishing him. What he had not expected, though, was that both the khagan of Kubrat and the marshal of Makuran would be speaking Videssian. What did it say when the Empire's two greatest foes had only its language in common?

"And while they're busy fighting the towers—" Maniakes was surprised again, not having expected to hear a third voice there. But, whether Bagdasares had given him anything to mark it or not, he had an affinity for Tzikas, an affinity of longtime common cause soured into near-murder and endless betrayal. Oh, yes, the two of them were connected.

But what did Tzikas know? What had he been trying to show the Kubratoi when Maniakes almost put a dart through him?

The Avtokrator did not find out. Abivard said, "Get the monoxyla over to us. You know the signal to use to let us know when they're coming?"

"I know the one you gave me," Etzilios answered. "Why that in particular?"

"Because it—" Abivard undoubtedly went on talking, but Maniakes heard no more. The arket and the hilt of the sword he was holding went hot in his hands. Weapon and coin both fell to the floor, the one with a clatter, the other chiming sweetly from the stone.

Bagdasares staggered slightly, then caught himself. "I crave pardon, your Majesty," he said. "The wizards warding them became aware that I had threaded my way through their defense, and cut off the thread after me."

"I wish they hadn't done it right then," Maniakes said. "If we'd learned what the Kubratoi signal is, our dromons would be waiting to pounce on their one-trunk boats. We'd slaughter them."

"No doubt you are right," Bagdasares said. "I promise you, I shall do everything I can to learn what this signal may be. But I cannot do it now; the enemy's wizards almost made me lose a good-sized piece of my soul in the escape."

"Go rest, then," Maniakes said. "You look like you need it." What Bagdasares looked as if he needed was something more than rest. Maniakes said nothing of that, in the hope rest would also restore what else was missing from the Vaspurakaner mage. And, on leaving, Bagdasares did indeed yawn enormously, as if his body, not his spirit, had put in a hard day.

Maniakes waited till Bagdasares was well clear of the room in which he'd worked before muttering a ripe oath. That might not have done him any good, if Bagdasares was listening with senses beyond those mundane five. The Avtokrator cursed again, more ripely yet.

"*So* close!" Maniakes said, slamming a fist down on a tabletop. Another sentence, two at the most, would have told him what he so desperately wanted—so desperately needed—to learn. Now all he knew was that the Kubratoi would in fact swallow their pride and get help from the men of Makuran, who were more experienced when it came to sieges.

He wished—how he wished!—Etzilios had been too headstrong to share what he hoped would be his triumph with his allies. But Etzilios was too practical for that, worse luck. Trim his beard and take him out of his furs and he would have made a pretty fair Videssian. On that depressing note, Maniakes also left the chamber where Bagdasares had worked his successful spell. *If only it had been a little more successful,* the Avtokrator thought.

Thrax rose from his prostration, eyeing Maniakes warily. "How may I serve your Majesty?" he asked. The ceremonial of the Grand Courtroom weighed on him, as it was meant to do.

"I summoned you here to make certain you have the fleet at the highest pitch of readiness over the next few days," Maniakes said from the throne, staring down at the drungarios of the fleet with no expression whatever on his face. The only way he could have sounded more imposing would have been to use the royal *we*, as Sharbaraz did—*probably even when he goes in unto his wives,* Maniakes thought, which amused him enough to make him have trouble holding his face still.

"The fleet is always at the highest pitch of readiness, your Majesty," Thrax said. "If the cockroaches come away from the wall, we'll step on 'em."

"I know you're ready to fight," Maniakes said. "That isn't quite what I meant."

"Well, what did you mean, then?" the drungarios of the fleet asked. A couple of courtiers muttered to one another at the imperfectly respectful way in which he framed the question.

Maniakes felt like muttering, too, but held onto his patience by main force. He knew how Thrax was. Knowing how Thrax was had made him convoke this ceremony. If the drungarios knew ahead of time exactly what he was supposed to do, he would do it, and do it well enough. If taken by surprise, he still might do well—but he also might do anything at all, with no way to guess beforehand whether for good or ill.

"I summoned you here to explain just that," the Avtokrator answered. "I expect that the Kubratoi will try to send a good many monoxyla over to the west side of the Cattle Crossing to bring back enough Makuraners to man the siege towers against us. Are you with me so far?"

"Aye, your Majesty," Thrax said confidently. Under that shock of shining silver hair, his bronzed, lined face was a mask of concentration.

"Good." Maniakes did his best to sound encouraging. Since he hadn't found anyone better than Thrax, he had to work as best he could within the man's limitations. He went on, "Before they sail, they'll signal, to let the Makuraners know they're coming. If we can spot that signal, too, we'll be able to get a running start on them, you might say. Wherever the main body of the fleet is, whether tied up at the piers or on patrol a little way off from the city, you have to be ready to get it out and covering the Cattle Crossing on the instant. Now do you understand what I'm saying?"

"I think so," the drungarios said. "You're saying you don't only want us ready to fight at a moment's notice, you want us ready to move at a moment's notice, too."

"That's it! That's perfect!" Maniakes felt like leaping down from the throne and planting a kiss on Thrax's cheek. Only the suspicion that that would fluster the drungarios more than it pleased him kept the Avtokrator in his seat. "Can you do it?"

"Oh, aye, I can, no doubt about that," Thrax said. "I'm still not sure I see the need, but I can."

"Seeing the need is my job," Maniakes said.

"Oh, aye," Thrax repeated. Unlike a lot of officers, he had no secret ambition to set his fundament on the throne Maniakes occupied. He might well have lacked the imagination to picture himself enjoying the power that would accrue to him on the seat. Cocking his head to one side, he asked, "How will you know what signal the Kubratoi are using?"

That was a good question. It was, in fact, *the* question of the moment. It wouldn't have been, had Etzilios' wizards—or perhaps Abivard's—not discovered Bagdasares' sorcery till another few moments had gone by. But they had discovered it, and now Maniakes had to live with—or perhaps die from—the consequences.

He said, "Our wizards are working on that," which had the twin virtues of being true and of satisfying Thrax. Also true was that the wizards had not had any luck whatever, but Maniakes did not tell the drungarios that.

The wizards' failure ate at the Avtokrator. So did the feeling they shouldn't have failed, or rather that their failure shouldn't have mattered. But matter it did. The Kubratoi, curse them, were not fools. Their wizards knew he'd been eavesdropping on Etzilios and Abivard. They knew he knew they intended to signal Abivard before their one-trunk boats dashed over the Cattle Crossing to ferry the Makuraners back to the eastern side of the strait to attack the walls of Videssos the city.

They also knew, or perhaps hoped, Maniakes did not know what the signal was supposed to be. And so they gave him every kind of signal under the sun. Fires sent columns of dense black smoke into the air by day. Fires crackled on the beach near the city by night. Kubratoi on horseback carried enormous banners of different colors back and forth. In among that welter of decoys the nomads might almost have hung out a sign—HERE WE COME, say, in letters fifty feet high—and had it pass with no special notice.

For the Videssians, in the frustrating absence of any sure knowledge of what the true signal would be, had to react to each and every one of them as if it was the real thing. Time after time, dromons would charge out into the Cattle Crossing, oars whipping the waves to foam, only to find no sign of the monoxyla they'd hoped to trap.

Inevitably, the false alarms began corroding the fleet's readiness. Maniakes had expected that to be a worse problem than it was. After a while, he realized why it wasn't so bad. He'd told Thrax he wanted the dromons ready to move at a moment's notice, no matter what. *No matter what* turned out to be more complicated and difficult than he'd expected. But he'd given Thrax an order, and the drungarios of the fleet was going to make sure that order got obeyed—period. Every once in a while, dogged mediocrity had its advantages.

Had Rhegorios suggested a sally now, Maniakes might have been more inclined to listen to him. The notion did not tempt him enough to order one on his own. He had more patience than his cousin—or so he kept telling himself, at any rate, though his record of moving too soon made it a dubious proposition.

The Kubratoi kept Videssos the city under blockade by land, and, away from it, their monoxyla picked off some of the merchantmen bringing supplies to the defenders. Grain did not grow scarce, but looked as if it would soon, which drove up the price in the markets.

Maniakes summoned a couple of the leading grain merchants. One of them, Boraides, was short and plump and smiled all the time. The other, Provhos, was tall and thin and doleful. Their looks and temperaments might have been different, but they thought alike.

Boraides said, "Not right to keep a man from turning an honest profit, heh heh."

"We are in a risky business, your Majesty," Provhos agreed. He cracked his knuckles with careful attention, one after another, his two thumbs last of all. The popping noises were startlingly loud in the small audience chamber of the imperial residence.

"I called you here to ask you to keep your prices down of your own free will," Maniakes said, "and to ask you to ask your colleagues to do likewise."

Boraides' eyes flicked left to Provhos, whose eyes were flicking right to him. Both men coughed at the same time. "Can't be done, your Majesty," Provhos said.

"Wish it could, but it can't," Boraides agreed. "Us grain sellers, we don't trust anybody. Why, I don't trust myself half the time, heh heh. I tell the other boys what you've just told me, they're liable to bump up prices on account of what you said, no better reason than that."

"They would be well advised not to do anything so foolish," Maniakes said.

Boraïdes started another breezy story. Provhos held up a hand. His fingers were long and, except at the joints, thin. Maniakes wondered whether that was because he cracked his knuckles. The lean grain merchant asked, "Why is that, your Majesty?"

"Because if they try to make an unfair profit off the people during this time of trouble—which is something the two of you would never even think of doing, of course—I would decide I had no choice but to open the imperial granaries to bring prices down again."

"You wouldn't do such a thing, your Majesty," Boraïdes said. "Why, it'd cost the grain merchants' goodwill for years to come."

Maniakes angrily exhaled through his nose. Some people's self-importance never failed to amaze him. He said, "Shall I have the soldiers take you out to the wall, distinguished sir? Do you want to go up there and see the Kubratoi and Makuraners with your own eyes? If that will convince you they're really there, I'll be happy to arrange it."

"I know they're there, your Majesty, heh heh," Boraïdes said. "It's only that—"

"If you know they're there, why don't you act like it?" Maniakes interrupted. "I don't want people going hungry while we're besieged, and I don't want people hating the men who sell them grain, either. Both those things are liable to make them fight worse than they would otherwise, and that's all I'm worried about. If the city falls, we're dead—for true, not metaphorically. Next to that, gentlemen, having the grain merchants angry at me is something I don't mind risking."

"But—" Boraïdes was ready to go on arguing.

Provhos seemed to have a better grip on reality. "It's no good, Bor," he said sadly. "He can do more things to us than we can do to him, and that's all there is to it." He bowed to Maniakes. "We'll keep prices down as low as we can, your Majesty. If you open the imperial granaries, you can always knock them down lower. That's what being Avtokrator is all about."

"That's right," Maniakes said. "I'm glad one of you has the wit to realize it, anyhow."

"Bah," Boraïdes said. "If we put enough people on the streets—"

"A lot of them will end up dead," Maniakes promised. "So will you. You may perhaps have noticed that we have an army's worth of soldiers in the city. If merchants protest now because they can't gouge, they will be sorry, as I said earlier. How long do you think they'll be able to go before soldiers start looting the shops of merchants who've been . . . troublesome, especially if they didn't think anyone would punish them afterward?"

Boraides still didn't seem ready to keep his mouth shut. Provhos hissed at him. They put their heads together. Maniakes let them mutter for as long as they liked. When they finished, he had trouble deciding which of them looked less happy. Provhos' long face had probably seemed mournful on the most joyous day of his life, and he wasn't joyous now. Boraides usually looked jolly even when he wasn't. He didn't look jolly at the moment.

"You're doing a terrible thing to us, your Majesty, keeping us from earning an honest return on our work," he said. "You can make us do it—Provhos is right about that—but you can't make us like it."

"I've never said you can't make your usual profit. I've said you can't gouge," Maniakes answered. "Think back. Pay attention to my words. I don't like the idea of food riots. I have enough trouble and to spare outside the city. If I can stop trouble inside the city before it starts, you'd best believe I'm going to do that."

Both grain merchants shook their heads. He'd overawed them. He hadn't convinced them. He was willing to settle for that. He was not the lord with the great and good mind, to reach inside a man's head and change the way he thought. If he could make his subjects act as he wished them to act, he'd be content.

He scowled. Up till now, he hadn't had much luck making the Makuraners and Kubratoi act as he wished them to act.

Provhos and Boraides took his frown as dismissal. He hadn't intended it that way, but it would do. As they rose, Kameas appeared in the doorway to escort them out of the imperial residence.

"How do you do that?" Maniakes asked when the vestiarios returned to see if he needed anything else.

"How do I do what, your Majesty?" Kameas asked in return.

"Know exactly when to show up," the Avtokrator said. "I've never caught you snooping, and neither has anyone else, but you're always in the right place at the right time. How do you manage?"

"I have a good notion of how long any particular individual is likely to require your attention," the eunuch said, which was not really an answer.

"If your sense of timing is as good as that, esteemed sir, maybe you belong on the battlefield, not in the palace quarter."

Maniakes hadn't meant it seriously, but Kameas sounded serious as he replied, "A couple of chamberlains with my disability have served their sovereigns as soldiers, your Majesty. I am given to understand that they did not disgrace themselves, perhaps for the very reason you cited."

"I didn't know that," Maniakes said, bemused. Eunuch generals would have to gain respect from their men by different means from entire men, that was certain. It wouldn't be easy, either; he could see as much. "I must say I admire them."

"Oh, so do we, your Majesty," Kameas replied. "Their memory is yet green within the palaces." Maniakes pictured old chamberlains telling young ones of the great deeds of their warlike predecessors, and then those young eunuchs growing old in turn and passing on the tales to those who came after them. Then Kameas rather spoiled his vision by adding, "And several historians and chroniclers also note their martial accomplishments."

"Do they?" Maniakes' reading, aside from endless parchments from the bureaucrats and soldiers who made the Empire of Videssos keep running even in the face of the dislocations of the Makuraner and Kubrati invasions, ran more to military manuals than to histories. And soldiers like Kalokyres, in explaining how a general was to go about doing the things he needed to do, never bothered mentioning whether testicles were essential for the job.

"They certainly do, your Majesty." The vestiarios showed more enthusiasm for the subject than Maniakes usually saw in him, no doubt because it touched him personally. He went on, "Should you so desire, I could show you some of the relevant passages. I have several of these scrolls and codices myself, copied out by very fine scribes, and I am gradually accumulating more as I discover documents in the archives."

"Is that what you do in your free time—search the archives, I mean?"

"One of the things, yes, your Majesty." Kameas drew himself straight with a pride that was liable to be twisted. "After all, things being as they are, I am hardly in a position to chase women."

Maniakes walked over and punched him in the shoulder, as he might have done with Rhegorios. "To the ice with me if I think I could joke about it," he said. "You're a good man, esteemed sir—

and you don't need a pair of balls for most of the things that make a good man."

"I have often thought as much myself, your Majesty, but I must tell you that it gives me a great deal of satisfaction to hear it from an entire man," Kameas said. "Some, I assure you, are less generous than that."

His mouth stretched out into a thin, hard, bleak line. He had been vestiarios for Genesios before Maniakes managed to rid Videssos of the tyrant. Every so often, Kameas let slip something that suggested Genesios' reign of terror had been even worse within the palace quarter than anywhere beyond. Maniakes had never questioned him or any of the other palace eunuchs about that, partly because he was as well pleased not knowing and partly because he did not want to pain the eunuchs by making them remember.

The vestiarios bowed. "Will there be anything further, your Majesty?"

"I don't think so," Maniakes said. As Kameas turned to go, the Avtokrator changed his mind. "Wait." The eunuch obediently stopped. Maniakes dug in his beltpouch. He found no gold there, only silver: a telling comment on the state of the Empire's finances. He tossed a couple of coins to Kameas. They shone in the air till the eunuch caught them. "For your copyist," Maniakes said.

Kameas bowed again, this time in a subtly different way: as himself now, not as vestiarios. "Your Majesty is gracious."

"What my Majesty is, is sick and tired of being hemmed into the city and waiting for the Makuraners to try swarming over the Cattle Crossing," Maniakes said. "We should know when they're going to do it, but we can't steal the signal that warns they're truly moving."

"If we keep responding to all the signals the Kubratoi have been putting forth—" Kameas began.

"We end up not responding well enough to any one of them," Maniakes broke in. "It will happen, sooner or later. It has to. But one day soon, one of those signals will be real, and, if we don't take that one seriously, we'll have a Makuraner army on this side of the . . ."

His voice trailed away. When he didn't go on after a minute or so, Kameas cleared his throat. "You were saying, your Majesty?"

"Was I?" Maniakes answered absently. His eyes and his thoughts were far away. "Whatever I was saying—" He had no memory of it. "—that doesn't matter any more. Had I had gold to give you, esteemed sir, I might not have known. But I do. Now I know."

"Your Majesty?" Kameas' voice was plaintive. Maniakes did not reply.

VII

"**Y**OUR MAJESTY!" THE MESSENGER SPOKE IN HIGH EXCITEMENT. He smelled of lathered horse, which likely meant he'd galloped his mount through the streets of Videssos the city to bring his word to Maniakes. "Your Majesty, the Kubratoi are flashing sunlight from a silver shield over the Cattle Crossing to the Makuraners!"

"Are they?" Maniakes breathed. As he had with Kameas, he reached into his beltpouch for money. He'd made sure he had gold there now, against this very moment. The messenger gaped when the Avtokrator pressed half a dozen goldpieces into his hand. Maniakes said, "Now give Thrax the word. He knows what to do." He hoped—he prayed—the drungarios knew what to do.

"Aye, your Majesty, I'll do that," the messenger said. "Immodios sent a man to him, too, but I'll go, in case poor Vonos fell off his horse and cracked his hard head or something." He hurried away.

His boots rang against the mosaic tiles on the hallway floor of the imperial residence. Rhegorios rose from his chair, stiffened to attention, and gave Maniakes a formal salute, right clenched fist over his heart. "You knew," he said, nothing but admiration in his voice.

Maniakes shook his head. "I still don't *know*," he answered. "But I think I'm right, and I think so strongly enough to gamble on it. When Abivard first came to Across and I parleyed with him, he asked me if the Imperial Guards carried silver shields, and he seemed disappointed when I said no. And then there was Bagdasares' magic—"

"Yes, you told me about that the other day," his cousin answered. "He managed to capture the words some Makuraner seer had given Abivard?"

"That's right, or I think that's right," Maniakes said. "Wherever

172

they came from, the words were clear enough." He shifted into the Makuraner tongue: " 'Son of the *dihqan*, I see a broad field that is not a field, a tower on a hill where honor shall be won and lost, and a silver shield shining across a narrow sea.' " Returning to Videssian, he went on, "Wherever the words came from, as I say, they meant—and mean—a great deal to Abivard. If he asked Etzilios for any one signal to start his army moving, that would be the one—or that's my guess, at any rate."

"I think you're right," Rhegorios said. "And so does your father. I've never seen Uncle Maniakes looking so impressed as he did when you set your idea in front of him—and he doesn't impress easily, either."

"Who, my father?" Maniakes said, as if in surprise. He gave that up; he couldn't bring it off. "I had noticed, thanks."

"I thought you might have," his cousin agreed.

Maniakes said, "I couldn't decide for the longest time whether I'd watch the sea fight from the palace quarter here or from the deck of a ship. At last I thought, if I was there on the land wall, I ought to be there on the sea, too. I've ordered Thrax to pick me up at the palace harbor. Will you come, too?"

"Aboard the *Renewal*?" Rhegorios asked. Maniakes nodded. His cousin said, "If I didn't drown in that one storm, to the ice with me if I think the Kubratoi can do me any harm. Let's go. We'd better hurry, too. If you've told Thrax to pick you up there, he'll wait around and do it even if you don't show up till next month, and he won't care a rotten fig for what that does to the plans for the sea fight."

Since Rhegorios was undoubtedly right, Maniakes wasted no time arguing with him. The two men hurried out of the imperial residence. A few guards peeled off from the entranceways to the building and trotted along with them, complaining all the while that they should have waited for more men to accompany them. Maniakes wasted no time arguing with the guards, either. He was reveling in having escaped his dozen parasol-bearers. He wondered how they would have done standing at the bow of the *Renewal* when it climbed up and over a one-trunk boat. With any luck, half of them would have gone into the drink and drowned.

He and Rhegorios reached the quays by the palaces none too soon. Here came the *Renewal*, oars rising and falling in perfect unison. The sun shining off Thrax's hair was almost as bright as it would have been, reflected from a silver shield.

As the imperial flagship picked up the Avtokrator and the Sevastos, more dromons—many more dromons—dashed out into the middle of the Cattle Crossing, ready to keep the Kubratoi from reaching the western shore and picking up their Makuraner allies. "If you're right, your Majesty, they've fallen into our hands," Thrax declared. He sounded confident. Maniakes had told him it would be thus and so. He was going to act on that assumption. If Maniakes was right, all would be well. If Maniakes was wrong, Thrax's blind obedience would make him wronger.

"Let's go get them," Maniakes said. He would assume he was right, too, and would keep on assuming it for as long as he could. If he was wrong, he hoped he'd notice quickly, because Thrax wouldn't.

One of the dromons far enough south for its captain to be able to see around the bulk of Videssos the city sent a horn call back toward the rest of the fleet. Other ships echoed it, spreading the word as fast as they were able. "That's *enemy in sight*," Rhegorios breathed.

"Yes, it is, isn't it?" Maniakes said. He looked up into the heavens and sketched Phos' sun-circle above his breast. He felt taller, quicker, more agile, as if an enormous weight had just fallen from his shoulders.

Thrax shouted to the oarmaster. The deep drum picked up the beat. The *Renewal* fairly leapt over the waves, speeding toward the foes who had shown themselves at last. Maniakes peered south and east, for once regretting Videssos the city's seawall, because for some little while it kept him from learning how great a threat he, the city, and the Empire faced.

"By the good god," he said when the *Renewal*, like that first dromon, had come far enough to let him get a good look at the foe. Dozens of monoxyla bobbed in the chop of the Cattle Crossing. Their paddles rose and fell, rose and fell, in almost the same rhythm as the dromons' oars. Since the wind came out of the west, their masts were down.

Thrax shouted again, this time to the trumpeter: "Blow *each ship pick its own foe*." The call rang out and quickly went through the fleet.

Spying the Videssian warships between them and their allies, the Kubratoi shouted to one another. "If you were in one of those boats, what would you do?" Rhegorios asked Maniakes.

"Me?" The Avtokrator considered. "I'd like to think I'd have the sense to go back to dry land and try again some other day." He shook his head. "I'd probably press on, though, figuring I'd come too far to turn back. I've made a lot of mistakes like that, so I expect I'd make one more."

"Here's hoping it *is* a mistake," Rhegorios said, to which his cousin could only nod.

Mistake or not, the Kubratoi kept coming. Now they shouted not just back and forth among themselves but also at the Videssians. Maniakes did not understand their language. He did not need to understand it to get the idea that they weren't paying him compliments. If the fists they shook at the Videssian dromons hadn't given him a clue, the arrows arcing toward his fleet would have.

Those first arrows fell short, splashing into the sea like flying fish. Most of the dromons carried dart-throwers that could shoot farther than any archer. When their darts missed, they kicked up bigger splashes than mere arrows. When they hit, as they did every so often, a couple of Kubratoi would suddenly stop paddling, slowing their monoxyla by so much.

As the one-trunk boats and the dromons drew nearer to one another, the Kubrati archers began scoring hits, too. Here and there, Videssians crumpled to the decking of their ships. One or two of them fell into the water. Maniakes saw one wounded man bravely strike out toward the shore less than half a mile away. He never found out whether the fellow made it.

More and more arrows rained down on the dromons. More and more men cried out in pain. "Is this going to give us a lot of trouble?" Maniakes asked Thrax.

The drungarios of the fleet shook his head, then brushed disarrayed silver locks back from his forehead. "This is like a mosquito bite, your Majesty. It itches. It stings. So what? Fights on the sea aren't like your fights on land. A bunch of silly arrows don't decide anything, not here they don't."

He sounded perfectly confident. Maniakes, knowing himself only a spectator on this field, could but hope the drungarios had reason for confidence.

Up ahead, the dromon that had first spotted the monoxyla raced straight toward one, seawater slicing aside from its ram. It struck the one-log boat amidships. The crunch of the bronze-shod ram striking home was audible across a couple of furlongs. The dromon backed oars. Water flooded into the monoxylon through the gash the ram had torn. The Videssian vessel rowed off toward another victim.

"That one!" Thrax pointed at a one-trunk boat. The men at the steering oars swung the *Renewal* in the direction he had ordered. He called out course corrections with calm certainty. He'd done this before, after the storm on the Sailors' Sea. Anything he'd done before, he did well.

But, however well he did, the monoxylon escaped him. Maybe its Kubrati captain had as much experience dodging dromons as Thrax had in running down the smaller vessels. As the one-log boat and the war galley closed on each other, the monoxylon put on a sudden burst of speed, so that the dromon's ram slid past its stern.

Thrax cursed foully. "He was lucky," Maniakes said, which was not strictly true—the Kubrati had shown both nerve and skill. The Avtokrator went on, "We have plenty of monoxyla left to hunt, and they can't all get away." *They'd better not all get away,* he added to himself.

"Phos bless you, your Majesty, for your patience," the drungarios of the fleet said.

While Thrax swung the *Renewal* toward the next nearest one-trunk boat, Maniakes turned to Rhegorios. "I've been patient with him, all right—patient to a fault. If I had anyone better—"

"You would have put him in Thrax's place a long time ago," Rhegorios broke in. "You know that. I know that. Maybe even Thrax knows that. But you don't. Sometimes there aren't enough good men to go around, and that's all there is to it. He's not bad."

Maniakes didn't answer. Having the fate of the Empire depend on a man who wasn't bad gnawed at him. But the sea fight, as it developed, didn't really depend on Thrax alone. It was every Videssian captain for himself, trying to crush enemy vessels that seemed as small and quick and elusive as cockroaches scuttling from one side of a room to the other.

One of those cockroaches would not get away. The *Renewal* rode up and over a monoxylon, capsizing it and spilling most of its warriors into the green-blue waters of the Cattle Crossing. The collision had slowed the dromon. Would it be able to reach the

next nearest one-trunk boat before the latter could speed off? Maniakes shouted in delight as the ram bit into the monoxylon near the
stern.

"Back oars!" Thrax shouted. The *Renewal* pulled free. The one-
log boat filled rapidly. It did not sink—it was, after all, only wood.
But the Kubratoi aboard, regardless of whether they eventually
managed to reach Across, would bring back no Makuraners to
attack Videssos the city.

Monoxylon after monoxylon was holed or capsized by the
Videssian fleet. The imperials did not quite have it all their own
way. Some of the Kubratoi shot fire arrows, as they had in Maniakes' earlier encounter with them. They managed to set a couple
of dromons afire. And four monoxyla converged on a war galley
that had trouble freeing its ram from the one-log boat it had struck.
The Kubratoi swarmed onto the dromon and massacred its crew.

"Ram them," Maniakes said, pointing to the nomads who exulted
on the deck of the dromon. Thrax, for once, did not need to be told
twice. The *Renewal* had not been too near the captured galley, but
quickly closed the distance. Thrax guided the flagship between
two of the one-log boats still close by the dromon. The Kubratoi
had barely got the unfamiliar ship moving by then. It moved no
more after the *Renewal*'s ram tore a gaping hole in its flank.

Maniakes peered toward the western shore of the Cattle Crossing. A couple of monoxyla had managed to make the crossing
despite all the Videssian fleet could do. Makuraner soldiers were
running toward them and scrambling inside. A lot of Makuraners
stood drawn up over there, awaiting transport over the narrow
strait to Videssos the city. By the way the sea fight was going,
most of them would wait a long time.

Together, Kubratoi and Makuraners shoved into the sea once
more one of the boats that had made the crossing. Before Maniakes could order the *Renewal* to the attack, two other Videssian
dromons raced toward the eastbound monoxylon. Abivard's men,
being armored in iron, went to the bottom faster than Etzilios'.
Otherwise, there was not much difference between them.

"It's a slaughter!" Rhegorios shouted, slapping Maniakes on
the back.

"By the good god, it is," Maniakes said in some astonishment.
Few uncapsized monoxyla still floated. Some of those that did,
having managed to escape the fighting, were paddling back toward

the shore from which they had come. Kubratoi bobbed in the water, a few still swimming or clinging to wreckage but most of them dead.

"Haven't I said all along, your Majesty," Thrax boomed proudly, "that if we ever got the chance to fight a big sea battle, dromons against monoxyla, I mean, we'd smash them to flinders? Haven't I said that?"

"So you have," Maniakes said. "It seems you were right." That Thrax had also said a fair number of things that had turned out to be wrong, he did not mention. The drungarios had redeemed himself today.

"I didn't think it would be *this* easy," Rhegorios said. He was looking at bobbing bodies, too.

"I did," Thrax said, which was also true. "These one-trunk boats, they're good enough to carry raiders, but they've always taken lumps when they went up against real war galleys. The Kubratoi know it, too; they aren't in the habit of getting into stand-up fights with us. They tried it here this once, and they've paid for it."

"That they have," Maniakes said. "If they haven't thrown away more men here on the sea than they did trying to storm the city's walls, I'll be astonished."

A ripple showed near one of the corpses floating in the Cattle Crossing. A moment later, it floated no more. Land battles quickly drew ravens and buzzards and foxes. Sea fights had their scavengers, too.

"Remind me not to eat seafood for a while," Rhegorios said.

Maniakes gulped. "I'll do that. And I won't do that for a while myself." His cousin nodded, having no trouble sorting through the clumsy phrasing.

The Avtokrator gauged the sun. It wasn't that far past noon, and it hadn't been long before noon when he and Rhegorios boarded the *Renewal*. In the space of a couple of hours, Etzilios' hopes, and those of Sharbaraz, too, had gone to ruin in the narrow sea between Videssos the city and Across.

"I wonder how much gold we've spent on the fleet over the years—over the centuries, by Phos," the Avtokrator said musingly. "So much of it must have looked like nothing but waste. However much we spent, though, what we did here today made every copper of it worthwhile."

"That's right, your Majesty. That's exactly right," Thrax said.

"And so next year, when I ask for gold for new ships and for keeping the old ones in the shape they should be, you'll give me all I ask for, won't you?"

Scratch a drungarios, find a courtier. In a mock-fierce voice, Maniakes growled, "If you ask me for so much as one Makuraner silver arket, Thrax, I will beat you with a club studded with nails. Is that plain?"

"Yes, your Majesty." Not even Thrax, naive and stolid as he was, could take the threat seriously.

Rhegorios said, "Etzilios' plans have gone down the latrine, and so have those of Sharbaraz King of Kings, may his days be long and his arse covered in boils. What about Abivard's plans?" The Sevastos pointed over toward Across, where Makuraner soldiers still waited near the shore for boats that would never come.

"I don't know," Maniakes said. "We'll have to find out. He can't do anything to the capital now. That, I think, is certain. He can still do quite a lot to the westlands—or he may pull back to the Land of the Thousand Cities against a move from us. No way to tell till it happens."

"I suppose not," Rhegorios said. "I wish we could pry him loose from Sharbaraz, the way he pried Tzikas loose from you."

"He didn't pry Tzikas loose from me. Tzikas pried himself loose from me," Maniakes answered. "When he didn't manage to kill me, taking refuge with the Makuraners looked like the best way to keep me from prying his head loose from his shoulders." He made a sour face. "It worked too bloody well."

"Abivard seems loyal." Rhegorios made it sound like a disease. Maniakes felt the same way, at least where Abivard was concerned. A disloyal Makuraner marshal would have been a great boon to the Empire of Videssos. Thinking of loyalty in such disparaging terms made Maniakes realize how completely a Videssian he'd become in spite of his Vaspurakaner heritage. His great-grandparents surely would have praised loyalty even in a foe. He shrugged. His great-grandparents hadn't known everything there was to know, either.

"What now, your Majesty?" Thrax asked.

Having thought himself a true Videssian, Maniakes had an idea of truly Videssian duplicity. "Let's go over to the shore near the Kubrati camp," he answered. "I want to deliver a message to Etzilios."

As he'd guessed, the sight of the *Renewal* cruising not far away brought a crowd of Kubratoi to the seaside to see why he was there. "What youse am wantings?" one of them shouted in Videssian so mangled that he recognized the speaker at once.

"Moundioukh, take my words to your khagan, the magnifolent Etzilios." Full of triumph, Maniakes used the contorted epithet without hesitation. "Tell him that, since my fleet has disposed of those poor, sorry toys he called boats, nothing now prevents me from shipping a force to the coast north of Videssos the city, landing it there, and making sure he never escapes from the Empire of Videssos."

"Youse am bluffing," Moundioukh shouted across the water. He did not sound confident, though. He sounded frightened.

"You'll see. So will Etzilios," Maniakes said, and then, to Thrax, "Move us out of bowshot now, if you'd be so kind."

"Aye, your Majesty," the drungarios replied. For a wonder, he understood exactly what Maniakes had meant, and said "Back oars!" loud enough to let the oarmaster know what was required but not so loud as to alert the Kubratoi on the shore.

"That's—demonic, cousin of mine," Rhegorios said admiringly. "By the good god, we really could do it, too."

"I know we could," the Avtokrator said. "Etzilios has to know it, too. We did it once, three years ago, and we almost put paid to him. He has to think we'd try it again. I'm not going to ship an army out of Videssos the city, on the off chance that he'd try using his siege towers again instead of retreating, and get inside because we'd weakened the garrison. But he won't know that, and I'm going to make it look as much as if we *are* moving troops as I can."

"What now, your Majesty?" Thrax asked again.

"Now we go back to Videssos the city," Maniakes answered. "We've sown the seed. We have to see what kind of crop we get from it."

Agathios the ecumenical patriarch called for a service of thanksgiving in the High Temple. He sent the call through Videssos the city without the least urging from Maniakes, who was almost as surprised as he was pleased. Agathios displayed initiative only a little more often than Thrax did.

Maniakes was also surprised at the fervor of the Videssians who flocked to the Temple to worship and to give thanks to the good god. A fair number of them also seemed willing to give him some credit for having smashed the Kubratoi at sea. They knew how desperate their situation had been, and knew also that, while the Kubratoi still besieged them, the risk of the Makuraners' joining the assault was gone.

And then, with timing Maniakes could not have hoped to emulate, a messenger rushed into the High Temple just as the service was ending and before more than a handful of people had filed out. "Your Majesty!" the fellow cried out in a great voice. "Your Majesty, the Kubratoi are withdrawing! They're burning their towers and engines and riding away!"

"We bless thee, Phos, lord with the great and good mind!" Agathios exclaimed, and his voice came echoing back from the dome wherein the great mosaic image of Phos stern in judgment looked down on his congregation. Even Phos' majestic face seemed less harsh at that moment, the Avtokrator thought.

"This I will see for myself," Maniakes declared. For the first time since marrying Lysia, he left the High Temple accompanied by cheers. Though judging those cheers aimed less at himself than at the news the messenger brought, Maniakes was glad of them all the same.

He saw long before reaching the city wall that the messenger had spoken the truth. Black clouds of smoke rose into the sky to the east. Maniakes had seen such clouds before, when the Kubratoi came down to raid as far as the wall. Then they had been Videssian fields and farmlands going up in flames.

This time, the Kubratoi had not merely come up to the wall. They had set foot on it, which no invaders in all the history of the Empire of Videssos had done before them. But, though they had done so much, they had done no more; the defenders and the great strength of the walls themselves had made sure of that. What they burned now was of their own substance, which they could not take with them lest it slow them in their retreat, and which they did not care to leave lest the Videssians take it and use it against them.

When Maniakes went up onto the wall, the picture became sweeter still. The siege towers the Videssians had not been able to set afire burned now. So did the stone-throwers the Makuraner engineers had taught the Kubratoi to build. "We would have saved those, had this been our campaign," a Videssian officer said, pointing out toward them.

"Aye, so we would," Maniakes answered. He'd carried a baggage train full of the parts needed for siege engines throughout the Land of the Thousand Cities. "They're nomads, though. They didn't bring supply wagons along with them, and they've been living off the countryside."

"They won't be back soon, not after this," the officer said. "They've failed against us twice running now, and they can't be happy about it. With any luck, they'll have a nice little civil war over what went wrong and who was to blame."

"From your mouth to Phos' ear," Maniakes said fervently. It didn't look as if any stone-throwers at all were going back north with the Kubratoi. He wondered if their artisans would be able to make new ones without models before them. They probably would, he thought with no small regret. Underestimating how clever his foes were did no good.

"Are we going to pursue, your Majesty?" the officer asked, avid as any Videssian to pick up news that was really none of his business.

"Right now, I think I'm willing to let them go," the Avtokrator said. The officer's disappointed look would have drawn applause had he been a mime in a Midwinter's Day show. So would the way he brightened with excitement when Maniakes added, "And I'll tell you why." He went on, "I don't want my soldiers chasing the Kubratoi away from what has to be the main center of action. The most important thing we can do is get the westlands back from the Makuraners. Chasing the Kubratoi, however delightful it might be, distracts us from what needs doing more."

"Ah." The captain saluted. "This I can understand." Videssians could be, and often were, ruthlessly pragmatic when it came to war.

Maniakes watched the Kubratoi engines smolder. The wind shifted, blowing harsh smoke into his face. His eyes stung. He coughed several times. And then he started to laugh. The officer stared at him for a moment. He started laughing, too. The sweet sound spread up and down the wall, till every soldier in the garrison seemed to be letting out his relief in one long burst of hilarity. Maniakes hoped the Kubratoi had not fled too far to hear that laughter. It would have wounded them almost as badly as the Videssians' stalwart defense had done. *Take that, magnifolent Etzilios,* the Avtokrator thought.

* * *

The elder Maniakes raised a silver winecup high. "Here's to half the battle won!" he said, and drained the cup.

Maniakes drank that toast without hesitation. It was exactly how he viewed the situation himself. Lysia, however, spoke with some asperity: "It's more than half the battle, I'd say. The Kubratoi and the Makuraners had the one chance to work together, and we've ruined it. They'll never put that alliance back together again, because we'll never let them."

"You're right, lass, you're right," the elder Maniakes said, making a placating gesture. "Every word you say is true—and far be it from me to argue with my daughter-in-law. My son would probably put my head up on the Milestone for that, with a big placard saying what a naughty fellow I'd been." He made as if to shrink from the Avtokrator.

"It would need to be a very big placard, to get all that on," Maniakes said with a snort. But even his father's drollery had calculation in it. Lysia had been the elder Maniakes' niece all her life. He did not mention that family tie now, as Rhegorios often did. He would not speak out against the marriage Maniakes had made, but he did not speak for it, either.

"You're right, Lysia—and you're wrong," Symvatios said. "Yes, we've forced the Kubratoi and the Makuraners apart again, and that's a very great triumph again. I don't say it isn't. But—" He pointed west. "—there's Abivard still, practically close enough to spit on. Till we drive him back where he belongs, we're missing a good piece from a whole victory."

"Will we sail back to Lyssaion, or through the Videssian Sea to Erzerum?" Rhegorios asked. "Getting late in the year to do either, worse luck."

"I'd like to," Maniakes said. "Now that we don't have to worry about the Kubratoi any more—or don't have to worry about them sacking the city, anyhow—we could."

He looked from his father to his uncle to his cousin to his wife. None of them seemed to think much of the idea. After a brief pause, the elder Maniakes said, "It's late in the year to hope to accomplish much unless you intend to winter in the Land of the Thousand Cities."

"I could," Maniakes said. "They bring in crops the year around. The army would eat well enough."

"Late in the year for a fleet to be setting out, too," Rhegorios observed. "We've been through one bad storm already this campaigning season. That's plenty for me."

"If I order Thrax to sail west, he will sail," Maniakes said.

"You can order Thrax to do whatever you please, and he will do it," the elder Maniakes put in. "That doesn't make him smart. It only makes him obedient."

"The Avtokrator of the Videssians can command his subjects as he pleases," Symvatios added, "but I've never heard that even the Avtokrator can order wind and wave to obey his will."

Maniakes didn't have such an inflated view of his own place in the world as to disagree with that. Had he had such an inflated view, the storm he and his cousin and the entire fleet barely survived would have made him revise it. He said, "I'll have Bagdasares check what sort of weather we'll have if we sail. He warned me of this storm coming home, and we couldn't get away from it no matter what we did. If he says the sailing will be good, we'll go. If not, not. Does it please you?"

Everyone beamed at him.

Bagdasares prostrated himself when Maniakes came into his sorcerous study. Having risen, the Vaspurakaner wizard said, "How may I serve you, your Majesty?"

If he did not know what Maniakes had in mind, the Avtokrator would have been astonished. Bagdasares would have needed no divination to know; palace gossip was surely plenty. But the forms had to be observed. Formally, Maniakes said, "I want to know if the fleet will enjoy good weather sailing west to Lyssaion later this campaigning season."

"Of course, your Majesty," Bagdasares said, bowing low. "You have seen how this spell is performed. If you will be good enough to bear with me while I assemble the necessary ingredients—"

He did that with such quick efficiency as to remove all doubt from Maniakes' mind as to whether he'd known this visit was coming. He even had several little wooden ships already made to symbolize the vessels of the fleet. Maniakes hid his smile. Had everyone served him as well as Bagdasares, he would have been the most fortunate Avtokrator in Videssian history.

Into the bowl went the ships carved from chips of wood. They rode the ripples there, as real ships would ride over the waves of the Sailors' Sea. Bagdasares began to chant; his hands moved in swift passes above the bowl.

Developments were not long in coming. Maniakes vividly remembered the storm the mage's spell had predicted for the return journey from Lyssaion. The miniature tempest Bagdasares raised this time was worse, with lightning like sparks and thunder like a small drum. One of the little lightning bolts smote a sorcerous ship, which burned to the waterline.

"Your Majesty, I cannot in good conscience recommend that you undertake this course," Bagdasares said with what struck Maniakes as commendable understatement.

"A pestilence!" Maniakes muttered under his breath. "All right— suppose we sail the Videssian Sea to Erzerum, then?" He didn't want to do that. It made for a longer journey to Mashiz, and one in which the Makuraners would have plenty of chances to slow and perhaps even stop him before he ever brought his army down into the Land of the Thousand Cities.

"I shall attempt to see what may be seen, your Majesty," the wizard replied. Like most in his art, he had a sober countenance, but now his eyes twinkled for a moment. "As this route would bring you close to Vaspurakan, so will the sorcery become more precise, more accurate."

"Really?" Maniakes asked, intrigued in spite of his annoyance at the earlier prediction; Bagdasares had never claimed anything like that before.

The Vaspurakaner mage sighed. "I wish it were true. Logically, it should be true, Vaspur the Firstborn and his descendants being the primary focus of Phos' activity here on earth. But if you order me to prove to you it is true, I fear I cannot."

"Ah, well," Maniakes said. "If you could, you'd have a lot of mages in the Sorcerers' Collegium—and in Mashiz, too, I shouldn't wonder—hopping mad at you. All right, you can't be more accurate about what happens on the Videssian Sea. If you can be as accurate, I'll take that."

What he meant was, *If you can show me how to do what I want to do, even if I have to do it in this inconvenient way, I'll take that.* Bagdasares spent some little while incanting over the bowl and the water and the little ships he had made—except for the one that had burned—sorcerously persuading them they now represented a fleet on the Videssian Sea, not one on the Sailors' Sea.

When he was satisfied the components of his magic understood their new role, he began the spell proper. It was almost identical to the one that had gone before, name and description of the new sea and new landing place being substituted for those he had previously used.

And, to Maniakes' dismay, the results of the incantation were almost identical to those that had gone before. Again, the Avtokrator watched a miniature storm play havoc with the miniature fleet. None of the little chip ships caught fire this time, but more of them capsized than had been true in the previous conjuration.

He asked the only question he could think to ask: "Are you certain you took off all the influence from the earlier spell?"

"As certain as may be, yes," Bagdasares answered. "But if it pleases you, your Majesty, I can begin again from the beginning. Preparing everything from scratch will take a bit more time, you understand, but—"

"Do it," Maniakes said.

Do it, Bagdasares did. He chose a new bowl, he prepared fresh— or rather, new—symbolic seawater, and he made a new fleet of toy ships. It did seem to take quite a while, though Maniakes reflected that his wizard was much swifter than his shipwrights. "I shall also use a different incantation this time," Bagdasares said, "to reduce any possible lingering effects from my previous spells." The Avtokrator nodded approval.

Bagdasares went about the new spell as methodically as he had with the preparations for it. The incantation was indeed different from the one he'd used before. The results, however, were the same: a tiny storm that sank and scattered most of the symbolic fleet.

"I am very sorry, your Majesty." Bagdasares' voice dragged with weariness when the spell was done. "I cannot in good conscience recommend sending a fleet to the west by way of the Videssian Sea, either." He yawned. "Your pardon, I crave. Three conjurations of an afternoon will wear a man down to a nub." He yawned again.

"Rest, then," Maniakes said. "I know better than to blame the messenger for the news he brings." Bagdasares bowed, and almost fell over. Wobbling as if drunk, he took his leave. Maniakes stood alone in the sorcerous workroom. "I know better than to blame the messenger for his news," he repeated, "but, by the good god, I wish I didn't."

* * *

With a screech of rusty hinges, the postern gate opened. It was not the gate through which Moundioukh had come when Maniakes tried to detach the Kubratoi from their alliance to Makuran. That one had been made quiet. Now silence and stealth no longer mattered. Maniakes could leave Videssos the city without fear, without worry; no enemy stood nearby.

Maniakes could not leave Videssos the city, however, without his guardsmen or without his full complement of twelve parasol-bearers. He might have vanquished Etzilios, he might have kept the Makuraners on the west side of the Cattle Crossing, but against entrenched ceremonial he struggled in vain.

Rhegorios said, "Don't worry about it, cousin your Majesty brother-in-law of mine." That he was using his whimsical mix of titles for Maniakes again said he thought the crisis was over for the time being. He went on, "They won't get in your way very much."

"Ha!" Maniakes said darkly. But, even with the demands of ceremony oppressing him, he could not hold on to his foul mood. Being able to leave the imperial city, even with his escort, felt monstrous good.

Seeing the wreckage of Etzilios' hopes up close felt even better. Videssian scavengers were still going over the engines and towers for scraps of timber and metal they could use or sell. Before long, nothing would be left.

"On this side of the Cattle Crossing, we're our own masters again," Rhegorios said, thinking along with him. The Sevastos' grin, always ready, got wider now. "And from where we are, the wall keeps us from looking over the Cattle Crossing at the Makuraners on the other side. We'll worry about them next, of course, but we don't have to do it now."

For once, Maniakes didn't try to peer around the wall to glare at Abivard's forces. He wasn't worrying about them now, but not for the reason Rhegorios had put forward. His worries, for the moment, were closer to him. Pointing toward the base of the wall, he said, "It was right around here somewhere."

"What was right around here?" asked Rhegorios, who hadn't asked why the Avtokrator was leaving Videssos the city before coming along with him.

"That's right," Maniakes said, reminding himself. "You weren't up on the wall then. Immodios and I were the ones who served the dart-thrower."

"What dart-thrower?" Rhegorios sounded like a man doing his best to stay reasonable but one unlikely to stay that way indefinitely.

"The one we used to shoot at Tzikas," the Avtokrator answered; he hadn't intended to thwart his cousin. "The renegade, may the ice take him, was showing the Kubratoi *something*—probably something he wanted them to know so they could hurt us with it. Whatever it is, I want to find it so we won't have to worry about it again."

"How could it be anything?" Rhegorios sounded calm, logical, reasonable—more like his sister than the way he usually sounded. "If something were here, wouldn't we know about it?"

"Who can say?" Maniakes replied. "We spent years in exile, our whole clan. Good thing Likinios sent us away, too, as it worked out; if we had been anywhere Genesios could have reached us, our heads would have gone up on the Milestone. But Tzikas was here in the city at least part of the time, before he went off to the westlands to fight the Makuraners and play his own games."

"Well, maybe," Rhegorios said grudgingly. "But if you're right, wouldn't *somebody* here besides Tzikas know about this whatever-it-is?"

"Well, maybe," Maniakes said, as grudgingly. "But maybe not, too. A lot of heads went up on the Milestone when Genesios held the throne. A lot of men died other ways, too, murdered or in battle or even in bed. And this thing would have been very secret. Not many people would have known about it in the first place, or we would have heard of it years ago."

"There's another explanation, you know," Rhegorios said: "How can you know about something that's not there?"

The guards and the parasol-bearers and Maniakes and even Rhegorios kept on going over the area again and again. Maniakes began to think his cousin was right. He shrugged. If that was so, it was so. Knowing it rather than merely hoping it would be a relief.

One of the guards, a big blond Haloga who wore his hair in a braid halfway down his back, called to Maniakes: "Lord, here the ground feels funny under my feet."

"Funny, Hafgrim?" The Avtokrator came over and stomped where the guardsman was standing. "It doesn't feel funny to me."

Hafgrim snorted. "One of me would make two of you, lord."

That wasn't true, but it wasn't so far wrong, either. The Haloga went on, "I say it feels funny. I know what I know." He folded his arms across his broad chest, defying Maniakes to disbelieve him.

With nothing better found—with nothing else found at all—Maniakes was willing to grasp at straws. "All right, to you it feels funny," he said agreeably. "Let's break out the spades and mattocks and find out why."

The guards set to work with a will. The parasol-bearers stood around watching. Maniakes didn't say anything about that, but he suspected several of those parasol-bearers would suffer accidents—accidents not too disabling, he hoped—around the palace in the near future.

He also suspected the diggers would find nothing more than that Hafgrim's weight had made damp ground shift under his feet. That made him all the more surprised when, after penetrating no deeper than a foot and a half, the diggers' tools thumped against wood. "What did I say, lord?" Hafgrim said triumphantly.

"What did I say, cousin of mine?" Maniakes said triumphantly. Rhegorios, for once, said nothing.

"It is a trapdoor, lord," the Haloga guardsman said after he and his companions had cleared more of it. "It is a trapdoor—and what would a trapdoor have under it?"

"A tunnel," Maniakes breathed, even before one of the guards dug the tip of a spade under the door and levered it up. "By the good god, a tunnel."

"Now, who would have wanted to dig a tunnel under the wall?" Rhegorios said. No possible doubt where the tunnel went: it sloped almost straight down, to dive beneath the ditch around the outer wall, and was heavily shored with timbers on all four sides.

An answer leapt into Maniakes' mind: "Likinios. It has to be Likinios. It would have been just like him to build a bolt-hole—the man could see around corners on a straight line. And Tzikas could easily have known about it." Maniakes shivered. "Good thing it came up so near the wall, where all our weapons would bear on it. Otherwise, Tzikas would have had the Kubratoi dig it open right away."

"He should have done it anyhow," Rhegorios said. "Getting the enemy inside the city would have been a dagger stabbing at our heart."

"When it comes to scheming, there's nobody to match Tzikas,"

Maniakes answered. "But when it comes to fighting, he's always been on the cautious side. We've seen that before. Me, now, I think you're right, cousin of mine. If that had been me out there, I'd have tried to break in no matter what kind of losses I took doing it. But I'm Tzikas' opposite. I can't plot the way he does, but I'll stick my neck out when there's a battle going on."

"Yes, and you've almost had a sword come down on it a time or two, too," Rhegorios said, which would have made Maniakes angry had he not known it was true. In musing tones, the Sevastos went on, "I wonder why Likinios never got to use the hole he made for himself."

"I wonder if we'll ever know," Maniakes said. "I have my doubts about that. We were just saying how most of the people who served Likinios are dead. Genesios made sure they were dead after he took over." He blinked. "Kameas was around, though, and he's still here." He snapped his fingers. "By the good god, I wonder if he's known about this tunnel all along. Have to ask him when we get back to the palaces."

"What do we do about it in the meantime?" Rhegorios asked, pointing down into the black mouth of the tunnel.

"Fill it up," Maniakes said at once. "It's more dangerous to us than it's ever likely to be useful."

Rhegorios plucked at his beard while he thought that over. After a few seconds, he nodded. "Good," he said.

"A tunnel, your Majesty?" Kameas' eyes grew round. The soft flesh under his beardless chin wobbled as he drew back in surprise. "No." He sketched Phos' sun-sign above his heart. "I never heard of such a thing. But then, you must remember, Likinios Avtokrator was always one to hold what he knew as close as he could."

"That's so," Maniakes said. Rhegorios looked to him for the agreement: the Sevastos had never known Likinios himself. The Avtokrator continued, "If the secret was so good even you didn't know it, esteemed sir, why didn't Likinios use it when he saw Genesios was going to overthrow him?"

"That, your Majesty, I may perhaps be able to answer," Kameas replied. "Throughout Genesios' rebellion, Likinios never took him seriously enough. He would call him 'commander of a hundred,' as if to say no one with such small responsibility could hope to cast down the Avtokrator of the Videssians."

"He must not have realized how much the army on the Astris hated him, there at the end," Maniakes said.

"And everyone else, there at the end," the vestiarios agreed. "The guards at the Silver Gate opened it to let Genesios' soldiers into Videssos the city. Nothing, they said, could be worse than Likinios." His eyes were far away, looking back across the years. "Soon enough, Genesios let them—let all of us—know they were mistaken."

"Likinios was clever," Maniakes said. "He had to have been clever, or he wouldn't have ruled the Empire for twenty years, he wouldn't have convinced a man as able as my father that he had no chance for the throne, and he wouldn't have used the war to restore Sharbaraz to the Makuraner throne to gain so much. But he was clever about things, about ideas, not so much about people and feelings. In the end, that cost him."

"We used to say, your Majesty—we of his court, I mean—that he thought like a eunuch," Kameas said. "It was neither compliment nor condemnation. But he seemed somewhat separated from most of mankind, as we are, and divorced from the passions roiling mankind as well."

"I suspect my father would agree with you," Maniakes answered. "I doubt he ever would have said so while Likinios was alive, though."

"The trouble with what Likinios did was that it needed him on the throne to keep it working," Rhegorios observed. "Once we had Genesios instead, it fell apart faster and worse than it would have if it were simpler." He turned toward Maniakes with that impudent look on his face. "I'm glad you're nice and simple, cousin of mine your Majesty."

"I'll simple you," Maniakes said. He and his cousin both laughed. The Avtokrator suddenly sobered. "Do you know, all at once I think I begin to understand Tzikas."

"I'm so sorry for you!" Rhegorios exclaimed. "Here, sit down and stay quiet, you poor fellow. I'll send for Philetos from the Sorcerers' Collegium and for Agathios the patriarch, too. Between the two of them, they ought to be able to exorcise whatever evil spirit's got its claws in you."

Maniakes laughed again, but persisted: "By the good god, I mean it. Tzikas must have learned a lot, serving under Likinios. He couldn't have helped it, sly as he was—still is, worse luck. I don't know whether he decided to be just like Likinios the way sons decide to be like their fathers, but I'd bet it was something like that. And he *is* just like Likinios—or rather, he's just what Likinios would have been without integrity."

"Your Majesty, I believe you are correct," Kameas said. "I admit, however, that my experience with Tzikas is limited."

"I wish mine were." But Maniakes refused to let himself get downhearted. "He's not my worry now, Phos be praised. He's Abivard's worry, there on the far side of the Cattle Crossing. Abivard's welcome to him, as far as I'm concerned."

The mention of Abivard brought silence in its wake, as it often did. "Why is he still sitting in Across?" Rhegorios said at last. "What will he do now that he knows he can't get over the strait and attack us?"

He and Maniakes and their kin had been asking one another the same question since they'd crushed the Kubratoi on the sea. "We still don't know, curse it," Maniakes said. "I've been trying to figure it out, these past few days. Maybe he thinks Etzilios will be able to bring the Kubratoi south again and start up the siege once more."

"He cannot be so foolish, can he, your Majesty?" Kameas said, at the same times as Rhegorios was vehemently shaking his head.

Maniakes spread his hands. "All right. I didn't really believe that myself. Etzilios is going to be lucky if someone doesn't take his head for leading the nomads into disaster." He spoke with the somber satisfaction any man can feel on contemplating his enemy's discomfiture. "But if that's not the answer, what is?"

Rhegorios said, "As long as he's over there—" He nodded west, toward the suburb of Videssos the city. "—he blocks our easiest way into the westlands."

"That's true," Maniakes said. "Still, with us having a fleet and him not, we can bring our men in wherever we want, whenever we want—if the weather lets us, of course. But even in the dark days, before we had any kind of army worth mentioning, we were using ships to put raiders into the westlands and get them out again."

"Not that we've stopped since," Rhegorios said.

"Hardly," Maniakes agreed. "We've had rather bigger things going on beside that, though." Rhegorios and Kameas both nodded. Maniakes went on, "Cousin of mine, you hold a piece of the truth, but I don't think you have all of it. As I say, I've been thinking about this ever since we saw that Abivard wasn't going anywhere."

"We all have," Rhegorios said. He grinned. "But do enlighten us, then, O sage of the age."

"I'll try, cousin of mine, though after that buildup whatever I say won't sound like much," Maniakes answered. He and Rhegorios both laughed. The corners of Kameas' mouth slid upward, too, slowly, as if the vestiarios didn't want that to happen but discovered he couldn't help himself. Maniakes continued, "The frightening thing about this siege is how close it came to working. The other frightening thing is that we didn't see it coming till it was here. Sharbaraz King of Kings—may the ice take him—prepared his ground ever so well."

"All true," Rhegorios said. "The lord with the great and good mind knows it's all true. If that messenger hadn't made it through the Land of the Thousand Cities—" He shivered. "It was a *good* plan."

"Aye," Maniakes said. "And Abivard did everything he could to make it work, too. He got engineers over the Cattle Crossing. He got Tzikas over the Cattle Crossing. By the good god, he crossed over himself. The only thing he couldn't do was get a good-sized chunk of his army across, and that wasn't his fault. He had to depend on the Kubrati fleet, and we smashed it."

"All true," Rhegorios said. "And so?"

"The planning was splendid. We all agree about that," Maniakes said. The Sevastos and the vestiarios both nodded. "Abivard did everything possible to get it to work." More nods. "But it didn't." Still more nods. Maniakes smiled, once more enjoying a foe's predicament. "When Sharbaraz King of Kings, being who he is, being what he is, finds out it didn't work, *what will he do*?"

"Phos," Rhegorios whispered.

"Not exactly," Maniakes said. "But he is the fellow who had a shrine for the God made over in his own image, remember. Anyone who'd do that isn't the sort of fellow who's likely to stay calm when things go wrong, is he? And who knows Sharbaraz King of Kings better than Abivard?"

"Phos," Rhegorios said again, this time most reverently. "He doesn't dare go home, does he?"

"I don't know whether I'd go that far," Maniakes answered. "But he has to be thinking about it. We would be, if that were us over there. The Makuraners may play the game a little more politely than we do, but it's the same game. Sharbaraz will be looking for someone to blame."

"He could blame Etzilios, your Majesty," Kameas said. "The fault, as you pointed out, lay in the Kubrati fleet."

"Yes, he could do that," Maniakes agreed. "He probably even does do that, or will when the news reaches him, if it hasn't got there yet. But how much good will that do him? Even if he blames Etzilios, he can't punish him. He was lucky to get an embassy to Kubrat. He'd never get an army there."

Rhegorios said, "Half the fun of blaming someone is punishing him for whatever he did wrong."

Maniakes hadn't thought of it as fun. He'd worried about what was practical and what wasn't. But his freewheeling cousin had a point. When you were King of Kings of Makuran—or, for that matter, Avtokrator of the Videssians—you could, if you wanted, do exactly *as* you wanted. Punishing those who failed you was one of the perquisites—sometimes one of the enjoyable perquisites—of the position.

Musingly, Kameas said, "I wonder how we could best exploit whatever disaffection may exist between Sharbaraz and Abivard, or create such disaffection if none exists at present."

Maniakes clapped the vestiarios on the back. "The Makuraners are always complaining about how devious and underhanded we Videssians are. Esteemed sir, if they heard that, it would prove their point. And do you know what else? You're exactly right. That's what we have to do."

"Send a messenger—secret but not *too* secret—to Abivard," Rhegorios said. "One of two things will happen. He may go along with us, which is what we have in mind. Or he may say no, in which case Sharbaraz will still get word he's been treating with Videssians. I don't think Sharbaraz would like that."

"I don't, either," Maniakes said. "I'll do it."

The messenger sailed out of Videssos the city the next day. He went behind a shield of truce. Abivard was better about honoring such shields than most officers on either side. Maniakes had reason to expect the messenger, a certain Isokasios, would return intact, if not necessarily successful.

Return Isokasios did, by noon that day. He was tall and lean, with a close-trimmed gray beard fringing a face thin to gauntness. After prostrating himself, he said, "Your Majesty, I failed. Abivard would not see me, would not hear my words, would have nothing to do with me whatever. He did send one message to you: that, since the westlands are, in his words, rightfully Makuraner territory, any Videssian warriors caught there will be treated as spies henceforth. Fair warning, he called it."

"Killed out of hand instead of slowly, you mean," Maniakes said. "They work their war captives to death, a digit at a time." He wondered if that had happened to his brother Tatoules, who had vanished in the Makuraner invasion of the westlands and not been seen since.

"I'm afraid you're right, your Majesty," Isokasios said.

"By Phos, I shall put a stop to that before it starts." Maniakes shouted for a scribe, saying, "I'd write this myself, but I don't want whoever he has reading Videssian for him puzzling over my scrawl." When the secretary arrived, the Avtokrator told him, "Take my words down exactly: 'Maniakes son of Maniakes to Abivard son of Godarz of Makuran: Greetings. Know that, should any Videssian soldier taken by your army within the bounds of the Videssian Empire at the time of the death of Likinios Avtokrator be slain as spies, any Makuraner soldiers captured by Videssos within those same bounds shall likewise be slain as brigands. My actions in this regard shall conform to those shown by you and your men.' " He made a slashing gesture to show he was finished. "Make a fair copy of that if the one you have there isn't, then bring it to me for my signature and seal."

"Yes, your Majesty." The scribe hurried away.

To Isokasios, Maniakes said, "When he comes back with that, you take it straight to Abivard. No secrecy this time. I want the Makuraners to know exactly what kind of trouble they're playing with and what we think about it."

"Aye, your Majesty," the messenger replied. Moments later, the scribe returned. Maniakes set down his name on the fair copy in the crimson ink reserved for the Avtokrator alone. He stamped his sunburst signet into hot wax, handed the message to Isokasios, and sent him off once more.

The messenger came back to Videssos the city at sunset with a written message from Abivard. When Maniakes broke the seal, he grunted in surprise. "It's in the Makuraner tongue. He doesn't usually do that." He clicked his tongue between his teeth. "I wonder if this is something he couldn't trust to a Videssian-speaking scribe. If it is, it might be interesting."

Since he did not read Makuraner himself, he summoned Philetos the healer-priest, who did. When the blue-robe arrived, Maniakes gave him the square of parchment. Philetos read through it once, his lips moving, then translated it: " 'Abivard son of Godarz, servant to Sharbaraz King of Kings of Makuran, good, pacific, beneficent—' "

"You can skip the titles," Maniakes said dryly.

"As you say, your Majesty. I resume: 'to Maniakes son of Maniakes: Greetings.' "

Before he could go on, Maniakes interrupted again: "He still won't admit I'm the legitimate Avtokrator, but at least he isn't calling me a usurper anymore." Sharbaraz maintained a puppet who pretended to be Likinios' eldest son, Hosios. Having seen the true Hosios' head, Maniakes knew Genesios had liquidated him along with the rest of Likinios' clan. The Avtokrator added, "Come to think of it, the Makuraners don't have the false Hosios along with them. I wonder if he's still alive."

"An interesting question, I am certain," Philetos said, "but would you not like to hear that which you summoned me to read?" Having regained Maniakes' attention, he went on, " 'The policy you question was instituted at the command of Sharbaraz King of Kings, may his years be many and his realm increase. I shall not put it into effect until after I have sent your response to the King of Kings for his judgment thereon.' "

Maniakes scowled in reluctant admiration. "I'd hoped for more," he said at last. "All he's saying is, 'This isn't my fault, and maybe I'll be able to get it changed. Meanwhile, don't worry about it.' "

"I should have thought that was exactly what you wanted to hear, your Majesty," Philetos said.

"No." The Avtokrator shook his head. "This gives me nothing I can grab, nothing I can use to separate Abivard from Sharbaraz. He's obeying the King of Kings and referring the question back to him. That's not what I need. I'd rather have him tell me Sharbaraz is flat-out wrong. Then I could either use that to detach him from the King of Kings or else send it on to Sharbaraz and detach him from Abivard."

"Ah. Now I understand more fully, your Majesty," the healer-priest said. "But if the brute fact of Abivard's failure to capture Videssos the city will not cost him the favor of the King of Kings, why should anything smaller have that effect?"

"I'd hoped for this failure to cost him that favor," Maniakes said, pronouncing the words with care; he wouldn't have liked to try it after a couple of cups of wine. "Since it doesn't seem to have done the job, I'm not too proud to try tossing pebbles onto the big boulder, in the hope that they'll tip the scale where it didn't. But Abivard didn't hand me any pebbles."

"Compose yourself in patience." Philetos sounded more like a priest than he usually did. "These things take time."

"Yes, holy sir," Maniakes said dutifully. On the one hand, he'd been patient throughout his entire reign—a necessity during much of it, when he was either desperately weak, beset on two fronts, or both. On the other hand, when he had seen chances to act, he'd often moved too soon, so perhaps he still needed instruction on the art of waiting.

"Will there be anything more, your Majesty?" Philetos asked.

"No. Thank you, holy sir," Maniakes answered. The healer-priest departed, leaving Abivard's letter behind. Maniakes stared in frustration at the document he could not read unaided. He consoled himself by remembering Abivard had written it himself, in the Makuraner script, so as not to have to reveal its contents to anyone else. That was something. It was not enough.

Philetos proved a fairly frequent visitor at the imperial residence over the next few weeks. The Videssian raiders who prowled the westlands had not the numbers to take on Makuraner armies. They observed and used shipborne messages to report back to Maniakes. They were, in fact, a good deal like spies if not the veritable beasts, a point on which the Avtokrator chose not to dwell.

They also made a habit of ambushing Makuraner couriers whenever they could. That always had the potential of being useful, as it had in the Land of the Thousand Cities. A lot of the messages they captured and sent back to Videssos the city were in the Makuraner tongue. The healer-priest had no trouble making sense of them.

Most, unfortunately, were not worth having, once captured. "Your Majesty, how do you profit by learning the garrison commander at Aptos has asked the garrison commander of Vryetion for the loan of some hay?" Philetos asked after translating a captured dispatch wherein the commander at Aptos had done just that.

"I could make a fancy speech about how learning that any one Makuraner garrison is low on supplies might be important," Maniakes replied. "I won't bother. The plain truth is, it doesn't do me any good I can see. They can't all be gems. When you're rolling dice, you don't get Phos' little suns—" Double ones counted as the winning throw in the Videssian game. "—every time out. But you never know what you'll get till you do throw the dice."

"I suppose so, your Majesty." Philetos sounded obedient but less than delighted. Whenever new messages from the westlands came into Videssos the city, he was called away from his sorcerous researches to translate them. "I might wish the Makuraners had the courtesy to write in Videssian."

"It would make our lives easier, wouldn't it?" Maniakes grinned at the healer-priest. "It would certainly make your life easier."

Every few days, one ship or another would bring in a dispatch or a handful of dispatches from out of the westlands. The hill country in the southeastern part of the peninsula had never been so firmly in Makuraner hands as the rest: it lay well away from the line of march toward Videssos the city. Makuraner commanders in the area were always howling about Videssian harassment and complaining to Abivard or to one another that they needed more men if they were not to be overwhelmed.

In the northern part of the westlands, Videssian land forces were weaker, but the fleet, now that pressure on the imperial city had eased, could swoop down and seize a port whenever it liked. The captured messages that came back to Videssos the city from that area were mostly warnings for Makuraner officers to remain ever alert and, again, unending and apparently unanswered pleas for reinforcements.

Studying Philetos' translations, the elder Maniakes said, "They haven't got enough men to do everything they have to do, not if they keep their field army at Across."

"True, but if they split up, they'll have a hard time putting it back together again," the Avtokrator said.

"The more I look at their position, the more I like ours," his father remarked. "They're sinking a little at a time, and the only way they can plug one hole is to let another one leak."

"And we've convinced them they don't dare bring any more

troops forward out of the Land of the Thousand Cities," Maniakes said. "If they try that, we *will* end up taking Mashiz, the way we could have this past campaigning season if Sharbaraz hadn't had his cursed clever idea."

"Too late in the year to send the fleet out now, even if your omens hadn't all been bad," the elder Maniakes said. "But there's next year, and the year after that if need be. The Kubratoi will leave us alone for a while. We can concentrate against Makuran."

"Sooner or later, though, we'll have to go up against the Makuraner field army," Maniakes said. "That's a lot of boiler boys to take on at once."

"Maybe you can split them up so you won't have to," his father answered. "And maybe you'll just beat them. Videssian armies *can* beat them, you know. If that weren't so, Makuran would have owned the westlands for hundreds of years by now."

"I understand that," Maniakes said. "But still—"

Throughout Genesios' unhappy reign, and throughout the opening years of his own, the Makuraners had regularly routed all the forces Videssos threw against them. The Makuraners had become convinced they could do it whenever they pleased—and so had the Videssians. Back in the Land of the Thousand Cities, Maniakes' troops had shown they could face the fearsome Makuraner heavy cavalry on something close to even terms. Facing the entire Makuraner field force, though, was different from facing a detachment from it. If something went wrong . . .

Kameas stuck his head into the chamber where the two Maniakai were talking and said, "Your Majesty, I beg pardon, but another handful of captured dispatches has just come in."

"Thank you, esteemed sir," Maniakes said. "Have them brought here and send someone to fetch Philetos, if you'd be so kind."

"I have taken the liberty of doing that already," the vestiarios said with the slightest hint of smugness.

Philetos arrived about a quarter of an hour later. After bowing to the elder Maniakes and prostrating himself before the younger, he went to work on the parchments Kameas had set on an alabaster tabletop. When he came to one of them, he stiffened and grew alert. "Your Majesty," he said in a tightly controlled voice, "we have something of importance here. This is from Sharbaraz King of Kings to Romezan son of Bizhan."

"Abivard's second-in-command," Maniakes breathed. "You're right, holy sir; that *is* important. What does it say?"

Philetos read through the parchment. When he looked up again, his eyes were wide and wondering. He said, "The gist is, Sharbaraz blames Abivard for failing to capture Videssos the city. This letter orders Romezan to take Abivard's head, send it back to Mashiz, and assume command of the field army himself."

VIII

Maniakes, his father, and Philetos stared at one another. The Avtokrator said, "I never imagined having anything so big fall into my lap. It's almost *too* big. How do we use it to best advantage?"

In a dry voice, the elder Maniakes said, "We've been looking for something that would pry Abivard loose from Sharbaraz. If an execution order won't do it, to the ice with me if I know what will."

Philetos said, "Might it not be best to refrain from interfering? The natural course of events, so to speak, would then remove Abivard from matters concerning us."

"And put Romezan in his place." Maniakes shook his head. "I've fought against Romezan. He's very good, and the soldiers like him. The Makuraners would be as dangerous with him in command as they are now."

"That's so," the elder Maniakes agreed. "By what I've seen, this Romezan is as nasty as Abivard commanding troops in battle, maybe worse, because he presses harder. Abivard is better at seeing past the nose on his face, though."

"Every word of that is true, Father, and it tells me what we need to do," Maniakes said. "If Abivard gone hurts Makuran only a little, what we have to have is Abivard angry at Sharbaraz."

"Like I say, showing him that letter ought to do the trick," the elder Maniakes rumbled.

"Just what I intend to do," the Avtokrator said. "I'll invite him into Videssos the city on the pretext of discussing a truce between his troops and mine. When he's in here—out comes the parchment."

"Will he not fear to come into Videssos the city?" Philetos said, "being worried lest you treat him as in fact his own sovereign intends to do?"

"I think he'll come," Maniakes said. "No matter what Sharbaraz has done, Abivard and I have fought hard but fair: no treachery on either side I can think of. And he must know we know how good Romezan is, and how little we'd gain by murdering him."

Philetos, still looking shaken at the magnitude of what he'd discovered, sketched Phos' sun-circle above his heart. "The good god grant that it prove as you desire."

A shield of truce at her bow, the *Renewal* bobbed in the chop within hailing distance of the beach at Across. Before long, a Makuraner soldier came forward and hailed the dromon in accented Videssian: "Who are you, and what do you want?"

Maniakes, gorgeous in full imperial raiment, stepped forward to show himself to the Makuraner. "I am Maniakes son of Maniakes, Avtokrator of the Videssians. I would speak with Abivard son of Godarz, your commander here. I want to invite him into Videssos the city, that we may confer on ways to end the war between us."

The Makuraner stared at him. "How do I know you're really Maniakes, not just some guy in a fancy suit?"

"Sharbaraz is the one who keeps imposters around his court—all the false Hosioi he's trotted out, for instance," Maniakes answered tartly. "Will you take my words to your commander? Tell him I promise his safety in the city and his free and safe return here the instant he requests it from me. Tell him also that I will give hostages if he doubts my word."

"I'll tell him," the Makuraner said, "or tell someone who'll tell him, anyhow." He hurried away.

Aboard the *Renewal*, Thrax breathed a sigh of relief. So did the shieldmen who had been poised to spring in front of Maniakes at the first sign of danger: a ship within hailing distance of the shore was also within easy arrow range. Abivard did not seem prone to murder even if it might help his cause, but what of his soldiers?

More and more of those soldiers came to stare at the dromon. At Thrax's order, the crew of the *Renewal* had a dart in the catapult at the bow. They'd done good work before, against Makuraners straying too close to the edge of the sea. Now, like Maniakes, they waited before moving.

Waiting ended when Abivard came riding up, sand spurting out from under the hooves of his horse. He swung down from the big, broad-shouldered animal—well suited for carrying a man in full armor, though the marshal wore a Makuraner caftan now—and peered out toward the *Renewal*. When he spied the imperial raiment, he called, "If you are the true Maniakes, what is my wife named?" He spoke in Makuraner so his men could understand.

"Her name is Roshnani," Maniakes replied in the same tongue. He knew he was mispronouncing the name, as he habitually did with Sharbaraz's: Videssian tongues would not wrap themselves around the *sh* sound.

"You are yourself, or else well coached," Abivard said. After a moment, he went on, "You are yourself; I know your voice, and your look. We've met often enough for that, over the years. What would you?"

"What I told your man." Of necessity, Maniakes kept his Makuraner simple. "I invite you to come to Videssos the city. I will give hostages, if you want hostages. What I want is to end the war between Makuran and Videssos. I think I see a way to do that."

"Tell me here and now." Abivard spoke more simply, responding to Maniakes' rusty use of his language.

"I have something you must see. It is in the city." Maniakes waved back over the Cattle Crossing to the imperial capital, the city Abivard had been unable to enter by force of arms. "Will you come?"

"I will come," Abivard declared. "Shall I swim to your ship, or will you send a boat?" He made as if to pull the caftan off over his head, as if expecting to have to swim.

"Get a boat in the water," Maniakes hissed to Thrax, who relayed the command to the sailors. To Abivard, Maniakes spoke in some surprise: "No hostages, marshal of Makuran? I will give them."

"No hostages." Abivard laughed. "If you make away with me, you have to deal with Romezan. I do not think you want the wild boar of Makuran rampaging through what you call the westlands." Maniakes waved to him across the strip of water between them, a gesture of respect: he and Abivard had made the identical calculation.

The boat grated up onto the beach. Abivard, after a few words to his men, got into it. One of the sailors pushed it back into the sea. The men rowed to the *Renewal* with remarkable celerity, as if delighted to get away from all the Makuraners by the seaside.

Maniakes did not blame them for that. He helped them and the man they had come to fetch clamber back up into the *Renewal*.

Maniakes studied the Makuraner marshal. Abivard was not far from his own age, perhaps a few years younger, with a long, thoughtful face, bushy eyebrows and liquid dark eyes, a nose straighter than Maniakes' but hardly less formidable, and a black beard into which the first strands of silver were working. Bowing to Maniakes, he said, "I would have treated the city differently if I had come into it without an invitation." He spoke Videssian now, using it more fluently than Maniakes did Makuraner.

The Avtokrator shrugged. "And the city would have treated you differently, too."

"That is also probably true," Abivard replied with an easy insouciance Maniakes had to admire. "But since I am not entering Videssos the city as a conqueror, why exactly am I entering it?"

"I can tell you that, if you like," Maniakes said. "I'd sooner show you, though. Can you wait? It's not far." He gestured over the water of the Cattle Crossing toward the imperial city, now visibly closer than it had been from the shore of the strait. He had not brought Sharbaraz's letter with him, lest a chance wave splash up over it and blur the evidence he needed to persuade Abivard.

"I have placed myself in your hands," the Makuraner general said. "I shall wait and see whatever it is. If I do not accept it, I rely on you to return me to my soldiers once more. You have fought hard against the armies of Sharbaraz King of Kings, may his years be many and his realm increase, but you have for the most part shown yourself honorable."

"For which I thank you," Maniakes said. "I've thought the same of you, by the bye. Had we started on the same side, I think we might have been friends."

"This thought has also crossed my mind," Abivard said, "but the God—" He dropped back into Makuraner to name his deity. "—chose my sovereign as he willed, not as I might have willed. Being only a mortal, I accept the God's commands."

"Your sovereign certainly knows you're only a mortal," Maniakes remarked. Abivard sent him a curious look. He pretended not to notice it. He did not need to pretend for long, for the *Renewal* came up to the little harbor in the palace quarter. Men stood on the quays to catch the ropes the sailors threw to them and to make the dromon fast to the pier.

Abivard watched the process with interest. "They know their business," he observed.

"They'd better," Maniakes answered. He waited till the gang-plank led from ship to pier, then strode up it, waving for Abivard to follow. "Come, eminent sir," he said, granting Abivard the highest rank of Videssian nobility. "Have a look at what you could not take."

Abivard did, with lively curiosity that grew livelier as they pressed into the palace quarter toward the imperial residence. "So this is what I could not see," he said when they turned a corner and a building hid the sea from sight. "Till now, I gained more detail on things I gazed at from afar. This, though, this is new to me."

Waiting at the residence stood Rhegorios, Symvatios, and the elder Maniakes. Abivard bowed to all three of them. The elder Maniakes held out his hand, saying, "Good to see you again when we're not trying to kill each other."

Abivard accepted the handclasp. "Indeed. Were it not for the army you once commanded, Sharbaraz would not be King of Kings today."

"He is King of Kings today, though, worse luck," the elder Maniakes growled. "But whether he'll be King of Kings tomorrow . . ." His voice trailed away.

Abivard's face went stiff, masklike. "If you have summoned me here to seek to make me rebel against Sharbaraz King of Kings, may his days be long and his realm increase, please take me back over the Cattle Crossing now. I will not betray my sovereign."

"No?" Maniakes led the Makuraner into the residence. Kameas came up to them, carrying a silver tray. Abivard looked at the vestiarios without curiosity; the Makuraner court used eunuchs, too. Considering the way the Makuraners so often mewed up their women, that was anything but surprising. Maniakes took the parchment off the tray and handed it to Abivard. "No?" he repeated. "Not even after this?"

Watching Abivard read it through, he could tell exactly when the Makuraner marshal came to the passage ordering his own elimination. Abivard did not shout or bellow or grow visibly angry. His face just set more firmly into nonrevelation. When he was through, he looked up at Maniakes. "How did you come by this?"

"Luck," the Avtokrator answered. "Nothing but luck. One of

our raiding parties happened to run into the messenger before he got to Across."

"Before I do anything about it," Abivard said, "I will want proof it is genuine, you know."

Maniakes nodded. "I thought you would say as much. You leave as little to chance as you can—I've seen that fighting you. I don't suppose you'll trust my wizards: I wouldn't, in your place. If you want to bring a Makuraner mage over here to test the truth, you may do so."

"That you make the offer goes a long way toward telling me this letter is genuine." Abivard let out a long sigh. "It doesn't surprise me. Sharbaraz has come close to taking my head before, as you may or may not have heard. But I will know for certain before I decide what to do next. One of my two chief mages is a Makuraner. The other is of Videssian blood."

"I knew that—or thought as much, anyhow," Maniakes broke in. "If it weren't so, the Voimios strap conjuration we used last year would have confused you longer than it did."

"Bad enough as things were." Abivard shook his head. "Ride into a canal, head for the other side, and come back out where you started—as I say, bad. But does the truce hold for Panteles, too?"

"Aye, it does," Maniakes answered. "He'll have to stay with you always, though. If he ever comes back into the Empire when he's not under your protection, his head goes up on the Milestone."

"I agree," Abivard said. "I would say the same if you had a Makuraner traitor in your midst, as Videssians have been known to do."

"Speaking of traitors, how's Tzikas these days?" Rhegorios asked.

"Alive," Abivard said. "Unfortunately. Sharbaraz thinks well of him, since he can't possibly aim to set his fundament on the throne of Mashiz."

"That may matter less in the way you look at the world than it did a little while ago," Maniakes observed.

"It may," Abivard agreed. "And, then again, it may not." He looked down at the parchment he was still holding and read through it again. "We shall see."

Bringing the wizards over the Cattle Crossing without arousing undue suspicion proved easier than Maniakes had expected. When his envoy said they were needed for the truce talks, the Makuraners accepted that not only without hesitation but also without further questions. Panteles and Bozorg hopped into a Videssian boat, were rowed out to the *Renewal*, and traveled back to Videssos the city in the course of a couple of hours.

"If you're vague enough," Maniakes said, watching the dromon tie up at the little palace-quarter harbor, "you can get away with anything."

"What do you mean, vague?" Rhegorios' voice rose in mock indignation. "We didn't even tell any lies."

Like Abivard, Maniakes was determined to observe the tests the Makuraner marshal's mages would use on the captured parchment. That meant he had to have his own mages present, lest those working for the other side try to turn their sorcery against him. He would have summoned Bagdasares and Philetos in any case, to make sure Panteles and Bozorg did not try to feed Abivard results that were not true.

Bozorg examined the parchment with the air of a man looking over a fish several days out of water. He was tall and thin and clever-looking, with the perfectly upright posture a column would have envied. At last, in grudging tones, he said, "It does have the look of a document that may perhaps—perhaps, I say, mind you—have come from the court of the King of Kings." As he himself had come from the court of the King of Kings to serve Abivard, that was no small admission.

Panteles said nothing at all. Though he'd been promised safety while in Videssos the city, he had the air of a man ready to flee at any moment. Coming to the imperial capital seemed to have reminded him he was a Videssian, and therefore an embarrassment to other Videssians.

His conscience is still breathing, Maniakes thought. *Coming here wouldn't bother Tzikas a bit.*

Abivard told his mages, "I want you to let me know whether Maniakes is being more clever than he has any business being—" He sent the Avtokrator a look full of mistrustful warmth. "—or whether Sharbaraz really does want Romezan to drop me into the Void."

"Lord, my own provenance will aid us in that," Bozorg said, speaking elegant Makuraner. "By the law of contagion, both this letter and I are in contact with the court of the King of Kings, and thus with each other."

"Go ahead, then. Do whatever you need to do," Abivard said. Maniakes nodded. His heart sped up in his chest. Once Abivard was convinced—if Abivard was convinced—Sharbaraz wanted to be rid of him . . . All manner of interesting things might happen then.

Bozorg set the captured letter on a table, then strode across the chamber in the imperial residence till he stood next to the wall farthest from that table. "Once in contact, always in contact," he said. "If this letter in fact emanates from the court of the King of Kings, the spell I am about to use will draw it to me once more. I begin."

Maniakes could follow spoken Makuraner, but caught only the occasional word of the wizard's chant. Philetos, though, was paying close attention, alert for any discrepancy from a spell and a type of spell evidently familiar to him.

Bozorg raised his hands and made a few passes with them: nothing complicated or ornate, which suggested to Maniakes that the spell was as basic as the arrogant Makuraner mage claimed. Bozorg called out in a loud, commanding voice—and the parchment flew across the room and came to rest on his right hand.

He looked from it to Maniakes to Abivard. Voice cautious, he said, "This does appear to indicate that the letter came from the court at Mashiz, as the Avtokrator of the Videssians has asserted." That was no small admission; coming from the court himself, he was more likely to be a creature of Sharbaraz's than of Abivard's.

Panteles walked over to him and took the parchment. Speaking Videssian, the mage said, "There is a simple test to see whether the letter is to be directly associated with the King of Kings." He fumbled in his beltpouch, eventually drawing forth a new-minted silver arket. "Using this coin with Sharbaraz' image, we can apply the law of similarity to determine the relationship of the parchment to the King of Kings."

"That is sound sorcery," Bagdasares said. Philetos nodded. After a moment, so did Bozorg.

Maniakes glanced at Bagdasares with a certain amount of amusement. Not so long before, Bagdasares had used a Makuraner coin himself when he sorcerously spied on Abivard's conference with Etzilios. Though in his person far away in Mashiz, Sharbaraz played a vital role here.

The Videssian wizard in Abivard's pay went about his business with matter-of-fact competence. His spell, though carried out in Videssian, seemed closely related to the one Bozorg had used. He set the coin on the table where the Makuraner mage had placed the letter. Holding the sheet in his left hand, he began to chant.

"Wait," Bagdasares said suddenly. He, too, produced a coin from his pouch: a goldpiece of Maniakes' minting. He put it on the table not far from the silver arket. "This will provide a check. If the parchment goes to it, you will know we seek to lead you astray."

Panteles nodded his agreement to the change in the sorcery. So did Abivard, who said quietly, "If you are so sure you can prove your own innocence here, that is no small sign of it."

Again, the Videssian mage began his chant. He let the parchment drop from his hand—but it did not fall to the floor. Floating in the air as if it were a wisp of smoke, it drifted toward the table on which rested the two coins, one Videssian, the other Makuraner. Even though Maniakes knew he had captured the message rather than fabricating it, he tensed. Maybe Panteles was clever enough to fool both Bagdasares and Philetos. Or maybe the magic would simply go wrong.

Softly, softly, the parchment descended on the arket blazoned with Sharbaraz's imperious profile. Maniakes heaved a sigh of relief. Abivard sighed, too: the sigh of a man who now had to choose a course he might have hoped to avoid. And all four mages in the chamber sighed as well, having shown their masters what was so and what was not.

Turning to Bozorg, Abivard spoke in his own language: "Tell me, my friend—do I deserve such treatment from Sharbaraz King of Kings?" He did not wish his overlord either long days or many years.

The Makuraner mage licked his lips. If he was from the court in Mashiz, he had to have risen under Sharbaraz's eye. And yet, by the way Abivard asked the question, Bozorg also seemed to have been with the Makuraner marshal for some time. Had that not been so, Abivard would have got rid of him on the instant—or Maniakes would have, in Abivard's position, to keep the mage from upsetting whatever plans he might make.

"Lord, I have seen you in war for some years now," Bozorg said slowly. "All that Sharbaraz has asked of you, all that a man could do: this you have done. For him to pay you back by ordering you treacherously slain . . . lord, there is no justice in that. Tell me what to do. In any way I can, I shall aid you. By the God and the Prophets Four I swear it. May I be lost forever in the Void if I lie."

"I stand with you, too, lord," Panteles said quickly. Abivard nodded in absentminded acknowledgment. The Videssian who served him had little choice but to stay loyal: he couldn't return to his homeland, and who else among the Makuraners was likely to want him?

Abivard spoke wonderingly: "So it comes to this at last. I could have rebelled against the King of Kings half a dozen times, and always I held back, out of loyalty and because my sister Denak is his principal wife. Now I have no choice, not if I want to go on breathing."

"Your sister had a son last year, I hear," Maniakes said.

"At last," Abivard agreed, "and, I daresay, to everyone's astonishment."

"As may be," Maniakes said. "You might go further among your own people as uncle and protector to the infant King of Kings than as an out-and-out usurper seizing power for no one but yourself."

"Mm, so I might." Abivard cocked his head to one side. "May I speak with you alone, your Majesty?"

"You may." Maniakes spoke without hesitation, finding Abivard a most unlikely assassin. The Avtokrator gathered up Philetos and Bagdasares by eye. They led their thaumaturgical counterparts out of the chamber in which they had proved the parchment genuine. Bagdasares closed the door behind him. Maniakes gestured for Abivard to say whatever he had in mind.

After coughing a couple of times, the Makuraner marshal came out with it: "Your Majesty, will you be so good as to invite my principal wife Roshnani—she may as well be my only wife, as I've not set eyes on any of the others for ten years and more—to Videssos the city? No one would think that odd in the least; everyone knows how fond she is of the easier way between men and women you Videssians have."

"Yes, I'll do that," Maniakes said at once. "By the way you ask, though, you sound as if you don't want me to invite her just for the sake of banquets where she can eat with you without scandalizing three quarters of your comrades."

"Half of them, I'd say." Abivard's eyes twinkled. "We have

come a little way, we Makuraners, from what we were when we crossed the Videssian border as refugees all those years ago, Sharbaraz and Denak and Roshnani and I." He grew intent once more. "But the reason we crossed to Videssos—that was Roshnani's idea, not Sharbaraz's or mine."

"Really?" Maniakes said in genuine surprise. Abivard nodded. "Isn't that interesting?" the Avtokrator murmured. "So the real reason you want her here is so the two of you can do a better job of plotting, is it?" Abivard nodded again. Maniakes went on, "There is, of course, the chance I take that you'll be plotting against me, but I'll risk it. She ought to get on well with Lysia, as a matter of fact."

"I can see that," Abivard agreed. "By all accounts, your marriage is as far removed from your customs as mine is from ours."

"Further, maybe," Maniakes said, with a bitterness that would not fade. After a moment, he tried for a more judicious view: "And maybe not, too. I look at mine from the inside and yours from the outside, so my view of the two is different. But I didn't bring you here to talk philosophy. I brought you here to talk rebellion. And if having your lady here will help that, eminent sir, have her you shall."

Roshnani's round, pleasant face proved to conceal a mind convoluted enough to have made her a great success as a Videssian logothete. "Romezan isn't going to want to believe this or to revolt on account of it," she said when Maniakes and Abivard had brought her up to date on why her husband and she had been asked to Videssos the city. "He's a high noble of the Seven Clans, the great families that support the King of Kings."

Maniakes looked at Abivard. "And you're not."

"Not even close." Abivard's smile had knives in it. "I'm just a jumped-up frontier *dihqan*—a minor noble, but one to whom Sharbaraz happens to owe his life, his freedom, his throne . . . minor details. To be just, Romezan doesn't fret about class the way so many Seven Clan nobles do. A good many officers under him would like to think of me as a cursed upstart, but I've started up so high, you might say, that they don't dare."

Roshnani's eyes lit up. "And you know who those officers are, too. You could make a long list of them."

"I could, yes, without any trouble," Abivard said. Roshnani

reached out and let her hand rest on his for a moment. Maniakes nodded thoughtfully. Yes, the Makuraner marshal and his wife were as isolated from their army as he and Lysia were from the people and clergy of Videssos the city.

In a small, innocent voice, Roshnani went on, "And you could add that list of officers from the high nobility—and some officers you know the King of Kings doesn't favor—to Sharbaraz's letter to Romezan, so that it would look as if he were supposed to kill every last one of them, not you alone."

"That's—fiendish," Maniakes said, his own voice full of aston-ished admiration. He turned to Abivard. "If a lot of Makuraner women are like this, I can see why you keep so many of them under lock and key—they'd be dangerous if you let them run around loose."

"Thank you, your Majesty," Roshnani said. "Thank you very much."

"I was right," the Avtokrator said. "You will get on well with Lysia. Will the two of you dine with us tonight?"

"Of course," Abivard said.

"We've grown fond of Videssian cooking," Roshnani added. "We've spent so much time at Across—"

Maniakes smiled back at her, but it wasn't easy. He'd thought he was making a joke with Abivard. Now, abruptly, he wasn't so sure.

When the only seafood the cook served that evening was raw oysters, Roshnani said, "Did you think we were only being polite when we said we liked Videssian food?"

"By no means," Maniakes answered. "I'm not eating fish or crabs or prawns myself these days." He explained why, and had the small satisfaction of watching Roshnani and Abivard turn green.

They recovered, however, to do justice to seethed kid and roast mutton with garlic. The only thing they would not do was pour fermented fish sauce over the mutton. "Has nothing to do with the sea fight," Abivard said. "But I found out how the stuff was made, not long after I came into the Empire of Videssos. I haven't been able to stomach it since."

Lysia said, "Some things are better if you don't look at them too closely. Politics are like that, a lot of the time."

"They certainly are in Makuran," Roshnani agreed. "Here, too?" Lysia nodded. Maniakes immediately thought of the bargain he'd made with Agathios the patriarch to get him to recognize the validity of his marriage to his cousin. He also thought of the scheme for altering Sharbaraz's letter that Roshnani had come up with. Neither of those would have stood examination in the clean, bright light of day, but the one had been extremely effective and the other gave every sign of equaling that.

He raised his goblet of wine in salute. "To Abivard son of Godarz, protector of his tiny nephew."

Abivard drank, but looked unhappy. He'd emptied his goblet once or twice already. "This isn't what I'd sooner be doing, you know," he said, as if the notion was likely to surprise Maniakes.

It didn't. "I understand that—you'd sooner take my head," the Avtokrator said, to which Abivard gave a jerky, startled nod. Maniakes went on, "But since Sharbaraz would sooner take your head . . ." He let his guest complete the sentence for himself.

"Sharbaraz has never given Abivard his due," Roshnani said bitterly. "If it weren't for Abivard, Sharbaraz would be dead or locked up in Nalgis Crag stronghold, and Smerdis would still be King of Kings." *And Makuran and Videssos wouldn't have had this war,* Maniakes thought. Roshnani pushed ahead in a different direction: "Whatever victories we've won in the fight against your people, Abivard's led our armies. And what thanks does he get from the King of Kings?"

"The same thanks Maniakes gets from the priests and the people of Videssos the city for whatever success he's had against Makuran," Lysia answered, every bit as bitterly. At least in the matter of the husbands they saw slighted, the two women did understand each other well.

Roshnani pointed to Lysia's swollen belly. "How are you feeling?"

"Pretty well," Lysia answered. "If I had my choice, though, I'd sooner be pregnant in winter, not through the hottest time of the year."

"Oh, yes," Roshnani exclaimed. That made Abivard smile; Maniakes guessed he'd heard the same complaint from her a time or twelve.

"As soon as you have that list ready, I'm going to want to see it," Maniakes told the Makuraner marshal.

"I expected you would," Abivard said. "I'll have it for you in a couple of days at the latest, I promise. Names have been running around my head all this time I've been eating your excellent food. One I know will top it, and that's Kardarigan. He stands next after me and Romezan."

"That's very good." Maniakes felt like clapping his hands together. "If Romezan thinks Sharbaraz wants him to purge all your officers—"

"—and if the officers think Sharbaraz wants Romezan to purge them," Roshnani interrupted.

"Yes," Maniakes said. "If that happens, Romezan won't be happy with the King of Kings, and the officers won't be happy with Romezan or the King of Kings." He nodded toward Abivard. "You should be able to pick up a few pieces from that, don't you think?"

"What do you have in mind?" Lysia asked. "Once Abivard makes the list of officers, are you going to have Bagdasares sorcerously splice it into the letter Sharbaraz sent, so it looks as if he wants Romezan to do away with all of them?"

"That's exactly what I want Bagdasares to do," Maniakes said. "If it turns out he can't, life gets more complicated."

"Life is liable to get more complicated anyhow," Lysia said. "Abivard's two wizards know what the letter looked like when we got it. If they want to, they can make liars of us."

"You're right," Maniakes said. "If they want to, they can do that." He turned to Abivard. "How do we keep them from doing that?"

"I'm not worried about Panteles," Abivard said. "His first loyalty is to me, not to Sharbaraz. But Bozorg, now—he could be trouble."

"What does he want?" Lysia asked with brisk practicality. "Gold? Titles? Whatever it is, promise he'll get all he ever dreamt of if he keeps his mouth shut at the right time."

"I can arrange that side of it," Abivard said. "I can also put him in fear. Wizards are stronger than soldiers—when they have the leisure to prepare their spells. When they don't, soldiers can skewer them before they're able to do anything about it."

"And, maybe most important of all, you can convince him he's doing the right thing for Makuran," Roshnani said. "By what you've told me, husband of mine, he didn't want to believe Sharbaraz could stoop so low as to send out orders for your murder."

"Sharbaraz has stooped lower than that," Maniakes said.

"I'd like to know how!" Roshnani said indignantly.

Maniakes told her and Abivard about the shrine to the God his soldiers had come across in the Land of the Thousand Cities—or rather, the shrine to Sharbaraz in the role of the God. The two Makuraners exclaimed in their own language and made signs Maniakes presumed were meant to ward off evil. Slowly, sadly, Abivard said, "This is the curse of the court of the King of Kings, who never hears the word *no* and who comes to decide he can do exactly as he pleases in all spheres. I shall pass it on to Bozorg. If he needs one more reason to reject Sharbaraz, he'll have it."

Roshnani said, "If you'd known about that, you would have rebelled against the King of Kings a long time ago."

"Maybe I would have, but I didn't know," Abivard answered; Maniakes got the feeling this was an old argument between them. Abivard went on, "It doesn't matter any more. I have to go into rebellion now."

Roshnani muttered something. Maniakes wasn't quite sure he heard it, but thought it was *about time*.

Abivard nodded to him. "I'll have that list for you as fast as I can write it. The longer we delay, the more it looks as if we're plotting something. Since we are, we can't afford to look like it." Maniakes gave him a thoughtful nod. With a bit of practice, he would have made a good Videssian himself.

Late the next afternoon, Abivard handed Maniakes a large sheet of parchment. "Here you are, your Majesty," the Makuraner marshal said. "If this doesn't do the job, nothing will."

"I thank you for your diligence," the Avtokrator answered. He looked down at the list Abivard had compiled. Because it was written in the Makuraner script, he could read not a name, not a title. Somehow that made it more impressive, not less: thanks in no small measure to its unintelligibility, it seemed magical to him.

But he knew the difference—and the distance—between what seemed magical and what was. Abivard had given him a tool through which he might accomplish his ends. To get the most from the tool, he had to understand how best to use it. He summoned Philetos from the Sorcerers' Collegium.

The healer-priest arrived promptly, no doubt expecting he would be called. He studied Abivard's list for a little while, then looked up at Maniakes and said, "He has been most thorough, your Majesty."

"I thought so," Maniakes said. "There's a lot of writing here, even if I can't make sense out of any of it."

"He begins with Kardarigan, who ranks just after Romezan, and continues through division commanders and regimental commanders, and he gets all the way down to troop leaders." Philetos looked awed. "If it is made to appear that Sharbaraz intended Romezan to execute all these officers, your Majesty, he would barely have enough high-ranking men left alive to let him lead the army."

"Good," Maniakes said. "That's the idea."

He carried the parchment to Bagdasares. The Vaspurakaner mage studied it. "It's longer than I thought it was going to be, your Majesty," he said. "That complicates things, because I'll have to sorcerously stretch the substance of the parchment on which Sharbaraz wrote so that it can accommodate all these names."

"Not a difficult spell, thanks to the law of similarity," Philetos murmured, which earned him a venomous glance from Bagdasares: like men of any other trade, mages did not appreciate being told how to do their jobs.

"It may not matter," Maniakes said. "We still have to see if Panteles and Bozorg will play along."

Leaving Bagdasares to prepare his spell, Maniakes approached the two wizards who had come to confirm for Abivard that the letter ordering his execution truly had come from the King of Kings. As he'd expected, Panteles gave no trouble; his loyalty and hopes rested with Abivard, for whom he was prepared to say almost anything.

Bozorg proved a tougher nut to crack. He stood stiff and erect, wearing not only his caftan but also a nearly palpable cloak of virtue. "A wanton lie is the surest way for a man's soul to fall into the Void and be lost forever," he said. "If Romezan son of Bizhan asks me whether the King of Kings included all these names on the letter, I shall have to tell him no."

He had spirit. He also, perhaps, had confidence that Maniakes could not afford to get rid of him before he'd spoken to Romezan. In that, he was unfortunately—at least from Maniakes' point of view—correct. Eyeing his stern face, Maniakes got the idea he would not be so amenable to bribery as Roshnani had suggested. Again, he wished a foe's principles more flexible.

Picking his words with care, the Avtokrator said, "If Romezan doesn't ask that exact question, you don't have to blurt out all you know, do you? You can truthfully say Sharbaraz did send this letter. You can say he ordered Abivard killed." He realized he should have brought a priest of Phos, to discuss with Bozorg the propriety of telling only part of the truth and lying by omission.

The Makuraner mage chewed on the inside of his lower lip. At last, he said, "I am of the opinion that Sharbaraz has acted unjustly in the matter of Abivard. If my silence helps justice be restored, then I am willing to be silent. But I tell you once more: I shall not lie."

Maniakes ended up agreeing to that, having no better choice. It left him discontented. It left him worse than discontented—it left him nervous. The whole plan rested on a gamble now: the gamble that Romezan would not ask the damning question. What they would do if Romezan did ask that question was something he knew he'd have to worry about, but not yet. Bagdasares' magic came first.

When the Avtokrator returned to the mage's chamber, Bagdasares had already succeeded in expanding the strip of parchment on which the order for Abivard's death was written to a size that would also let it hold the names from the Makuraner marshal's list.

"Not a difficult sorcery, your Majesty," he said when Maniakes praised him. He'd grown angry when Philetos had said the same thing, but now he was extolling his own skill, which was a different matter altogether. "Instead of changing the substance of the parchment, as I had first planned, I merely fused its edge with another, having taken care to secure a good match in appearance."

Picking up the extended sheet, Maniakes nodded. Neither his eyes nor his fingernail could detect the join. A sorcerer probably would have been able to do so, but he counted on no sorcerers analyzing the document till it was too late to matter.

"And now," Bagdasares said, "if you will forgive a homely metaphor, I aim to cut the list of names and ranks from the parchment whereon Abivard wrote it and to paste it into the appropriate place on the one written by Sharbaraz' scribe. I shall attend to the cutting first, as is but fitting."

The parchment Abivard had given to Maniakes lay on a silver tray. Bagdasares had set a silver arket with a portrait of Sharbaraz on top of the parchment. Now he began to chant and to make passes above it. Some of the chanting was in the old-fashioned Videssian of the divine liturgy, the rest in the Vaspurakaner tongue.

Sweat ran down Bagdasares' face. Pausing for a moment, he turned to Maniakes and said, "I have created the conditions wherein cutting is possible and practical. Now for my instrument."

Instead of producing an ensorceled knife, as Maniakes had expected, the mage walked over to a cage and pulled out a small, gray mouse. The little animal sat calmly in his hand, and did not try to escape even when he dipped its tail into a bottle of ink.

"You understand, your Majesty, that the animal is acting under my sorcerous compulsion," Bagdasares said. Maniakes nodded. The wizard went on, "It will—the good god and Vaspur the First-born willing, it will—precisely pick out the text to be shifted from one document to the other."

He removed the arket from Abivard's list, then set the mouse at the head of the parchment. Whiskers twitching, the mouse ran down to the bottom of the list. Maniakes feared its inky tail would smear Abivard's writing. Nothing of the sort happened. Bagdasares' sorcery must have kept anything of the sort from happening. Instead, the unintelligible—at least to Maniakes—characters Abivard had written now turned a glowing white, while the parchment beneath them went black as soot.

Bagdasares let out a sigh of relief. Evidently, that was the effect he had wanted to achieve. Maniakes let out a sigh of relief, too, because he had achieved it. The mage said, "Now to paste."

He coaxed the mouse back up into the palm of his hand. It stared at him with beady little black eyes. Maniakes wondered what, if anything, it thought of its role in the sorcery. One more thing he'd never know.

Bagdasares carried the silver arket of Sharbaraz' over to the letter the King of Kings had sent to Romezan. "I have learned enough of the Makuraner script to be able to recognize Abivard's name," he said, "and I am going to set this coin immediately after it, so as to indicate the insertion point for the text to be shifted."

That done, he put the mouse back in its cage. It began to lick the ink off its tail with a tiny pink tongue. Bagdasares began another incantatory chant. His long-fingered hands moved in swift passes. His tone went from beseeching to serious to demanding. He shifted into throaty Vaspurakaner, a good language for demanding if ever there was one.

Maniakes exclaimed. There, starting where the arket lay, were the names and titles to be shifted to Sharbaraz' letter. The characters in which those names and titles were written remained white, though, and the portion of the parchment on which they appeared, black.

"Here," Bagdasares said, "we have an exact copy of the list Abivard wrote."

"Too exact, maybe," Maniakes observed, examining the document. "For one thing, the margins of the added text are different from those of the letter from Sharbaraz to Romezan."

"I have not yet completed the sorcery," Bagdasares said with a touch of annoyance. The Avtokrator waved for him to go on. He did, muttering now in Videssian, now in the Vaspurakaner tongue. When he stabbed out his forefinger at the parchment, the region of white characters on black grew longer and narrower; names and titles seemed to crawl downward to accommodate themselves to the change.

Watching words move made Maniakes vaguely seasick. Once having written, he expected what he wrote to stay put. But the result was no small improvement over what had been there before. It was, however, not yet perfect. Pointing, Maniakes said, "I don't read Makuraner, but even I can tell two different hands did the writing here."

Bagdasares exhaled through his nose—and a fine nose he had for exhaling, too. With the air of a man clutching for patience as it slipped through his fingers, he said, "I am aware of this, your Majesty. I have a remedy for it." He walked over to the cage to which he had returned the mouse. After he took it out once more, he let out another exasperated exhalation. "A pestilence! The foolish creature has done too good a job of cleaning itself. I shall have to reink it."

He dipped the mouse's tail into the jar of ink again, all the while murmuring the cantrips that made the black liquid part of his sorcery rather than a messy nuisance. That done, he set the mouse at the top of the document, allowing its sorcerously inked tail to slide across a couple of lines of text there.

"That should do it," he said, and picked up the little beast again. "Now we apply the law of similarity to the names pasted onto the parchment . . ."

He set the mouse down at the top of the area where the words were still white and the parchment black. His magic made it walk down the black area to the very end, its tail twisting this way and that till it touched all the names and titles in Abivard's pasted list. And as its tail touched them, they—changed. Now they were written in the same style as the words of the document to which they had been appended.

Once the change of scripts was complete, Bagdasares again caged the mouse. He turned to Maniakes. "Is this indeed how you wish the final document to appear, your Majesty?"

"Well, I'd be happier if it were all black on white instead of half the other way around," the Avtokrator answered.

Bagdasares snorted. "The reversal shows that part of the text still remaining mutable. Has it now been changed to your satisfaction?"

"Yes," Maniakes said. "I hope turning it back into black on white isn't too complicated for you."

"I think I can manage that, your Majesty," Bagdasares said with a smile. Tongue between his teeth, he made a single sharp clicking sound. All at once, white letters turned black, black parchment white. "There you are: one long, bloodthirsty letter, ready to befuddle Romezan."

Maniakes studied the letter. As far as he could tell, it might have come straight from the chancery of the King of Kings. The only trouble was, he couldn't tell much. "We'll let Abivard have a look at it and see what he thinks," Maniakes said. Bagdasares nodded.

When the Avtokrator stepped out of the wizard's workroom, Kameas stood waiting for his command. Half of him was surprised to find the vestiarios there; the other half would have been surprised had Kameas been anyplace else. "I shall bring him here directly," the eunuch said, almost before Maniakes could tell him what he wanted.

Bozorg came up the hallway of the imperial residence with Abivard. Maniakes was glad both of them would be reviewing the document before Romezan set eyes on it. Abivard looked at it first. He read it through, read it again, and then read it a third time. Having done that, he delivered his verdict: "Romezan will have kittens."

"May I see, lord?" Bozorg asked. Abivard passed him the altered letter. He studied it even longer than the Makuraner marshal had done. When he was finally finished, he looked not to Maniakes but to Bagdasares. "This is very fine work," he said, admiration in his voice.

Bagdasares bowed. "Your servant."

"You must tell me how you achieved such a perfect match of the script between the original and that which was written afterward," the Makuraner mage said. "I do not slight my own skill, but I am far from certain I could do the like."

"I'd be delighted," Bagdasares said, preening; he was never shy about receiving praise. "The method employs—"

Maniakes coughed. Bagdasares checked himself. Had he not checked himself, Maniakes might have trodden on his toes. The Avtokrator said, "It might be better if the details remain private." That seemed a politer way of putting it than, *If our magic is better than theirs, let's keep it that way, since we've been at war with them for the last ten years or so.*

Abivard coughed in turn. That worried Maniakes. If the Makuraner marshal insisted that his wizard learn Bagdasares' document-altering technique, Maniakes would have an awkward time gainsaying him. But Abivard contented himself with remarking, "We have our secrets, too, which we would be well advised not to let you Videssians learn."

"Fair enough," Maniakes said. Abivard was dead right in that, and the Empire of Videssos had almost died because Sharbaraz had kept his alliance with the Kubratoi secret so long.

Bagdasares said, "The document does meet with full approval, then?"

"Oh, yes," Abivard answered. "It will serve in every particular."

Bozorg said, "It is the best forgery I have ever seen." Bagdasares preened again. The Makuraner mage went on, "It will make me look at new techniques, it truly will, for nothing with which I am now familiar could produce such a fine linkage between two documents. The joining of new parchment to old is also quite good, but that I know I can equal."

Bagdasares bristled, offended at the notion any other mage was sure he could equal him at anything. Maniakes hid a smile. When he'd first met Bagdasares at the start of the uprising against Genesios, the Vaspurakaner mage had been a journeyman back in Opsikion, and, though proud of his skill, hadn't reckoned it extraordinary.

He'd come a long way since. So had Maniakes. Rising with the

Avtokrator had let—had sometimes made—Bagdasares deal with sorceries more elaborate than those he would have seen had he stayed in Opsikion. It had also let him largely discard *Alvinos*, the Videssian-sounding name he'd been in the habit of using then. Now he truly was a sorcerer as good as any in the world—and ever so aware of it.

Maniakes sobered. Bagdasares' blind spot was easy enough for him to recognize. What of his own? He'd noted his habit of moving too soon and too hard in the direction he wanted to go. But if he didn't spot his own weaknesses, who would tell him about them? He was the Avtokrator, after all. And how could he hope to notice his own blind spots if he was blind to them?

Lost in that unprofitable reverie, he realized he'd missed something Abivard had said. "I'm sorry?"

"You were thinking hard about something there," Abivard remarked with a smile. "I could tell. What I said was, I want to see the expression on Romezan's face when he looks at this letter."

"That will be interesting," Maniakes agreed. "The other thing that will be . . . interesting is the expressions on the faces of all the other officers you've added to the list." His attention suddenly sharpened. "Did you put Tzikas' name there, by any chance?"

"Tzikas' name is on your list, your Majesty, and the God knows he's on my list, but he'd never, ever be on Sharbaraz's list, so I left him off," Abivard said, real regret in his voice. "Sharbaraz trusts him, remember."

"You could tell that story as a joke in every tavern in the Empire of Videssos, and you'd get a laugh every time," Maniakes said. "I'll tell you this: the notion of *anyone* trusting Tzikas is pretty funny to me."

"And to me," Abivard said. "But, in some strange ways, it does make sense. As I said before, Sharbaraz is the one person in the whole world Tzikas can't hope to overthrow. Anyone below Sharbaraz—me, for instance—certainly. But not the King of Kings. Besides, Tzikas knew, or claimed he knew, something that would have given us a better chance to take Videssos the city."

"He did know something," Maniakes said. "I can even tell you what it was." He did, finishing, "It doesn't matter that you know, because the tunnel is filled in by now."

"It does sound like Likinios to have made such a thing," Abivard said. "If Likinios had ever told me about it, I would have used it against you—and then, with Tzikas no longer useful to me . . ." He smiled again, this time as cynically as any Videssian might have done.

"What we ought to do next," Maniakes said, "is get Romezan over here as fast as may be. One of the things we don't know is how many copies of that letter Sharbaraz sent to him. If the authentic version falls into his lap before he's seen this one . . ."

"Life gets difficult," Abivard said. "All those years ago, when Sharbaraz and I came into Videssos, I wondered if we were going into exile. If Romezan sees the authentic letter, I know perfectly well I am." His face clouded. "And my children are all on the far side of the Cattle Crossing."

"We'll attend to it," Maniakes said.

Isokasios rose from his prostration and said, "Your Majesty, Romezan won't come to this side of the Cattle Crossing. I asked him every way I could think of, and he flat-out won't do it."

Maniakes stared at his messenger in dismay. "What do you mean, he won't do it? Did he tell you why? Is it that he doesn't trust us?"

"Your Majesty, that's exactly what it is," Isokasios answered. "He said that, as far as he was concerned, we were just a pack of sneaky, oily Videssians trying to separate the Makuraner field army from its generals. Said he didn't like the chances of his coming back to Across in one piece, and so he'd stay where he was."

"To the ice with him!" Maniakes exclaimed. "I'm not the one who mistreats envoys from the other side—that's Sharbaraz."

Abivard coughed. "Your Majesty, what I've seen since we came into the Empire of Videssos is that there are two kinds of Makuraners. Some of us, like me—and like Roshnani more than me— have grown fond enough of your ways to ape some of them. The rest of us, though, keep all our old ideas, and cling to them harder than ever so we don't have to look at anything different. Romezan is in the second bunch. He's smoother about it than a lot of the other officers who think that way, but he is one."

"He would be," Maniakes said, a complaint against the way the world worked, a complaint against the way the world had worked against him since he'd had the Avtokrator's crown set on his head.

"What do we do now?" Rhegorios asked.

Abivard said, "I will go back over to the western side of the Cattle Crossing and tell him that he needs to come here with me."

"That's—one idea," Maniakes said. Romezan did not want to come to Videssos the city, for fear of what the Videssians might do to him and Abivard. Maniakes was less than keen on Abivard's return to the Makuraner field army, for fear of what he might do with it. He'd finally succeeded in splitting Abivard from Sharbaraz—or rather, Sharbaraz had done it for him—and he neither wanted the breach repaired nor for Abivard to go off on his own rather than acting in concert with him.

He found no way to say any of that without offending Abivard, which was the last thing he wanted to do. He wondered if he could find any polite way to use Roshnani as a hostage against the Makuraner marshal's return. While he was casting about for one, Rhegorios said, "If Romezan will come here, I'll go there. That should convince them we're serious about this business."

"If he wants hostages, he has my children," Abivard said, in a way anticipating Maniakes. He sounded serious, serious to the point of bleakness.

"They don't matter," Rhegorios said, and then, before Abivard could get angry, "As far as he knows, you and he are still on the same side. If he wants one of us over there while he's over here, I'll go."

"He doesn't need you, cousin of mine," Maniakes said. "If he wants a hostage against Videssos, he has the westlands."

"That doesn't matter, either," Rhegorios insisted. "As far as he knows, the westlands belong to Makuran by right. You offered hostages when Abivard came here. Why not now?"

Maniakes stared at him. "You *want* to do this."

His cousin nodded. "I do. Right now, it's the most useful thing I can do, and it's something *only* I can do: I'm a hostage Romezan has to take seriously. That means I'd better do it."

What he said wasn't strictly true. The elder Maniakes or Symvatios would have made as fitting a hostage. Maniakes, however, would not have sent his father or uncle into the hands of the Makuraners, not when they'd proved themselves liable to mistreat high-ranking Videssians. He would not have sent his cousin, either, but Rhegorios plainly thought the risk worth taking.

Abivard said, "Romezan is a man of often fiery temper, but he is also, on the whole, a man of honor."

"On the whole?" Maniakes did not like the qualification. "What if he gets an order from Sharbaraz to execute every hostage he has? Wouldn't he be as likely to obey that order as the one that called for him to kill you?"

Abivard coughed and looked down at his hands, which led Maniakes to draw his own conclusions. But Rhegorios laughed, saying, "What are the odds the King of Kings will send just that order at just this moment? It's a gamble, but I think it's a good one. Besides, as soon as Romezan sees what we've cooked up here—" He pointed to the augmented parchment. "—he's not on Sharbaraz' side any more, right? From then on, he's ours. By the good god, he'd better be ours from then on."

Maniakes hadn't even thought what might happen if Romezan read the altered documents and said something like, *Well, if that's what Sharbaraz wants me to do, I'd better do it.* Thrax might have done something like that, if faced with an order from Maniakes.

But Abivard said, "Romezan might well carry out an order aimed at me alone. He will not try to carry out an order aimed at me and half the officers in the army. He is headstrong, but he is no fool. He could see for himself that in moments we would be fighting among ourselves harder than we ever fought you Videssians."

That did make sense, and went a long way toward easing Maniakes' mind—at least about the prospect of Romezan's turning once he saw the letter. About Rhegorios' going over to Across . . . he felt no easier about that, not even a little.

With his cousin determined to go, though, the Avtokrator saw no way to stop him, not if his going made Romezan agree to come over the Cattle Crossing in return. "I'll send Isokasios back to Romezan," Maniakes said. "If he agrees to cross . . ." He sighed. "If he agrees to cross, you may go over there."

Rhegorios looked surprised, as if needing Maniakes' permission had not occurred to him. It probably hadn't; Rhegorios was used to doing as he pleased. Evidently concluding this was not the moment to argue for his own freedom of action, he said, "Very well, your Majesty," as if he were in the habit of obeying his cousin without question all the time.

When Maniakes ordered Isokasios back to Across yet again, the messenger gave him an impudent grin. "You ought to pay me by the furlong, your Majesty," he remarked.

"I'll pay your tongue by the furlong," Maniakes retorted. Back in his days of exile on the island of Kalavria, a messenger would have stuck out the organ in question after a crack like that. Maniakes watched Isokasios' eyes light up. He wanted to be difficult; Maniakes could see as much. But he didn't dare, not when he was dealing with the Avtokrator of the Videssians. Maniakes sighed to himself. The ceremonial upon which the Empire was founded made life less interesting in a multitude of ways.

Traveling openly in the *Renewal*, Isokasios went off to visit Romezan the next morning. Rhegorios stood with Maniakes at the foot of the piers in the palace quarter, watching the imperial flagship glide over the waters of the Cattle Crossing, oars rising and falling in smooth unison.

Rhegorios said, "When I get over there, I'll feel as if the reconquest of the westlands has started."

"You can feel any number of different things," Maniakes replied. "If feeling them made them real, life would be easier."

"Ah, wouldn't it?" his cousin agreed. "And if what we felt about Tzikas could make him feel what we feel he ought to feel . . ."

"I dare you to say that again," Maniakes broke in. "In fact, I defy you to say that again."

Rhegorios started to, but tripped on his tongue before he made it through. Unlike Isokasios, he was of rank exalted enough to be rude to the Avtokrator. Both men laughed.

Maniakes, though, soon grew serious. "If we do manage to drive a wedge between Sharbaraz and his field army, we also need to figure out how we can take best advantage of that." He listened to his own words, then shook his head in bemusement. "By the good god, I sound like poor Likinios." He sketched the sun-circle over his heart to avert any possible omen connecting his fate to that which his unfortunate predecessor had suffered.

His cousin also made the sun-sign. "You're right," he said. His eyes narrowed in thought. "Maybe I will be the first step in taking back the westlands—taking them back without losing a man."

"You're right with me," Maniakes said. "I don't know if that will work; I don't know what Abivard will choose to do. But we have our best chance now. Which reminds me—I ought to have our army ready to move whenever it needs to. The Makuraners may take more convincing than words can give."

"They always have up till now, that's certain," Rhegorios said.

"That's another reason I need to go over to Across." Maniakes grimaced, annoyed at his cousin for making a connection he hadn't seen himself.

The *Renewal* brought Isokasios back, with the sun not far past noon. The messenger said, "Your Majesty, you and Romezan have a bargain. When I said his Highness—" He glanced over to Romezan. "—would come to Across to guarantee his safety, he looked at me as if I'd started speaking the Haloga language. I needed a little while to convince him I meant it."

Maniakes turned to Rhegorios. "There. You see? Romezan thinks you're crazy, too." Rhegorios laughed at him.

Isokasios went on, "Once Romezan understood you were serious, he swore by his heathen God that no harm would come to the Sevastos in Across, so long as no harm came to *him* in Videssos the city. And he said he'd sail back here on the *Renewal* as soon as the Sevastos got there."

"He won't wait long, then," Rhegorios said. "I'm ready now, which means Romezan will be here this afternoon." He grinned at Maniakes. "And won't he have himself a surprise when he gets here?"

The Avtokrator embraced his cousin. "I still wish you weren't going. The lord with the great and good mind go with you." He and Rhegorios—and Isokasios, too—sketched Phos' sun-circle above their hearts.

Watching the *Renewal* glide west over the Cattle Crossing with Isokasios on board had been easy enough. Watching the dromon sail west with Rhegorios on board was something else entirely. Had Maniakes not had such a desperate need to see Romezan, he would not have let his cousin go. Had he not had desperate needs of one sort of another, he would not have done a lot of the things he had done since the ecumenical patriarch set the crown on his head. He was sick of acting from desperation rather than desire.

When the *Renewal* came back toward the imperial city, Maniakes shaded his eyes with his hand, half hoping he would see Rhegorios in the bow, a sign Romezan had decided not to keep the bargain, after all. He didn't see his cousin. He did see a large caftan-clad man who did not look familiar, though the Avtokrator might have seen him on one battlefield or another.

Sailors made the *Renewal* fast to a wharf. Abivard came up

beside Maniakes. "They're very quick and smooth at what they do," he remarked. "They put me in mind of well-trained troops—which in their own way I suppose they are."

"Etzilios would think so," Maniakes agreed absently. He waited for the sailors to run the gangplank out between the dromon and the shore. Romezan came across it first. When he did, Maniakes could see why his countrymen called him the wild boar of Makuran: he was not only tall but, unusual for a Makuraner, thick through the shoulders as well. He had a fierce, handsome, forward-thrusting face, with his mustache and the tip of his beard waxed to sharp points.

Politely, he prostrated himself before Maniakes, then kissed Abivard on the cheek, acknowledging the marshal's higher rank: no small concession for a noble of the Seven Clans to yield to a man raised over him from the lower nobility. "Lord," he said to Abivard before turning to Maniakes, whom he addressed in the Makuraner tongue: "Majesty, you've made my curiosity itch as much as a flea in my drawers would do for my bum. What can be so important that you'd use your cousin as surety for my safe return? The sooner I know, the happier I'll be."

Having at last lured Romezan over the Cattle Crossing, the Avtokrator now temporized. "Come to my residence," he said. "What you need to learn is there, and I have food and wine waiting, too."

"To the Void with food and wine," growled Romezan, who would have been blunt-spoken as a Videssian and made a truly startling Makuraner. Had Maniakes' Haloga guardsmen understood his tongue, they would have reckoned him a kindred spirit.

Once back at the residence, though, he did accept wine and honey cakes, and greeted Symvatios and the elder Maniakes with the respect their years deserved. To the latter, he said, "When I was first going to war, you taught me Videssians are enemies not to be despised."

"I wish you'd remembered the lesson better in later years," Maniakes' father answered, at which Romezan loosed a deep, rolling chortle.

The Makuraner general soon grew restless again. He prowled along the corridors of the residence nodding approval at the hunting mosaics on the floor and the trophies of victories past. Maniakes and Abivard accompanied him, the Avtokrator answering questions as they walked. When Maniakes judged the time ripe, he handed Romezan Sharbaraz' altered orders. "Here," he said without preamble. "What do you plan to do about this?"

IX

Romezan read through the entire document with the headlong intensity he seemed to give to everything. He kept his face as still as he could, but the more he read, the higher his eyebrows rose. "By the God," he said when he was through. He looked up at Maniakes. "Majesty, I crave pardon for doubting you. You were right. This is something I had to see."

"Now you have seen it," Abivard said before the Avtokrator could reply. "What *do* you plan to do about it?" His voice had an edge that required no pretense; Sharbaraz truly had ordered his execution.

"I'm not going to yank out my sword on the spot and carve slices off you, if that's what you mean," Romezan answered. "If this is real, Sharbaraz has fallen over the edge." His gaze sharpened, as if, on horseback, he had spotted a new target for his lance. "*Is* this real, or is it some clever forgery the Videssians have cooked up?"

He spoke without regard for Maniakes, who stood only a couple of feet away from him. Maniakes was better at holding his features quiet than the Makuraner. Behind the stillness, he was laughing. The only true answer to Romezan's question was *both*; part of the parchment was real, part clever forgery, though Abivard had had as much to do with that as any Videssian.

"It's real," Abivard said, playing the part that benefited Videssos because it also benefited him. "My mages have shown that's so—it's why I summoned them to this side of the Cattle Crossing."

"I will hear as much from them," Romezan said.

Maniakes nodded to Kameas. Bowing to Romezan, the vestiarios glided out of the audience chamber. He returned in short order with Panteles and Bozorg. Bowing again, he said, "Here they are, eminent sir."

To Abivard, Romezan said, "That's right, you brought your tame Videssian along, didn't you?" He dismissed Panteles with a wave of his hand. "Go on, sirrah; what you have to say interests me not at all, for you'll say whatever your master wants you to say."

"That is not so," the Videssian mage replied with dignity.

Since Maniakes knew perfectly well it was so, he was not surprised to discover Romezan did, too. The Makuraner general said, "Go on, I tell you," and Panteles perforce went. Romezan turned his attention to Bozorg. "Do you really mean to tell me Sharbaraz was this stupid?"

The Makuraner mage nodded. "Can you reckon wise any man who would treacherously seek to compass the death of his finest marshal?" He did not say anything about the deaths of all the other officers whose names had been transferred to the King of Kings' letter. Maniakes noted the omission. He had to hope Romezan would not.

"He truly did send that order?" Romezan sounded thoughtful and, unless Maniakes read him wrong, sad.

Bozorg nodded. "He did. My magic—and also that of Panteles—confirmed it." What the wizard said was the truth, as he had promised it would be. What he did not say, and would not say unless specifically asked . . .

No doubt intending to keep Romezan from asking the questions Bozorg was liable to answer truthfully, Abivard said, "You still haven't answered the question I put to you when I first showed you this. What do you plan to do about it?"

"If I do as the King of Kings commanded me, this whole army goes straight into the Void," Romezan observed, and Abivard nodded. "But if I don't do as the King of Kings commanded me," Romezan went on, "that by itself makes me into a traitor, and means some other officer—"

"Tzikas," Abivard interrupted. By the way he said it, he didn't expect Romezan to like Tzikas. Maniakes wondered whether anyone in the civilized world besides Tzikas liked Tzikas.

"Some other officer will get a letter like this one," Romezan finished, as if Abivard had not spoken. "But he won't have orders to get rid of you. He'll have orders to get rid of me." Romezan sighed. Those broad shoulders sagged. "I never thought I would have to turn away from Sharbaraz King of Kings, may his—" He broke off the honorific formula in the middle. "And to the Void with that, too. May his fundament be removed from the seat of the chair he occupies in Mashiz." He went down on his belly before Abivard. "Majesty," he said. "There. Now my rebellion is official."

"I hadn't planned to—" Abivard broke off. The logical consequences of being in the situation came crashing down on him. If he stayed loyal to Sharbaraz, he offered his neck to the chopping block. Beside that, rebellion became the more attractive choice.

Maniakes offered the alternative he'd suggested before: "If you don't care to be King of Kings in your own name, there's still your baby nephew to protect."

Still down on hands and knees, Romezan laughed wolfishly, an effect enhanced by his posture. "I've heard a lot of stories about men who rebel in the name of babies," he said. "Maybe I've heard one where the baby lived and got to rule when he grew up. Maybe I haven't, too."

"I don't have to decide that right away," Abivard answered. "What matters is that I'm in rebellion against Sharbaraz King of Kings—and so are you." He bent down and tapped Romezan on the shoulder. "Get up."

Romezan rose, that wolfish look still in his eye. "By this time tomorrow, the whole field army will be in arms against Sharbaraz. We'll march back to Mashiz, throw him out, get rid of him, put you on the throne, and—" His vision of the future ran out at that point. "And everything will be fine then," he finished.

Abivard did indeed look farther ahead than the noble from the Seven Clans. He glanced toward Maniakes. "It's . . . not going to be quite that simple, I don't think," he said.

"No, it's not," Maniakes agreed. He had been hoping for, and been planning for, a moment like this ever since he became Avtokrator of the Videssians. He had also spent a large stretch of time wondering if it would ever come. He spoke not to Abivard but to Romezan: "What do you propose to do with your garrisons in the westlands while the field army goes up against Sharbaraz?"

"Leave them there," Romezan answered at once. "Why not? We'll be back next year, and—" The difficulty Abivard had seen at once now became apparent to him, too. He looked at Maniakes with no great warmth. "Oh. If we leave, you'll start taking those cities back."

The Avtokrator shook his head. "No, I won't do anything of the sort," he answered. Romezan stared at him, angrily suspicious. Even Abivard looked surprised. He didn't blame them. Liberating the cities in the westlands after the Makuraner field force pulled out had been his first plan. Instead of using it, though, he said, "If you leave the garrisons behind, I'll burn everything in front of the field army and I'll attack it the first chance I get."

"Why would you want to do a stupid thing like that?" Romezan burst out. "If you do, our campaign against Sharbaraz goes into the latrine."

"He knows that," Abivard said, as if to a child. "He doesn't care—or he doesn't care much. What he wants is to get the westlands back under Videssian rule."

"That's right," Maniakes said. "Agree to put the border back where it was before Likinios Avtokrator got murdered, and I'll help you every way I can. Try to fight your civil war and hold on to the westlands, too, and I'll hurt you every way I can—and I can hurt you badly now."

"Suppose we don't march on Mashiz?" Romezan said. "Suppose we just stay where we are? What then?"

"Then Sharbaraz finds out you didn't execute Abivard," Maniakes said, a touch of wolf in his own smile. "Then somebody—Kardarigan, maybe, or Tzikas—gets the order to execute *you*, not for failure, but for rebellion. You said as much yourself."

Already swarthy, Romezan darkened further with anger. "You dare to take advantage of our squabbles among ourselves and use them to steal from us?"

Maniakes threw back his head and laughed in Romezan's face. The noble from the Seven Clans could not have looked more astonished had Maniakes dashed a bucket of cold water over him. The Avtokrator said, "By the good god, Romezan, how do you think you got the westlands in the first place? You marched into them when Videssos looked more like a catfight than an empire, after Genesios murdered Likinios and every general thought he could steal the throne for himself, or at least keep his neighbor from having it. Taking back what was mine is not stealing, not here it isn't."

"He's right," Abivard said, and Maniakes inclined his head to him, respecting his honesty. "I don't like him getting the westlands back, and if I can find any way to keep him from getting them back, I will use it. But trying to get them back doesn't make him a thief."

"I don't think you can find such a way," Maniakes said. "I don't think you have very long to spend looking for one, either of you. You can bargain with me or you can try to bargain with Sharbaraz. If you have any choices past those two, I don't see them."

"You are enjoying this," Romezan said, as if he were accusing the Avtokrator of lapping soup from a bowl like a dog.

Again, Maniakes met the challenge straight on. "Every minute of it," he agreed. "You Makuraners have spent my whole reign, and the one before mine, humiliating Videssos. Now I get a chance to get my own back—literally. You can either give it up and go back to your own land to deal with the King of Kings who put you in this predicament, or you can try to keep it, try to go back, and get chewed up along the way. The choice is yours."

"We have no choice," Abivard said. "Let the borders be as they were before Likinios Avtokrator was murdered." Romezan looked mutinous but said nothing.

"That was the start of the trouble between us," Maniakes said.

But Abivard shook his head. "No. Likinios paid gold to the Khamorth tribes north of the Degird to raid into Makuran. When Peroz King of Kings, may the God cherish his spirit, moved against them, he was defeated and slain, which let Smerdis usurp Sharbaraz's throne, which let Likinios interfere in our civil war, which . . . You know the tale as well as I. Finding a beginning for the strife between us is not easy."

"Nor will finding an end to that strife be easy," Romezan rumbled: a plain note of warning.

"For now, though, on these terms, we can stop," Maniakes said.

"For now." Abivard and Romezan spoke together.

Abivard and Roshnani scrambled down into a boat from the *Renewal*. The sailors swiftly rowed them over the narrow stretch of water separating the imperial flagship from the beach at Across. When they got out of the boat on the beach, Rhegorios got into it. The sailors brought him back to the dromon.

"I am well," he said to Maniakes. "Is all well here?"

"Well enough," his cousin answered. The Avtokrator nodded to Romezan. "Your turn now."

"Aye, my turn now," the noble from the Seven Clans said heavily. "And I shall make the most of it." He got down into the boat. So did Bozorg and Panteles. The Videssian mage in Makuraner pay looked as if he wished he could sit farther from Romezan than the boat permitted.

After Romezan and the two wizards had got out of the boat again and strode up the beach toward Across, Thrax spoke up: "I expect you'll want to get back to the imperial city now, eh, your Majesty?"

"What?" Maniakes said. "No, by the good god. Hang about here—a bit out of bowshot, if that suits you. This is where things that matter are going to happen today. I want to be here when they do."

"Why not just hop out of the dromon and go on into the Makuraners' camp yourself, then?" Thrax laughed.

All Maniakes answered was, "No, not yet. The time isn't ripe." The drungarios of the fleet stared at him; Maniakes was used to having Thrax stare at him. After the fleet had kept the Kubratoi from getting over the Cattle Crossing to join with the Makuraners, he begrudged Thrax his limitations less than he had.

"I presume we're waiting for the cheers that mean Abivard is reading the letter to a joyous and appreciative audience?" Rhegorios asked, grinning at his own irony.

"That's what we're waiting for, all right," Maniakes said. "I asked Abivard to meet with his officers by the seaside, but he said no. He doesn't care to remind them they're going to be cooperating with us any more than he has to, not right now he doesn't. Put that way, he has a point."

"Aye, likely so," Rhegorios agreed. "I'll be glad when we do get back to the city, though; I'll tell you that. They wanted to honor me, so they gave me a Makuraner cook. I've been eating mutton without garlic ever since I traded myself for Romezan. I think the inside of my mouth has fallen asleep."

"If that's the worst you suffered, you came through well," Maniakes said. "I'm just bloody glad the Makuraners let you go again."

Thrax pointed toward Across. "Looks like something's going on there, your Majesty. To the ice with me if I can make out what, though."

Trees and bushes and buildings—some standing, others ruins—screened most of the interior of the suburb from view from the sea, but Thrax was right: something was going on there. Where things had been quiet, almost sleepy, before Abivard and Romezan returned to the Makuraner field force, now suddenly men were moving through the streets, some mounted, others afoot. As Maniakes watched, more and more soldiers started stirring.

Shouts rang out, someplace he could not see. To his annoyance, he could not make out the words. "Move closer to shore," he told Thrax. Reluctantly, the drungarios obeyed the order.

A couple of horsemen came galloping out of Across. Maniakes and Rhegorios looked at each other. No way to tell what that meant. Had the *Renewal* come any closer to the shore, she would have beached herself. Maniakes should have been able to make out what the Makuraners were shouting. The trouble was, they weren't shouting anything after that first brief outcry. Only the slap of waves against the dromon's hull broke the quiet.

He waited, wishing he could be a fly on the wall wherever the Makuraners had gathered instead of uselessly staying here on the sea. After a moment, he thumped his forehead with the heel of his hand. Bagdasares' magic might have let him be that fly on the wall, as he had been for a little while listening to Abivard and Etzilios and, unexpectedly, Tzikas.

Mages on the other side had soon blocked his hearing then. But two of the chief mages for the other side were at least partly on his side now. On the other hand, magic had a way of falling to pieces when dealing with, or trying to deal with, inflamed passions—that was why both battle magic and love magic worked so seldom. And he suspected that passions at the Makuraner assemblage, if not inflamed now, would be soon.

Hardly had the thought crossed his mind when a great, furious roar arose somewhere near the center of Across. He could make out no words in it, but found himself less annoyed than he had been before. He did not think that angry baying *had* any words in it, anymore than a pack of hounds cried out with words when they scented blood.

On and on went the roar, now getting a little softer, now rising again to a new peak of rage. Rhegorios chuckled. "What do you want to bet they're reading through the whole list Abivard came up with?" he said.

"You're likely right," Maniakes answered. "When they shout

louder it must be because they've just come across some especially popular officer."

Abivard had come up with more than three hundred names. Reading them all took a while. At last, silence fell. A moment later, fresh outcry broke out. Now, for the first time, Maniakes could make out one word, shouted as part of a rhythmic chant: the name of the Makuraner King of Kings.

"If that's not 'Dig up Sharbaraz's bones!' in Makuraner, I'm a shave-pated priest," Rhegorios exclaimed.

Maniakes nodded. "Aye, that's the riot call, no doubt about it." He did several steps of a happy dance, right there on the deck, and slammed his fist into his open palm. "By the good god, cousin of mine, we did it!"

Where he was uncharacteristically delighted, Rhegorios was as uncharacteristically restrained. "We may have done it," he said. "We've done part of it, anyhow. But there are still thousands of boiler boys sitting right here next to the Cattle Crossing, only a long piss away from Videssos the city. Getting the buggers out of the westlands and back where they belong is going to take a deal of doing yet."

A Makuraner burst out from among the buildings of Across and ran along the beach. He utterly ignored the presence of the *Renewal* not far offshore—and well he might have, for three of his countrymen were at his heels, their caftans flapping about them like wings as they ran. The swords in their hands glittered and flashed in the sun.

The fleeing Makuraner, perhaps hearing them gaining on him, turned at bay, drawing his own sword. As with most fights of one against three, this one did not last long. He lay where he had fallen, his blood soaking the sand.

"Maybe their whole army will fall apart," Rhegorios said dreamily. "Maybe they'll have their civil war here and now."

"Maybe," Maniakes said. "I don't think enough Makuraners will stay loyal to Sharbaraz to make much of a civil war, though."

"Mm, something to that," Rhegorios admitted. "For so long, though, we've got less than our due that I don't think the good god will be angry with me if I hope for more than our due for a change." He shifted from theology to politics, all in one breath: "I wish I knew which side the dead man was on, and which the three who killed him."

Maniakes could not grant that wish, but the three Makuraners did, almost as soon as it was uttered. They waved to the *Renewal*, and bowed, and did everything they could to show they were well inclined to Videssos. One of them pointed to the body of the man they had killed. "He would not spit on the name of Sharbaraz Pimp of Pimps!" he shouted, his voice thin across the water of the Cattle Crossing.

"Sharbaraz Pimp of Pimps." Now Maniakes, echoing the Makuraners, sounded dreamy, his mind far away across the years. "When Sharbaraz was fighting Smerdis, that's what his men called the usurper: Smerdis Pimp of Pimps. Now it comes full circle." He sketched Phos' sun-sign, a circle itself, above his heart.

"We have the rebellion," Rhegorios said. Solemnly, he and Maniakes and Thrax clasped hands. As Rhegorios had said, success seemed strange after so many disappointments.

The Makuraners on the beach were still shouting, now in bad Videssian instead of their own language: "You Avtokrator, you come here, we make friends. No more enemies no more."

"Not yet," Maniakes shouted back. "Not yet. Soon."

A little breeze flirted with the scarlet capes of the Halogai and Videssians of the Imperial Guard as they formed three sides of a square on the beach near Across. The sun mirrored off their gilded mail shirts. Almost to a man, they looked wary, ready to fight: all around them, drawn up in far greater numbers, stood the warriors of the Makuraner field force.

The waters of the Cattle Crossing formed the fourth side of the square. Sailors decked out in scarlet tunics for the occasion rowed Maniakes and Rhegorios from the *Renewal* to the shore. One of them said, "Begging your pardon, your Majesty, but I'd sooner jump in a crate full of spiders than go over there."

"They won't do anything to me or the Sevastos." Maniakes kept his voice relaxed, even amused. "If they do, they'll have our fathers to deal with, and they know it." That was true. It was, however, the sort of truth that would do him no good if it came to pass.

Sand grated under the planks of the boat. Maniakes and Rhegorios stepped out. As they did so, the Makuraner army burst into cheers. Rhegorios' grin was wide enough to threaten to split his face in two. "Did you ever imagine you'd hear that?" he asked.

"Never once," Maniakes replied. The Imperial Guards, without moving, seemed to stand easier. They might yet have needed to defend the Avtokrator against being trampled by well-wishers, but not against the murderous onslaught they'd dreaded, knowing they were too few to withstand it if it came.

Out among the Makuraners, deep drums thudded and horns howled. The axe-bearing Halogai and the Videssians with swords and spears tensed anew: that sort of music commonly presaged an attack. But then an iron-lunged Makuraner herald cried: "Forth comes Abivard son of Godarz, Makuran's new sun now rising in the east!"

"Abivard!" the warriors of the field army shouted over and over again, ever louder, till the marshal's name made Maniakes' head ring.

Only a handful of his own soldiers understood what the outcry meant. Not wanting fighting to start from panic or simple error, the Avtokrator called to them: "They're just announcing the marshal."

Slowly, Abivard made his way through the crush of Makuraners till he stood before the Imperial Guards. "May I greet the Avtokrator of the Videssians?" he asked a massive Haloga axeman.

"Let him by, Hrafnkel," Maniakes called.

Without a word, the Haloga stood aside. So did the file of guardsmen behind him. Abivard strode past them into the midst of the open space their number defined. As the Makuraner field force could have overwhelmed the Imperial Guards and slain Maniakes before help could reach him, so the guards could have slain Abivard before his men could save him. Maniakes nodded, appreciating the symmetry.

Abivard came up to him and held out his hand for a clasp. That was symmetry of another sort: the greeting of one equal to another. The only equals in all the world the Avtokrators of the Videssians acknowledged were the King of Kings of Makuran.

Maniakes clasped Abivard's hands, acknowledging that equality. As he did so, he asked, "What was your herald talking about—the new sun of Makuran? What's that supposed to mean?"

"It means I still haven't decided whether I'm going to overthrow Sharbaraz on my own account or in the name of my nephew," Abivard answered. "If I call myself King of Kings now, I've taken the choice away from myself. This way, I keep it."

"Ah," Maniakes said. "Fair enough. The more choices you have, the better off you are." He inclined his head to Abivard. "Over the years, you've given me too bloody few of them."

"As you well know, I am not excessively burdened with choices myself at the moment," Abivard answered tartly.

"Shall we get on with the ceremony, your Majesty, your—uh—Sunship?" Rhegorios said with a grin. "The sooner we have it out of the way, the sooner we can find someplace quiet and shady and drink some wine."

"A splendid notion," Abivard agreed. Till then, he, the Avtokrator, and the Sevastos had been speaking quietly among themselves while the Imperial Guards and the Makuraner warriors peered in at them and tried to make out what they were saying. Now Abivard raised his voice, as he might have on the battlefield: "Soldiers of Makuran, here is the Videssian Avtokrator, who has dealt honestly and honorably with us. Who is a better friend for us, Maniakes or that mother of all assassins, Sharbaraz Pimp of Pimps?"

"Maniakes!" the soldiers shouted. Again, the Avtokrator had the bewildering sensation of hearing himself acclaimed by men who, up till a few days before, had bent all their efforts toward slaying him and sacking his city.

"If Sharbaraz Pimp of Pimps wants to slaughter half our officers, what do we tell him?" Abivard asked.

A majority of the men in the field force shouted, "No!" That was the one word Maniakes could make out clearly. The other answers to Abivard's question were far more various, and blurred together into a great din. But, although Maniakes could make little sense of them, he did not think they would have delighted the heart of Sharbaraz back in Mashiz.

Abivard asked the next question: "Shall we make peace with Videssos, then, and go home and settle the man who's tried to ruin all Makuran with this war?"

"Aye!" some of the warriors shouted. Others cried, "Peace!" Other shouts mixed in with those, but Maniakes did not think any of them were cries of dissent.

"On going home," Abivard continued, "is it agreed that we empty out our garrisons to secure the peace and do no more harm to this country than we must to keep ourselves fed?"

"Aye!" the Makuraners shouted again, not with the heartfelt enthusiasm they'd put into the first couple of questions, but, again, without any complaints Maniakes could hear.

"There you have it," Abivard said to the Avtokrator. "What you and I agreed to in Videssos the city, the army agrees to as well. Peace lies between us, and we shall evacuate the westlands to seal it."

"Good enough," Maniakes said, "or rather, almost good enough. Can you give me one present?—an advance payment on the peace, you might say."

Abivard might have styled himself the new sun of Makuran, but his face clouded over. "I have carried out our bargain in every particular," he said stiffly. "If you are going to add new terms to it now—"

"Hear me out," Maniakes broke in. "I don't think you'll object."

"Say on." Every line in Abivard's face expressed doubt.

Smiling, Maniakes made his request: "Give me Tzikas. You have no need to withhold him from me now. Since he's Sharbaraz's creature, you ought to be all the gladder to yield him up, in fact."

"Ah." Abivard relaxed. "Yes, I could do that in good conscience."

He said no more. He had already shown he spoke Videssian well, and could get across subtle shades of meaning in the language of the Empire. Taking note of that, Maniakes said, "You *could* yield him up, eh? Not, you *can* yield him up?"

"Just so," Abivard spread his hands in angry regret. "As soon as I learned Sharbaraz had betrayed me, I realized his protection over the traitor mattered no more—the reverse, as you say. One of the first things I did, even before I announced to the assembled soldiers what Sharbaraz had done, was to send two men to seize him. I would have dealt with him myself, you understand. The two men did not come back. I have not seen Tzikas since that day."

"Did he slay them?" Rhegorios asked.

"Not so far as I know," Abivard answered. "I meant exactly what I said—the two men did not come back. Neither did Tzikas. The only thing I have thought of is that he and they escaped together."

"That is not good," Maniakes said, one of his better understatements since assuming the imperial throne. "If he's escaped with them—"

"Very likely he's on his way to Sharbaraz, to let him know I'm on my way, too," Abivard broke in. Maniakes started to glare: how dared this fellow interrupt him? But if Abivard was a sovereign, too, he was not interrupting a superior, only an equal, which might have been rude but wasn't lese majesty. Abivard went on, "I've sent riders after the three of them. The God willing, they'll pull them down."

"And if they don't?" Maniakes asked. "Tzikas, may Skotos torment him in the ice forevermore, has got out of more trouble than anyone in his right mind would ever get into."

Abivard shrugged. He waved in the direction of the bearded men in caftans staring in at him from beyond the thin cordon of Maniakes' Imperial Guards. "This is the field force of Makuran. It is, I think, the finest army we have ever put in the field. Do you deny it, Maniakes Avtokrator?"

"I'd be a fool if I did," Maniakes answered. "It's taken me my whole reign to build my army up to the point where it can stand against your cursed boiler boys." He finally had troops who could do that, too, but not so many of them as Abivard had gathered here.

"Just so," Abivard said, waving again. "These are the best warriors of all Makuran. Since that is so, where will Sharbaraz Pimp of Pimps come up with their like? We may start the fight against him a little farther east than otherwise, but what of it?"

"Something to that," Maniakes admitted.

"Something," Rhegorios said, "but not enough. If you're not worried about what Tzikas is doing or where he's going, why did you send men after him?"

"Because I wanted him dead," Abivard snapped, sounding very much like a man who would be King of Kings. "And," he added grudgingly, "because with Tzikas and Sharbaraz, you never know, not for certain, not till too late."

"*I* certainly found that out about Sharbaraz," Maniakes said with feeling.

"He was a good man, or as good a man as a pampered prince could be, when he got his throne back a dozen or so years ago." Abivard sighed. "The court and the eunuchs and the women's quarters all worked together to ruin him."

"He had something to do with it, too—what he is, I mean," Maniakes said. "My court is as stifling as the one in Mashiz; you've seen my eunuch chamberlains, and how many women you can choose from doesn't matter all that much, I don't think."

"You give me hope," Abivard said.

"Take it where you find it," Maniakes said. "Plenty of times when I've had to look for it under flat stones myself, so to speak. But Tzikas, now . . . whatever Tzikas does, it will be for himself first. As long as you understand that, you have a portrait of the man."

"This I have seen with my own eyes, I assure you," Abivard answered. For the second time, he waved out to the men of the Makuraner field army. "Do you want to say something to them? They'd like to hear you, I think. The times we've met before haven't been times for talk."

"Haven't been for talk, indeed." Maniakes snorted; Abivard had an unsuspected gift for understatement himself. "My Makuraner is only fair at best." Abivard shrugged, as if to say, *So what?* Maniakes took a deep breath and raised his voice: "Men of Makuran!" Silence rippled outward from the warriors closest to the Imperial Guards. "Men of Makuran!" Maniakes called again. "For years, I have pursued and chased after peace. I fought, but I never wanted this war. Sharbaraz forced it on me—and on you. Now, then, let us take up weapons against each other no more. Let us welcome the peace we have found. Let us put out the flame of war, before it burns us all."

He wondered how that would go over. The Makuraners were proud and fierce; they might take the longing for peace as an admission of weakness. When they stayed quiet after he finished speaking, he feared that was what they had done.

Then the cheering started. The Makuraners pressed harder on the Videssian guards than they had when tension curdled the air. They pressed so hard, they broke through, which they might not have done so fast had they and the guardsmen used weapons against one another. They swarmed toward Maniakes, Rhegorios, and Abivard.

Maniakes wore at his side the sword he commonly carried into battle. He did not draw it: what point to drawing it? With so many Makuraners bearing down on him, if one of them was a murderer, the fellow would have his way. If Tzikas had planned for this very moment, Maniakes was in peril.

No blows came. Tzikas, never popular himself, had apparently failed to imagine an outpouring of affection from the Makuraners for a Videssian Avtokrator. Maniakes had trouble thinking him obtuse for that. He'd never imagined such a thing, either.

A Makuraner shouting his name grabbed him around the waist. The fellow was not trying to wrestle him to the ground. Instead, grunting, he hoisted Maniakes up onto his shoulders. Once up there, the Avtokrator discovered that Rhegorios and Abivard had been similarly elevated. The cheering got louder than ever.

The Makuraners passed the two Videssians and their own almost King of Kings back and forth among themselves. It would have been scandalous if . . . Maniakes shook his head. It *was* scandalous, but he, like the soldiers, was having too much fun to care.

Presently, he discovered he was riding atop one of his own Haloga guards rather than a Makuraner. "Put me down!" he shouted, trying to make himself heard through the din.

The Haloga shook his big blond head. "No, your Majesty," he boomed in slow, sonorous Videssian. "You need this. Soldiers need this." As if Maniakes weighed nothing, he tossed him through the air to a couple of Makuraners who caught him and kept him from smashing to the ground below.

They, in turn, threw him to some of their friends. He nearly did fall then; one of the Makuraners grabbed him around the waist in the nick of time. "Careful, Amashpiit!" exclaimed another Makuraner nearby. "Don't drop him."

"I didn't," Amashpiit answered. "I won't." The fellow who'd warned him helped him lift Maniakes up above them once more. Then the two of them—and other eager, shouting, grinning Makuraners—propelled the Avtokrator through the air again.

In the course of his wild peregrinations, he passed close enough to Rhegorios to yell, "If Kameas saw me now, he'd fall over dead." His cousin laughed—or so he thought, though the crowd swept him away almost before he could be sure.

At last, when he was certain every boiler boy had bounced him through the air at least one and most of them two, three, or four times, his feet touched the ground. The couple of men closest to him, instead of seizing him and hurling him up onto yet another bumpy road, helped straighten him. "I thank you," he told them, most sincerely.

Someone was shouting his name: Abivard. By what had to be luck, the Makuraner marshal had alighted not far from him.

"Whew!" Maniakes said when they clasped hands again. "As part of our ritual for crowning the Avtokrator, his soldiers lift him onto a shield—but they don't throw him around afterward."

"That wasn't part of our ritual, either," Abivard answered. "Just something that happened. That's what life is, you know: just one cursed thing after another."

"I wouldn't call this a cursed thing," Maniakes said in judicious tones. "More on the lines of—interesting. There's a good word." He looked around. "What happened to Rhegorios? Did they fling him into the Cattle Crossing?"

He and Abivard—and, soon, the men around them—raised their voices, calling for his cousin. Rhegorios turned out to be about as far from them as he could have been while remaining on the same beach. When they finally rejoined one another, the Sevastos said, "Now I know how a horse feels when it's ridden for the first time. All jumps and bounds and hard landings—have we got an imperial masseur?"

"I've never asked for one," Maniakes said, "but one of the eunuchs or another will know who the best in the city is." Taking stock of his body, he realized he was going to be bruised and sore in some unusual places. "Cousin of mine, that's not a bad idea."

Abivard brought matters back to the business at hand. "For the moment, we are friends, you and I, you and my army," he said. "If we Makuraners are going to leave the westlands, we had best do it quickly, while that friendship holds. Will you in your turn do all you can to keep us supplied as we travel, or will you understand when we take what we may need from the countryside?"

"As Videssos hasn't held most of the westlands since before I became Avtokrator, I don't know how much I can do to resupply you," Maniakes said. "As for the other, you know the difference between requisitioning and plundering, or I hope you do."

"Certainly," Abivard said at once. "Requisitioning is what you do when someone is watching you." He dipped his head to Maniakes. "Since we are friends—for the moment—and since you will be watching, we shall requisition. Does that suit you?"

Maniakes opened his mouth, then closed it again on realizing he had nothing to say. He had, for once, met his match in the cynicism that came with ruling or aspiring to rule a great empire.

Later, sailing back to Videssos the city, Rhegorios remarked,

"Smerdis King of Kings didn't suit us, so we helped the Makuraners get rid of him and put Sharbaraz King of Kings on the throne. Sharbaraz turned out to be more dangerous than Smerdis ever dreamt of being, which meant he didn't suit us, either. So now we're helping the Makuraners get rid of *him* and put Abivard King of Kings, or whatever he ends up calling himself, on the throne. And Abivard is liable to turn out to be . . ." He let Maniakes finish the progression for himself.

"Oh, shut up," Maniakes said loudly and sincerely. Rhegorios laughed. So did the Avtokrator. They both sounded nervous.

The Videssian army exercised on the meadow near the southern end of the city wall. The soldiers rode and hurled javelins and shot arrows from horseback into bales of straw with more enthusiasm than Maniakes had ever known them to show. Immodios said, "They didn't care for being cooped up in the siege, your Majesty. They want to be out and doing."

"So I see," the Avtokrator said. "They would have been doing in Mashiz, if only Sharbaraz hadn't turned out to be more clever than we thought." Rhegorios' comment went through his mind. Resolutely, he ignored it. If Genesios hadn't overthrown Likinios, Sharbaraz would have been a good enough neighbor to the Empire of Videssos. Since no one was going to overthrow *him* . . . He laughed, though it wasn't very funny. He knew how lucky he was to remain on his own throne.

Immodios said, "We won't have quite the numbers the boiler boys do, once we go over into the westlands."

"I know we won't," Maniakes answered. "Their army will get bigger as they go, too, because they'll be adding garrison troops to it. But that'll make them slow, less likely to up and strike at us: not that they aren't already aimed at Sharbaraz. And besides, I expect we'll recruit a few men of our own once we get over there."

"Oh, aye, no doubt," Immodios said, "men who used to be Videssian soldiers, but who've been making their living as bandits and robbers while the Makuraners held the westlands. The ones who can recall what they used to be will be worth having. The others—"

"The others will end up short a hand, or maybe a head," Maniakes broke in. "That will be what they deserve, and it'll help the better ones remember what they're supposed to be."

He put his horse through its paces. Antelope was glad to run, glad to rear and lash out with iron-shod hooves, glad to halt and stand steady as a rock while Maniakes shot half a quiver of arrows into a hay-bale target. Since other riders gave way for Maniakes, Antelope was convinced their horses gave way for *him*. For all Maniakes knew, they did.

Maniakes enjoyed putting himself through his paces, too. As long as he was up on Antelope, using his body as he'd been trained to do from as far back as his memory reached, he didn't have to think about how best to shepherd the Makuraners out of the westlands. He didn't have to remember the scorn so much of the city mob and so much of the ecclesiastical hierarchy felt for him. He didn't have to do any thinking, and he didn't. His body did what needed doing without his worrying about it.

He came back to himself some while later, returning to awareness when Antelope started breathing hard. His next conscious thought was startlement at how far the sun had moved across the sky. "Been at it for a bit," he remarked to Immodios.

"Yes, your Majesty, you have." Immodios was a sobersides, and sounded full of somber approval. If he reckoned anything more important than readying himself for war, Maniakes didn't know what it was.

Having stopped, the Avtokrator realized how tired he was. "I'll be stiff and sore tomorrow, too," he grumbled, "even if it's not from being thrown all over the landscape. I don't do this often enough to stay in the shape I should." After a moment's reflection— thought, once back, would not be denied—he added, "I'm not so young as I used to be, either." He was tempted to start exercising again, to drive that thought away. But no. The alternative to getting older was *not* getting older, which was worse.

Accompanied by a squad of guardsmen, Maniakes rode up to the Silver Gate and then back along Middle Street toward the palace quarter. The guards were there only to protect him. They took no special notice of the hot-wine sellers and the whores, the scribes and the thieves, the monks and the mendicants who filled the street. But the crowds noticed them. They were the nearest thing to a parade Videssos the city had at the moment, which of itself made them worthy of attention.

A few people, safely anonymous among others, shouted obscenities at the Avtokrator. He ignored them. He'd had plenty of practice ignoring them. Several men in the blue robes of the priesthood turned their backs on him, too. Agathios might have granted him his dispensation, but lacked the will for the ecclesiastical civil war enforcing it on the clergy would have required. Maniakes ignored the priests' contempt, too.

And then, to his astonishment, a blue-robe standing under a colonnade bowed to him as he rode past. Some priests did acknowledge Agathios' dispensation, but few till this moment had been willing to do so publicly. The Avtokrator waited for some outraged rigorist, layman or priest, to chuck a cobblestone at this fellow.

Nothing of the sort happened. Perhaps a furlong farther up Middle Street, someone shouted, "Good riddance to those Makuraner bastards, your Majesty!" The fellow waved to Maniakes.

He waved back. He'd always hoped success in war would bring him acceptance. Till recently, he hadn't had enough success in war to put the idea to the test. Maybe, earlier appearances to the contrary notwithstanding, it was true after all.

Someone yelled a lewd joke that suggested Lysia was his own daughter, not a cousin close to his own age. For a moment, he wanted to draw his sword and go after the ignorant loudmouth as fiercely as he'd practiced earlier in the day. But he surprised his bodyguards, and himself, too, by throwing back his head and laughing instead.

"You are well, your Majesty?" one of the Halogai asked.

"By the good god, I *am* well," he answered. "Some of them still hate me, aye, but most of those are fools. The ones who know what I've done know I haven't done too badly." It was, he thought, the first time he'd not only said that but also believed it.

"How a man judges himself, this lies at the heart of things," the northerner said with the certainty his people commonly showed. "A man who will let how others judge him turn how he judges himself—that is the man whose judgment is not to be trusted."

"If only it were so easy," Maniakes said with a sigh. The Haloga stared at him, pale eyes wide in perfect incomprehension. For him, it *was* that easy; to the Halogai, the world seemed a simple placc. Maniakes saw it as much more complex than he could ever hope to understand. In that, even if not in blood, he was very much a Videssian.

The Haloga shrugged, visibly putting the matter out of his mind. Maniakes worried about it and worried at it all the way back to the imperial residence. There, he supposed, both he and his guardsman were true to the pictures they had built up of their world. But which of them was right? And how could you judge? He didn't know.

Videssian soldiers began filing out of merchantmen onto the beaches near Across. Sailors began persuading horses to leave barges and ships they'd persuaded the animals to board not long before. They'd had trouble getting the horses on; they had trouble getting them off. Curses, some hot as iron in a smith's forge but more resigned, floated into the morning sky.

Not far away, a detachment of Makuraner heavy cavalry stood waiting, watching. When Maniakes, Lysia on his arm and Rhegorios behind him, walked down the gangplank from the *Renewal* to the sandy soil of the westlands, the Makuraners swung up their lances in salute.

Rhegorios let out a soft whistle. "Here we are, landing in the westlands with the boiler boys watching," he said in slow wonder.

"I never thought it would be like this," Maniakes agreed.

"No," Lysia said. "Otherwise, you would have made me stay in the *Renewal* till you'd beaten them back from where you landed."

Was that resentment? Probably, Maniakes thought. He glanced over at his wife's bulging belly. "You wouldn't be at your best right now, not shooting the bow or flinging javelins from horseback," he remarked.

"I suppose not," Lysia admitted. In tones suggesting she was trying to be just, she went on, "You use that sort of excuse less than most men, from all I've seen and heard. You don't leave me behind when you go on campaign."

"I never wanted to leave you behind, going on campaign," he answered.

A single Makuraner in full armor rode toward the Videssians. All Maniakes could see of his flesh were the palms of his hands, his eyes, and a small strip of forehead above those eyes. Iron and leather encased the rest of him, from gauntlets extending up over his fingers to a chain-mail veil protecting most of his face.

Coming up to Maniakes, he spoke in his own language: "Majesty, you know that Tzikas the traitor fled our encampment, accompanied by two others he suborned to treason."

"Yes, I know that," Maniakes answered. Emerging from behind that metal veil, the Makuraner's voice took on iron overtones, too. And hearing his words without seeing his lips was disconcerting; it was almost as if he were disembodied and reanimated by sorcerous arts. But all that paled before the possible import of his message. "I know that," Maniakes repeated. "Are you telling me you've caught the son of a whore?"

"No, Majesty. But one of the patrols sent out by Abivard King of Kings, may his days be long and his realm increase—" Though Abivard did not yet claim the Makuraner royal title, this soldier was doing it for him. "—did run down a confederate of his. The wretch now stands before the God for consignment to the Void."

"That's good news, though not so good as I would have hoped," Maniakes said.

"Wait," Rhegorios put in. "This patrol caught only one of the men who went west with Tzikas?"

"Just so, lord," the Makuraner messenger replied.

Maniakes saw the import there as readily as his cousin. "They've split up to make it harder for your men to catch them," he said, "and easier for them to get the word through to Sharbaraz. That is not good." Tzikas had a way of making his life—and evidently Abivard's life, too—difficult.

"Abivard judges this in the same way," the Makuraner said. "His view is that he will reckon himself rid of Tzikas for good when he sees the traitor's head on a pole—provided it does not answer when he speaks."

"Mm, yes," Maniakes said. "If anyone could bring that off, Tzikas is the man. Your task is the same, either way, though: whether or not Tzikas gets to Mashiz ahead of you, you still have to beat Sharbaraz."

"This is also true, Majesty," the messenger agreed. "But I can swim the Tutub naked, or I can swim it, or try to swim it, in my corselet here. Swimming it naked is easier, as taking Sharbaraz unawares is also easier."

Now Maniakes nodded, yielding the point. "The faster Abivard moves, then, the better his chances of doing that."

"Again I think you speak the truth," the Makuraner said. "The bulk of his army has already headed west." He waved back to his comrades. "We are a guard of honor for your men—and a force that can harm you if you go against the agreement you have made. You are Videssians, after all."

"We are your comrades in this, since it works for our good as well as yours," Maniakes said.

The Makuraner nodded; that was logic he could understand. "And we are your comrades. Know, *comrade,* that we shall always watch you to make sure we stay friends and you do not try to move into a position where you can harm us."

Maniakes smiled at him, none too sweetly. "Even after you drove our armies out of the westlands, we've always watched you. We'll keep on doing it. And tell Abivard for me that I am not the one who has harmed him and I am not the one who intends to harm him."

"I shall deliver your words, just as you say them." The Makuraner rode back toward the force of heavy cavalry waiting for him.

Lysia sighed. "I wish we could come to trust each other."

"We've come further now than we ever did before," Maniakes answered. "If I had to guess, I'd say we've come about as far as we can. Abivard is welcome to keep an eye on me, I'll keep an eye on him, and maybe we can stretch two generations of peace out of that instead of one. Worth hoping for, anyhow." In earnest of that hope, he sketched the sun-circle over his heart.

Close by Across, the countryside had been fought over several times, and looked it. Many little farming villages were nothing but charred ruins, many fields full of nothing but weeds because the peasants who should have worked them were dead or fled. Seeing the wreckage of what had been prosperous farmland saddened Maniakes without surprising him.

What did surprise him was how normal things seemed as soon as his army moved away from areas war had ravaged. The Videssian force traveled behind and a bit north of Abivard's army; had it followed directly in back of the Makuraners, it would have found the land largely eaten bare before it arrived.

As things were, the quartermasters attached to the Videssian army had a harder time keeping it fed than they'd expected. "The cursed peasants get word we're on the way, your Majesty," one of them said indignantly, "and they light out for the nearest hills they can find. And what's worse, they lead all their livestock with them and bury their grain in the ground in jars. How are we supposed to find it then?"

"Magic?" Maniakes suggested.

The quartermaster shook his head. "We've tried it, your Majesty. It does no good. Passion is magic's foe. When the peasants hide their food, they aren't thinking kind thoughts about the people from whom they're hiding it—"

"I wonder why that is," Maniakes said.

"I don't know," the quartermaster answered, showing he was better suited to counting sacks of beans than to understanding the people who grew them. "The net result, though, is that we haven't got as much as I wish we did."

"Have we got enough?" Maniakes asked.

"Oh, aye, a sufficiency," the quartermaster sniffed, "but we should do better than that." Even in matters of supply, he wanted to turn a profit.

"A sufficiency will, uh, suffice," Maniakes said. "After all, if everything goes as we want, after this campaign—which isn't even a fighting campaign, at that—we'll have the westlands back. If we can't get a surplus with the whole Empire restored, that will be time enough for worry." The quartermaster's nod was reluctant, but it was a nod.

Everything went smoothly till the army came to Patrodoton, a good-sized village a couple of days' ride east of the Eriza, a south-flowing tributary of the Arandos, the biggest river in the westlands. Patrodoton, though not large enough to boast a city wall, had hosted a Makuraner garrison, a couple of dozen men who'd made sure the local peasants gave a share of their crops and animals, and the handful of local merchants a share of their money, to support the Makuraner occupation.

Getting the garrison to leave Patrodoton was not the problem. The Makuraners had already pulled out by the time Maniakes' outriders neared the village. Three of the occupiers had married Videssian women, apparently intending to settle down in the area for good. Two of those brides headed back toward Makuran with their husbands, and the father of one of them left with the garrison, too. That was the start of the problem, right there.

The village *ypepoptes*, or headman, was a gray-bearded miller named Gesios. After performing a proskynesis before Maniakes, he said, "It's a good thing you're here, your Majesty, to settle all the treason that's gone on in this town while the heathen Makuraners were running things. If Optatos hadn't run off with Optila and the heathen she gave herself to, I expect you'd already have shortened him by a head. He was the worst, I reckon, but he's a long way from the only one."

"Wait." Maniakes held up a warning hand. "I tell you right now, a lot of this I don't and won't want to hear about. Once the westlands are in our hands again, we're all going to have to live with one another. If someone turned his neighbors over to the Makuraners to be killed, that's treason, and I'll listen to it. If people went on quietly living their lives, I'm going to let them keep on doing it. Have you got that?"

"Aye, your Majesty." Gesios sounded more than disappointed. He sounded angry. "What about the priest, then? These past years, Oursos has been preaching the worst nonsense you ever did hear, about Vaspur the Firstborn and all sorts of heresy, enough to make your beard curl. Boiler boys made him do it."

Maniakes didn't bother mentioning that his own father still clung to the Vaspurakaner beliefs that Makuraners had tried to impose on Videssos. What he did say was, "Now that the boiler boys are gone, will the holy Oursos return to the orthodox faith? If he will, no one will punish him for what he preached under duress."

"Oh, he will," Gesios said. "He's already done it, matter of fact. Thing of it is, though, he's been preaching the other way for so long now, about one in four has decided it's the right way to believe."

You could plunge a burning torch into a bucket of water. That would put out the fire. What it wouldn't do was restore the torch to the way it had been before the fire touched it. And having the Makuraners pull out of the westlands would not restore them to what they had been, either. They'd been tormented for years. They wouldn't heal overnight.

"Have the holy Oursos talk with them," the Avtokrator said with as much patience as he could find. "The good god willing, he'll bring them back to orthodoxy in a while. And if he doesn't—well, that's something to worry about later. Right now, I've got more to worry about than I can hope to handle, and as for later—" He laughed, though he didn't think Gesios saw the joke.

Not only he, but also Rhegorios and nearly every other officer above the level of troop leader, was bombarded with claims from the locals while the army spent the night outside Patrodoton. The officers dismissed a lot of claims out of hand—which meant Maniakes found out about them only afterward, and was sure he never found out about them all—but some got passed up the line till they came to him.

Next morning, he looked at the villagers, all of them in the best tunics that were too often the worst and only tunics they owned. "I am not going to punish anyone for fraternizing with the Makuraners," he said. "I wish that hadn't happened, but the boiler boys were here for years because we were so weak. So—if those are the complaints you have to make, go home now, because I will not hear them."

An old man and his wife left. Everyone else stayed. Maniakes listened to charges and countercharges and to peasants calling one another liars till long after he should have been in bed. But that was the price that came with the return of Videssian authority, and he was Videssian authority personified.

The hardest and ugliest case involved a man named Pousaios and his family. What made it even harder and uglier than it would have been otherwise was that he was obviously the richest man in Patrodoton. By the standards of Videssos the city, he would have been a small fish, but Patrodoton was farther from Videssos the city than the few days' travel getting from one to the other took. That had been true before the Makuraners seized the village, and was all the truer now.

Everyone loudly insisted Pousaios had got his wealth by licking the occupiers' boots or some other, more intimate, portions of their persons. As loudly, the prosperous peasant denied it. "I didn't do anything the rest of you didn't," he insisted.

"No?" Gesios questioned. "What about those two troopers—*our* troopers—who rode into town in the middle of the night six or eight years ago? Who told the Makuraners which house they were hiding in? Who's living in that house today, because it's finer than the one he used to have?"

Pousaios said, "Blemmydes was my wife's cousin. Why shouldn't I have moved into his house after he died?"

That produced fresh outcry. "He didn't just die," Gesios said shrilly. "A boiler boy killed him, and nobody ever saw those two soldiers again."

"I don't know anything about it," Pousaios insisted. "By Phos the good god, I swear I don't. Nobody ever proved a thing, and the reason's simple: nobody can prove a thing, because there's nothing to prove. Your Majesty, you can't let them do this to me!"

Maniakes bit his lip. The case cried out for slow, careful investigation, but that was the last thing the people of Patrodoton wanted. They were out for vengeance. The question was, did they deserve to get it?

Since he couldn't be sure, not on what he'd heard so far, he didn't give it to them, saying, "I'll be gone from here tomorrow, but from this day forth the land here is under Videssian rule once more. I swear by the good god—" He sketched the sun-circle over his heart. "—to send in a team of mages to learn the truth here by sorcery. When they do, I shall act as their findings dictate, with double punishment for the side that turns out to have been lying to me."

Both Gesios and Pousaios complained about that, loud and long. At last, Maniakes had to turn his back on them, a bit of dramatic rudeness that silenced them where nothing else had.

When he got up the next morning, one of his guardsmen, a Videssian named Evethios, said, "Your Majesty, half the people from this little pisspot of a town have been trying to wake you up since a couple of hours before sunrise. Finally had to tell 'em I'd shoot arrows into 'em if they didn't shut up and go away and leave you alone till you decided all by your lonesome to get out of bed. Nothing—" He spoke with great conviction. "—*nothing* that happens here is worth getting you out of bed two hours before sunrise."

"You're probably right, but don't tell the Patrodotoi I said so," Maniakes answered. Through Evethios' laughter, he went on, "I'm up now, so bring them on. I expect the army can get ready to move out without my looking at everything every moment."

"If we can't, we're in trouble, your Majesty, and not just with you," Evethios said, the last few words delivered over his shoulder as he went off to fetch the contingent from Patrodoton.

They came on at a dead run, almost as if they were so many Makuraner boiler boys charging with leveled lances. As soon as Maniakes saw Gesios baying in the van, he knew what must have happened. He could have delivered the village headman's speech for him, idea for idea if not word for word. He tried to tell that to the local, but Gesios was in no mood to listen.

"Your Majesty, Pousaios has run off, the son of a whore!" the headman cried.

"Run off!" the villagers behind him echoed, as if he were soloist and they chorus.

"His house is empty, and his stable's empty, too."

"Empty," the villagers agreed.

"He's fled to the Makuraners, may the ice take them, him, and all his worthless clan."

"Fled to the Makuraners."

"That proves what I was telling you last night was so, don't it?"

"Don't it?"

The choral arrangement got disconcerting in a hurry. Maniakes' head kept whipping back and forth between Gesios and his followers. But the message, delivery aside, was clear enough. He didn't even have to turn his back to get Gesios to stop; holding up a hand sufficed.

"By his own actions, Pousaios has proved himself a traitor," he said. "Let his lands and house and other property be divided equally among all those who have plots adjoining his, with no tax on those lands for two years."

"You can catch him now!" Gesios exclaimed, clenching his fists with bloodthirsty glee. "Catch him and kill him!" The chorus broke down. Instead of speaking as one, the villagers each suggested some new and different way to dispose of Pousaios. Before long, they got ingenious enough to have horrified Sharbaraz's executioners.

"Wait," Maniakes said again, and then again, and then again. Eventually, the Patrodotoi waited. Into something resembling silence, save that it was a good deal noisier, the Avtokrator went on, "As far as I'm concerned, the Makuraners are welcome to as many of our traitors as they want to keep. Sooner or later, they'll be sorry they have them. Traitors are like adulterers: anyone who cheats on one wife will likely cheat on another one, too."

What that got him was an earful of village gossip, some of it going back a couple of generations. The scandals of Patrodoton, he discovered without any great surprise, were much the same as those that titillated Videssos the city. The only differences he noted were that less money was involved here and that fewer people talked about these.

Thinking of traitors, inevitably, made him think of Tzikas. Every couple of days, Abivard would send a courier up to the Makuraner army with news of what he'd learned of the location of the Videssian renegade and the Makuraner Tzikas had talked into riding with him. Every couple of days, the answer was the same: nothing. That didn't strike Maniakes as answer enough.

Although the Patrodotoi would cheerfully have gone on telling him who'd been sleeping with whom and why and sometimes for how much till everything turned blue, he brought that to a halt, saying, "I'm sorry, my friends, but this isn't the only town in the Empire whose affairs—however you want to take that—I have to settle." They gaped at him: surely he could see they were the true center of the world?

He couldn't. The army moved out on time, and he rode with it. Pousaios had given the villagers some tasty new scandal with which they could regale visitors a hundred years from now. And, for all he knew, a couple of his cavalry troopers might have caused some adultery during their brief stay here, women being no more immune to it than men.

West of Patrodoton, a wooden footbridge had spanned the Eriza. Only burned remnants on either side of the river stood now. He didn't think the retreating garrison had torched the bridge; it looked to have been down longer than that. Ypsilantes was of the same opinion. "Aye, your Majesty," the chief engineer said. "Likely tell, some band of Videssian irregulars did the job, one of those years when the boiler boys were lording it over the westlands. Well, no matter."

Some of the timbers his men used to build the temporary bridge were still stained with the mud of the Land of the Thousand Cities. Since it wasn't being built against opposition, the bridge swiftly crossed the Eriza. Waiting, Maniakes reflected that he could have listened to more gossip from Patrodoton, after all.

Ypsilantes was the first to cross by the temporary bridge, to show it could be safely done. The rest of the army followed. Antelope snorted and shied, as he always did when setting foot on a bridge, especially one where the timbers shifted under his hooves as these did. But, having let his master know what he thought of things, he crossed when he found out Maniakes insisted. Maniakes looked back over the Eriza with something like amazement. "One corner of the westlands ours again," he said, and rode on.

X

Aʙɪᴠᴀʀᴅ's ᴀʀᴍʏ, ᴏɴ ʀᴇᴀᴄʜɪɴɢ ᴛʜᴇ Eʀɪᴢᴀ ᴀᴛ ᴀ ᴘʟᴀᴄᴇ ᴀ couple of days' march south of Patrodoton, did not cross the river. Instead, it proceeded south along the Eriza's eastern bank till it came to Garsavra, which lay at the confluence of the Eriza and the Arandos, where the lush coastal lowlands gave way to the west-lands' central plateau.

Maniakes hovered northwest of Garsavra, waiting to see what the garrison there would do. It was one of the shackles the Maku-raners had used to bind the westlands to them; if the soldiers in the town declared for Sharbaraz, the Makuraners were liable to start fighting their civil war on Videssian soil, which was not what Mani-akes wanted.

But the messenger Abivard sent to the Videssian encampment was all smiles. "The garrison unites in denouncing and renounc-ing Sharbaraz Pimp of Pimps," he said, spitting on the ground in a gesture of rejection he'd surely learned inside Videssos. "Nowhere has anyone a good word to say for the tyrant who sent us forth in this useless war."

"Good news, and I'm glad to hear it," Maniakes said. The phrase *this useless war*, though, would not leave his mind once heard. Had the Makuraners taken Videssos the city along with their Ku-brati allies, no one among them, not even Abivard, would be cursing Sharbaraz now. They cared nothing about the injustice of his invasion of Videssos. All that mattered to them was his an-gry reaction when they failed to bring the war to a satisfactory end. And even that, unbeknownst to them, Maniakes had needed to amplify.

He shrugged, not feeling the least bit guilty about his own chi-canery. When he tossed the Makuraner messenger a goldpiece, the fellow praised him as if he were somewhere in rank between the

King of Kings and one of the Four Prophets. That was chicanery, too, designed to squeeze another goldpiece—or maybe even two—out of him at the messenger's next visit. Pretending to believe it, Maniakes waved the rider out of his camp.

He stayed in that camp for the next several days. While there, he got another reassuring sign, for Abivard recalled to his own army the force that had been shadowing the Videssians as the Videssians had shadowed his main body. Augmented by those men and by the Garsavra garrison, Abivard began his journey up the Arandos toward Amorion. "When he gets to Amorion—better yet, when he leaves the place—we'll truly have come full circle," Maniakes told Rhegorios.

"Aye, that's the truth," his cousin answered. "That's the town that held the Makuraners out of the Arandos valley for so long. Once it's in our hands, where it belongs, we can hold them out again if they ever try to come back."

"That's so," Maniakes said. "And the general who held them out before was Tzikas. He's bound to have friends there still. I wonder if he'll be waiting for Abivard—or for us."

"Now there's an interesting thought." Rhegorios raised an eyebrow. "Whom do you suppose he hates worse, you or Abivard?"

"Good question." Maniakes plucked at his beard as he thought. "I have the title he wanted most, of course, but, to balance that, Abivard is going after a title he can't hope to claim. Both of us should have executed him when we had the chance, and neither one of us did it, the bigger fools we. Dishonors are about even, I'd say."

"I'd say you're right," his cousin answered. "I'd also say that means you and Abivard had both better watch yourselves."

"Oh, yes." Maniakes nodded vehemently. "Phos only knows what would happen to the Makuraner army if Abivard came down with a sudden case of loss of life."

He didn't know what would happen in Videssos if he himself vanished from the scene without warning, either. He didn't bring that up with Rhegorios for a couple of reasons. For one, he wouldn't be around to worry about it if that did happen. For another, the succession would be disastrously complicated. Likarios was his legal heir, but Likarios' mother was years dead. Lysia might push her children's claims instead. But they were all young, young. And Rhegorios, as cousin to the Avtokrator, brother to the Empress, and

Sevastos in his own right, would have a formidable claim of his own: certainly more formidable in law than Abivard's to the throne of Makuran.

Rhegorios said, "Here's hoping he's not lurking there. Here's hoping he's not lurking anywhere. Here's hoping his horse slipped on a mountainside road and he broke his snaky neck in a fall. Here's hoping you never have to worry about the two-faced son of a whore again."

"Aye, here's hoping," Maniakes said. "But something tells me that's too much to hope for. Tzikas is too much of a nuisance to disappear just because we wish he would."

Abivard's army stuck close to the northern bank of the Arandos, eating their way along the river like a swarm of locusts. His riders were not the only ones who came north bringing news to Maniakes. Several peasants and herders came up, begging him to keep the Makuraners from emptying the countryside of everything edible.

He sent them away unhappy, saying, "Abivard's men are our allies now, and I do not begrudge our allies the supplies they need." Having to answer in that way left him unhappy, too. *How many times have the Makuraners despoiled the westlands since Likinios fell?* he wondered. At last, though, his distress eased. *However many times, this is the last.*

He kept his army a couple of days' march north of the Arandos. Up on the plateau, that meant making sure he had enough grain and water before he crossed one south-flowing tributary to be certain he could reach the next. The country was scrubby between streams.

In spite of complaints from his countrymen, he admitted to himself that Abivard could have done far worse than he was doing. The Makuraner wanted to give Maniakes no excuse to attack him, just as the Avtokrator wanted to give him no excuse to break their partnership. Mutual fear might have made a strange foundation for an alliance, but it seemed to work.

The Arandos and the Ithome joined east of a range of hills, the Arandos flowing up from the southwest, the Ithome down from the northwest. Amorion lay on the north bank of the Ithome, three or four days' travel west of the meeting place of the two rivers. It

was the most important town in the westlands, even if the Garsav-
rans probably would have argued the distinction. It had anchored
Videssian possession of the Arandos valley and, once lost to Makuran, anchored the invaders' occupation.

For all those reasons, and also because of its central location,
it held the largest Makuraner garrison in the westlands. Maniakes
worried that the garrison would stay loyal to Sharbaraz and require a siege to make it yield. The siege wouldn't be Abivard's
problem, either—the Makuraner marshal would no doubt keep on
moving west against the King of Kings he'd renounced. Amorion
was Maniakes' city, and it would likely be Maniakes' job to take
it back.

And so, when a rider from Abivard came up to the Videssian
army, the Avtokrator tensed. But the horseman cried, "Good news
twice, your Majesty! The garrison of Amorion joins everyone else
in rejecting Sharbaraz. And the soldiers of the garrison captured
the second Makuraner rider who went with Tzikas the traitor to let
the Pimp of Pimps know his murderous wickedness has been laid
bare before the entire world."

"That *is* good news," Maniakes agreed. "What happened to this
second rider?"

"Nothing lingering or unusually interesting." The messenger
sounded almost disappointed. "The garrison commander, knowing Abivard's reputation for leniency, questioned him for a time
and then took his head. Very simple, very neat."

Maniakes wasn't used to thinking of the esthetics of executions.
"All right," he answered, faintly bemused. "Did he learn by which
roads Tzikas was going, so we can send pursuit down them?"

"Not in all the detail he should have liked, Majesty," the Makuraner answered. "The two of them had separated some time before. The rider believed Tzikas was traveling south of the Arandos,
but knew no more than that."

"All right," Maniakes said. It wasn't, but he couldn't do anything about it. He knew too well how little Tzikas could be relied
upon once out of sight. Like as not, the renegade had headed north
as soon as he thought his departing comrade thought he was going
south. He was a connoisseur of deceit, as some men were con-
noisseurs of wine, and had a fine and discriminating palate for it.

Or, of course, knowing Maniakes knew of his deceitfulness, he
might have thought to deceive by doing exactly what he'd said

he would do, reckoning the Avtokrator would assume he'd done the opposite. Or . . . Maniakes shook his head. Once you started floundering in those waters, the bewildering whirlpool would surely drag you under.

Maniakes did move down to Amorion once Abivard's forces and the Makuraner garrison abandoned it. Not only did he intend to place a small garrison of his own there, he also wanted to see the town for the first time since becoming Avtokrator. His previous push up the Arandos toward Amorion had been rudely interrupted by Abivard's capture of the place.

Finding the wall intact was the first surprise. The Makuraners had breached it, after all; otherwise, they never would have taken the city. Afterward, they'd repaired the breaches with new stone, easy to tell from what had been there before because it was so much less weathered. One of the city gates was also new, and arguably stronger than the Videssian work it replaced.

Once inside Amorion, though, Maniakes saw what several years of occupation by hostile masters had done. A good many buildings had been burned or otherwise wrecked in the sack. If any of them had been repaired since, he would have been astonished. And many of the buildings that had survived the Makuraners' entry were simply empty. Maybe the people who had lived in them had fled before the Makuraners stormed in. Maybe they had been expelled afterward, or simply left. Maybe they were dead.

"We're going to have to rebuild," Maniakes said. "We're going to have to bring in people from parts of the Empire that haven't taken such a beating."

"We're going to have to find parts of the Empire that haven't taken such a beating," Rhegorios said, exaggerating only a little.

"There'll always be Vaspurakaners trickling out of their mountains and valleys, too," Maniakes said. "The Makuraners don't treat them well enough to make them want to stay . . . and after a while, they start turning into Videssians."

"Can't imagine what you're talking about," his cousin said with a chuckle.

Here and there, people did come out and cheer the return of Videssian rule—or at least acknowledge it. "Took you long enough!" an old man shouted, leaning on his stick. "When Tzikas was here, things was pretty good—not perfect, mind you, but pretty good.

You'll have to go some to beat him, whatever your name is, and that's a fact."

"I'll do my best," Maniakes answered. Riding along next to him, Rhegorios giggled: not the sort of noise one would expect to come from the august throat of a Sevastos. The Avtokrator ignored him.

When he got to what had been the *epoptes'* palace, he found it in better shape than any other building he'd seen. The servants who trooped out to greet him looked plump and prosperous, where everyone else in the city seemed skinny and shabby and dirty. In answer to Maniakes' question, one of them said, "Why, yes, your Majesty, the Makuraner garrison commander did live here. How did you know?"

"Call it a lucky guess," Maniakes answered dryly.

Across the central square from the residence, the chief temple to Phos seemed to have taken all the abuse and neglect the residence had avoided. Like a lot of chief temples in provincial towns, it was modeled after the High Temple in Videssos the city. It hadn't been the best of copies before; now, with weeds growing all around, with the stonework of the exterior filthy and streaked with bird droppings, and with every other windowpane bare of glass, it was nearer nightmare vision than imitation.

A blue-robed priest came out of the temple and looked across the square at Maniakes. Recognizing the Avtokrator's raiment, he dashed over the cobblestones toward him, sandals flapping on his feet. When he got close, he threw himself down on the cobblestones in front of Maniakes in a proskynesis so quick and emphatic, he might almost have fallen on his face rather than prostrating himself.

"Mercy, your Majesty!" he cried, his face still pressed down against the paving stones. "Have mercy on your holy temple here, so long tormented by the savage invaders!"

"Rise, holy sir," Maniakes said. "You are—?"

"I am called Domnos, your Majesty," the priest replied, "and I have had the honor—and, I assure you, the trial—of being prelate of Amorion these past three years, after the holy Mavrikios gave up this life and passed to Phos' eternal light. It has not been an easy time."

"Well, I believe that," Maniakes said. "Tell me, holy Domnos—

did you preach Vaspurakaner dogmas when the Makuraners ordered our priests to do that?"

Domnos hung his head. He blushed all the way up to the top of his shaven crown. "Your Majesty, I did," he whispered. "It was that or suffer terrible torment, and I—I was weak, and obeyed. Punish me as you will." He straightened, as if eagerly anticipating that punishment.

But Maniakes said, "Let it go. You'll preach a sermon on things you had to do under duress, and then you and your fellow priests will talk to the people who've accepted the Vaspurakaner doctrines as better than our own—I know you'll have some. We won't push them back into orthodoxy all at once. After that, you can go on with life as it was before the invasion." He knew it wouldn't be that easy. If Domnos didn't know, he'd find out soon enough.

Now Domnos stared at the Avtokrator. He'd asked for mercy. Maniakes had given it to him, a large dose of it, but he didn't seem to want it as much as he'd claimed. "Yes, your Majesty," he said, rather sulkily.

Maniakes, however, had more important things to worry about than a priest put out of temper. He chose a question touching on the most important of those things: "Has Tzikas, the former commander here, passed through this town in the last few days?"

Domnos' eyes widened. "No, your Majesty." After a moment, he qualified that: "Not to my knowledge, at any rate. If he came here in secret, I might not know it, though I think I should have heard. But why would he have needed to come in secret?"

"Oh, he'd have had his reasons," Maniakes answered, his voice drought-dry. He reflected that Amorion under Makuraner rule had been a town wrapped up in wool batting, a town caught in a backwater while the world went on around it. By the look on Domnos' face, he still thought of Tzikas as the stubborn general who had held Abivard away for so long, and he had no reason to think otherwise. Yes, sure enough, the world had passed Amorion by.

"You will know better than I, your Majesty," Domnos said. "Will you come see the temple and learn the relief we need?"

"I'll come," Maniakes said, and followed Domnos across the square.

He had not gone more than a couple of paces before his guardsmen, Videssians and Halogai both, formed a square around him. "No telling who or what all's waiting in there, your Majesty," a

Videssian guard said, as if defying him to order the warriors to step aside. "Might even be this Tzikas item you're worrying about."

That comment, delivered in the streetwise dialect of Videssos the city, might have been one of Bagdasares' magic words, so effectively did it shut off any argument the Avtokrator might have made. The plain truth was, the guardsman was right. If Tzikas struck, it would have to be from ambush. What more unexpected place to set an ambush than one of Phos' holy temples?

Up the steps and into the exonarthex, Domnos led Maniakes. The priest pointed to a mosaic of a bygone Avtokrator presenting Amorion's temple to Phos as a pious offering. "Do you see, your Majesty?" the priest said. "The infidel Makuraners chiseled out every gold tessera from the costume of Metokhites II."

"I do see." Maniakes didn't know how much gold the Makuraners had realized from their chiseling, but they must have thought the results worth the labor.

In the next chamber in from the entrance, the narthex, Domnos sadly pointed out where silver lamps had been torn from the ceiling. "They took the great candelabrum, too," he said, "thinking its polished brass gold. Even after they found they were wrong, they did not return it."

"Brass is useful," Maniakes said. He didn't need to say much to keep the conversation going. Domnos talked enough for any two ordinary people, or possibly three.

Tzikas had not lurked in the exonarthex or narthex. Maniakes' guardsmen preceded their charge into the main worship area. No renegade, no band of bravos, crouched in ambush behind the pews. The guards gave their permission for Maniakes to enter. He was sovereign in the Empire of Videssos, but hardly in his own household.

"You see?" Domnos said again. "Gold, silver, brass, semiprecious gems—all gone."

"Yes," Maniakes said. Even before the Makuraners had come, the temple here in Amorion had been a copy of the High Temple in the capital, but a poor man's copy. Despoiled by the invaders, it was, as Domnos had claimed, poorer still.

Maniakes glanced upward toward the dome in the central altar. The mosaic image of Phos in the dome was not perfectly stern in judgment, as it was in Videssos the city; here, he looked more nearly petulant. And the gold tesserae that had surrounded his image were gone, survived only by the rough gray cement in which they had been mounted. That made Phos' image seem even more lifeless than it would have otherwise.

"Aye, they even stripped the dome," Domnos said, following Maniakes' gaze. With a certain somber satisfaction, he added, "And three of their workmen died in the doing, too; may Skotos freeze their souls forevermore." He spat on the marble floor in rejection of the dark god.

So did Maniakes. He asked, "How much money do you think you'll need to restore the temple to the way it was?"

Domnos clapped his hand. A less senior priest in a plainer blue robe came running. "The accounts list," the prelate snapped. His subordinate hurried off, returning shortly with three leaves of parchment held together at one corner by a small iron ring. Domnos took it from him, then presented it to Maniakes with a flourish. "Here you are, your Majesty."

"Er—thank you," Maniakes said. He flipped through the document. His alarm grew with every line he read. Domnos had the cost of full repairs calculated down to the last copper, in materials and labor both. The sum at which he'd finally arrived looked reasonable in light of the damage done to the temple—and altogether appalling in light of the damage done to the Empire's finances.

"Well, your Majesty?" Domnos said when Maniakes gave no sign of pulling goldpieces out of his ears.

"Well, holy sir, all I can say right now is that yours isn't the only temple to have suffered, and I'll have to see what other needs we have before I can think of paying you this entire sum." Maniakes knew he sounded weak. He didn't know what else to say, though. Tzikas hadn't been lurking inside the temple, no, but he'd been ambushed just the same.

Domnos' acquisitive instincts aside, reestablishing Videssian control over Amorion proved easier than Maniakes had expected. Most of the locals who had collaborated with the Makuraner occupiers had fled with them. The ones who were left were loudly repentant. As he had elsewhere, Maniakes forgave more than he punished.

Being a good-sized town, Amorion had had its own small Vaspurakaner community before it fell to the Makuraners, a community with its own discreetly sited temple. That let the Avtokrator send the Videssian locals who had converted to Vaspurakaner usages during the occupation and now refused to abandon them to a place where they could continue to worship in the fashion they had come to find fitting.

"But, your Majesty," Domnos protested, "the goal is to return them to orthodoxy, as you said, not to confirm them in their error. One Empire, one true faith: it is a law of nature."

"So it is," Maniakes said. "As time goes by, holy sir, I think almost all of them *will* return to orthodoxy. We make that the easier path, the preferred path, just as the Makuraners made the dogma of Vaspur the Firstborn the way to move ahead. You lay under the Makuraner yoke for years; you've been free a few days. Not everything happens at once."

"I certainly see *that*, your Majesty," Domnos said, and stalked off, robe swirling about him.

Rhegorios eyed his retreat with amusement. "Do you know, cousin of mine, I don't think you're one of his favorite people right now."

"I noticed that, thanks." Maniakes made a sad clucking sound. "I wouldn't empty the treasury to repair the temple here this instant, and I wouldn't burn heretics without giving them a decent chance to come back to orthodoxy, either. See what a wicked fellow that makes me?"

"Sounds bloody wicked to me," Rhegorios agreed. "Not giving someone all the money he wants the instant he wants it—why, if that doesn't rank right up there for wickedness with ordering your best general executed, I don't know what does." He paused, looking thoughtful. "But since you're your own best general, that would complicate the whole business a bit, wouldn't it?"

"Complicate? That's one way to put it, anyhow." Maniakes sighed. "Here's Amorion back under Videssian rule. I didn't have to fight to get it back, so the town isn't burned or wrecked any worse than it was before I got here. The Makuraners didn't take anybody with them who didn't want to go. And what thanks do I get? I haven't made everything perfect right away, so of course I'm nothing but a tyrant."

Rhegorios plucked at his beard. "If it's any consolation, cousin your Majesty brother-in-law of mine, I'll bet the people here were grumbling about the Makuraners the same way till the day the boiler boys pulled out." His voice rose to a high, mocking falsetto: " 'The nerve of that cursed Abivard. To the ice with him, anyway!

He has gall, he does, going off to try and conquer Videssos the city when his supply wagons have left such big potholes in *our* streets.' " He looked and sounded like an indignant chicken.

Maniakes opened his mouth to say something, but he'd already started laughing by then, and almost choked to death. When he could speak, he pointed an accusing forefinger at his cousin: "You, sirrah, are a demon from a plane of being the Sorcerers' Collegium hasn't yet stumbled onto, the reason being that it's too absurd for such calm, careful men to contemplate."

"Why, thank you, your Majesty!" Rhegorios exclaimed, as if the Avtokrator had just conferred a great compliment upon him. From his point of view, maybe Maniakes had done just that.

"It's a good thing Uncle Symvatios passed all the silliness in his line of the family down to you and not to Lysia," Maniakes said.

"Oh, I don't know about that." Rhegorios studied him. "My sister puts up with you, doesn't she?"

Maniakes considered. "You may have something there," he said at last, and flung his arm over his cousin's shoulder. They walked back to the *epoptes'* residence together.

While Maniakes settled affairs in Amorion to his satisfaction, if not always to that of the town's inhabitants, Abivard kept marching steadily to the west, and took a good-sized lead on the Videssian force that had been following him. On the day when Maniakes was finally ready to head west from Amorion himself, a courier from Abivard brought a message to the Avtokrator.

"Majesty," the fellow said, "the general has decided to swing up a bit to the northwest, to pick up some detachments on garrison duty in Vaspurakan. It won't cost but a couple of days of time, and will add some good soldiers to his army."

"Whatever he thinks best," Maniakes said, though he would not have been diverted from the shortest road to Mashiz. "I hope the soldiers turn out to be worth the delay."

"Through the Prophets Four, we pray the God they so prove," the messenger replied, and rode back toward Abivard's army. Maniakes stared after him.

So did Rhegorios, who said, "I wouldn't have done that. I'd have gone for Sharbaraz's throat with what I have here."

"I was thinking the same thing," Maniakes agreed. "That's what I'd have done. So would my father. I have no more doubt of that than I do of the truth of Phos' holy creed. And yet—" He laughed ruefully. "When Abivard and I have met each other on the battlefield, he's come off the winner as often as I have, so who's to judge which of us is wiser?"

"Something to that—I hope," his cousin said. "The other side of the goldpiece is, if Abivard has swung to the northwest, we're going to have to swing farther northwest than we thought we would, or else we'll be feeding ourselves from the crumbs the Makuraners leave behind."

"That's so," Maniakes said. "You've thought of it sooner than I did, for which I thank you. I'll change the marching orders. You're right; we'd get hungry in a hurry if we came straight down the path the Makuraners had just used."

The first settlement of decent size northwest of Amorion was Aptos, which, like Patrodoton farther east, lay on the border between town and village. Unlike Patrodoton, Aptos knew it wanted to be a town: when Maniakes and the Videssian army arrived, the folk of the area had started running up a rammed-earth core for what would be a wall around it.

The headman, a baker named Phorkos, was proud of the initiative his town was showing. "Your Majesty, we never imagined the Makuraners would come so far or stay so long," he said. "If that ever happens again—which Phos prevent—they won't find us so ripe for going into their oven."

"Good," Maniakes said. "Excellent, in fact. I have to tell you, I don't have a lot of money right now. I'll do what I can to help you pay for your work, but it won't be much and it may not be soon."

"We're taking care of it, your Majesty," Phorkos said. "One way or another, we'll manage."

"I wonder if you could go down to Amorion and talk with Domnos the priest for a while," Maniakes murmured. Phorkos' blank look said he didn't know what the Avtokrator was talking about. That, Maniakes decided, was probably as well: if Phorkos did talk with Domnos, the priest was liable to persuade him he deserved an enormous subsidy.

That Phorkos and his fellow townsfolk were undertaking this labor on their own, that they'd presented Maniakes with what they were doing rather than asking permission of him to do it, said they'd got used to being out from under the stifling weight of Videssian bureaucracy, one of the first good things the Avtokrator had found to say about the Makuraner invasion. He didn't think he'd come up with many more.

From Aptos, the army continued northwest for another couple of days to the town of Vryetion. Vryetion, already having a wall, was what Aptos aspired to be. Having a wall, however, had not kept it from falling to the Makuraners. Maybe it had made seizing the place more difficult, and cost the boiler boys more wounded and dead. Maniakes hoped so.

He lodged in what had been the *epoptes'* residence, a house a medium-sized linen dealer in Videssos the city would have rejected as inadequate. The Makuraner garrison commander had made his home there during the occupation, and left several graffiti expressing his opinion of the place. So Maniakes guessed, at any rate, though he didn't read the Makuraner language. But the scribbled drawings accompanying a couple of the inscriptions were anything but complimentary.

Like it or not, though, that garrison commander had been forced to make the best of it. So did Maniakes, who spent a day hearing petitions from the locals, as he'd done in other towns through which he passed.

Those were, for the most part, straightforward. As had happened in other towns farther east, few collaborators were left; however many there had been, they'd fled with the Makuraner garrison. The officer who'd led that garrison seemed to have done a more conscientious job than many of his peers, and the folk of Vryetion tried to get the Avtokrator to overturn only a couple of his rulings.

"To the ice with me if I know whether I like that or not," Maniakes said behind his hand to Rhegorios. "He didn't torment them, and most of them were as happy with him in charge as with one of their own."

"He's gone now," Rhegorios answered, to which Maniakes nodded.

A woman a few years younger than the Avtokrator came before him along with her son, who was a little older than the eldest of his own children. She and the boy both prostrated themselves, a bit more smoothly than any of the other locals had done.

"Rise," Maniakes said. "Tell me your name, and how I may help you."

"My name is Zenonis," the woman said. She looked from Maniakes to Rhegorios and back again. She would have been attractive—

she might even have been beautiful—had she not been so worn. "Forgive me, your Majesty, but why is my husband not with you?"

"Your husband?" Maniakes frowned. "Who is your husband?"

Zenonis' eyebrows flew upward. He'd either astonished or insulted her, maybe both. Probably both, from her expression. "Who is my husband, your Majesty? My husband is Parsmanios—your brother. And this—" She pointed to the boy. "—this is your nephew Maniakes."

Beside the Avtokrator, Rhegorios softly said, "Phos."

Maniakes felt like making the sun-sign himself. He didn't, schooling himself to stillness. Parsmanios had mentioned that he'd married in Vryetion, and mentioned his wife's name as well. But Parsmanios had not been anyplace where he could speak to Maniakes for four years and more, and the Avtokrator had spent all that time trying to forget the things his younger brother had told him. He'd succeeded better than he'd guessed.

"Why is Parsmanios not here with you?" Zenonis asked again. She probably had some Vaspurakaner blood in her—not surprising, this close to the princes' land—for she was almost as swarthy as Maniakes and Rhegorios. Beneath that swarthiness, she went pale. "Is my husband dead, your Majesty? If he is, do not hide it from me. Tell me the truth at once." Her son, who looked quite a bit like Likarios, started to cry.

"By the good god, lady, I swear Parsmanios is not dead," Maniakes said. He got reports from Prista, on the peninsula depending from the northern shore of the Videssian Sea, several times a year. When last he'd heard, at any rate, his brother had been well.

Zenonis' smile was as bright as her frown had been dark. "Phos be praised!" she said, sketching the sun-circle and then hugging little Maniakes. "I know how it must be: you have left him back in the famous city, in Videssos the city, to rule it for you while you take the westlands back from the wicked Makuraners."

Rhegorios started to have a terrible coughing fit. Maniakes kicked him in the ankle. The woman before him was plainly no fool and would realize how badly she was mistaken. Maniakes wanted to give her that news as gently as he could; what her husband had done was not her fault. The Avtokrator would not lie to her, though: "No, he is not back in Videssos the city. My father—his father—has the authority there while I am in the westlands."

Zenonis' frown returned, though it was not so dark as it had been a moment before. "I do not understand," she said.

"I know you don't," Maniakes told her. "The explanation will take a while: no help for that. Come here at sunset for supper with me and Lysia, my wife, and with Rhegorios here—my cousin, the Sevastos."

"Both of you have something of the look of Parsmanios," Zenonis said. "Or maybe he has your look, I don't know." Her frown got deeper. "But if your cousin is Sevastos, what rank does Parsmanios hold?"

Exile, Maniakes thought. Aloud, he replied, "As I said, the explanation isn't quick or simple. Let me handle the matters here that are simple. At supper, I promise I'll tell you everything you need to know. Is that all right?"

"You are the Avtokrator. You have the right to command," Zenonis said with considerable dignity. "As you say, so shall it be." She led her son away. The next petitioner stepped forward.

Before dealing with the fellow, Maniakes sent Rhegorios a stricken glance. "I'd forgotten all about this," he said. "It won't be easy."

"You aren't the only one who forgot," his cousin answered, which did not make him feel any better. Rhegorios went on, "You're right. It won't be easy."

Lysia grimaced. She spoke severely to her belly: "Stop that." The baby in there didn't stop wiggling; Maniakes could see movement where her swollen middle pressed against her gown. She grimaced again. "He's kicking my bladder. Excuse me. I need to use the pot again."

"It won't be long now," Maniakes remarked when she came back.

"No, not long," Lysia agreed.

Silence fell. Maniakes broke it with a sigh, and then said, "I'd sooner have an aching tooth pulled than go through with this supper, but I don't see any way not to do it."

"Neither do I," Lysia answered. "We'll tell her the truth and see how things go from there, that's all. I don't know what else we can do."

"Send her into exile to keep my brother company?" Maniakes suggested. But he shook his head and held his hands out in front of him before Lysia could say anything. "No, I don't mean it. What Parsmanios did wasn't her fault."

"No, it wasn't." Lysia sighed, too. "And we'll have to explain about ourselves again: better she should hear it from us than from anyone else. I get tired of explaining sometimes."

"I know. So do I." Maniakes spread his hands once more. "We fell in love with each other. I didn't expect it, but . . ." His voice trailed off.

"I didn't, either," Lysia said. "I'm not saying it hasn't been worth the fight over the dispensation and the explanations and everything else. But I do get tired."

Rhegorios knocked on the door of the chamber they were sharing and said, "Zenonis is here. She's nervous as a cat. I gave her a big cup of wine. I hope that will settle her down. If it doesn't, she'll jump up to the ceiling when the two of you come down to the dining hall."

"We'd better get on with it." Maniakes stood aside to let Lysia precede him through the door. Hand in hand, the two of them followed Rhegorios downstairs.

Zenonis did jump when Maniakes came into the dining hall, enough to make a little wine slop out of the cup she was holding. She'd left young Maniakes at home. She started to prostrate herself before the Avtokrator. He waved for her not to bother. "Your Majesty is gracious," she said, her voice under tight control. She wanted to scream questions at him—Maniakes had heard that kind of restraint before, often enough to recognize it here.

To forestall her, at least for a bit, the Avtokrator said, "Zenonis, let me present you to my wife, the Empress Lysia, who is sister to the Sevastos Rhegorios." There. There it was, all in a lump.

At first, she simply heard the words. Then she figured out what they meant. Rhegorios was Maniakes' cousin. Lysia was Rhegorios' sister. That meant . . . Zenonis took a deep breath. Maniakes braced himself for trouble—thought there would surely be trouble of one sort or another tonight. "I am allied with this family by marriage," Zenonis said after a visible pause for thought. "I am allied with all of it."

"Well said, by the good god!" Rhegorios exclaimed.

Lysia took Zenonis' hands in hers. "We do welcome you to the family," she said. "Whether you'll be so glad of us after a while may be another question, but we'll get to that."

The cooks brought in bread and a roasted kid covered with powdered garlic and a sharp, pungent cheese. They also presented the diners with a bowl of golden mushrooms of a sort Maniakes had never seen before. When he remarked on them, one of the cooks said, "They don't grow far from Vryetion that I know of, your Majesty. We've sautéed them in white wine for you."

They were delicious, with a flavor half nutty, half meaty. The kid was falling-off-the-bone tender, no easy trick with goat. And yet, however good the supper proved, Maniakes knew he was enjoying it less than he should have. He kept waiting for Zenonis to stop picking at the lovely food and start asking the unlovely questions he would have to answer.

She lasted longer than he'd thought she would. But, when he showed no signs of volunteering what she wanted to know, she took a long pull at her cup of wine and said, "Parsmanios lives, you tell me." Maniakes nodded, taking advantage of a full mouth to say nothing. His new-met sister-in-law went on, "He is not here. You said he was not in Videssos the city." She paused, like a barrister building a case in a law court. Maniakes nodded again. Zenonis asked the first of those blunt questions: "Where is he, then?"

"In Prista," Maniakes answered, giving blunt for blunt.

But he was not blunt enough. "Where is that?" Zenonis said. "I never heard of it. Is it important? It must be. Is he your viceroy there?"

"No, he is not my viceroy there," Maniakes said. "Prista is a little town on the northern shore of the Videssian Sea." It was, in its way, an important place, for it let the Empire of Videssos keep an eye on the Khamorth tribes wandering the Pardrayan steppe. But that wasn't what Zenonis had meant, and he knew it.

"That's—at the edge of the world," she exclaimed, and the Avtokrator nodded yet again. "Why is he there and not here or in the capital?"

Yes, that was *the* blunt question, sure enough. "Why, lady?" Maniakes echoed. He found no way to soften his reply: "Because he and one of my generals conspired to slay me by magic. The general got away; I still haven't caught up with him. But Parsmanios—"

"No." Zenonis' lips shaped the word, but without sound. Then she said it again, aloud this time: "No." She shook her head, as if brushing away a buzzing fly. "It's not possible. When Parsmanios was here in Vryetion with me after you became Avtokrator, your

Majesty, he would talk about going to Videssos the city so he and you and your brother Tatoules could run things the way they—"

Maniakes held up his hand. "I don't know where Tatoules is. He never came to Videssos the city, and no one knows what's happened to him. If I had to guess, I'd say the Makuraners captured him in the early days of their invasion, while Genesios was still Avtokrator. Most of my family was in exile on Kalavria then. To the boiler boys, he'd have been just another officer, just another prisoner. They probably worked him to death."

"I am sorry," Zenonis said; she'd already shown she had good manners. "I didn't know. Parsmanios didn't know, either, of course. He would go on and on about how you three brothers would set the Empire to rights and get rich doing it, too."

"He was welcome to help me set the Empire to rights," Maniakes said. "By the good god, it's needed setting to rights. He did help, some. But he wanted to be promoted without having earned it, just because he was my brother. When I told him no, he didn't like that."

Rhegorios wriggled in his seat, then held up his winecup. A servant hurried to fill it. Rhegorios hurried to empty it. The title Parsmanios had wanted was Sevastos, the title he owned. The Avtokrator had kept him in preference to his own brother. No wonder he felt a little uneasy here.

Zenonis said, "I can't believe he would turn on his own flesh and blood."

"I couldn't believe it, either," Maniakes answered. "Unfortunately, it happens to be true, and I nearly died from it. He always claimed he did it because he thought my marriage with Lysia was wrong and wicked. Maybe he was even telling the truth; I don't know. It doesn't matter. What he did matters, and that's all. Phos, I wish he hadn't done it."

Zenonis' gaze flicked from him to Lysia and back again. Parsmanios' wife had spirit; Maniakes could tell she was going to challenge him. When she did, she picked her words with great care, but challenged nonetheless: "By the teachings of the holy temples, the two of you are within the prohibited degrees of kinship, and so—"

"No." Maniakes made his voice flat. "We have a dispensation from Agathios, the most holy ecumenical patriarch. My father— Parsmanios' father—has accepted the wedding." That was true, as far as it went. The elder Maniakes didn't like the wedding, but he accepted it. "Lysia's father has accepted it, too." That was also true, with the same reservations. "None of them tried to overthrow me or take the throne for themselves." Most important of all, that was true, too. "Neither did Rhegorios here."

"Me?" Rhegorios' eyebrows shot upward. "I've seen what all the Avtokrator has to do. Looks too much like work for my taste."

Lysia snorted. So did Maniakes. Rhegorios had a hard time keeping his own face straight. He enjoyed affecting the role of a useless, gilded fop. When he was younger, the affectation might have covered some truth. No more, though. Maniakes knew that, if he fell over dead tomorrow, his father and Rhegorios would keep the Empire running as smoothly as it could in these troubled times.

He also knew Rhegorios would do nothing to try to make him fall over dead, and everything in his power to keep him from falling over dead. There, in a sentence, was the difference between his cousin and the brother he'd had to exile.

"If the ecumenical patriarch says it is acceptable, then it is," Zenonis said, as if stating a law of nature. If it was a law of nature, Maniakes wished more clerics and citizens were familiar with it. His sister-in-law bowed her head. "Thank you for sparing his life."

"You're welcome," Maniakes answered. He started to say something more, but stopped. He started again, and again left it unspoken. Whatever comments he might make about not having the stomach to spill a brother's blood would only cause him to seem smug and self righteous, because Parsmanios had shown *he* had the stomach to try doing just that.

"What will you do with me?" Zenonis asked.

"I don't intend to do anything with you," Maniakes answered. "And, in case you're still wondering, I don't intend to do anything to you, either. If you want to stay here in Vryetion, you may do that. If you want to come to Videssos the city, you may do that. If you want to go into exile with Parsmanios, you may do that, too. But think carefully before you choose that road. If you go to Prista, you will never come back."

"I don't know what to do now," Zenonis said. "These past few years, I've wondered whether my husband was alive. To find out he is, to be raised to the heights by that, and then to learn what he'd done and to plunge into the depths again . . . I don't know where I am now." She looked down at her hands again.

Gently, Lysia said, "After this, you may not want anything to do with our clan any more. If you should decide to dissolve the marriage, the clerics will give you no trouble, not with your husband a proved traitor. None of us would hold it against you, I know that." She glanced to Maniakes and Rhegorios for confirmation. Both quickly nodded.

"I don't know," Zenonis repeated.

"You don't have to decide right away," Maniakes said. "Take your time to find what you think is best. The Makuraners aren't going to run us out of Vryetion again tomorrow, nor even the day after." He sketched the sun-circle above his heart to make sure Phos was paying attention to his words.

"What's best for me may not be best for Maniakes—my Maniakes, I mean," Zenonis said, thinking out loud. "And what's best for me may not be best for Parsmanios, either." She looked up at Maniakes, half-nervous, half-defiant, as if daring him to make something of that.

Before he could reply at all, Rhegorios asked, "What was it like, living here under the Makuraners when you were the Avtokrator's sister-in-law?"

"They never knew," Zenonis answered. "Half the people in Vryetion know who my husband is, but none of them ever told the boiler boys. I was always afraid that would happen, but it never did."

"Interesting," Maniakes said. That meant Zenonis was widely liked in the town. Otherwise, someone eager to curry favor with the occupiers would surely have betrayed her, as had happened so often at so many other places in the westlands. It also meant no one had hated Parsmanios enough to want to strike at him through his family, a small piece of favorable information about him but not one to be ignored.

"You are being as kind to me as you can," Zenonis said. "For this, I am in your debt, so much I can never hope to repay."

"Nonsense," Maniakes said. "You've done nothing to me. Why should I want to do anything to you?"

That question answered itself in his own mind as soon as he spoke it. Genesios would have slaughtered Parsmanios in the name of vengeance, and disposed of Zenonis and little Maniakes for sport. Likinios might have got rid of them merely for efficiency's sake, to leave no potential rivals at his back. Not being so vicious as Genesios nor so cold-blooded as Likinios, Maniakes was willing to let his sister-in-law and nephew live.

"You will let me think a while on what I should do?" Zenonis said, as if she still had trouble believing Maniakes. After he had reassured her yet again, she rose and prostrated herself before him.

"Get up," he said roughly. "Maybe people whose great-grandfathers were Avtokrators before them got used to that, but I never have." The confession would have dismayed Kameas, but Kameas was back in Videssos the city. The vestiarios had accompanied Maniakes on his ill-fated journey to buy peace from Etzilios. Maniakes had almost been captured then. Kameas had been, though Etzilios later released him. Since then, he'd stuck close to the imperial city.

With still more thanks, Zenonis made her way out of the city governor's residence. Maniakes looked at Rhegorios. Rhegorios looked at Lysia. Lysia looked at Maniakes.

Being the Avtokrator, he had the privilege of speaking first. He could have done without it. "That," he said, "was ghastly. If I'd known it was coming, that would have been hard enough. To have it take me by surprise this afternoon . . . I knew Parsmanios had lived in Vryetion. I didn't think about everything that would mean."

"You did as well as you could," Lysia said.

"Yes, I think so, too," he answered without false modesty. "But I think I'd sooner have been beaten with boards."

Thoughtfully, Rhegorios said, "She's nicer than I thought she'd be. Not bad-looking at all, a long way from stupid . . . I wonder what she saw in Parsmanios."

"No telling," Maniakes said wearily. "He wasn't a bad fellow, you know, till jealousy ate him up from the inside out."

A servant came in with a platter of pears, apricots, and strawberries candied in honey. He looked around in some surprise. "The lady left before the sweet?" he said in faintly scandalized tones.

"So she did." Maniakes' imperturbability defied the servitor to make something of it. After a moment, the Avtokrator went on, "Why don't you set that tray down? We'll get around to it sooner or later. Meanwhile, bring us a fresh jar of wine."

"Meanwhile, bring us two or three fresh jars of wine," Rhegorios broke in.

"Yes, by the good god, bring us two or three fresh jars of wine," Maniakes exclaimed. "I hadn't planned to get drunk tonight, but then, things can change. Till this afternoon, I hadn't planned on entertaining the wife of my traitorous brother tonight, either."

Lysia yawned. "I've had enough wine already," she said. "I'm going upstairs to bed. I'll see what's left of the two of you in the morning."

"She's smarter than either one of us," Maniakes said. That judgment didn't keep him from using a small knife to scrape the pitch out from around the stopper of one of the wine jars with which the servant had presented him. Once the stopper was out, the fellow took the jar from him and poured his cup and his cousin's full.

Rhegorios lifted the goblet, spat on the floor in rejection of Skotos, and drank. "Ahh," he said. "That's good." He took another pull. "You forget, your magnifolent Majesty—" He and Maniakes both laughed at that. "—I grew up with Lysia. I've known for a long time that she's smarter than I am. And while I wouldn't commit lese majesty for anything . . ."

"I get your drift." Maniakes drank, too, and ate a candied strawberry. Then he shook his head. "What a night. You know how the laundresses batter clothes against rocks to get the dirt out? That's how I feel now."

"Life is full of surprises," Rhegorios observed.

"Isn't it, though?" Maniakes drained his cup and filled it again before the servant could. "I'd thought the Kubratoi and the Makuraners—to say nothing of Tzikas, which is generally a good idea—had long since taught me all I needed to know of that lesson. I was wrong."

"I don't think Zenonis is out to kill you or overthrow the Empire—or to kill you *and* overthrow the Empire," Rhegorios said.

"I don't think so, either," Maniakes agreed. "But when you've been wrong before, you can't help wondering. I've given her a powerful reason to dislike me."

"That's so," his cousin admitted. "Times like this, you almost begin to understand how Genesios' ugly little mind worked."

"I had that same thought not very long ago," Maniakes said. "Frightening, isn't it?" He looked down into his goblet. It was empty. *How did that happen?* he wondered. Since no drunken mice staggered across the floor, he must have done it himself. He filled the cup again. "If I'd had some warning, I would have handled it better."

"You did fine, cousin of mine," Rhegorios said. "If you won't listen to Lysia, listen to me. I don't see what else you could have done. You explained what Parsmanios did, you explained what you did afterward, and you explained why. You didn't get angry during any of it. I would have, I think."

"I doubt it," Maniakes said. "You probably would have pardoned Parsmanios, too. I'm sterner than you are."

"Not for things like that," Rhegorios declared. "I would have advised you to take his head—but it wasn't my place to advise you of anything, not with him wanting my job and being blood of my blood both. I thought you'd do right on your own, and you did."

"Poor Zenonis, though," the Avtokrator said. "If her being here took me by surprise, what I told her must have hit like a—like a—" He began to feel the wine, which made groping for a simile hard. He found one anyhow: "Like a jar of wine in a tavern brawl. Life shouldn't work that way."

"A lot of things that shouldn't happen, happen to happen." Rhegorios stared reproachfully at the winecup he was holding, as if shocked that the ruby liquid it contained had betrayed him into saying something so absurd. Then he giggled. So did Maniakes. They both let loose gales of laughter. With enough wine, the world looked pretty funny.

When Maniakes woke up the next morning, nothing was funny any more. He felt as if a thunderstorm were rattling his poor abused brains. Every sound was a crash, every sunbeam a bolt of lightning.

Lysia, who'd had a full night's sleep and only a little wine, was less than properly sympathetic. "You look like you're going to bleed to death through your eyes," she said. "And you ought to comb your beard, or maybe iron it—it's pointing off to one side."

"Oh, shut up," he mumbled, not very loud.

His wife, heartless creature that she was suddenly revealed to be, laughed at him. "Remember, you've got another full day ahead of you, sorting through who was doing what to whom here and why, all the way through the Makuraner occupation."

He groaned and sat up in bed. That prompted another groan, more theatrical than the first. Then he groaned yet again, this time in good earnest. "Phos, Zenonis is going to be back here this morning, telling me what she wants to do."

"If she sees you like this—" Lysia hesitated. "No, come to think of it, maybe she went home and got drunk after dinner last night, too. You could hardly blame her if she did."

"No, but she'll blame me," Maniakes said. "I'm the Avtokrator. That's what I'm for—getting blamed, I mean."

He breakfasted on a little bread and honey and a cautious cup of wine. Splashing cool water on his face helped. So did combing the tangles out of his beard. Lysia studied him, then delivered her verdict: "Amazingly lifelike." Maniakes felt vindicated. He also felt human, in a glum sort of way.

Sure enough, by the time he came downstairs, petitioners were lined up in front of the city governor's residence. He dealt with them as best he could. Approving some and denying others made some people glad and others angry, but no one seemed to think the decisions he made especially idiotic.

Rhegorios bravely stuck his head into the chamber where Maniakes was passing his judgments. "I wondered if you could use some help," he said, his voice a rasping croak.

"I'm managing," Maniakes answered.

"I see you are," his cousin said. "In that case—" He withdrew. Whatever he'd done to fight his hangover, the hangover had won the battle.

Zenonis and little Maniakes came into the chamber about halfway through the morning. They both prostrated themselves before the Avtokrator, even though he waved for them not to bother. In a way, that relieved his mind, as a sign that Zenonis took his sovereignty seriously . . . unless, of course, she was dissembling. Life, he decided with the mournful clarity the morning after a drunken night could bring, was never simple.

"Have you decided what you would like to do?" he asked after his sister-in-law and nephew had risen.

"Yes, your Majesty," Zenonis said. "By your leave, we—" She put her arm around little Maniakes' shoulder. "—will travel to Videssos the city." She hesitated. "Maybe, later on, we will sail across the sea to Prista. I still have to think on that."

"Good enough," Maniakes said. "I think you are wise not to go to Prista at once, but I wouldn't have stood in your way if that was what you wanted to do. I'll give you an escort to go to the city, and I'll send a courier ahead to let my father know you're coming and to ask him to show you every kindness. He would anyway, for your husband's sake."

He watched Zenonis' eyes when he spoke of Parsmanios. As best he could tell, she looked sad, not angry. All the same, he'd also quietly ask his father to keep an eye on her while she was in the capital.

Zenonis said, "Your father is also Maniakes, not so?"

Maniakes nodded. "Yes. I suppose he's the one for whom your son is named, not me."

"No," Zenonis said, "or not altogether. When Maniakes—or little Maniakes, I should say—was born, my husband named him for the two of you. Now he's met one of his namesakes, and soon he'll meet the other."

"What do you think of that?" Maniakes asked his nephew.

"I don't know," little Maniakes answered. "It's all right, I guess, but I want to see my papa. That's what I really want to do."

Beside him, Zenonis began, very quietly, to weep. Obviously, she hadn't told her son what Parsmanios had done. Maniakes found himself unable to blame her for that. Sooner or later, little Maniakes would have to find out. It didn't have to be right away, though. To him, Maniakes said, "Maybe you will, one of these days. You *will* meet your grandfather, though. Isn't that good?"

"I don't know," his nephew said again. "Is he nicer than Gramps here in Vryetion?"

Maniakes hadn't even thought about Zenonis' father. Taken aback, he said, "Well, you can ask him for yourself when you get to Videssos the city. I'll bet he tells you yes." His nephew gravely puzzled away at that. Though tears still streaked her face, Zenonis managed a smile.

More claims about collaboration and treason kept the Avtokrator busy the rest of the day. Vryetion hadn't been occupied so long as some of the other Videssian towns up on the plateau, and it had been fortunate in having a relatively decent Makuraner overlord. Maybe that was why so many people had, or were accused of having, collaborated with the occupiers. Maniakes fought through the cases, one by one.

As in other Videssian towns through which he'd passed in the wake of the retreating Makuraners, temple affairs were in turmoil here. Vryetion wasn't far from the border with Vaspurakan. Some of the locals had Vaspurakaner blood; even some of those who didn't had looked kindly on Vaspurakaner doctrines before those were imposed on them.

A priest named Salivas said, "Your Majesty, your own clan reveres Vaspur the Firstborn. How can you condemn us for doing the same?"

"I follow the orthodox creed of Videssos," Maniakes answered, which was not a thorough denial of what the priest had said. He went on, "And you, holy sir, you were orthodox before the Makuraners ordered you to change the way you preached. You were happy enough then, not so? Why doesn't orthodoxy content you any more?"

"Because I believe with all my heart the doctrines I preach now are Phos' holy truth." Salivas drew himself up to his full height. He was tall, and also thin, which made him look even taller. "I am ready to die to defend the truth of the dogma of Vaspur."

"Nobody said anything about killing you, holy sir," Maniakes replied, which seemed to surprise and disappoint the priest—not the first time the Avtokrator had seen that, either. He went on, "I have another question for you: if you're so bloody eager to martyr yourself for faith in Vaspur the Firstborn, why didn't you let the boiler boys slaughter you when they made you change *from* orthodoxy?" *Then I wouldn't have had to deal with you,* he added to himself.

Salivas opened his mouth and closed it without saying anything. As far as Maniakes was concerned, that was a triumph almost as satisfying as holding the Kubratoi and Makuraners out of Videssos the city. Then, dashing it, Salivas tried again to speak, and succeeded. What he said, though, made the Avtokrator feel victorious after all: "Your Majesty, I don't know."

"May I offer a suggestion?" asked Maniakes, who had observed this phenomenon a couple of times before, too. Since Salivas could hardly refuse his sovereign, the Avtokrator continued, "You were orthodox all your life. You took orthodoxy for granted, didn't you?" He waited for Salivas to nod, then pressed ahead: "The Vaspurakaner doctrines are new to you. They're exciting on account of that, I think, as a man will find a new mistress exciting even though there's nothing whatever wrong with his wife except that she's not new to him any more."

Salivas flushed to the shaven crown of his head. "That is not a comparison I would have chosen to use," he said stiffly. Reminding Videssian priests of the celibacy required of them was bad manners.

Maniakes didn't care about bad manners, except insofar as he preferred them to religious rioting and other civil strife. "Use whatever comparison you like, holy sir. But think hard on it. Remember that you'd been perfectly content while you were orthodox. Remember that the other priests here—" *Most of them, anyhow,* he qualified mentally, and the couple of others who still inclined to Vaspurakaner views were wavering. "—have gone back to orthodoxy now that the Makuraners have left."

"But the Vaspurakaner views are—" Salivas began.

He was probably going to be stubborn. Maniakes didn't give him the chance. "Are imposed on you by foreigners who wanted to ruin Videssos," he said firmly. "Do you want to help Sharbaraz King of Kings win this fight even after his soldiers have left the Empire?"

"No," Salivas admitted, "but neither do I want to spend eternity in Skotos' ice for having misbelieved."

What Maniakes wanted to do was punch the stubborn priest, or possibly hit him over the head with a large stone in the hope of creating an opening through which sense might enter. With more patience than he'd thought he owned, he asked, "Didn't you believe you would be bathed in Phos' holy light before the Makuraners made you change your preaching?"

"Yes, but I have changed my mind since then," Salivas answered.

"If you changed it once, do you think you might change it again?" the Avtokrator said.

"I doubt that," Salivas told him. "I doubt that very much."

"Before the boiler boys made you reject orthodoxy, did you ever think you would change your mind about that?" Maniakes asked.

"No," the cleric said.

"Well, then—" Maniakes waited for Salivas to make the connection. He waited, and waited, and waited some more. The connection remained unmade. Salivas remained convinced that what he believed now, he would believe forever. Maniakes became convinced the priest was a perfect blockhead, but the only thing he could do about that was hope the people of Vryetion would notice it, too.

Seeing his discontent without fully recognizing its source, Salivas said, "I shall pray for you, your Majesty."

"For that much I thank you," Maniakes said wearily. Vryetion was going to be a town with Vaspurakaner-style heretics in it for some time to come. There were a lot of towns like that in the west-lands. The ecumenical patriarch wouldn't be happy about it. Mani-akes wasn't happy about it himself; it disturbed his sense of order. But plunging the westlands back into strife just after getting them back from the Makuraners disturbed his sense of order even more.

He dismissed Salivas, who departed with the air of a man who, having nerved himself for the worst, was more angry than relieved at not having suffered it. The next case that came before the Av-tokrator was a complicated stew of forgery, where property bounds lay, and whether Makuraner officials had been bribed to make them lie there. It involved no theology, just skulduggery. Mani-akes attacked it with great relish.

XI

ABIVARD BOWED IN THE SADDLE TO MANIAKES. "IF THE GOD IS kind," the Makuraner marshal said, "the next message you have from me will be that Mashiz has fallen into my hands."

"May it be so," Maniakes said. "Then we shall be equals: two jumped-up generals sitting on the thrones of our lands."

"Yes," Abivard said. "I suppose so." He still had his little nephew with whom to concern himself. Denak's son had a more nearly legitimate claim to the Makuraner throne than he did. Had the boy been Sharbaraz's get by another woman, the answer would have been easy. Disposing of his sister's child, though . . .

Judging it wiser to shift the subject a bit, Maniakes said, "So you have the men you need out of Vaspurakan?"

"Oh, yes," Abivard answered. "And I have three regiments of Vaspurakaners, all of them eager to cast down Sharbaraz."

"You'll take their help, but you won't take me?" Maniakes jabbed.

"Of course," Abivard said easily. "They are our subjects. If you were a Makuraner subject now, Sharbaraz would be well pleased with me, and I'd have had no need to rebel against him. The Vaspurakaners weren't invading the Land of the Thousand Cities earlier this year, either."

"A point," Maniakes said. "Two points, as a matter of fact. Good luck go with you. Cast down Sharbaraz; give him everything he deserves for all the sorrows he's brought to Videssos and Makuran both. And then, by the good god, let's see how long we can live in peace."

"Long enough to rebuild everything that's been destroyed, here and in Makuran," Abivard said. "That should take a few years, or more than a few—you weren't gentle between the Tutub and the Tib."

"I can't even say I'm sorry," Maniakes said. "The only way I could find to get you out of my land—where you weren't always gentle, either—was to ravage yours."

"I understand," Abivard said. "It worked, too. Maybe, if the God is kind, we'll have got out of the habit of fighting each other once we have everything patched. And the two of us, we know what this war was like, and why we don't want another one."

"Maybe we can even make our sons understand," Maniakes said hopefully. Abivard's nod was tighter and more constrained than the Avtokrator would have liked to see. The hesitation worried him till he remembered that Abivard was still pondering whether to rule as King of Kings or as regent for his nephew.

Maniakes drew the sun-circle, lest his thinking past Abivard's victory prove a bad omen for winning that victory. He rode forward, holding out his hand. The Makuraner marshal clasped it. Then Abivard surprised him, saying, "I want you to tell your father something for me."

"What's that?" the Avtokrator said.

"Tell him that if the Khamorth nomads hadn't killed Godarz—my father—I think the two of them would have got on famously together."

"I'll remember," Maniakes promised. "They might even have fought against each other, back when we were small or before we were born."

"That's so." Abivard looked bemused. "They might have. I hadn't thought of it, but you're right. And we certainly have. If the God is kind, our sons won't." He gave what might have been a sketched Videssian salute or might as easily have been a jerky wave, then used his knees and the reins to turn his horse and ride back toward his own army. His guards, who, like Maniakes', had halted out of earshot of their masters, fell in around him.

After watching him for most of a minute, Maniakes turned Antelope in the direction of the Videssian army. He heaved a long sigh as he trotted up to Rhegorios, who had ridden out a little way to meet him.

"It's over," Maniakes said in wondering tones. "It's really over. After all these years, the Makuraners really are leaving the westlands. We're at peace with them—unless Sharbaraz beats Abivard, of course. But even then, the King of Kings would have to think three times before he dared a new war with us. The Kubratoi aren't going to fight us any time soon, either. We're at peace, and we have the whole Empire back."

"Well, don't let it worry you too long," his cousin said. "The Khatrishers may decide to get bold, or the Halogai might gather a fleet together and attack Kalavria, or, for that matter, some people none of us has ever heard of might appear out of nowhere, for no better reason than to cause Videssos trouble."

"You do so relieve my mind," Maniakes said.

Rhegorios laughed. "Happy to please, your Majesty. You were looking so bereft there without anybody to fight, I thought I'd give you someone."

"People appearing out of nowhere? In the middle of the Empire, I presume? No, thank you," Maniakes said with feeling. "If you're going to wish for something absurd, wish for the Halogai to invade Kubrat instead of Kalavria. That would actually do us some good."

"You've won the war," Rhegorios said. "What will you do now?"

"What I'd like to do," Maniakes answered, "is go back to Videssos the city, enjoy my children and the rest of my family for a while, and have the people in the city not throw curses at me when I go out among 'em. Too much to ask for, I suppose."

"Now you're feeling sorry for yourself," Rhegorios said. "I'm not going to let you get away with that. I need to remind you that you just drove the invincible Makuraner army out of the westlands, and you didn't lose a man doing it. Go ahead and blubber after *that*."

Maniakes chuckled. "There you have me. Only goes to show, I suppose, that forgery beats fighting."

Rhegorios whipped his head around in sudden anxiety, or an excellent simulation thereof. "You'd better not let any Makuraners hear you say that."

"Of course not," Maniakes said. "If Romezan ever finds out all those other names weren't on the order Sharbaraz sent him, the whole civil war over there—" He pointed in the direction of the withdrawing army. "—might still unravel."

"That isn't what I mean," his cousin said. "You were talking like one of the sneaky Videssians they always complain about."

"Oh," the Avtokrator said. "I *am* a sneaky Videssian, but I don't suppose they have to know about that. They can think of me however they like—as long as they do it from a great distance."

"Do you plan on going back to the capital right away?"

"No." Maniakes shook his head. "Once I'm sure the boiler boys are gone for good—or at least for this campaigning season—I'll send back half, maybe even two thirds, of the army. Until I find out how the fight between Abivard and Sharbaraz goes, though, I'm going to stay in the westlands myself. If you can't stand being away from the fleshpots of the city, I'll send you back with the part of the army I release."

"What, and let you find out who wins the Makuraner civil war a couple of weeks before I do?" Rhegorios exclaimed. "Not likely. Send Immodios. If he's not killing Makuraners himself, he hasn't got the imagination to worry about what happens to 'em."

"All right, I'll do that," Maniakes said with a laugh. "My father and yours will be jealous of both of us, because we'll know when they don't."

"So they will." Rhegorios' eyes twinkled. "And they'll both say it's the first time in the history of the world we ever knew anything they don't already, even for a little while. That's what fathers are for."

"So it is," Maniakes said. "And pretty soon I'll be able to treat my boys the same way. See how life goes on?"

As Rhegorios had predicted, Immodios made not the tiniest protest when Maniakes ordered him to take half the imperial army back toward Videssos the city. The Avtokrator had decided not to give him more than half, on the off chance that he might take whatever he had into rebellion with him. Maniakes trusted him further than anyone not of his own immediate family; but someone inside his own immediate family had conspired against him, so that said little.

And no sooner had Immodios led the detachment back toward Videssos the city than Maniakes wished the army reunited. That, though, had nothing to do with fears about Immodios' loyalty or lack of same. It had to do with news a messenger brought up from the south.

"I'm sorry to have to tell you this, your Majesty," the fellow said, "but the Makuraner garrison in Serrhes hasn't pulled out of the town. They keep insisting they're loyal to Sharbaraz."

"Oh, they do, do they?" Maniakes sounded half-angry, half-resigned. "Well, I suppose I should have expected that would happen somewhere. I wish it hadn't happened at Serrhes, though."

The garrison town's main reason for existing was to plug that stretch of frontier between Makuran and the Empire of Videssos. He and his father had set out from Serrhes along with Abivard and Sharbaraz to return the latter to the Makuraner throne. That seemed a lot longer before than twelve or thirteen years.

"What will you do, your Majesty?" the messenger asked.

"What can I do?" Maniakes returned. "I'll go down to Serrhes and pry the Makuraners out of it." He paused. "How big a Makuraner garrison does the place have in it?"

"About a thousand men, or so I hear," the messenger said.

"I still have four times that many with me," the Avtokrator mused aloud. Having sent Immodios' detachment back toward the capital, he did not want to recall those troops. "Maybe I can get away with just using what I've got."

Intending to try it, he moved south with his half of the army. They hadn't had to march quickly since they'd left the Land of the Thousand Cities; the journey through the westlands had been a parade. The roads down toward Serrhes weren't good, and had been little traveled during the Makuraner occupation. The Videssians pressed rapidly along them nonetheless.

Before they got to Serrhes, the corrugated central plateau of the westlands began to give way to the scrubby semidesert lying between Videssos' western border and the Tutub River. Back in the long-ago days of his reign, Likinios Avtokrator had complained about almost every expense he ever had to meet. Trying not to meet one, finally, had cost him his throne and his life. So far as Maniakes knew, he'd never complained about keeping Serrhes supplied.

Approaching the town, Maniakes wondered how—or if—the Makuraners had managed that. Had they fed Serrhes off the countryside? The countryside yielded little. A few cattle grazed it, but not enough grew nearby to support more than a few. Over the dry country from the Land of the Thousand Cities? If so, the supply line was either already broken or easily breakable.

Looking at Serrhes' thick walls, looking at the citadel on the high ground in the center of town, Maniakes quickly decided he did not want to try storming the place. He rode forward behind a shield of truce to parley with the garrison commander.

Tegin son of Gamash came to Serrhes' western gate and looked down at the Avtokrator of the Videssians. He was a solidly built man with a gray beard and an impressive nose. "You're wasting your time," he called to Maniakes. "We won't yield to you."

"If you don't, you'll be sorry after I break into Serrhes," Maniakes said, threatening to do what he least wanted to do. "We outnumber you at least six to one. We'll show no mercy." *Assuming we're lucky enough to get onto or through those works,* he thought. Serrhes had been built with admirable skill to hold the Makuraners at bay. Now it threatened to do the same to the folk who had built it in the first place.

"Come do your worst," Tegin retorted. "We're ready for you."

Maniakes concluded he was not the only one running a noisy bluff. "What do you propose to eat in there?" he demanded.

"Oh, I don't know," Tegin said airily. "We have a deal of this and that. What do you propose to eat out there?"

It was, Maniakes had to admit, a good question. Supplying an army surrounding Serrhes had all the drawbacks of supplying the town itself. He wasn't about to let the Makuraner know he'd scored a hit, though. "We have all the westlands to draw on," he said. "Yours is the last Makuraner garrison hereabouts."

"All the more reason to hold it, then, wouldn't you say?" Tegin sounded as if he was enjoying himself. Maniakes wished he could say the same.

What he did say was, "By staying here, you violate the terms of the truce Abivard made with us."

"Abivard is not King of Kings," Tegin said. "My ruler is Sharbaraz King of Kings, may his years be many and his realm increase."

"All the Makuraners in the westlands have renounced Sharbaraz," Maniakes said.

Tegin shook his head. "Not all of them. This one hasn't, for instance."

"A pestilence," Maniakes muttered under his breath. He should have expected he'd come across a holdout or two. Things could have been worse; Romezan could have stayed resolutely loyal to Sharbaraz. But things could also have been better. The Avtokrator had no intention of letting Serrhes stay in Makuraner hands. He said, "You know Sharbaraz ordered Abivard and most of his generals slain when they failed to take Videssos the city."

"I've heard it said," the garrison commander answered. "I don't know it for a fact."

"I have seen the captured dispatch with my own eyes," Maniakes said. He had also seen the document transformed into one more useful for Videssian purposes, but forbore to mention that, such forbearance also being more useful for Videssian purposes.

Tegin remained difficult. "Majesty, begging your pardon, I don't much care what you've seen and what you haven't seen. You're the enemy. I expect you'd lie to me if you saw any profit in it. Videssians are like that."

Since Maniakes not only would lie but to a certain degree was lying, he changed the subject: "I point out to you once more, excellent sir, that you are at the moment commanding the only Makuraner garrison left in the westlands."

"So you say," Tegin replied, still unimpressed.

"If there are others all around, how have I fought my way past them to come to you?" Maniakes asked.

"If they've all gone over to Abivard, you don't need to have done any fighting," Tegin said.

"That's true, I suppose," Maniakes said. "And what it means is, I can concentrate my entire army—" He did not think Tegin needed to know that Immodios was leading half of it back to Videssos the city. "—against you holdouts in Serrhes." He waved back toward his encampment. It was as big as . . . an army. He did not think Tegin was in a position to estimate with any accuracy how many men were in it.

And, indeed, the garrison commander wavered for the first time. "I am surrounded by traitors," he complained.

"No, you're surrounded by Videssians," Maniakes answered. "This is part of the Empire, and we are taking it back. You've probably heard stories about what we've done to the walls of the Thousand Cities. Do you think we won't do the same to you?"

He knew perfectly well they couldn't do the same to Serrhes. The walls of the towns between the Tutub and the Tib were made of brick, and not the strongest brick, either. Serrhes was fortified in stone. Breaking in wouldn't be so easy. If Tegin had time to think, he would realize that, too. Best not give him time to think, then.

Maniakes said, "Excellent sir, I don't care how brave you are. Your garrison is small. If we once get in among 'em, I'm afraid I can't answer for the consequences. You'll have made warnings of that sort yourself, I expect; you know how soldiers are."

"Yes, I know how soldiers are," Tegin said somberly. "If I had more men, Majesty, I would beat you."

"If I had feathers, I'd be a tall rooster," Maniakes replied. "I don't. I'm not. You don't, either. You'd better remember it." He started to turn away, then stopped. "I'll ask you again at this hour tomorrow. If you say yes, you may depart safely, with your weapons, like any other Makuraner soldiers during the truce. But if you say no, excellent sir, I wash my hands of you." He did not give Tegin the last word, but walked off instead.

At his command, Videssian engineers began assembling siege engines from the timbers and ropes and specialized metal fittings they carried in the baggage train, as if they were intending to assault one of the hilltop towns in the Land of the Thousand Cities.

"We'd be able to run up more, your Majesty," Ypsilantes said, "if the countryside had trees we could cut down and use. We can only carry so much lumber."

"Do the best you can with what you have," Maniakes told the chief engineer, who saluted and went back to his work.

From the walls of Serrhes, Makuraner soldiers watched dart- and stone-throwers spring up as if by magic, though Bagdasares had nothing whatever to do with them. They watched the Videssian engineers line up row upon row of jars near the catapults. They no doubt had their own store of incendiary liquid, but could not have been delighted at the prospect of having so much of it rained down on their heads.

Seeing all those jars, Maniakes summoned Ypsilantes again. "I didn't know we were *that* well supplied with the stuff," he said, pointing.

Ypsilantes coughed modestly. "If you must know, your Majesty, most of those jars used to hold the wine we've served out to the troops when we weren't drawing supplies from a town. They're empty now. We know that. The Makuraners don't."

"Isn't that interesting?" Maniakes said with a grin. "They fooled me, so I expect they'll fool Tegin, too."

Ypsilantes also put ordinary soldiers to work dragging stones into piles. Those were perfectly genuine, though Maniakes wouldn't have put it past the chief engineer to have a few deceptive extras made of—what? stale bread, perhaps—lying around in case he needed them to befuddle an opponent.

A little before the appointed hour the next day, Tegin threw wide the gates of Serrhes. He came out and prostrated himself before Maniakes. "I would have fought you, Majesty. I wanted to fight you," he said. "But when I looked at all the siege gear you have with you, my heart failed me. I knew we could not withstand your army."

"You showed good sense." Maniakes made a point of not glancing toward Ypsilantes. The veteran engineer had served him better in not fighting this siege than he had in fighting a good many others. "As I told you, you may depart in peace."

Out filed the Makuraner garrison. Seeing it, Maniakes started to laugh. He wasn't the only one who'd done a good job of bluffing. If Tegin had even three hundred soldiers in Serrhes, he would have been astonished. He'd thought the garrison commander led three times that many, maybe more. Tegin might have fought an assault, but not for long.

Seriously, respecting the foe who had tricked him, Maniakes said, "If I were you, excellent sir, I'd keep my men out of the fight between Sharbaraz and Abivard. You can declare for whoever wins after he's won. Till then, find some little town or hilltop you can defend and stay there. That will keep you safe."

"Did you find 'some little town or hilltop' during Videssos' civil wars?" Tegin's voice dripped scorn.

But Maniakes answered, "As a matter of fact, yes." Tegin's jaw dropped. The Avtokrator went on, "My father was governor of the island of Kalavria, which is as far east as you can go without sailing out into the sea and never coming back. He sat tight there for six years. He would have thrown himself and his force away if he'd done anything else."

"You and your father took the course you judged wise," Tegin said tonelessly. "You will, I hope, forgive me if I say that this course goes straight against every Makuraner noble's notion of honor."

"Makuraner notions of honor didn't stop you people from kicking Videssos when we were down," Maniakes said.

"Of course not," Tegin replied. "You are only Videssians. But I cannot sit idly by in a fight among my countrymen. The God would judge me a faintheart without the will to choose, and would surely drop my soul into the Void after I die."

"There are times," Maniakes said slowly, "when I have no trouble at all dealing with Makuraners. And there are other times when I think we and you don't speak the same language even if we do use the same words."

"How interesting you should remark on that, Majesty," Tegin

said. "I have often had the same feeling when treating with you Videssians. At times, you seem sensible enough. At others—" He rolled his eyes. "You are not to be relied upon." That sounded as if he were passing judgment.

"No, eh?" Maniakes knew his smile was not altogether pleasant. "I suppose that means nothing would stop me from ignoring the truce we agreed to and scooping up your men now that they're out from behind the walls of Serrhes." Tegin looked appalled. Maniakes held up his hand. "Never mind. *I* think I have honor, whether you do or not."

"Good," Tegin said. "As I told you, sometimes Videssians are sensible folk. I am glad this is one of those times."

At the head of his little army, the garrison commander rode off to the west. He had a jauntiness to him that Maniakes didn't usually associate with Makuraners. Maniakes hoped he wouldn't have to throw his small force into the fight between the King of Kings and his marshal.

Like many other provincial towns, Serrhes centered on a square with the city governor's residence and the chief temple to Phos on opposite sides. Maniakes settled down in the residence and, as he had in so many other towns, began sorting through the arguments left behind after Tegin and his troopers were gone.

Some of those quarrels were impressively complicated. "He cheated me, your Majesty!" one plump merchant exclaimed, pointing a finger at another. "By Phos, he diddled me prime, he did, and now he stands there smooth-faced as a eunuch and denies every word of it."

"Liar," the second merchant said. "They were going to make you a eunuch, but they cut off your brain instead, because it was smaller."

"Ahem, gentlemen," Maniakes said, giving both the benefit of a doubt neither seemed likely to deserve. "Suppose, instead of insulting each other, you tell me what the trouble is."

"Actually," Rhegorios murmured from beside him, "I wouldn't mind hearing them insult each other a while longer. It has to be more interesting than the case, don't you think?"

"Hush," Maniakes said, and then, to the first merchant, "Go ahead. You say this other chap here cheated you. Tell me how." The second merchant started to howl a protest before the first could begin to speak. Maniakes held up a hand. "You keep quiet. I promise, you'll have your turn."

The first merchant said, "I sold this whipworthy wretch three hundred pounds of smoked mutton, and he promised to pay me ten and a half goldpieces for it. But when it came time for him to cough up the money, the son of a whore dumped a pile of trashy Makuraner arkets on me and said I could either take 'em or stick 'em up my arse, because they were all I'd ever see from him."

Maniakes' head started to ache. He'd run into cases like this before. With many parts of the westlands in Makuraner hands for more than a decade, it was no wonder that silver coins stamped with the image of the King of Kings were in wide circulation thereabouts. The methodical Makuraners had even made some of the provincial mints turn out copies of their coins rather than those of Videssos.

"May I speak now, your Majesty?" the second merchant asked.

"Go ahead," Maniakes said.

"Thank you," the merchant said. "The first thing I want to tell you is that Broios here can give himself piles when he sneezes, his head is so far up his back passage. By the lord with the great and good mind, your Majesty, you must understand what money of account is. Am I right, or am I right?"

"Oh, yes," Maniakes answered.

"Thank you," the merchant said again. "When I told this chamberpot-sniffing jackal I'd give him ten and a half goldpieces, that was money of account. What else could it be? When was the last time anybody in Serrhes saw real goldpieces? Whoever has 'em, has 'em buried where the boiler boys couldn't find 'em. We all buy and sell with silver these days. We coin our silver at twenty-four to the goldpiece, so if I'd given Broios two hundred and fifty-two pieces of silver—Videssian silver, mind you—for his smoked mutton, that would have been right and proper. You see as much, don't you, your Majesty?"

Maniakes had a good education—for a soldier. He would sooner have given himself over to a torturer than multiplied twenty-four by ten and a half in his head. But, since Broios wasn't hopping up and down like a man who needed to visit the jakes, the Avtokrator supposed the other merchant—whose name he still didn't know— had made the calculation correctly.

"If Vetranios had given me two hundred and fifty-two of our

silverpieces, I wouldn't be fussing now," Broios said, thereby giving Maniakes the missing piece.

"I couldn't give you that many of our silver pieces, because I didn't have them, you ugly twit," Vetranios said. "I gave you as many as I had, and paid the rest of the scot in Makuraner arkets—I had plenty of those."

"Of course you did," Broios shouted. "All the time the boiler boys were here, you did nothing but lick their backsides."

"Me? What about you?" Vetranios swung at the other merchant, awkwardly but with great feeling. Broios swung back, with rather greater effect. A couple of Haloga guards grabbed them and pulled them away from each other.

"Gently, gentlemen, gently," Maniakes said. "Did you come before me to fight or to get this dispute settled?" The question was rhetorical, but neither of the merchants quite had the nerve to say he would sooner have fought the other. Maniakes took their silence as acquiescence. "Let us continue, then. You, Vetranios, how many Videssian silver pieces did you pay to Broios here?"

"Forty," Vetranios answered at once. "That was all the Videssian silver I had. I made up the other two hundred and twelve with arkets. They're silver, too."

"You only gave me seventy-seven of them," Broios howled.

"That's how many I was supposed to give you, you boil on the scrotum of stupidity," Vetranios retorted. The Haloga who was holding him let go to clap his hands together to applaud the originality of the insult. The merchant ignored that, saying, "It takes eleven Videssian silver pieces to make four arkets, weight for weight, so I gave you the proper payment; you're just too stupid to see it."

Maniakes would have needed pen and parchment and infinite patience to be sure whether Vetranios had done his calculations right. He decided for the time being that they were when Broios didn't protest. "This *was* the correct pay, then?" he asked the merchant who claimed he'd been defrauded.

"No, your Majesty," Broios answered. "This *would have been* the right pay, if this dung beetle who walked like a man hadn't cheated me. All the arkets he gave me were so badly clipped, there wasn't sixty arkets' worth of silver in the seventy-seven."

"Why, you lying sack of moldy tripes!" Vetranios said.

"To the ice with me if I am," Broios said, "and to the ice with you if I'm not." He handed Maniakes a jingling sack of silver. "Judge for yourself, your Majesty. The cursed cheat's clipped the coins, and kept for himself the silver that was round the rim."

Opening the sack, Maniakes examined the silver arkets it held. They were indeed badly clipped, one and all. "May I see those, your Majesty?" Vetranios asked. When Maniakes showed them to him, his face darkened in anger—or, perhaps, in a convincing facsimile thereof; Maniakes could not for the life of him tell which. The merchant said, "These aren't the coins I gave to Broios. I gave him perfectly good silver, by Phos. If anybody clipped them, he did it himself."

Now Broios turned purple, as convincingly as Vetranios had done a moment before. "By the lord with the great and good mind, your Majesty, hear how this sack of manure farts through his mouth." Vetranios tried to punch him again; the Haloga guards kept them apart.

"Each of you says the other is a liar, eh?" Maniakes said. Both merchants nodded vehemently. Maniakes continued, "Each of you says the other clipped these coins, eh?" Both men nodded again. The Avtokrator's face went stern. "Both of you no doubt know that clipping coins comes under the same law as counterfeiting and carries the same unpleasant penalties. If I have to get all the way to the bottom of this, I fear that one of you will regret it very much."

Both merchants nodded again, as vigorously as before. That surprised Maniakes. He'd expected one of them—he didn't know which—to show some sign of alarm. They had nerve, these two.

He said, "If whichever of you is lying makes a clean breast of it now, I swear by the lord with the great and good mind to make the penalty no greater than a fine of seventeen Makuraner arkets and an oath binding you never to clip coins again on penalty of further punishment."

He waited. Vetranios and Broios both shook their heads. Each glared at the other. Maniakes didn't know whether to be annoyed or intrigued at their stubbornness. He would sooner have had no trouble from the newly reoccupied westlands. That hadn't happened. He hadn't thought it would. Here, at least, was a dispute more interesting than the common sort, where truth was easy to find.

"Very well, gentlemen," he said. "For the time being, I shall keep these arkets, since they are evidence—of what sort remains to be seen—in the case between you. Come back here tomorrow at the start of the eighth hour, after the midday meal. We shall see what my sorcerer makes of this whole strange business."

Before the merchants returned the next day, Rhegorios came up to Maniakes and said, "I've done some of my own investigating in this case, cousin of mine."

"Ah?" Maniakes said. "And what did you find?"

"That Broios has a very tasty daughter—not shaped anything like him, Phos be praised." Rhegorios' hands described curves in the air. "Her name's Phosia. I think I'm in love." He let out a sigh.

"What you're in, cousin of mine," Maniakes retorted, "is heat. I'll pour a bucket of water on you, and you'll feel better."

"No, wetter," Rhegorios said. He ran his tongue across his lips. "She really is beautiful. If her father weren't a thief . . . Maybe even if her father is a thief . . ." Since Rhegorios had made similar noises in almost every town the Videssian army visited, Maniakes took no special notice of these.

Broios and Vetranios returned to the city governor's residence within a couple of minutes of each other at the eighth hour. Maniakes had looked for that; to merchants, punctuality was hardly a lesser god than Phos. What the Avtokrator had not looked for was that each of the men from Serrhes brought his own wizard with him.

Broios' champion, a certain Sozomenos, was as portly as his principal, and resembled him enough to be his cousin. Phosteinos, who represented Vetranios' interests, was by contrast thin to the point of emaciation, as if whoever had invented food had forgotten to tell him about it.

Bagdasares looked down his long nose at both of them. "Have you gentlemen—" As Maniakes had with the merchants, he sounded like a man graciously conferring the undeserved benefit of the doubt. "—been involved in this matter from the outset?"

"Of course, we have," Phosteinos said in a thin, rasping voice. "Vetranios hired me to keep Broios from cheating him, and the wretch countered by paying this charlatan here to help him go on bilking my client."

"Why don't you blow away for good?" Sozomenos demanded. Phosteinos responded with a skeletal smile. Sozomenos ignored it, turning to Maniakes and saying, "See how they misrepresent me and my principal both?" He shrugged his plump shoulders, as if to say, *What can you do?* The Avtokrator was suddenly certain each merchant had spent a great deal more on this case than the seventeen arkets' worth of silver allegedly at issue.

Bagdasares took Maniakes aside and whispered, "Your Majesty, getting to the bottom of this will be harder than we thought. These two bunglers will have muddied the waters till no one can hope to tell where the truth lies and where the lies start."

"Just go ahead," the Avtokrator answered. "Make it as impressive as you can." He looked from merchant to merchant. "Makes you wonder if we shouldn't have let the Makuraners keep this place, doesn't it?"

Bagdasares let out a loud sniff, perhaps at the notion of having to associate with wizards who, in Videssos the city, would surely have starved for lack of trade; Phosteinos looked to be on the point of starving anyhow, but Maniakes blamed that on personal asceticism rather than want of business: his robe looked expensive.

"Very well," Bagdasares said, that sniff having failed to make his sorcerous colleagues vanish. "We have to determine two things today: whether the coins Broios presented to his Majesty—" He had them in a bowl. "—are in fact those Vetranios paid to him, and, if so, who was responsible for clipping the aforesaid coins."

"We know *that*," Broios and Vetranios said in the same breath with the identical intonation. They glared at each other.

"First," Bagdasares went on as if they had not spoken, "we shall use the law of similarity to determine whether Broios is honestly representing these arkets to be the ones he received from Vetranios."

"Now see here," Sozomenos said, "how can we trust you not to have it in for Broios? When the Makuraners were here, by the good god, a little coin in the right places would make magic turn out any way the chap who was paying had in mind."

Bagdasares started to answer. Maniakes cut him off, saying, "*I* will deal with this." He glowered at the mage. "Do you think either of your clients is important enough in the scheme of things to buy off the Avtokrator of the Videssians and his chief sorcerer?"

Before Sozomenos could say anything, Phosteinos broke in with a loud, startled cackle of laughter. Sozomenos glowered at his thin colleague, then coughed a couple of times. "Put that way, probably not, your Majesty," he said.

"Good. See that you remember it." Maniakes nodded to Bagdasares. "Proceed, eminent sir. These fellows here are welcome to watch you to make sure you do nothing to favor Broios or Vetranios—not that you would—but they are not to interfere with your magic in any way." He gave Phosteinos and Sozomenos a severe look. "Is that understood, sorcerous sirs?"

Neither of the mages from Serrhes said no. Maniakes nodded again to Bagdasares. The Vaspurakaner wizard said, "The first thing I intend to do, as I said a little while ago, is to find out whether Broios presented to his Majesty coins he actually received from Vetranios. Vetranios, if you have an arket in that pouch on your belt, please hand it to Broios. Broios, you will then hand it to me."

"I just might have an arket or two," Vetranios said, chuckling. "Yes, sir, I just might." He opened the pouch and took out a shiny silver coin. "Not clipped at all, you'll note," he remarked as he handed it to Broios.

The other merchant took it from him as if it smelled bad. He handed it to Sozomenos, who in turn passed it to Bagdasares.

Bagdasares looked pained. "We'll do that again, with a new arket," he said, tossing the first one aside. Vetranios' eyes hungrily followed it. So did Broios'. So did those of both local wizards. "No more foolishness," Bagdasares told them. "Anyone who fails to follow my instructions will be deemed to have forfeited his case."

Under Bagdasares' watchful eye, Vetranios got out another arket. This one was also unclipped, but he didn't boast about it. He gave it to Broios. Broios gave it to Bagdasares without presuming to let another wizard handle it in between.

"That's better," Bagdasares said. Maniakes hid a smile; the mage spoke with the authority of a provincial governor. The Avtokrator was suddenly thoughtful. He would need new governors for the provinces of the westlands—he would need to repair the whole system of provincial administration here, in fact. He could do much worse than Bagdasares.

Muttering to himself, the Vaspurakaner mage dropped Vetranios' arket in among the coins Broios claimed to have received from the other merchant. It clinked sweetly; the Makuraners coined little gold, but their silver was as pure as anything from a Videssian mint.

Bagdasares began to chant. Phosteinos and Sozomenos both pricked up their ears. They evidently knew the spell he was using. Maniakes watched as the mage made several swift passes over the coins. Phosteinos nodded what looked like approval of Bagdasares' technical skill.

After one final pass, Bagdasares cried out in a commanding voice. Some of the coins in the bowl began glowing with a soft, bluish radiance. Others remained simply—coins. "Your Majesty," Bagdasares said, "as you may judge for yourself, some of this money has indeed passed from Vetranios to Broios, as we see by the aid of the law of similarity. Some of the coins, however, did not take this route."

"Isn't that interesting?" Maniakes studied Broios, who seemed to be doing his best to disappear while remaining in plain sight. Gloating glee filled Vetranios' chuckle. The Avtokrator turned a mild and speculative eye on the merchant who'd brought the charges against his fellow in the first place. "Well, Broios, what have you got to say for yourself?"

"Y-y-your M-majesty, maybe I—I mixed in a few arkets that weren't from Vetranios by—by mistake." Broios' voice firmed. "Yes, that's it. I must have done it by mistake."

Vetranios walked over to look at the arkets more closely. "Likely tell," he jeered. "You can see that all of these 'mistaken' coins are clipped." He struck a pose so overblown, Maniakes wondered if he'd gotten it from some mime in a Midwinter's Day troupe.

Broios said, "They're not the only ones that are clipped, though, by Phos!" He came up to the bowl and pointed to some of the shining coins. "Look at that arket there, and that one—and that one. That one's cut so bad, you can hardly see the King of Kings' face at all. They were like that when I got 'em, too."

"Liar!" Vetranios shouted. He turned to Maniakes. "You hear with your own ears, you see with your own eyes, what a liar he is. I don't think there's any bigger liar in the whole Empire than Broios."

"Liar yourself," Broios retorted. "You have your wizard here, your Majesty. He can show you who stuck the silver from the rims of these arkets into his pouch."

"Yes, why don't you go ahead and show me that, Bagdasares?" Maniakes said. "I confess, by now I'm curious. And nothing about this case would surprise me any more, except perhaps finding an honest man anywhere in it."

Phosteinos stirred. "Your Majesty, I resent the imputation. You have proved nothing illicit about my actions."

"That's true," Maniakes admitted, and the scrawny wizard preened. Then the Avtokrator brought him down to earth: "I haven't proved anything yet." That got a laugh from Sozomenos, a laugh that cut off very sharply when Maniakes glanced over at the sorcerer who'd been helping Broios.

At a nod from Maniakes, Bagdasares handed Vetranios a small sharp knife and said, "I presume you have in your pouch yet another unclipped arket." Most unhappily, the merchant nodded. "Excellent," Bagdasares declared. "Be so good as to trim the silver from the edges, then, that we may have a comparison against which to set these arkets in the bowl."

Vetranios looked as if he would sooner have stuck the knife into Bagdasares. He shot Phosteinos a hunted glance. Almost imperceptibly, the emaciated mage shook his head: he could do nothing— or, more likely, nothing Bagdasares wouldn't detect. Vetranios deflated like a popped pig's bladder. "Never mind," he mumbled. "You don't need to go through the rigmarole. I clipped some of those arkets—*just like every other merchant around*." Now he might have wanted to stab Broios.

Broios took no notice of his hate-filled glare. "Who's the biggest liar in the Empire *now*?" he said, for all the world like one small boy scoring a point against another.

"You're both wrong," Maniakes said. "Neither one of you knows the biggest liar in the Empire. His name is Tzikas."

Broios pointed at Vetranios. "*He* knows this Tzikas. I've heard him talk about the fellow, plenty of times."

Suddenly, everyone in the room was staring at Vetranios. "So you know Tzikas, do you?" Maniakes said in a soft voice. "Tell me about Tzikas, Vetranios. When did you see him last, for starters?"

Vetranios knew something was wrong, but not what, nor how much. Serrhes was far from Videssos the city, and had been in Makuraner hands since the earliest days of Genesios' disastrous reign. The merchant answered, "Why, it must have been about three weeks before you came, your Majesty. He's been through the town now and again, these past few years. I've sold him this and that, and we've drunk wine together every now and then. That's about the size of it, I'd say."

Maniakes studied not him but Broios. If Vetranios' enemy accepted that tale, it was likely to be true. If, on the other hand, Broios found more to say . . . But Broios did not find more to say. Maniakes didn't know whether to be glad or disappointed.

"I can understand why you wouldn't like having a Videssian

working for the boiler boys," Vetranios said, sympathy oozing from him like sticky sap from a cut spruce. "He's not the only one, though."

"He's the only one who's tried to overthrow me," Maniakes said. "He's the only one who's tried to murder me. He's the only one who's betrayed both sides in this war more times than I can count. He's the only one who's—" He made a disgusted gesture. "Why go on?"

Broios and Vetranios were both staring at him. He could see exactly what was going on behind Broios' eyes as the merchant realized he should have done a more thorough job of slandering Vetranios. He could also see Broios realizing that now was too late, and growing furious at his own lapse.

"Why did Tzikas come here?" Maniakes asked Vetranios.

"I don't know for certain," the merchant answered. "He spent a lot of time closeted with Tegin, I know that much. It had something to do with the squabbles the Makuraners are having, didn't it? They both favored Sharbaraz King of Kings, may his days be long and his realm increase." He spoke the honorific formula without noticing he'd done so. Serrhes *had* been in Makuraner hands a long time.

Letting that ride, Maniakes said, "So you know about whom Tzikas favored, do you?" Vetranios gave a tiny nod, as if expecting hot pincers and thumbscrews to follow upon the admission. Maniakes asked the next question: "What exactly did he say to you when the two of you talked?"

"Let's see." Vetranios was ready to cooperate freely, if for no better reason than to keep himself from having to cooperate any other way. "He bought ten pounds of the smoked mutton I had of this wretch here." He pointed to Broios. "Then he said something about how hard life had been lately, and how nobody appreciated his true worth. I told him I did. For some reason, he thought that was funny."

Maniakes thought it was funny, though he didn't say so. If a cheat of a merchant was the only one who appreciated Tzikas, what did that say about the ververversatile Videssian officer? Idly, the Avtokrator asked, "When you sold him the ten pounds of mutton, how badly did you bilk him?"

"Not a barleycorn's worth," Vetranios answered, wide-eyed. "He killed a man here who gave him short weight last year."

"I remember that!" Broios exclaimed: such a calamity had obviously created a lasting impression on the merchants of Serrhes. "I didn't know the name of the fellow who did it."

Thoughtfully, Bagdasares said, "Ten pounds of smoked mutton? That's traveler's food, something somebody would want if he was going on a long journey."

"So it is." Maniakes was thoughtful, too. "The timing strikes me odd, though. You're sure he was here only three weeks before I came to Serrhes, Vetranios? It wasn't longer ago than that?"

"By the lord with the great and good mind I swear it, your Majesty." To emphasize his words, Vetranios sketched Phos' sun-circle over his heart.

"I wish you'd said longer." Maniakes wondered if Vetranios, like a lot of merchants, would change his story to suit his customer better. But the plump trader shook his head and drew the sun-sign again. Maniakes drummed the fingers of one hand on a tabletop. "It doesn't fit. He wouldn't have dawdled here in the westlands so long, not if he was all hotfoot to warn Sharbaraz. Phos, he could have gone to Mashiz and come back here in that time. But why on earth would he do that?"

It was a rhetorical question. He hoped Bagdasares, one of the mages from Serrhes, or one of the merchants would answer it nonetheless. No one did. Instead, Bagdasares added more questions of his own: "And if he did do it, what need would he have for smoked mutton? He could have stayed here with Tegin and gone west with the Makuraner garrison. We'd be none the wiser."

"I didn't see him here after he bought the mutton from me," Vetranios said. "If he'd stayed with the garrison, I might not have seen him, but I think I would."

Phosteinos coughed to draw attention to himself and then said, "I also know this man somewhat. I agree with my principal in this matter: the visit to Serrhes was but a brief one."

Maniakes' glance toward the local wizard was anything but mild and friendly. "You know Tzikas, eh?" he asked. Phosteinos nodded. The Avtokrator interrogated him as he had with Vetranios: "Did you ever perform any magical service for him?" Phosteinos nodded again. Maniakes pounced: "And what sort of service was that, sirrah?"

"Why, to use the laws of similarity and contagion to help him find one of a pair of fancy spurs early this year, your Majesty," Phosteinos answered.

"Nothing else?" Maniakes' voice was cold.

"Why, no," Phosteinos said. "I don't understand why—"

"Because when the son of a whore tried to murder me, he did it with a wizard's help," the Avtokrator interrupted. Phosteinos' eyes went big in his pinched face. Maniakes pressed on: "Now, are you sure this was the only sorcerous service he ever had of you?"

Phosteinos was as eager to swear by Phos as Vetranios had been. Maniakes reckoned both those oaths as being worth only so much: a man might easily prefer risking Skotos' ice in the world to come to the Avtokrator's wrath in the world that was here. But then Sozomenos spoke up: "May it please your Majesty, I have no great love for my scrawny colleague here, but in all our years of acquaintance I have never known him to work magic to harm a man's health, let alone seek his death."

To Bagdasares, Maniakes said, "I'd sooner have your word on that than the word of someone I don't know if I can trust."

Sozomenos looked affronted. Maniakes didn't care. Bagdasares looked troubled. That worried the Avtokrator. Bagdasares said, "Judging a wizard's truthfulness by sorcerous means is different from gauging that of an ordinary man. Mages have too many subtle ways to confuse the results of such examinations."

"I was afraid you were going to say something like that," Maniakes said unhappily. He studied Phosteinos and Sozomenos. Both of them fairly radiated candor; had they been lamps, he would have had to shield his eyes against their glow. What Bagdasares told him meant he would have to gauge whether they were telling the truth by his usual, mundane complement of senses—either that or try to drag truth out of them by torture. He wasn't fond of torture; under the lash or more ingenious means of interrogation, people were too apt to say whatever they thought likeliest to make the pain stop.

Reluctantly, he decided he believed the two sorcerers from Serrhes. That left one last thing to do. Turning to Broios and Vetranios, he said, "And now to deal with the two of you."

Both merchants started. Both, Maniakes guessed, had hoped he'd forgotten about them. "What—what will you do with us, your Majesty?" Broios asked, his voice trembling.

"I don't know which of you is worse," Maniakes said. "You're both liars and cheats." He stroked his beard while he thought, then suddenly smiled. Broios and Vetranios quailed under that smile. Maniakes took an ignoble but very real pleasure in passing sentence: "First, you are fined fifty goldpieces each—or their weight in *perfect* silver—for tampering with the currency. The money is due tomorrow. And second, both of you shall be sent out to the center of the square here between the city governor's residence and Phos' holy temple. There in the square, a Haloga will give each of you a sturdy kick in the arse. If you can't get honesty through your heads, maybe we can send it up from the other direction."

"But, your Majesty, publicly humiliating us will make us laughing-stocks in the city," Vetranios protested.

"Good," Maniakes said. "Don't you think you deserve to be?"

Neither merchant answered that. If they agreed, they humiliated themselves. If they disagreed, they contradicted the Avtokrator of the Videssians. Given those choices, silence was better.

Maniakes escorted them out of the room where Bagdasares had performed his sorcery. When he told the guardsmen outside about the sentence, they shouted approval and almost came to blows in their eagerness to be the two who would deliver the kicks.

The Avtokrator came back into the chamber. He found Bagdasares talking shop with Phosteinos and Sozomenos. That convinced him the wizards shared his view of the two merchants from Serrhes. To those two, he said, "I presume you were doing nothing to threaten me. Because of that, you may go."

They thanked him and left in a hurry, giving him no chance to change his mind. "What was Tzikas doing here so recently?" Bagdasares asked again as soon as they were out of earshot.

"To the ice with me if I know," Maniakes answered. "It makes no more sense to me now than it did when we first found out about it." He scowled at Bagdasares even more fiercely than he had at Vetranios and Broios. "But I'm sure of one thing."

"What's that?" Bagdasares asked.

"It makes sense to Tzikas."

For as long as Maniakes stayed in Serrhes, he heard no more from his squabbling merchants. That suited him fine; it meant they were on their best behavior. The other alternative was that it meant they were cheating so well, no one was catching them and complaining. Maniakes supposed that was possible, but he didn't believe it: neither Broios nor Vetranios was likely to be that good a thief.

Rhegorios did keep sighing over Phosia. Maniakes kept threatening him with cold water. After a while, his cousin fell silent.

As long as Abivard had stayed in the Videssian westlands, he'd sent streams of messengers to Maniakes. Once he crossed back into territory long Makuraner, though, the stream shrank to a trickle. Maniakes worried that something had gone wrong.

"What's likely wrong," Rhegorios said, one day when the Avtokrator had been fretting more than usual, "is that Tegin has got between us and Abivard. The little garrison force couldn't do anything much against Abivard, mind you, but it's big enough to pick off a courier or two."

"You're right about that, of course," Maniakes said. "And you're probably right that that's what's causing the trouble. I should have thought of it for myself." Thinking of everything was part of what went with the Avtokrator's job. That it was impossible didn't make it any less necessary. Every time Maniakes missed a point, he felt bad for days.

He cheered up when a rider did come from out of the west. The fellow wore the full panoply of a Makuraner boiler boy; either he'd worried about running into Tegin's men or about running into Maniakes'. His armor clattered about him as he prostrated himself before the Avtokrator of the Videssians.

"Majesty," he said, rising with noisy grace, "know that the forces led by Abivard the new sun of Makuran have encountered those foolishly loyal to Sharbaraz Pimp of Pimps in the Land of the Thousand Cities. Know further that Abivard's forces have the victory."

"Good news!" Maniakes exclaimed. "I'm always glad to hear good news."

The messenger nodded. His chain-mail veil rattled. Above that veil, all Maniakes could see of the man himself were his eyes. They snapped with excitement. "We have Sharbaraz on the run now, Majesty," he said. "A good part of his army came over to ours, which made him flee back to Mashiz."

"That's better than good news," Maniakes said. "Press hard and he's yours. Once his forces start crumbling, they'll go like mud brick in the rain."

"Even so, or so we hope," the messenger said. "When I was

detached to come east to you, the field force was making ready to follow Sharbaraz's fugitives to the capital."

"Press hard," Maniakes repeated. "If you don't, you give Sharbaraz a chance to recover." From behind the messenger's veil came an unmistakable chuckle. "What's funny?" the Avtokrator asked.

"Majesty, you speak my language well," the messenger answered. Maniakes knew he was politely stretching a point, but let him do it. The fellow went on, "No one, though, would ever take you for a Makuraner, not by the way you say the name of the man Abivard will overthrow."

Maniakes proved his command of the Makuraner tongue left something to be desired by needing a moment to sort through that and figure out what the messenger meant. "Did I say *Sarbaraz* again?" he demanded, and the man nodded. Maniakes snapped his fingers in chagrin. "Oh, a pestilence! I've spent a lot of time learning how to pronounce that strange sound you use. His name is . . . is . . . *Sarbaraz*!" He started to raise a hand in triumph, then realized he'd failed again. Really angry now, he concentrated hard. "Sar . . . Sar . . . *Shar*baraz! There."

"Well done!" the messenger said. "Most of you hissing, squeaking Videssians never do manage to get that one right, try as you will."

"You can tell a Makuraner by the way he speaks Videssian, too," Maniakes said, to which the messenger nodded. Maniakes went on, "You haven't—or Abivard hasn't—by any chance got word of where Tzikas is lurking these days?"

"The traitor? No, indeed, Majesty. I wish I did know, though I'd tell Abivard before I told you. He's offering a good-sized reward for word of him and a bigger one for his head."

"So am I," Maniakes said.

"Are you?" The Makuraner's eyes widened. "How much?" His people claimed to scorn Videssians as a race of merchants and shopkeepers. Maniakes' experience was that the men of Makuran were no more immune to the lure of gold and silver than anyone else. And when Maniakes told him how much he might earn for finding Tzikas, he whistled softly. "If I hear anything, I'll tell you and not Abivard."

"Tell whichever of us has the best chance of catching the renegade," Maniakes said. "If he is caught thanks to you, get word to me and I'll make good the difference between Abivard's reward and mine, I promise. Tell all your friends, too, and tell them to tell their friends."

"I'll do that," the messenger promised.

"Good," Maniakes said. "If I had to guess, I'd say he's somewhere not far from here, but I know that could be wildly wrong." He explained what he'd learned from Vetranios and Phosteinos.

"He is more likely to be here than he is in the Land of the Thousand Cities or in Mashiz, I think," the messenger said. "Here, at least, he can open his mouth without betraying himself every time he does it."

"When Tzikas opens his mouth, he betrays other people, not himself," Maniakes said, which made the messenger laugh. "You think I'm joking," the Avtokrator told him. He was, but only to a degree. And the Makuraner's comments made him thoughtful. If Tzikas wanted to disappear in the westlands, he could. Maniakes had found it impossible to imagine a Tzikas who wanted to disappear. He admitted to himself he might have been wrong.

He gave the messenger a goldpiece, warned him about Tegin's small force of men still loyal to Sharbaraz, and sent him back to Abivard with congratulations. That done, he went outside the city governor's residence instead of getting on to the next order of business in Serrhes.

Everything looked normal. A few peasants from the surrounding countryside were selling sheep and pigs and ducks. Some other peasants, having made their sales, were buying pots and hatchets and other things they couldn't get on their farms. One of them was showing a harlot some money. The two went off together. If the peasant's wife ever found out about that, Maniakes could think of at least one thing the fellow wasn't likely to get on the farm.

So many people: tall, short, bald, hairy, young, old. And, if Tzikas had decided to disappear instead of trying to get his revenge, he might have been about one out of three of the men. The thought was disquieting, freighted as it was with a heavy burden of anticlimax.

Maniakes had needed to hold off the Kubratoi and Makuraners. He'd done that. He'd needed to find a way to get the Makuraners out of the westlands. Thanks to some unwitting help from Sharbaraz, he'd done that, too. And now, either Abivard would beat Sharbaraz or the other way round in the Makuraner civil war he'd helped create. Whichever happened, he'd know, and handle what came next accordingly.

Sharp, decisive answers—like anyone, he was fond of those. He already had ambiguity in his life: he'd never found out, and doubted he ever would find out, what had happened to his brother Tatoules. He knew what was most likely to have happened to him, but that wasn't the same.

Getting rid of Tzikas would be a sharp, decisive answer. Even knowing what had happened to Tzikas, regardless of whether he'd had anything to do with it, would be a sharp, decisive answer. Never learning for certain whether Tzikas was alive or dead, or where he was or what he was doing if he was alive . . . Maniakes didn't care for that notion at all.

He understood only too well how dangerous ambiguity could be when connected to Tzikas. He might be riding down a street in Videssos the city ten years from now, having seen or heard nothing of the renegade in all that time, having nearly forgotten him, only to be pierced by an arrow from a patient enemy who had not forgotten *him*. Or he might spend those ten years worrying about Tzikas every day when the wretch was long since dead.

"No way to know," he muttered. A writer of romances would not have approved. Everything in romances always came out neat and tidy. Avtokrators in romances were never foolish—unless they were wicked rulers being overthrown by someone who would do the job right. Maniakes snorted. He'd done exactly that, but, somehow, it hadn't kept him from remaining a human being.

"No matter how much I want the son of a whore dead, I may never live to see it." That was another matter, and made him as discontented as the first. If Tzikas chose obscurity, he could cheat the headsman. Would obscurity be punishment enough? It might have to be, no matter how little Maniakes cared for the notion.

He kicked at the dirt, angry at himself and Tzikas both. This should have been the greatest triumph of his career, the greatest triumph any Avtokrator had enjoyed since the civil wars the Empire had suffered a century and a half before cost it most of its eastern provinces. Instead of being able to enjoy the triumph, he was still spending far too much of his time and energy fretting over the loose end Tzikas had become.

He knew one certain cure for that. As fast as he could, he went back to the city governor's residence. "The Empress, your Majesty?" a servant said. "I believe she's upstairs in the sewing room."

Lysia wasn't sewing when Maniakes got up there. She and some of the serving women of the household were spinning flax into thread and, by the laughter that came from the sewing room as Maniakes walked down the hall toward it, using the work as an excuse for chat and gossip.

"Is something wrong?" Lysia asked when she saw him. She set the spindle down on the projecting shelf of her belly. The serving women exclaimed in alarm: he wasn't supposed to be there at this time of day.

"No," he answered, which was on the whole true, his worries notwithstanding. He amplified that: "And even if it were, I know how to make it better."

He walked over to her and helped her rise from the stool on which she sat: the baby wouldn't wait much longer. Then, standing slightly to one side of her so he wouldn't have to lean so far over that great belly, he did a careful and thorough job of kissing her.

A couple of the serving women giggled. Several more murmured back and forth to one another. He noticed all that only distantly. Some men, he'd heard, lost desire for their wives when those wives were great with child. Some of the serving women had made eyes at him, wondering if he felt like—and perhaps trying to provoke him into feeling like—amusing himself elsewhere while Lysia neared the end of her pregnancy. He'd noticed—he'd never lost his eye for pretty women—but he hadn't done anything about it.

"Well!" Lysia said when the kiss finally ended. She rubbed at her upper lip, where his mustache must have tickled her. "What was that in aid of?"

"Because I felt like doing it," Maniakes answered. "I've seen how many layers the bureaucracy in the Empire has, but I've never yet seen anything that says I have to submit a requisition before I draw a kiss from my wife."

"I wouldn't be surprised if there was such a form," Lysia answered, "but you can probably get away without using it even if there is. Being Avtokrator has to count for something, don't you think?"

If that wasn't a hint, it would do till a real one came along. Maniakes kissed her again, even more thoroughly than he had before. He was so involved in what he was doing, in fact, that he was taken by surprise when he looked up at the end of the kiss and discovered the serving women had left the room. "Where did they go?" he said foolishly.

"It doesn't matter," Lysia said, "as long as they're gone." This time, she kissed him.

A little later, they went back to their bedchamber. With her so very pregnant, making love was an awkward business. When they joined, she lay on her right side facing away from him. Not only was that a position in which she was more comfortable than most others, it was also one of the relatively few where they *could* join without her belly getting in the way.

The baby inside her kicked as enthusiastically then as at any other time, and managed to be distracting enough to keep her from enjoying things as much as she might have done. "Don't worry about it," she told Maniakes afterward. "This happened before, remember?"

"I wasn't worried, not really," he said, and set his hand on the smooth curve of her hip. "We'll have to make up for things after the baby's born, that's all. We've done that before, too."

"Yes, I know," Lysia answered. "That's probably why I keep getting pregnant so fast."

"I've heard the one does have something to do with the other, yes," Maniakes said solemnly. Lysia snorted and poked him in the ribs. They both laughed. He didn't think about Tzikas at all. Better yet, he didn't notice he wasn't thinking about Tzikas at all.

XII

Having settled affairs in Serrhes, Maniakes rode west with about half his army, so as to be in a position to do something quickly if the civil war in Makuran required. He sent small parties even farther west, to seize the few sources of good water that lay in the desert between Videssos' restored western frontier and the Land of the Thousand Cities.

"See, here you are, invading Makuran the proper way, the way it should be done, instead of sneaking up from the sea," Rhegorios said.

"If we didn't have control of the sea, we wouldn't be here on land now," Maniakes said. "Besides, what could be better than coming up from an unexpected direction?"

"The last time I asked a question like that, the girl I asked it of slapped my face," his cousin said.

Maniakes snorted. "I daresay you deserved it, too. When we go back to Videssos the city, I'm going to have to marry you off, let one woman worry about you, and put all the others in the Empire out of their fear."

"If I'm as fearsome as that, brother-in-law of mine, do you think being married will make any difference to me?" Rhegorios asked.

"I don't know if it will make any difference to you," Maniakes said. "I expect it will make a good deal of difference to Lysia, though. If you tomcat around while you're single, you get one kind of name for yourself. If you keep on tomcatting around after you're married, you get a name for yourself, too, but not one you'd want to have."

"You know how to hit below the belt," Rhegorios said. "Considering what we're talking about, that's the best way to put things, isn't it? And you're right, worse luck: I wouldn't want Lysia angry at me."

"I can understand that." Maniakes looked around. "I wonder if we could put a town anywhere around here, to help seal the border."

"Aye, why not?" Rhegorios said. "We can call it Frontier, if you like." He waved a hand, as if he were a mage casting a spell. "There! Can't you just see it? Walls and towers and a grand temple to Phos across the square from the *hypasteos'* residence, with barracks close by."

And Maniakes *could* see the town in his mind's eye. For a moment, it seemed as real as any of the cities in the westlands he'd liberated from the Makuraners. It was, in fact, as if he *had* liberated the hypothetical town of Frontier from the Makuraners, and spent a couple of days in that *hypasteos'* residence digging through the usual sordid tales of treason, collaboration, and heresy.

But then Rhegorios waved again, and said, "Can't you see the dust-herders bringing their flocks into the market for coughing—I mean, shearing? Can't you see the rock farmers selling their crops to the innkeepers to make soup with? Can't you see the priests of Phos, out there blessing the scorpions and the tarantulas? Can't you see the vultures circling overhead, laughing at the men who set a town three weeks away from anything that looked like water?"

Maniakes stared at him, stared at the desert through which they were traveling, and then started to laugh. "Well, all right," he said. "I think I take your point. Maybe I could put a town not too far from here, somewhere closer to water—though we're less than a day from it, not three weeks—to help seal the border. Does that meet with your approval, your exalted Sevastosship, sir?"

Rhegorios was laughing, too. "That suits me fine. But if I'm going to be difficult, wouldn't you rather I had fun being difficult, instead of looking as if I'd just had a poker rammed up my arse?" He suddenly assumed an expression serious to the point of being doomful.

"Do you know what you look like?" Maniakes looked around to make sure no one could overhear him and his cousin, then went on, "You look like Immodios, that's what."

"I've been called a lot of hard names in my time, cousin of mine, but that's—" Rhegorios donned the stern expression again, and then, in lieu of a mirror, felt of his own face. As he did so, his expression melted into one of comically exaggerated horror and dismay. "By the good god, you're right!"

He and Maniakes laughed again. "That feels so good," Maniakes said. "We spent a good many years there where nothing was funny at all."

"Didn't we, though?" Rhegorios said. "Amazing how getting half your country back again can improve your outlook on life."

"Isn't it?" Instead of examining the ground from which the town of Frontier would never sprout, Maniakes looked west toward Makuran. "Haven't heard from Abivard in a while," he said. "I wonder how he's doing in the fight against Sharbaraz."

"I'm not worrying about it," Rhegorios said. "As far as I'm concerned, they can hammer away at each other till they're both worn out. Abivard's a good fellow—I don't deny that for a moment—and Sharbaraz is a right bastard, but they're both Makuraners, if you know what I mean. If they're fighting among themselves, they'll be too busy to give us any grief."

"Which is, I agree, not the worst thing in the world," Maniakes said.

"No, not for us, it's not." Rhegorios' grin was predatory. "About time, don't you think, some bad things happen to the Makuraners? Things ought to even out in this world, where we can see them happen, not just in the next, where Phos triumphs at the end of days."

"That would be fine, wouldn't it?" Maniakes' tone was wistful. "For a long time, I wondered if we'd ever see things even out with the boiler boys."

Rhegorios pursued his own thought: "For instance, we might even be able to cast down that villain of an Etzilios and do something about the Kubratoi. The good god knows what they've been doing to us all these years."

"Oh, wouldn't that be sweet?" Maniakes breathed. "Wouldn't that be fine, to get our own back from that liar and cheat?"

The memory of the way Etzilios had deceived him, almost captured him, and routed his army came flooding back, as if the years between that disaster and the present were transparent as glass. The Makuraners had done Videssos more harm, but they'd never inflicted on him a humiliation to match that one.

"We did give him some," the Avtokrator said. "After our fleet crushed the monoxyla, the way he fled from the city was sweet as honey to watch. But he's still on his throne, and his nomads are still dangerous." He sighed. "Getting the westlands back in one piece counts for more, I suppose. I rather wish it didn't, if you know what I mean."

"Oh, yes," Rhegorios said. "The pleasure of doing what you want to do—especially of paying back somebody who's done you wrong—can be more delicious than just doing what needs doing."

"That's it exactly." Maniakes nodded. "But I'm going to do what needs doing." His grin was wry. "I'd better be careful. I'm in danger of growing up."

The Makuraner heavy cavalryman dismounted, walked toward Maniakes in a jingle of armor, prostrated himself before the Avtokrator, and then, with a considerable display of strength, rose smoothly despite the weight of iron he wore. "What news?" Maniakes demanded. "Is Sharbaraz overthrown?" He would have paid a pound of gold to hear that, but didn't tell the boiler boy in front of him. If the word was there, that would be time enough for rewards.

Regretfully, Abivard's messenger shook his head. "Majesty, he is not, though we drive his forces back toward Mashiz and though more and more men from the garrisons in the Land of the Thousand Cities declare for us each day. That is not why the new sun of Makuran sent me to you."

"Well, why did he send you, then?" Maniakes said, trying to hide his disappointment. "What news besides victory was worth the journey?"

"Majesty, I shall tell you," the Makuraner replied. "In the Land of the Thousand Cities, in a barren tract far from any canal, we found another of the blasphemous shrines such as the one you described to my master." The man's eyes were fierce behind the chain-mail veil that hid the lower part of his face. "I saw this abomination for myself. Sharbaraz may act as if he is the God in this life, but the God shall surely drop him into the Void in the next."

"I burned the one my men came across," Maniakes said. "What did Abivard do with this one?"

"The first thing he did was send every squadron, every regiment of his army through the place, so all his men could see with their own eyes what kind of foe they were facing," the messenger said.

"That was a good idea," Maniakes said. "I used the one we discovered to rally my men's spirits, too."

"If a blasphemy is so plain that even a Videssian can see it, how did it escape the notice of the King of Kings?" the messenger asked rhetorically. He failed to notice the casual contempt for Videssians that informed his words. Instead of getting angry, Maniakes wondered how often he'd offended Makuraners without ever knowing it. The messenger finished, "Once everyone had seen that the Pimp of Pimps reckoned himself the God of Gods, the shrine was indeed put to the torch."

"Best thing that could have happened," Maniakes agreed. "Pity Abivard couldn't have taken Sharbaraz's soldiers through the place instead of his own. I wonder how many would have fought for Sharbaraz after they saw that. Not many, I'd wager."

"Aye, that would have been most marvelous." The Makuraner sighed in regret. "In any case, Majesty, the balance of this message is that, while Abivard the new sun of Makuran did not reckon you a liar when you told him of a shrine of this sort, he did reserve judgment until he saw such with his own eyes. Now he knows you were correct in every particular, and apologizes for having doubted you."

"For one thing, he hid the doubt very well," Maniakes replied. "For another, I can hardly blame him for keeping some, because I had trouble believing in a place like that even after I saw it."

"I understand, Majesty," the messenger said. "If the God be gracious, the next you hear from us will be when the wretch has been ousted from the capital and the cleansing begun."

"I hope that news comes soon," Maniakes said, whereupon the messenger saluted him and rode back toward the west. Maniakes smiled at the Makuraner's armored back. So Abivard intended to cleanse Mashiz, or perhaps only the court at Mashiz, did he? That struck Maniakes as a project liable to go on for years. He liked the idea. As long as the Makuraners were concentrating on their internal affairs, they would have a hard time endangering Videssos.

When he told Rhegorios of the message from Abivard, his cousin's smile might almost have been that of a priest granted a beatific vision of Phos. "The boiler boys can cleanse, and then countercleanse, and then countercountercleanse, for all of me," the Sevastos said. "They're welcome to it. Meanwhile, I expect we'll head back to Serrhes."

"Yes, I suppose so." Maniakes gave Rhegorios a sharp look. "You're not usually one who wants to go backward."

His cousin coughed. "Well—er—that is—" he began, and went no further.

Seeing Rhegorios tongue-tied astonished Maniakes—but not for long. He thought back to the conversation he'd had with his cousin not long before. "Have you found a woman there?"

Knowing his cousin's attitude, he hadn't intended the question as more than a probe. But then Rhegorios said, "I may have."

Maniakes had all he could do not to double over with laughter. When someone like Rhegorios said he might have found a woman, and especially when he said it in a tone of voice suggesting he didn't want to admit it, even to himself, it was likely he'd fallen hard. Maybe Maniakes wouldn't have to worry about his tomcatting through the Empire, after all. "Who is she?"

Rhegorios looked as if he wished he'd kept his mouth shut. "If you must know," he said, "she's that Phosia I was telling you about, Broios' daughter."

"The larcenous merchant?" Now Maniakes did laugh. "If it hadn't been for you, I'd never have known he had a daughter."

"I make a point of investigating these things." Rhegorios did his best to sound dignified. His best was none too good. "The lord with the great and good mind be praised, she takes after her mother in almost everything—certainly in looks."

"Well, all right. All I can say is, she'd better." Thinking of Broios still irked Maniakes. "She doesn't want to slide a knife between your ribs because I had her father's backside kicked in public?"

"Hasn't shown any signs of it," Rhegorios said.

"Well, good enough, then." Maniakes reached out and gave his cousin an indulgent poke in the shoulder. "Enjoy yourself while we're in Serrhes, and you can find yourself another friend, or another cartload of friends, when we get back to Videssos the city."

By everything Maniakes knew of his cousin, that should have made Rhegorios laugh and come back with a gibe of his own. Instead, the Sevastos said, "I may have my father talk with Broios when we get back to the city."

If Maniakes had been startled before, he gaped now. "What?" he said again. "I've never heard you talk like that before." He wondered if his cousin had taken their earlier conversation to heart and resolved to marry. Then he wondered if this Phosia, or maybe

Broios himself, had prevailed upon their wizard to work love magic on—or maybe against—Rhegorios. He would have found that easier to believe had such sorcery been easier to use. Passion made magic unreliable.

"Maybe it's time, that's all," Rhegorios said. His wry grin was very much his own. "And maybe, too, it's just that I'm fascinated by the idea of a girl who says no. I don't see that every day, I'll tell you."

"Mm, I believe you," Maniakes said. His cousin was handsome, good-natured, and the man of second-highest rank in the Empire of Videssos. The first two would have been plenty by themselves to find him lots of female friends. The prospect of the riches and power his position added didn't hurt his persuasiveness, either.

"I think she's what I want," Rhegorios said.

Maniakes wondered if she was what he wanted precisely because she hadn't let him have her. Was her reluctance altogether her own? The Avtokrator doubted Broios was clever enough to come up with such a scheme. He knew nothing about the merchant's wife, though. Not trusting his own judgment, he asked, "Have you told Lysia about this?"

"Some if it," Rhegorios answered. "Not the whole."

"I think you should do that," Maniakes said. "She will have a clearer view about Phosia and her family than either one of us. She's not assotted with the girl, as you are." He ignored his cousin's indignant look. "And she's—not quite—so worried about the Empire as a whole as I am."

"By the good god, though, she's my sister," Rhegorios said. "How can I talk about matters between man and woman with my sister? It wouldn't be decent."

"For one thing, I daresay she has more sense than either one of us," Maniakes replied. "And, for another, if you can't talk about these things with her, with whom can you talk of them? I know what you were thinking of doing, I'll wager, and never mind this yattering about having Uncle Symvatios talk with Broios: go ahead and marry this girl and then tell me about it afterward, when I couldn't do anything. Am I right or am I wrong?"

Rhegorios tried for dignified silence. Since he wasn't long on dignity under most circumstances, nor, for that matter, on silence, Maniakes concluded he'd read his cousin rightly.

"We'll be heading back to Serrhes soon—as you guessed, cousin of mine," the Avtokrator said. "It'll have to do as our frontier outpost for now. And while we're waiting there to hear from Abivard, we won't have anything better to do than sort through this whole business. Doesn't that put your mind at ease?"

"No," Rhegorios snarled. "You're taking all the fun out of it. The way you're treating it, it's a piece of imperial business first and a romance afterward."

Maniakes stared again. "Cousin of mine, everything we do is imperial business first and whatever else it is afterward."

"Oh, really?" Rhegorios at his most polite was Rhegorios at his most dangerous. "Then how, cousin of mine your Majesty brother-in-law of mine, did you happen to end up wed to your own first cousin? If you tell me that was good imperial business, by Phos, I'll eat my helmet. And if you get to have what you want for no better reason than that you want it, why don't I?"

Maniakes opened his mouth, then shut it again in a hurry on realizing he had no good answer. After a bit of thought, he tried again: "The one thing I can always be sure of with Lysia is that she'll never betray me. Can you say the same about this woman here?"

"No," Rhegorios admitted. "But can you say you wouldn't have fallen in love with Lysia if you weren't so sure of that?"

"Right now, I can't say anything about might-have-beens," Maniakes answered. "All I can say is that when we get back to Serrhes, we'll see what we have there, I expect."

After a while out in the semidesert that marked the Empire's western frontier, Serrhes seemed almost as great a metropolis as Videssos the city, a telling measure of how barren that western country really was. Maniakes did not invite Broios and Phosia and her mother to dine with him right away. Instead, he did some quiet poking around.

So did Lysia, who said, "What your men don't hear, my serving women will, in the marketplace or from a shopkeeper or from a shopkeeper's wife."

"That's fine," Maniakes said. "You're right, of course; women do hear any number of things men miss." He grinned. "Some of those things, some of the time, might even be true."

Lysia glared at him, showing more anger than she probably felt.

"You know I'll remember that," she said. "You know I'll make you pay for it one of these days, too. So why did you say it?"

"If I give you something you can sharpen your knives on," he said, as innocently as he could, "you won't have to go out looking for something on your own." The dirty look he got for that was more sincere than the earlier one. He went on, "You never have said much about what you think of your brother's choice. Does that mean what I'm afraid it means?"

Lysia shook her head. "No, not really. It means I paid no attention to this Phosia when we were here before." Now she sank a barb of her own, aimed not so much at Maniakes in particular as at his half of the human race: "A pretty face is less likely to distract me."

"Less likely to distract you than what?" he asked, and then held up a hasty hand. "Don't answer that. I don't think I want to know." By the dangerous gleam that had come into his wife's eye, he knew he'd changed course in the nick of time.

Sure enough, gossip about Phosia, about Broios, and about Broios' wife—whose name was Zosime—began pouring in. A lot of it had to do with the way Broios ran his business. Vetranios had been able to cheat him, but he'd evidently managed to be on the giving as opposed to the receiving end of that a good many times himself. Maniakes didn't quite know how much weight to give such reports. A lot of merchants thought first of themselves and then, if at all, of those with whom they dealt. He couldn't gauge whether Broios was typical of the breed or typical of the breed at its worst.

His men and Lysia's serving women also brought in a lot of reports claiming Broios had been hand in glove with the Makuraners while they held Serrhes. Again, he had trouble deciding what those meant. If Broios hadn't cooperated with the occupiers to a certain degree, he wouldn't have been able to stay afloat. No one said he'd betrayed any of his fellows, and the Avtokrator had consistently forgiven those who'd done nothing worse than get on with their lives regardless of who ruled the westlands. But did that mean he wanted such people in his family? That was a different question.

No one seemed to say anything bad about Phosia. People who disliked her father thought she was nice enough. People who liked her father—there were some—thought she was . . . nice enough.

Everyone agreed her mother talked too much. "If that's a vicious sin, Skotos' ice will be even more crowded than the gloomiest priests claim," Lysia said.

"True enough," Maniakes said. "Er, true." His wife laughed at him for editing his own remarks.

Once he was back in Serrhes, he naturally started judging cases again. His first stay in the city had scratched the surface of what had gone on in better than a decade of Makuraner rule, but had not done much more than that. As he lingered in the westlands waiting for word from Abivard, he had time to look at cases he had not considered before. And, seeing him do that, others who had not presented matters to him in his earlier stay now hauled them out, dusted them off, and brought them to his notice.

Enough new cases and accusations and suits came before him to make him hand some of them over to Rhegorios. His cousin, instead of making his usual protests about doing anything resembling work, accepted the assignment with an alacrity Maniakes found surprising. After a little thought, it wasn't so surprising any more. When Rhegorios was fighting his way through the intricacies of a case involving fine points of both Videssian and Makuraner law, he wasn't thinking about Phosia.

His decisions were good, too: as thoughtful as the ones Maniakes handed down. As day followed day, the Avtokrator grew more and more pleased with the Sevastos. Rhegorios had been a good second man in the Empire even when he grumbled about having to do his job. Now that he was doing it without the grumbling, he was as fine a second man as anyone could have wanted.

As day followed day, he also grew more confident in his decisions and made ever more of them on his own, without checking with Maniakes till after the fact. Thus he startled the Avtokrator when he came in one afternoon and said, "Your Majesty, a matter has come to my notice that I think you should handle in my place."

"It will have to wait a bit," Maniakes said. "I'm in the middle of an argument here myself." He nodded at the petitioner standing before him. "As soon as I'm done, I'll deal with whatever perplexes you. You ought to know, though, that I think you're up to fixing it, whatever it happens to be."

"Your Majesty, it would be better in your hands," Rhegorios said with unwonted firmness. Maniakes shrugged and spread those hands, palms up, in token of puzzled acquiescence.

Having disposed of the petitioner—and having annoyed him by denying his request for land that had belonged to a monastery till the Makuraners razed it to the ground and slaughtered most of the monks—Maniakes sent a secretary to Rhegorios to let him know he could bring his unusual case, whatever it was, up into the chamber the Avtokrator was using.

As soon as the Sevastos and the man who had come before him walked into the room, Maniakes understood. Broios walked up to the high-backed chair Maniakes was using as a throne and prostrated himself before his sovereign. "Rise," the Avtokrator said, at the same time sending his cousin an apologetic look. Had he been assotted of Broios' daughter, he wouldn't have wanted to deal with a case involving the merchant, either. He asked Broios, "Well, sir, how may I help you today? Not more clipped arkets, I hope."

"No, your Majesty," Broios said. "I don't fancy another week with a sore fundament, thank you very kindly all the same."

"Good," Maniakes said. "What *can* I do for you, then?"

"Your Majesty, I beg your pardon if I give you great offense, but I hear from a lot of people that you've set men and women to asking questions about me and my family," Broios said. "You can say whatever you like about me, Emperor; Phos knows you have the right. But if you're going to say I have treason in mind, it isn't so, and that's all there is to it. All the men and women you sent out won't find it when it's not there. Remember, your Majesty, Vetranios is the one who took a shine to that Tzikas item, not me."

Maniakes turned to Rhegorios. "Well, cousin of mine, you had the right of it after all: this one wasn't for you to judge." He gave his attention back to Broios. "I wasn't trying to find out about you because I think you're a traitor. I'm trying to make certain you aren't."

"I don't understand, your Majesty," Broios said.

Sighing, Maniakes found himself explaining what he would rather have kept dark a while longer. "My cousin here, his highness the Sevastos Rhegorios, has . . . conceived an interest in your daughter, Phosia. I need to know if there are any scandals in your family that would keep it from being joined to mine."

Broios wobbled on his feet. For a moment, Maniakes feared he would faint. The merchant coughed a couple of times, then found words: "Your Majesty, I crave your pardon in a different way. I

know his Highness has seen my daughter, but—" His voice broke
like that of a youth whose beard was beginning to sprout. What he
was probably thinking was something like, *I knew Rhegorios
wanted to dally with her, but* . . . "—I had no idea that—that—"
He ran down again.

"Since you are here, since you have come to me," Maniakes
said, "I want you to tell me anything that might be an impediment
to this union. If you tell me here and now, no penalty and no blame
will come to you, even if we decide not to make the match. But if
you conceal anything and I learn of it for myself, not only is the
match forfeit, you will regret the day you were born for having
lied to me. Do you understand, Broios?"

"Yes, your Majesty." Broios drew himself to his full unimpres-
sive height. "Your Majesty, to the ice with me if I can think of any
reason—except the late kick in the arse, of course—for you not
to take my tender chick under your wing." His voice rang with
sincerity.

His voice had also rung with sincerity when he denied having
mixed in some arkets Vetranios hadn't given him before taking the
coins to the Avtokrator. He'd been lying then. Was he lying now?
Maniakes couldn't tell. A successful merchant got to the point where
he could dissemble well enough to deceive anyone who didn't have
a sorcerer at his side.

The Avtokrator wondered if he should summon Bagdasares. For
the moment, he decided against it. He'd given Broios the warning.
"Remember what I said," he told the merchant. "If you don't speak
now—"

"I have nothing to say," Broios answered, a statement normally
so improbable that Maniakes thought it stood some chance of being true.

He dismissed the merchant and then asked Rhegorios, "And
what do you think of your prospective father-in-law?"

"Not bloody much," his cousin replied at once. "But I'm not
interested in marrying him, the lord with the great and good mind
be praised. He's Zosime's problem, which suits me down to the
ground."

"Only shows you've never been married," Maniakes said. "Your
wife's family is your problem." He grinned at Rhegorios. "Take
my brother-in-law, for instance."

"Who, him? He's a prince among men," Rhegorios said, laughing. "Why, he's even a prince among princes." The reference to the Vaspurakaner blood the two of them shared made Maniakes laugh, too.

But he did not laugh long. He said, "Do we really want Broios in the family with us?"

"No, that's not the question," Rhegorios said. "The question is, is Broios so revolting, we can't stand to have him in the family no matter how much I want Phosia in it?"

As far as Maniakes could tell, the question wasn't how much Rhegorios wanted Phosia in it, the question was how much he wanted it in Phosia, the *it* being different in the two cases. He didn't say that, for fear of angering his cousin instead of amusing him. Taken on its own terms, what Rhegorios asked was reasonable. Recognizing that, Maniakes said, "We shall see, cousin of mine. We shall see."

Excitement on his face, a Videssian trooper led one of Abivard's boiler boys before Maniakes. "He's got news for you, your Majesty," the imperial exclaimed as the Makuraner went down on his belly in a proskynesis.

"Rise, sir, rise," Maniakes said. "Whatever you tell me, I am certain it will be more interesting than the endless arguments I've been hearing here in Serrhes."

"I think this is small praise, not great," the Makuraner said, his dark eyes sparkling with amusement above the chain mail veil he wore. "But yes, Majesty, I have news indeed. Know that Abivard son of Godarz, the new sun of Makuran, now holds Mashiz in the hollow of his hand, and know further that he also holds in the hollow of his hand Sharbaraz Pimp of Pimps, and awaits only the decree of the Mobedhan-Mobhed concerning the said Sharbaraz's infamous and impious practices in regard to religion before ending his life and consigning him to the Void forevermore." The Mobedhan-Mobhed, the leading servant of the God, held a place in the Makuraner hierarchy close to that of the ecumenical patriarch in Videssos.

Maniakes clapped his hands together. "He has the capital and he has his foe, eh?" The Makuraner messenger nodded. Maniakes went on, "That's very wise, getting your chief cleric to condemn him. Taking his head won't seem so much like murder then: more as if he's getting his desserts."

"Majesty, he is," the Makuraner said angrily. "To start so great a war and then to lose it, to leave us with nothing to show for so much blood and treasure spent—how can a man who fails so greatly deserve to live?"

Again, none of the Makuraners blamed Sharbaraz for starting the war against Videssos. They blamed him for losing it. Had Videssos the city fallen, no one would have lifted a finger against the victorious, all-conquering figure Sharbaraz would have become. He would have ruled out his span of years with unending praise from his subjects, who might even have come to think he deserved deification as much as he did. He probably would have found some convenient excuse to get rid of Abivard so no one shared the praise. Success would have concealed a multitude of sins; failure made even virtues vanish.

"It's over, then," Maniakes said in wondering tones. He would still have to see if and how he could live at peace with Abivard. But even if they did fight, they wouldn't go to war right away. The struggle that had begun when Sharbaraz used Genesios' overthrow of Likinios as an excuse to invade and seek to conquer Videssos was done at last.

Abivard's messenger construed Maniakes' three words in the sense in which he'd meant them. "Majesty, it is," he said solemnly, giving back three words of his own.

"I presume your master is tying up loose ends now," Maniakes said, and the messenger nodded. The Avtokrator asked, "What of Abivard's sister—Denak, was that her name? She was Sharbaraz's wife, not so?"

"His principal wife, yes," the messenger answered, making a distinction about which the monogamous Videssians did not need to bother.

"What does she think of the changes in Mashiz?" Maniakes chose his words with care, not wanting to offend either the messenger or Abivard, to whom what he said would surely get back.

The Makuraner boiler boy replied with equal caution: "Majesty, as pledges have been given that no harm shall come to her children, and as these past years she had not always been on the best of terms with him who was King of Kings, she is said to be well enough pleased by those changes."

Maniakes nodded. Abivard, then, was not inclined simply to dispose of his little nephew. Maniakes liked him better for that.

Still, he wondered how happy Denak would be when she fully realized the child of her flesh would not succeed to the throne. But that was Abivard's worry, not his own. He had plenty that were his, and chose to air one: "Any sign of Tzikas in Mashiz?"

"The Videssian traitor?" The Makuraner spoke with unconscious contempt that would have wounded Tzikas had he been there to hear it. "No. I am told he was in Mashiz at some earlier time, but Abivard the new sun of Makuran—"*Abivard the man with a new fancy title*, Maniakes thought wryly. "—finds no trace of him there at present, despite diligent searching."

"What a pity." Maniakes sighed. "It can't be helped, I suppose. For the good news you do bring—and it's very good news indeed—I'll give you a pound of gold."

"May the God and the Prophets Four bless you, Majesty!" the Makuraner exclaimed. Coming from a nation that coined mostly in silver, he, like most of his countrymen, held Videssian gold in great esteem.

When Maniakes went to tell Rhegorios that Sharbaraz had been cast down, he discovered his cousin already knew. He was flabbergasted for a moment, but then remembered the grinning Videssian soldier who had brought the messenger into his presence. That grin said the Videssian had already heard the news—and what one Videssian knew, a hundred would know an hour later, given the imperials' unabashed love for gossip. By sunset tomorrow, all of Serrhes would have all the details of Abivard's entry into Mashiz. Some of the people might even have the right details.

"It doesn't matter that I heard it from other lips than yours," Rhegorios said soothingly. "What matters is that it's so. Now we can start putting the pieces back together again."

"True," Maniakes said. With more than a little reluctance, he added, "I still haven't heard anything out-of-the-way about Phosia."

"Neither have I," Rhegorios said. "I don't expect to hear anything bad about her, either. What I do worry about is hearing something so bad about Broios that I wouldn't want him in the family if he had ten pretty daughters."

"Ten pretty daughters!" Maniakes exclaimed. "What would you do with ten pretty daughters? No, wait, don't tell me—I see the gleam in your eye. Remember, cousin of mine, the Makuraners are trying to get away from the custom of the women's quarters.

What would your sister say if she found out you'd started that custom on Videssian soil?"

"Something I'd rather not hear, I'm sure," Rhegorios answered, laughing. "But you needn't worry. Having a whole raft of wives may sound like great fun, but how is any man above the age of eighteen—twenty-one at the outside—supposed to keep them all happy? And if he doesn't keep them all happy, they'll be unhappy, and whom will they be unhappy about? Him, that's whom. No, thank you."

The grammar in there was shaky. The logic, Maniakes thought, was excellent. Idly, he said, "I wonder what will happen to all of Sharbaraz's wives now that he isn't King of Kings anymore. For that matter, if I remember rightly, Abivard has a women's quarters of his own, up at Vek Rud domain, somewhere off in the far northwest of Makuran."

"Yes, he does, doesn't he?" Rhegorios said. "He never talks about his other wives back there, though. He and Roshnani might as well be married the way any two Videssians are."

"Which is all very well for the two of them, no doubt," Maniakes said. "But Abivard has spent most of his time the past ten years and more here in Videssos, and none of it, so far as I know, up in Vek Rud domain. I wonder what the other wives have to say about him, yes, I do."

"That could be intriguing." Rhegorios got a faraway look in his eyes. "He's not in Videssos any more. He's not going to come back here, either, not if Phos is kind. Now that he's the new lead horse in Makuran, wouldn't you say he's likely to be going through the plateau country, to make himself known to the *dihqans* and such up there? Wouldn't you guess he'll probably find his way back to his own domain one day?"

"I wouldn't mind being a fly on the wall when he did." Maniakes wondered if Bagdasares could make magic stretch that far. After a moment, he realized it didn't matter: he would have no way of knowing exactly when Abivard returned to his old domain. *Too bad,* he thought. *Too bad.*

Fat and sweating with nervousness as well as heat, Vetranios prostrated himself before Maniakes. "I pray that you hear me out," he said to the Avtokrator after he had risen. "It is true, your Majesty, isn't it, that you've been trying to find out what sort of games Broios has been playing with his daughter?"

"Yes, that is true," Maniakes said, "and what's also true is that I'll land on you like an avalanche if you're lying to score points off your rival. If you know something I should hear, why didn't I hear it two weeks ago?"

"I got back into Serrhes only day before yesterday," Vetranios answered with some dignity. "I went over to Amorion to see if I could collect on a debt owed me since before the Makuraners took the town."

"Any luck?" Maniakes asked, genuinely curious.

"Alas, no. The merchant who owed me the payment walked the narrow bridge of the separator during the years of the Makuraner occupation, and is now settling up accounts with either Phos or Skotos." Vetranios sounded sad, not so much because his debtor had died but because he'd died without paying him back. As if to prove that, the merchant went on, "I was unable to locate any of his heirs or assigns, either. Most distressing, and a most slipshod way of doing business, too."

"War does have a habit of making people's lives difficult," Maniakes said. Vetranios nodded; the Avtokrator's irony sailed right past him. Reflecting that he should have known better, Maniakes returned to the matter at hand: "Very well. You haven't been in Serrhes for a bit. I thought the town seemed quieter than usual. What do you know about Broios and Phosia that I haven't already heard?"

"Since I don't know what you've already heard, your Majesty, how can I tell you that?" Vetranios asked. Given his past record, the question struck Maniakes as altogether too reasonable to have come from his lips. Vetranios went on, "I can tell you, though, that Broios betrothed Phosia to Kaykaus, Tegin's second-in-command, while the Makuraners were occupying Serrhes."

"What?" Maniakes stared. "By the good god, sir, you'd better give me a good answer as to how you know that when no one else in this city has breathed a word of it to me. If you're lying, the Halogai may be kicking your head through the city square, not your arse."

"I am not lying." Vetranios sketched the sun-circle above his heart. Of course, he'd done the same thing during his earlier dispute with Broios. He'd been lying then. So had Broios, who had sworn just as hard he was telling the truth. "As for how I know . . . Your Majesty, I have a daughter, too. Her name is Sisinnia. Kaykaus and I were dickering over an engagement when all at once he broke off the talks, saying he preferred Phosia—by which I take it he meant her dowry. So news of this will not have got round the town."

"I—see," Maniakes said slowly. "Don't leave Serrhes again without getting my consent first, Vetranios. I may have to use magic to find out whether you're telling the truth."

"Your Majesty!" The merchant assumed an expression of injured innocence. "How could you possibly doubt me?"

"Somehow or other, I manage," Maniakes said, another shot that sailed over Vetranios' head. "Never mind. Go home. Stay there. If I need you again, I'll summon you."

After the merchant left the city governor's residence, Maniakes hunted up Rhegorios and gave him the news. "That doesn't sound good, does it?" Rhegorios said with a scowl. "Not that he wanted to make the marriage—that would be easy enough to forgive. But trying to make it and then not telling us about it . . . Master Broios has some explaining to do, I fear."

"So he does. And unless he's got a bloody good explanation . . ." Maniakes strode over and set his hand on Rhegorios' shoulder. "I know you're sweet on this girl, cousin of mine, but unless her father has a bloody good explanation, I don't want to be connected with him."

"I'm not arguing with you," Rhegorios said. "I wish I could argue, but I can't." He laughed in self-mockery. "If I were fifteen years younger, I'd be sure as sure I couldn't possibly live without her, and my life would be ruined forever. And I'd probably yank out my sword and try and make you change your mind—either that or I'd run off with her the way I was thinking of doing anyhow, get a priest to say the words over us, and leave you to make the best of it. But do you know what, cousin your Majesty brother-in-law of mine? If what Vetranios says is true, I'm not dead keen on having an old reprobate like Broios in the family."

"Don't despair," Maniakes said. "There may be a perfectly innocent explanation for this."

"So there may," Rhegorios said. "To the ice with me if I can think of one, though." Maniakes thumped him on the shoulder again. He couldn't think of an innocent explanation, either.

* * *

Broios' proskynesis was so smooth, he must have been prac-icing back at his own home. The robes he wore were of a cut, and of a quality of silk, above those to which even a prosperous merchant might normally aspire. Maniakes didn't know where he'd gotten them, but he looked to be ready for his role as father-in-law to the Sevastos of the Empire of Videssos.

"Good evening, your Majesty," he wheezed to Maniakes as he rose. "A pleasure to be in your company, as always."

Maniakes raised an eyebrow. "As always. As I recall, you weren't so glad to see me the second time we met."

"Only a misunderstanding," Broios said easily. The impression he gave was that Maniakes had done the misunderstanding, but that he was generously willing to overlook the Avtokrator's error. He let a little petulance creep into his voice as he went on, "I had hoped, your Majesty, that you might have chosen to honor my wife and daughter with an invitation to this supper tonight. After all—" He gave Maniakes a coy, sidelong glance. "—you'll be seeing a lot of them in times to come."

"No need to hurry, then, wouldn't you say?" Maniakes replied.

Broios looked to Rhegorios for support. Finding none, he said, "Well, however you like, of course." Again, he managed to make it sound as if the Avtokrator was obviously in the wrong, but he, out of his splendid magnanimity, was willing to overlook the breach in decorum.

One of the servants at the city governor's residence came in and announced that supper was ready. Maniakes found himself unenthusiastic about breaking bread with Broios, but he knew he would have to endure it. "Do try the wine," the servant urged.

Everyone did. Broios' eyes widened. "That's potent stuff," he said, and tossed back his cup. "Good, mind you, but potent. Are you planning on serving supper *under* the table tonight, eh, your Majesty?" He laughed loudly at his own joke.

"I hope not," Maniakes answered, although he would not have minded seeing Broios drunk so his tongue would wag freer. To further that end, he'd ordered the cooks to do up a salty casserole of mutton and cabbage, the better to encourage thirst.

Broios was not shy about drinking wine. Broios, as well as Maniakes could tell, was not shy about anything, whether that meant making deals or telling lies. But the merchant, while refilling his cup several times, gave no sign the wine was doing anything to him water would not have done.

"It is a pity, your Majesty, that Phosia couldn't taste this vintage," he said. "I don't know where in town you found it, but it's very fine."

"I'm glad you like it," Maniakes said, and then, given an opening of sorts, went on, "You must be very proud of your daughter."

"Oh, I am," Broios said with the same fulsome sincerity with which he invested every pronouncement. "Nothing too good for my little girl, that's the truth. Not that I've spoiled her, you understand," he added hastily. "Nothing like that. She won't be difficult for his Highness the Sevastos, not in any way she won't." He glanced over toward Rhegorios. "You've not said much tonight, your Highness."

Rhegorios went on saying not much. Broios looked puzzled, but then shrugged and went back to his supper.

"Nothing too good for Phosia, you say?" Maniakes asked, as if unsure he'd heard correctly. Broios' emphatic nod said he had no doubts on that score. Thoughtfully, Maniakes went on, "Not even the Sevastos of the Empire of Videssos?"

"Your Majesty has been generous and gracious enough to let me believe such a match might not be impossible," Broios said.

Since that was true, Maniakes nodded meditatively. And, meditatively, he asked, "Nothing is too good for Phosia, eh? Not even the—" He plucked the perfect word out of the air. "—magnifolent Kaykaus, second-in-command of the Makuraner garrison here?"

Broios stared at him. When the merchant spoke, he might almost have had reproach in his voice: "Ah, your Majesty, where could you have heard about that?"

"Never you mind where I heard about it," Maniakes answered. "That is not the point. The point, sirrah, is why I didn't hear of it from you weeks ago, when I asked if any obstacles or embarrassments stood between your daughter and my family. Wouldn't you say that an engagement to a Makuraner officer is an embarrassment of sorts?"

"If she'd been married to him, your Majesty, that would have been an embarrassment," Broios said. Whatever he knew of embarrassments, he plainly knew at second hand, for he was impervious to them himself.

Maniakes said, "Having her engaged to this officer may not be

o much of a much; you're right about that." Broios looked re-
ieved. But then the Avtokrator went on, "Not telling me about the
ngagement, though, is something else again. I asked you if there
vere problems. You said no. That was a lie. I don't think we want
iars in our clan."

"Your Majesty!" Broios cried. He turned to Rhegorios. "Your
Highness!"

Rhegorios shook his head. "No. You have a lovely daughter,
Broios, and I think she's a sweet girl, too. If I were marrying just
her, I'd be more than happy enough. But you don't marry just a
girl—you marry her whole family." Maniakes had to keep himself
from clapping his hands in glee. His cousin had listened to him
after all! Rhegorios went on, "While I'd like to have Phosia for a
wife, I'd sooner have a snake in my boot than you for a father-in-
law."

Maybe the strong wine Broios had drunk had loosened his tongue,
after all. He shouted, "You're the Avtokrator's cousin, so you think
you can pick any girl you want and she'll be glad to have you. If
you weren't his cousin, there's not a woman in the Empire would
look at you twice."

"Yes, I am the Avtokrator's cousin," Rhegorios agreed, "and
you're right, the rules for me are different because of it. If I weren't
the Avtokrator's cousin, I might even put up with the likes of you
for the sake of getting Phosia. But I can pick and choose, and so I
will." He stood up and looked down his nose at Broios. "But I will
say this, sir: when I was an exile on the island of Kalavria, I had
no trouble at all getting women to look at me twice—or getting
them to do more than that, either, when the mood took them. And
it did."

Maniakes knew that was true. One of the reasons Rhegorios
remained unwed was precisely that he did so well for himself without making any permanent promises. "You are dismissed, Broios,"
the Avtokrator said, more than a little sadly. "We'd have to watch
you closer than the Makuraners, and that's all there is to it. If you
like, once things settle down in Mashiz, you have my leave to
write Kaykaus and see if you can bring that match back to life."

"Bah!" Pausing only to empty his winecup one last time and
pop a couple of candied apricots into his mouth, Broios stormed
out of the dining hall. The city governor's residence shook as if in
a small earthquake as he slammed the door behind him.

"I'm sorry, cousin of mine," Maniakes said.

"So am I," Rhegorios answered. "I am going to be a while finding someone who suited me as well as Phosia. But Broios—' He shook his head again. "No, thank you." He suddenly looked thoughtful. "I wonder what Vetranios' daughter is like." Seeing Maniakes' expression, he burst out laughing. "I don't mean it, cousin of mine. If Broios is a snake in my boot, Vetranios is a scorpion. We're well shut of both of them."

"Now you're talking sense." Maniakes sketched the sun-circle to emphasize how much sense Rhegorios was talking. Then he eyed the wine jar. "That *is* a good vintage. Now that we've started it, we may as well finish it. After all, you're drowning your sorrows, aren't you?"

"Am I?" Rhegorios said. "Well, yes, I suppose I am. And by the time we get to the bottom of *that*, I expect they'll be so drowned, I'll have forgotten what they are. Let's get started, shall we?"

Broios was not seen in public for the next several days. The next time he was seen, he sported a black eye and a startling collection of bruises elsewhere about his person. When Maniakes heard the news, he remarked to Lysia, "I'd say his wife wasn't very happy to have the betrothal fall through—or do you suppose Phosia was the one who did the damage?"

"I'd bet on Zosime," Lysia said. "She knows what she lost, and she knows who's to blame for losing it, too."

By her tone, she would have given Broios the same had she been married to him rather than to Maniakes. The Avtokrator suspected it wasn't the last walloping the merchant would get, either. Videssians breathed the heady atmosphere of rank almost as readily as they breathed the ordinary, material air. To have a chance at a union with the imperial family snatched away ... no, Broios wouldn't have a pleasant time after that.

Maniakes kept waiting for news out of the west. He wondered again if one or more of Abivard's messengers had gone missing— if, perhaps, Tegin's garrison force, heading back toward Makuran from Serrhes, had waylaid the riders. If that was so, Tegin would have to know the King of Kings whose cause he still espoused had failed, and that he would be well advised to make whatever peace he could with the new powers in his land.

Tegin, at least, would know. Not knowing, Maniakes kept coming up with fresh possibilities in his own mind, each less pleasant than the one before. Maybe Sharbaraz had somehow rallied, and civil war raged across the Land of the Thousand Cities. That would account for no messengers' having reached Serrhes in a while.

Or maybe Abivard had won a triumph so complete and so easy that he repented of his truce with the Videssians. Maybe he'd stopped sending messengers because he was gathering the armies of Makuran with a view toward renewing the war against the Empire.

"I don't think he'd do that," Rhegorios said when Maniakes raised the horrid prospect aloud. The Sevastos looked west, then went on thoughtfully, "I don't think he *could* do that, not this campaigning season. We're too close to the fall rains. His attack would bog down in the mud before it got well started."

"I keep telling myself the same thing." Maniakes' grin conveyed anything but amusement. "I keep having trouble making myself believe it, too."

"That's why you're the Avtokrator," Rhegorios said. "If you believed that all of the Videssos' neighbors were nice people who wanted to do us a favor, you wouldn't be suited for the job."

"If I believed that all of Videssos' neighbors were nice people who wanted to do us a favor, I'd be out of my bloody mind," Maniakes exclaimed.

"Well, that, too," Rhegorios said. "Of course, if you believe all our neighbors are out to get us all the time, the way it must sometimes look if you're sitting on the throne, that's liable to drive you out of your bloody mind, too, isn't it?"

"I expect it is," the Avtokrator agreed. "And yes, it does look that way a lot of the time, doesn't it? So what have we got? If believing an obvious falsehood means you're out of your bloody mind, and if believing an equally obvious truth can send you out of your bloody mind, what does that say about sitting on the throne in the first place?"

"It says you have to be out of your bloody mind to want to sit on the throne, that's what." Rhegorios studied Maniakes. "Judging from the specimen at hand, I'd say that's right enough. Cousin of mine, I want you to live forever, or at least until all your sons have beards. I don't want the bloody job. Sevastos is bad enough, with leeches like Broios trying to fasten on to me."

"Fair enough," Maniakes said. "I—" Before he could go on one of his Haloga guardsmen came in from outside. "Yes? What is it, Askbrand?"

"Your Majesty, a boiler boy waits in the plaza," the big blond northerner answered. "He would have speech with you."

"I'll come," Maniakes said happily. "About time we've had some news from Abivard. Phos grant it be good."

"Just hearing from him is good news," Rhegorios said. "Now you can stop having dark suspicions about what he's up to."

"Don't be silly," Maniakes said. "I'm the Avtokrator, remember? It's my job to have dark suspicions."

"One more reason not to want it, as I said before," Rhegorios replied.

Maniakes walked out of the city governor's residence and onto Serrhes' central square. After the gloom of indoors, he blinked several times against the bright sunshine. The messenger bowed in the saddle when he saw the Avtokrator; the rings of his chain-mail veil rattled faintly. "Majesty," he said in the Makuraner.

"What word?" Maniakes asked.

The messenger rode closer. "Majesty, the word is good," he said. "Abivard bids me tell you that he has at last decided the fate of Sarbaraz Pimp of Pimps. Sarbaraz is to be—"

Maniakes had been listening intently for the news, so intently that he missed the first time the horseman mispronounced the name of the overthrown King of Kings. When the fellow made the same mistake twice in two sentences, though, he blurted, "You're a Videssian, aren't you?"

By then, the messenger had come quite close, almost alongside him. With a horrible curse, the fellow yanked out his sword and cut at Maniakes. But the Avtokrator, his dark suspicions suddenly roused, was already springing away. The tip of the blade brushed his robe, but did not cleave his flesh.

Cursing still, the messenger pressed forward for another slash. That fell short, too. The boiler boy wheeled his horse and tried to get away. Askbrand's axe came down on the horse's head. The animal was wearing the scale mail with which the Makuraners armored their chargers. Against arrows, the mail was marvelous. Against a stroke like that, it might as well not have been there. The horse crashed to the cobblestones. Guardsmen swarmed over the rider.

"Don't kill him!" Maniakes shouted. "We'll want answers from him."

"So we will," Rhegorios said grimly. "If Abivard is sending murderers instead of messengers, we have a new war on our hands right now."

"I don't think he is," Maniakes said. "Didn't you hear the way the fellow talked?"

"I didn't notice," his cousin answered. "You speak Makuraner better than I do. I was just trying to understand him."

The guards had gotten the would-be assassin's sword away from him. Roughly, one of them yanked off his helmet. Maniakes knew well the furious, clever, narrow face that glared at him. "Almost, Tzikas," he said. "Almost. You might have managed to let the air out of me and then get away—if I didn't make the same mistakes speaking Makuraner that you do."

"Almost." The renegade officer's mouth twisted bitterly. "The story of my life. Almost. I almost held Amorion. I almost got you the first time, as I should have. Once I went over to the other side, I almost had Abivard's position. And I almost had you now."

"So you did," Maniakes said. "I admit it—why not? If you think you can take it with you for consolation when you go down to Skotos' ice, I'd say you're wrong. The dark god robs the souls he gets of all consolation." He spat on the cobblestones in rejection of Phos' eternal foe, and shivered a little on reflecting how easily his blood rather than his spittle might have flowed among them.

"I prefer to believe I'll fall into the Void and be—nothing— forevermore." Tzikas still had a smile left in him. "I worshiped the God of the Makuraners as fervently as ever I prayed to Phos."

"I believe that." Maniakes held up one hand, palm out flat, then the other. "Nothing here—and nothing here, either. It's not *almost* that's the story of your life, Tzikas, it's *nothing*. You were always good at seeming to be whatever you liked, because it was all seeming and nothing real, nothing at the bottom of you to make you truly any one particular kind of person."

"Oh, I don't know," Rhegorios put in. "He's always been a particular kind of bastard, if anyone cares about what I think."

"Make your jokes. Take the last word," Tzikas said. "You can. You're the Avtokrator and the Sevastos. You've won. You even got away with swiving your cousin, Maniakes. Aren't you proud? My dying curse on you."

"As a matter of fact, I *am* proud," Maniakes said. "I've done what I've done, and I've never tried to hide it, which is more than you could say if you lived another thousand years—which you won't." He raised his voice: "Askbrand!"

The Haloga's axe rose and fell. Blood gushed from the great gash that split Tzikas' head almost in two. *Almost,* Maniakes thought. The renegade's feet drummed a brief tattoo and then were still.

Rhegorios sketched the sun-circle. "Don't fear his curse, cousin of mine," he said. "You had the right of it, and that curse won't stick, because it has nothing behind it."

"Nothing now." Blood flooded down through Tzikas' gray beard. Maniakes shook his head. "I feared him alive—feared him as much as anyone, because I never knew what he would do. He was quicksilver come to life: bright, shiny, able to roll any which way, and poisonous. And now he's gone, and I'm not, and I'm bloody glad that's the way things turned out."

"Now you can go through doors without checking behind them first to make sure he's not lurking there," Rhegorios said.

"Now I can do all sorts of things," Maniakes said. "I would have done them anyway, I think, but slower, always looking over my shoulder. Now I can live my life a free man." *Or as free from custom and danger as the Avtokrator ever gets, which isn't very far.*

The first thing he did to celebrate his new freedom was order Tzikas' head, already badly the worse for wear, hewn from his body and mounted on a spear for the edification of the people of Serrhes. At least he didn't have to do the hewing himself, as he had with Genesios when his vicious predecessor was captured. Askbrand and his axe took care of the business with a couple of strokes. Tzikas wasn't moving or fighting any more, which made things easier, or in any case neater.

The next thing Maniakes did was give Askbrand a pound of gold. The Haloga tried to decline, saying, "You already pay me to guard you. You do not need to pay me more *because* I guard you."

"Call it a reward for doing a very good job," Maniakes said. Askbrand's fellow guardsmen who happened to be Videssians urgently nodded, whispered in the northerner's ears, and seemed on the point of setting fire to his shoes. No imperial in his right mind—and bloody few out of it—turned down money for no reason, and the Videssians feared that, if one bonus was turned down, no more would be forthcoming. At last, reluctantly, Askbrand agreed to let himself be rewarded.

Drawn by the commotion in the square, Lysia came out then. She listened to the excited accounts, took a long look at Tzikas' still-dripping and very mortal remains, said, "Good. About time," and went back into the city governor's residence. At times, Maniakes thought, his wife was so sensible, she was unnerving.

A moment later, he sent one of the guardsmen into the residence, after not Lysia but a secretary. The fellow with whom the guard emerged did not take a headless corpse, an impaled head, and a great pool of blood on the cobbles in stride. He gulped, turned fishbelly pale, and passed out.

Gleefully, the guards threw a bucket of water over him. That brought him back to himself, but ruined the sheet of parchment on which he'd been about to write. When at last both the scribe and his implements were ready, Maniakes dictated a letter: "Maniakes Avtokrator to Abivard King of Kings, his brother: Greetings. I am pleased to tell you that—"

"Excuse me, your Majesty, but is 'King of Kings' Abivard's proper style?" the secretary asked.

Maniakes hid a smile. If the fellow could worry about such minutiae, he was indeed on the mend. "I don't know. It will do," the Avtokrator said, as much to see the scribe wince as for any other reason. "I resume: Greetings. I am pleased to tell you that Tzikas will trouble our counsels no more. He tried to murder me while in the guise of one of your messengers, and suffered what failed assassins commonly suffer. If you like, I will send you his head, so you can see it for yourself. I assure you, he looks better without it." He held up a hand to show he was done dictating. "Give me a fair copy of that for my signature before sunset. This is news Abivard will be glad to have."

"I shall do as you require, your Majesty," the scribe said, and went back indoors—*where he belongs,* Maniakes thought—in a hurry.

"By the good god," the Avtokrator said, taking another long look at what was left of Tzikas, "here's another step toward making me really believe the war is over, the westlands are ours again, and that they're liable to stay that way."

"If that's what you think, why don't we head back toward Videssos the city?" Rhegorios said. "The fall rains aren't going to hold off forever, you know, and I'd much sooner not have to slog through mud on the road."

"So would I," Maniakes said. "So would Lysia, no doubt." He didn't want her giving birth on the road. He knew she didn't want to give birth on the road, either. Having done that before, she did not approve of it.

"And besides," Rhegorios went on, "by now the people of Videssos the city are probably itching for you to get back so they can praise you to the skies. Phos!" The Sevastos sketched the suncircle. "If they don't praise you to the skies after this, I don't know when they ever will."

"If they do not praise the Avtokrator to the skies after this—" Askbrand began. He didn't finish the sentence, not in words. Instead, he swung through the air the axe he'd used to take Tzikas' head. The suggestion was unmistakable.

"I'll believe it when I see it." Maniakes' laugh held less bitterness than he'd expected. "As long as they don't riot in the streets when I ride by, I'll settle for that."

"You may be surprised," his cousin said. "They were starting to give you your due back there before you went into the westlands."

"*You* may be surprised," Maniakes retorted. "That was just because they were glad they had me in the city instead of Etzilios and Abivard. If a goatherd saves a pretty girl who's fallen down a well, she might go to bed with him once to say thanks, but that doesn't mean she'd want to marry him. And the city mob in the capital is more fickle than any pretty girl ever born."

"Which only goes to show, you don't know as much about pretty girls as you think you do," Rhegorios said.

"I'm sure there are a great many things you can teach me, O sage of the age," Maniakes said. "I'm sure there are a great many things you can teach most billy goats, for that matter." Rhegorios made a face at him. He ignored it, continuing, "But one thing you can't teach me about, by the good god, is the mob in Videssos the city."

"We'll see," was all his cousin said. "If I'm wrong, I may ask to borrow Askbrand's axe."

"Honh!" the guardsman said. "An these stupid city people give not the Avtokrator his due, maybe he will turn all the Halogai loose on them. They would remember that a long time, I bet you."

He swung the axe again. His pale, intent eyes lit up, perhaps in anticipation.

"I don't think so," Maniakes said hastily. "There are ways to be remembered, yes, but that's not one I care for. We'll go home and see what happens, that's all. Whatever it is, I can live with it."

XIII

IT RAINED ON MANIAKES' PARADE. IT HAD RAINED THE DAY before, and the day before that, too. It was liable to keep on raining for the next week.

He didn't care. He'd returned to Videssos the city before the fall rains began, which meant traveling had been easy. He'd ordered the parade more because he thought the city mob expected one than because he had anything spectacular to display. The sole disadvantage of having peacefully reacquired the westlands was the absence of captured siege gear, dejected prisoners in chains, and most of the other elements that made a procession dramatic and worth watching.

Without prisoners and booty, Maniakes paraded his own soldiers. Without those soldiers, he never would have been able to take the war to Makuran or to defend Videssos the city against the Makuraners and Kubratoi. They deserved the credit for the victories that would go down in the chronicles as his.

He'd thought the rain and the relatively mundane nature of the parade—which he'd taken pains to announce beforehand—would hold down the crowd. He didn't mind that. If only dedicated paradegoers came out, he'd reasoned, fewer of the people lining Middle Street would be of the sort who amused themselves by hissing him and shouting obscenities at Lysia.

Looking at the way men and women packed the capital's chief thoroughfare, though, he turned to Rhegorios and remarked, "More folk came out than I expected. Must be the colonnades—I'd forgotten how they let people stay dry even in wet weather."

Rhegorios didn't answer right away. Like Maniakes, he was busy waving to the people as he rode along. Unlike Maniakes', most of his waves seemed aimed at the pretty girls in the crowd; he hadn't let his disappointment over Phosia dishearten him for long. At last,

e said, "Cousin of mine, you may as well get used to it: they've
ecided they like you after all."

"What? Nonsense!" Maniakes exclaimed. He'd grown so used
o being an object of derision in Videssos the city that any other
ole seemed unnatural.

"All right, don't listen to me," Rhegorios said equably. "You're
he Avtokrator; you don't have to do anything you don't want to
do. But if you don't pay attention to what's going on around you,
ou're in a pretty sorry state, wouldn't you say?"

Stung by that, Maniakes did listen harder. A few shouts of "In-
cest!" and "Vaspurakaner heretic!"—this despite his orthodoxy—
did come out of the crowd. He always listened for shouts like that.
Because he always listened for them, he always heard them.

Now, though, along with them and, to his amazement, nearly
drowning them out, came others: "Maniakes!" "Huzzah for the
restorer of the westlands!" "Maniakes, conqueror of Kubrat and
Makuran!" "Thou conquerest, Maniakes!" He hadn't heard that
last one since his acclamation as Avtokrator. It was shouted during
acclamations as a pious hope. Now he'd earned it in truth.

"Maybe I really have convinced them," he said, as much to
himself as to Rhegorios. He'd hoped victory would do that for
him—hoped and hoped and hoped. Up till this past campaigning
season, he hadn't won enough victories to put the theory to a
proper test.

"You're a hero," Rhegorios said with a grin. "Get used to it."
The grin got wider. "So am I. I like it."

"There could be worse fates," Maniakes admitted. "We almost
found out about a good many of them, these past few months."

"Didn't we, though?" Rhegorios said. "But it came right in the
end. Why, the mime troupes may even leave you alone this Midwinter's Day."

Maniakes considered that. He didn't need long. "I don't believe
it for a minute," he said. "The mime troupes don't ever leave anybody alone: that's what they're for. And if you're the Avtokrator,
you have to sit on the spine of the Amphitheater and pretend it's
funny. On Midwinter's Day, that's what the Avtokrator's for." After a moment, he added in a wistful, almost hopeful voice, "Maybe
they won't bite quite so hard this year, though."

He didn't even believe that, not down deep. Midwinter's Day

was still a couple of months away. By then, renewed familiarity would surely have blunted the respect the city mob felt for him now.

Rhegorios said, "Enjoy this while it lasts, anyhow." By the way he spoke, he didn't think it would last indefinitely, either.

In the crowd, a man held up a little baby in one hand, pointed to it with the other, and shouted, "Maniakes!"—he'd named the boy for the Avtokrator.

"Take him home and get him out of the rain, before he comes down with the croup," Maniakes called. Several nearby women— including, by the look of things, the infant Maniakes' mother— expressed loud and emphatic agreement with that sentiment.

Agathios the patriarch, who was riding a mule just behind Maniakes and Rhegorios, said, "Today, everyone delights in honoring you, your Majesty."

"Yes. Today," Maniakes said. But being honored was better than being despised; he couldn't deny that. Having experienced both, he could compare them.

And he was still despised, here and there. From the margins of the crowd, a priest cried, "Skotos' ice still awaits you for your lewdness and the travesty you have made of the marriage vow."

Maniakes looked back over his shoulder toward Agathios. "Do you know, most holy sir," he said in thoughtful tones, "just how badly we need priests to preach against the Vaspurakaner heresy in the towns and villages of the westlands? A passionate fellow like that is really wasted in Videssos the city, wouldn't you say? He would do so much better in a place like, oh, Patrodoton, for instance."

Agathios was not an astute politician, but he knew what Maniakes had in mind when making a suggestion like that. "I shall do my utmost to find out who that, ah, intrepid spirit is, your Majesty, and to translate him to a sphere where, as you rightly remark, his zeal might be put to good use."

"Speaking of good use, you'll get that out of the westlands," Rhegorios murmured to his cousin. "Now that we have them back, you've got a whole raft of new places to dump blue-robes who get on your nerves."

"If you think that's a joke, cousin of mine, you're wrong," Maniakes said. "If priests don't care to deal with sinful me in this sinful city, they can—and they will—go off somewhere quiet and out of the way and see how they like that."

A certain bloodthirsty gleam—or maybe it was just the rain—came into Rhegorios' eyes. "You ought to send the really zealous ones up to Kubrat, to see if they can convert Etzilios and the rest of the nomads. If they do, well and good. If they don't, the lord with the great and good mind will have some new martyrs, and you'll be rid of some old nuisances."

He'd intended only Maniakes to hear that. But he spoke a little too loudly, so that it also reached Agathios' ears. In tones of reproof, the ecumenical patriarch said, "Your Highness, mock not martyrdom. Think on the tale of the holy Kveldoulphios the Haloga, who laid down his life in the hope that his brave and glorious ending would inspire his people to the worship of the good god."

"I crave your pardon, most holy sir," Rhegorios said. Like any other Videssian, he was at bottom pious. Like any other Videssian high in the government, he also thought of the faith as an instrument of policy, holding both views at the same time without either confusion or separation.

Maniakes turned back and said to Agathios, "But the Halogai follow their own gods to this day, and the holy Kveldoulphios lived—what?—several hundred years ago, anyhow. Long before the civil wars that tore us to pieces."

"Your Majesty is, of course, correct." The patriarch let out a sigh so mournful, Maniakes wondered if he shed a tear or two along with it. In the rain, he could not tell. Agathios went on, "But he went gloriously to martyrdom of his own free will, rather than being hounded into it by the machinations of others."

"Very well, most holy sir. I do take the point," Maniakes said. Patriarchs were, in their way, government functionaries, too. Each one of them, though, had a point beyond which his obligations to Phos took precedence over his obligations to the Avtokrator. Maniakes realized the talk of deliberately creating martyrs had pushed Agathios close to that point.

"Thou conquerest, Maniakes!" "Maniakes, savior of the city!" "Maniakes, savior of the Empire!" Those shouts, and more like them, kept coming from the crowd. They didn't quite swallow up all the other shouts, the ones that had been hurled at Maniakes since the day he married his first cousin, but there were more of them and fewer of the others. If he hadn't won any great love, the Avtokrator had gained respect.

* * *

Pacing the floor, Maniakes said, "I hate this." In the Red Room, Zoïle the midwife was with Lysia, and custom binding as manacles kept him from being there. Having lost his first wife in childbed, he knew only too well the dangers Lysia faced.

His father set a hand on his shoulder. "Hard for us men at a time like this," the elder Maniakes said. "Just don't let your wife ever hear you say so, or *you* won't hear the last of it. It's the difference between watching a battle and going through one yourself, I suppose."

"That's probably about right," Maniakes said. "How many people here were watching from the seawall when our fleet beat the Kubratoi? They could drink wine and point to this and that and say how exciting it all was, but they weren't in any danger." He paused. "Of course, they would have been if we'd lost the sea fight instead of winning it."

"Nobody's going to lose any fights, by the good god," Symvatios said. "Lysia's going to give you another brat to howl around this place so a man can't get a decent night's sleep here."

"Ha!" The elder Maniakes raised an eyebrow at his brother. "You're more likely to be looking for an indecent night's sleep, anyhow."

Symvatios growled something in mock high dudgeon. Maniakes, his own worries forgotten for a moment, grinned at his father and uncle. They'd been bickering like that since they were boys, and enjoying it, too. Maniakes and Rhegorios bickered and bantered like that. Maniakes had done the same with Parsmanios . . . when they were boys. But between the two of them, the jealousy that had grown up was real.

As if picking the thought from his son's mind, the elder Maniakes said, "Your nephew, the little fellow who's named for the two of us, seems a likely lad."

"I hope so, for his sake," Maniakes said. "Zenonis and her boy have been here a good deal longer than I have, so you'll have seen more of them than I have. They don't seek me out, either." The corners of his mouth turned down. "You're her father-in-law, but in her mind—and I suppose in the boy's mind, too—I'm the chap who sent her husband into exile across the sea."

"Couldn't be helped, son," the elder Maniakes said heavily. "Af-

er he did what he undoubtedly did to you, I don't see that you had
any choice. I've never held it against you—you know that."

His heavy features got a little heavier. He'd had three sons. One,
his namesake, was a great success. But one was a proved traitor,
and one long years missing and surely dead. A great weight of sor-
row had to lurk there, though he spoke of it but seldom.

Symvatios said, "Sometimes there isn't any help for the things
that happen, and that's all there is to it. You do the best you can
with what you've got and you go on."

One of the things that had happened, of course, was Lysia and
Maniakes falling in love with each other. Symvatios tolerated Maniakes as son-in-law as well as nephew, as the elder Maniakes was
resigned to having Lysia as daughter-in-law. The marriage had been
one of the things—though jealousy of Rhegorios played a bigger
role—pushing Parsmanios away from the rest of the family and
toward Tzikas' plot. Neither Maniakes' father nor his uncle had
ever blamed him for that, not out loud. He was grateful to them for
so much.

With a sigh, he said, "We always were a tight-knit clan. Now
we're knitted tighter than ever." That was his doing, his and Lysia's.
But the world, as far as he was concerned, wasn't worth living in
without her.

Kameas came in. "Wine, your Majesty, your Highnesses?"
he said.

"Yes, wine," Maniakes said. Wine would not take away the worry.
Nothing would take away the worry. But, after three or four cups,
it got blurry around the edges. That would do.

The vestiarios glided away, looking as he always did as if he
propelled his vast bulk without moving his feet up and down when
he walked. He returned a few moments later with that same ponderous grace. "I have an extra cup here, if his Highness the Sevastos should join you," he said.

"You think of everything," Maniakes said. Kameas nodded
slightly, as if to say that was part of his job. Suddenly Maniakes
wished this were his fourth cup of wine, not his first. He forced out
a question: "Have you seen to Philetos?"

"Oh, yes, your Majesty. One of the prominent sirs—" He used
the palace term for a lower-ranking eunuch. "—is attending to
him, down by the Red Room." Kameas sketched Phos' sun-circle

above his breast. "We all pray, of course, that the holy sir's presence shall prove unnecessary."

"Aye, we do, don't we?" Maniakes said harshly. That Philetos was a priest was not why, or not precisely why, he'd been summoned to the imperial residence when Lysia's pangs began. He was also a healer-priest, the finest in Videssos the city. If anything went wrong . . . If anything went wrong, he might be able to help, and then again he might not. He hadn't been able to help when Niphone died giving birth to Likarios.

With a distinct effort of will, the Avtokrator forced his thoughts away from that track. He spat on the floor in rejection of Skotos, at the same time raising his cup toward Phos and his holy light. The elder Maniakes and Symvatios did as he did. Then Maniakes drank. The wine, golden in a silver cup, slid down his throat smooth as if it were sunlight itself.

"Well," Rhegorios said indignantly, walking into the little dining hall where his kinsfolk waited. "Shows the importance *I* have around here, when people start drinking without me."

Maniakes pointed to the extra cup Kameas had left behind. "We don't have a long start on you, cousin of mine—not like the one Abivard got on us when he moved against the city while we were sailing to Lyssaion. If you apply yourself, I expect you can catch up."

"Apply myself to wine?" Rhegorios raised an eyebrow. "Now there's a shocking notion." He used the dipper to fill the cup.

"*I'm* not shocked at it," Symvatios said. Rhegorios winced, rhetorically betrayed by his own father. After a perfectly timed pause, Symvatios went on, "I daresay you get it from me."

The elder Maniakes said, "It's a gift that runs in the family, I expect. Father certainly had it." Symvatios nodded at that. The elder Maniakes went on, "He had so much of it, sometimes he needed two or three tries before he could make it through a door."

"He was right when it mattered, though," Symvatios said. "When he did his drinking, it was when he didn't have to do anything else." He paused again. "Well, most of the time, anyhow."

"You're scandalizing your children, you know, the two of you," Rhegorios told his father and uncle. "Maniakes and I don't remember Grandfather all that well, so if you tell us he was an old soak, we'll believe you."

"What else will you believe if we tell it to you?" Symvatios asked. "Will you believe *we're* as wise and clever as we say?"

"Of course not," Rhegorios replied at once. "We *do* know you."

Both Maniakai, father and son, laughed. So did Symvatios. Kameas brought in a tray full of little squid sautéed in olive oil, vinegar, and garlic. They went well with the wine. Before too long, the jar was empty. The vestiarios fetched in another of the same vintage. For a little while, Maniakes managed to enjoy the company of his kin enough to take his mind off what Lysia was going through in the Red Room.

But time stretched. If Maniakes didn't intend to emulate his grandfather—or the account of his grandfather his father and uncle gave—he had to keep from drinking himself blind. And if he slowed his drinking so as to keep his wits about him, those wits kept returning to his wife.

Lysia had begun her labor around midmorning. The sun was sinking toward late autumn's early setting when Zoïle strode into the little dining hall and thrust a blanket-wrapped bundle at Maniakes. "Your Majesty, you have a daughter," the midwife announced.

Maniakes stared down at the baby, who was staring up at him. Their eyes met for a moment before those of the tiny girl wandered away. She was a dusky red color, and her head wasn't quite the right shape. Maniakes had learned all that was normal enough. He asked the question uppermost in his mind: "Is Lysia all right?"

"She seems very well." If Zoïle disapproved of his having married his cousin, she didn't show it. Since Maniakes had the strong impressions she was as frank as a Haloga, he took that for a good omen. The midwife went on, "She has been through this business a time or two, you know."

"Three, now," Maniakes corrected absently. "May I see her?" When it came to matters of the Red Room, even the Avtokrator of the Videssians asked the midwife's leave.

Zoïle nodded. "Go ahead. She'll be hungry, you know, and tired. I think Kameas has already gone to get her something." She pointed toward the baby Maniakes was still holding. "What will you name her, your Majesty?"

"Savellia," Maniakes said; he and Lysia had chosen the name not far into her pregnancy.

"That's pretty," Zoïle said, as quick and sharp in approval as in everything else. "It's the Videssian form of a Vaspurakaner name, isn't it?"

"That's right." The elder Maniakes spoke for his son, whose

command of the language of his ancestors was sketchy. "The original is Zabel."

"Forgive me, your highness, but I like it better in Videssian disguise," Zoïle said—no, she wasn't one to hide her opinions about anything.

Maniakes carried Savellia down the hall to the Red Room. The baby wiggled in the surprisingly strong, purposeless way newborns have. If he stepped too hard, it would startle his daughter, and she would try to throw her arms and legs wide, though the blanket in which she was wrapped kept her from managing it. Frustrated, she started to cry, a high, thin, piercing wail designed to make new parents do whatever they could to stop it.

She was still crying when Maniakes walked into the Red Room with her. "Here, give her to me," Lysia said indignantly, stretching out her arms but not rising from the bed on which she lay. She looked as exhausted as if she'd just fought in a great battle, as indeed she had. She didn't sound altogether rational, and probably wasn't. Maniakes had seen that before, and knew it would last only a couple of days.

He handed her Savellia. She set the baby on her breast, steadying the little head with her hand. Savellia didn't know much about the way the world worked yet, but she knew what the breast was for. She sucked greedily.

A serving woman wiped Lysia's face with a wet cloth. Lysia closed her eyes and sighed, enjoying that. Other maidservants cleaned up the birthing chamber. They'd already begun that before Maniakes got there. Even so, the place still had an odor to it that, like Lysia's worn features, put him in mind of the aftermath of a battle. It smelled of sweat and dung, with a faint iron undertone of blood he tasted as much as he smelled it.

Being here, smelling those smells—especially the odor of blood—also made him remember Niphone, and how she had died here. To put his fears to rest, he asked, "How do you feel?"

"Tired," Lysia answered at once. "Sore. When I walk, I'm going to walk all bowlegged, as if I've been riding a horse for thirty years like a Khamorth nomad. And I'm hungry. I could eat a horse, too, if anyone would catch me one and serve it up with some onions and bread. And some wine. Zoïle wouldn't let me have any wine while I was in labor."

"You'd have puked it up," the midwife said from the doorway, "and you'd have liked giving it back a lot less than you liked drinking it down."

She stood aside then, for Kameas came gliding into the Red Room, carrying a tray whose delicious aromas helped cover the ones that had formerly lurked in the birthing chamber. "Tunny in leeks, your Majesty," he said to Lysia, "and artichokes marinated in olive oil and garlic. And, of course, wine. Congratulations. Savellia—did I hear the name rightly?"

"Yes, that's right," Lysia said. The eunuch set the tray down beside her on the wide bed. She smiled at him. "Good. Now I won't have to eat the horse, after all." He looked confused. Maniakes hid a smile. Lysia went on, "Oh, and you've gone and cut everything up into little bite-sized bits for me. Thank you so much." She sounded on the edge of tears with gratitude. Maybe she was. For the next little while, her emotions would gust wildly.

"I am glad your Majesty is pleased," Kameas said. The Avtokrator wondered how he felt about being in the presence of new life when he could never engender it himself.

"Here." Maniakes sat down on the bed, carefully, so as not to jar Lysia. "Let me do that." He picked up the spoon and started feeding his wife.

"Well!" she said after he'd given her a few bites. "You're the one who's supposed to have beautiful slaves dropping grapes into your mouth whenever you deign to open it, not me."

"I'm afraid beautiful is rather past my reach," Maniakes said, "and it's too late in the year for fresh grapes, but if Kameas will bring me some raisins, I'll see what I can do for you."

Kameas started to leave the Red Room, no doubt on a quest for raisins. "Wait!" Lysia called to him. "Never mind. I don't want any." She laughed, which made her wince. "Aii!" she said. "I'm still very sore down there." Her eyes traveled to Savellia, who had fallen asleep. "And why do you suppose that is?"

Rhegorios, Symvatios, and the elder Maniakes made themselves visible in the hall outside the open door to the Red Room. Maniakes waved for them to come in. "Ha!" Rhegorios said when he saw his cousin feeding Lysia. "We've finally gone and run out of servants, have we?"

"You be quiet," Lysia told him. "He's being very sweet, which is more than you can say most of the time." Maniakes knew Rhegorios would give him a hard time about that in due course, but he couldn't do anything about it now.

"Are you all right?" Symvatios asked his daughter.

"Right now? No," Lysia answered. "Right now I feel trampled in every tender place I own, and every time I have a baby, I seem to discover a couple of tender places I never knew I did own before. But if everything goes the way it should, I will be all right in a few weeks. I don't feel any different from the way I did the first two times I went through this."

"Good. That's good," Symvatios said.

" 'Went through this,' eh?" the elder Maniakes rumbled. He nodded to his son. "Your own mother talked that way, right after she had you. It didn't keep her from having your brothers, mind you, but for a while there I wondered if it would."

Maniakes did his best to make his chuckle sound light and unforced. Even what was meant for family banter could take on a bitter edge, with one of his brothers in exile and the other likely dead. He went back to feeding Lysia. Rhegorios' teasing him about that would not bite so close to the bone.

Lysia finished every morsel of tunny and every chunk of artichoke heart. She also drank down all the wine. Maniakes wondered if she would ask Kameas for raisins, after all. Instead, she yawned and pulled Savellia off her breast and said, "Will someone please put the baby in a cradle for a while? I'd like to try to sleep till she wakes up hungry again. It's been a busy day."

Both grandfathers, her husband, and her brother reached for Savellia. She gave the new baby to Symvatios, who smiled as he held his granddaughter, then laid her in the cradle so gently, she did not wake.

"You could have a wet nurse deal with her," Maniakes said.

"I will, soon," Lysia answered. "The healer-priests and physicians say mother's milk is better for the first week or so, though. Babies are funny. They're tough and fragile, both at the same time. So many of them don't live to grow up, no matter what we do. I want to give mine the best chance they can have."

"All right," Maniakes said. She was right, too. But mothers were also tough and fragile, both at the same time. He leaned over and kissed her on the forehead. "Get what rest you can, then, and I hope she gives you some."

"She will," Lysia said. "She's a good baby." Maniakes wondered how she could tell. He wondered if she could tell. One way or the other, they'd find out soon enough.

Savellia was a good baby. She slept for long stretches and wasn't fussy when she woke. That helped Lysia mend sooner than she might have. The new princess' brothers and half brother and half sister stared at her with curiosity ranging from grave to giggly. When they realized she was too little to do anything much, they lost interest. "She doesn't even have any hair to pull," Likarios remarked, like a judge passing sentence.

"She will," Maniakes promised. "Pretty soon, she'll be able to pull yours, too." His son by Niphone—his heir, as things stood—looked horrified that anyone could presume to inflict such an indignity on him. Maniakes said, "She's already done it to me," which surprised Likarios all over again. "So did you, for that matter," the Avtokrator added. When a baby got a handful of beard . . . His cheeks hurt, just thinking about it.

Likarios went off. Maniakes watched him go. He plucked at his own beard. He'd wondered how Abivard would handle the problem of Denak's son by Sharbaraz. But Abivard was not the only one with family problems relating to the throne. Maniakes wondered what he'd do if Lysia ever suggested moving her sons ahead of Likarios in the succession. She never had, not yet. Maybe she never would. Succession by the eldest son born of the Avtokrator was a strong custom.

But strong custom was not the same as law. What if he saw young Symvatios, or even little Tatoules, shaping better than Likarios? He sighed. The answer suggested itself: in that case, when he hoped above all else for simplicity, his life would get complicated once more, in new and incalculable ways.

His mouth twisted. Parsmanios hadn't cared anything for the strong custom of rule by the eldest. That made a disaster for Parsmanios, and nearly one for the whole clan. It was liable to be as nothing, though, next to what could happen if his sons got to squabbling among themselves.

Later that day, he wondered if his thinking of Parsmanios was what made Kameas come up to him and say, "Your Majesty, the lady Zenonis requests an audience with you, at your convenience." The eunuch's voice held nothing whatsoever: not approval, not its reverse. Maybe Kameas hadn't made up his mind about Pars-manios' wife. Maybe he had and wasn't letting on, perhaps not even to himself.

"I'll see her, of course," Maniakes said.

Formal as an ambassador, Zenonis prostrated herself before him. He let her do it, where for other members of the family he would have waved it aside as unnecessary. Maybe he hadn't made up his mind about Zenonis, either. Maybe she was just tarred with Parsmanios' brush.

"What can I do for you, sister-in-law of mine?" he asked when she'd risen.

She was nervous. Seeing that was something of a relief. Had she been sure of herself, he would have been sure, too: sure he needed to watch his back. "May it please your Majesty," she said, "I have a favor to beg of you." She licked her lips, realized she'd done it, and visibly wished she hadn't.

"You are of my family," Maniakes answered. "If a favor is in my power to grant, you must know I will."

"I am of your family, yes." Zenonis licked her lips again. "Considering the branch of it I'm in, how you must wish I weren't."

Speaking carefully, Maniakes answered, "I have never put my brother's crimes on your page of the account book, nor on your son's. That would be foolish. You did not know—you could not have known—what he was doing."

"You've been gracious, your Majesty; you've been kind and more than kind," Zenonis said. "But every time you see me, every time you see little Maniakes, you think of Parsmanios. I see it in your face. How can I blame you? But the thing is there, whether you wish it or not."

Maniakes sighed. "Maybe it is. I wish it weren't, but maybe it is. Even if it is, it won't keep me from granting you whatever favor you ask."

"Your Majesty is also just." Zenonis studied him. "You work hard at being just." The way she said it, it was not altogether a compliment: mostly, but not altogether. She took a deep breath, then brought out her next words in a rush: "When spring comes and ships can cross the Videssian Sea without fearing storms, I want you to send my son and me to Prista."

"Are you sure?" Maniakes asked. Regret warred in him with something else he needed a moment to recognize: relief. That he felt it shamed him, but did not make it go away. Fighting against it, he said, "Think three times before you ask this of me, sister-in-law of mine. Prista is a bleak place, and—"

To his surprise, Zenonis laughed. "It's a provincial town, your Majesty, not so? All I've ever known my whole life long is a provincial town." She held up a hand. "You're going to tell me that, if I go, I can't come back. I don't care. I never set foot outside Vryetion till I came to Videssos the city. If I'm in Prista with my husband, that will be company enough."

Maniakes spoke even more carefully than he had before: "Parsmanios will have been in exile some little while by the time you arrive, sister-in-law of mine."

"He'll be the gladder to see me, then, and to see his son," Zenonis replied.

She didn't see what Maniakes was aiming at. Having been several years in Prista, Parsmanios was liable to have found another partner. Why not? He could hardly have expected his wife to join him, not when, up till this past summer, Vryetion had been in Makuraner hands. Maniakes got reports on his banished brother's doings, but those had to do with politics, not with whom Parsmanios was taking to bed. Maniakes expected he could find out whom, if anyone, Parsmanios was taking to bed, but that would have to wait till spring, too.

He said, "Don't burn your boats yet. If, when sailing season comes, you still want to do this, we can talk about it then. Meanwhile, you and your son are welcome here, whether you believe me or not."

"Thank you, your Majesty," Zenonis said, "but I do not think my mind will change."

"All right," he answered, though it wasn't all right. He was settled into being Avtokrator, too, and taken aback when anyone met his will with steady resistance. "Only remember, you truly can't decide now. If, come spring, you want to go to Prista, I will give you and your son a ship, and to Prista you shall go, and to . . . to my brother. But you and little Maniakes and Parsmanios will never come back here again. I tell you this once more, to make certain you understand it."

"I understand it," she said. "It gave me pause for a while, but no more. I am going to be with my husband. Little Maniakes is going to be with his father."

"If that is what you want, that is what you shall have," Maniakes answered formally. "I do not think you are making the wisest choice, but I will not rob you of making it."

"Thank you, your Majesty," Zenonis told him, and prostrated herself once more, and went away. Maniakes stared at her back. He sighed. He thought—he was as near sure as made no difference—she was making a bad mistake. Did he have the right to save his subjects from themselves, even when they wouldn't thank him for it? That was one of the more intriguing questions he'd asked himself since he took the throne. He couldn't come up with a good answer for it. Well, as Zenonis had time to think on her choice, so did he.

Courtiers, functionaries, bureaucrats, soldiers, and, for all Maniakes knew, utter nonentities who chanced to look good in fancy robes packed the Grand Courtroom. The Avtokrator sat on the throne and stared down the long colonnaded hall to the entranceway through which the ambassador from Makuran would come and make obeisance before him.

When Makuran and Videssos changed sovereigns, they went through a ritual, as set as the figures in a dance, of notifying each other. In the scheme of things, that was necessary, as each recognized only the other as an equal. What the barbarians around them did was one thing. What they did with each other was something else again, and could—and had—set the civilized world on its ear.

No hum of anticipation ran through the assembled Videssian dignitaries when the ambassador appeared in the doorway. On the contrary: the courtiers grew still and silent. They looked straight ahead. No—their heads pointed straight ahead. But their eyes all slid toward that small, slim figure silhouetted against the cool winter sunshine outside.

The ambassador came gliding toward Maniakes, moving almost as smoothly—no, a miracle: moving as smoothly—as Kameas. At the proper spot in front of the throne, he prostrated himself. While he lay with his forehead pressed against the polished marble, the throne rose with a squeal of gearing till it was several feet higher off the ground than it had been. The effect sometimes greatly impressed embassies from among the barbarians. Maniakes did not expect the Makuraner to be overawed, but custom was custom.

From his new altitude, the Avtokrator said, "Rise."

"I obey," Abivard's envoy said, coming to his feet in one smooth motion. His face was beardless, and beautiful as a woman's. When he spoke, in good Videssian, his voice was silver bells. He must have been gelded early in life, for it never to have cracked and changed.

"Name yourself," Maniakes said, continuing the ritual, though the ambassador had already been introduced to him in private.

"Majesty, I am called Yeliif," the beautiful eunuch answered. "I am come to announce to Maniakes Avtokrator, his brother in might, the accession of Abivard King of Kings, may his years be many and his realm increase: divine, good, peaceful, to whom the God has given great fortune and great empire, the giant of giants, who is formed in the image of the God."

"We, Maniakes, Avtokrator of the Videssians, vicegerent of Phos on earth, greet with joy and hope the accession of Abivard King of Kings, our brother," Maniakes said, granting Abivard the recognition Sharbaraz—who had claimed the Makuraner God was formed in *his* image—had consistently refused to grant him. "Many years to Abivard King of Kings."

"Many years to Abivard King of Kings!" the assembled courtiers echoed.

"Majesty, you are gracious to grant Abivard King of Kings the boon of your shining countenance," Yeliif said. However lovely and well modulated his voice, it held no great warmth. He spoke, not with Kameas' impassivity, but with what struck Maniakes as well-concealed bitterness. He was, of course, a eunuch, which certainly entitled any man—or half man—to be bitter. And his features, however beautiful, had the cold perfection of statuary, not the warmth of flesh.

"May we live in peace, Abivard King of Kings and I." That was also part of the ritual, but Maniakes spoke the words with great sincerity. Videssos and Makuran both needed peace. He dared hope they might find some small space of it.

Abivard King of Kings, he thought. The man who was, or could have been, his friend, the warrior who had made such a deadly foe, and now the ruler who had in the end chosen to reign in his own name, not that of his nephew, his sister's son by Sharbaraz.

That brought to mind another question: "What has befallen Sharbaraz the former King of Kings, esteemed sir?" the Avtokrator asked, giving Yeliif the title a high-ranking eunuch in Videssos would have had.

"Majesty, the God judges him now, not mortal men," Yeliif answered. "Not long before I set out for this city, his successor had his head stricken from his body." Was that regret? Yeliif had presumably been at court throughout Sharbaraz's reign. However little use most Makuraners might have had for Sharbaraz at the end, he might have been sorry to see his sovereign overthrown.

Well, Maniakes thought, *that's not my worry.* Aloud, he said, "I have gifts for you to take to Abivard King of Kings on your return to Makuran." That, too, was ritual.

But then affairs in Makuran became Maniakes' worry, for Yeliif broke with ritual by prostrating himself again. "Majesty, may it please you, I cannot return to Makuran, save only that my head should answer for it, as Sharbaraz's did for him," the beautiful eunuch said. "Abivard King of Kings sent me here not only as embassy but also as exile." He sighed, a wintry sound. "He was, in his way, merciful, having had it in his power to slay me out of hand."

"*I* won't slay you out of hand," Maniakes promised. "I'm sure I'll be able to learn a great deal about Makuran from you." *I'll squeeze you dry,* was what he meant. Yeliif nodded to show he understood and assented—not that he had much choice. Maniakes went on, "For now, esteemed sir, you may reckon yourself enrolled among the eunuchs of the palaces."

"Majesty, you are gracious to an exile," Yeliif said. "I shall have a great deal to say about everyone I know, I assure you."

"I'm sure you will," Maniakes said. "I'm sure you will." Betrayal was the coin with which the beautiful eunuch would buy his welcome in Videssos the city. Abivard must have known as much and exiled him anyhow, which was . . . interesting. And Yeliif did not have to have it spelled out for him. Maniakes studied the limpid dark eyes, the elegant cheekbones, the sculptured line of jaw. Though a man only for women himself, he recognized the danger in that loveliness. Yes, Yeliif would know about betrayal. And, of course, someone in Yeliif's early days had given him over to be castrated. What worse betrayal than that?

The Avtokrator bowed his head, signifying the audience was ended. Yeliif prostrated himself, rose, and backed away from the throne till he could turn around without showing disrespect. A great many eyes followed him as he withdrew from the Grand Courtroom.

* * *

"Yes," Yeliif said, "of course, the lady Denak was furious when Abivard chose to rule as King of Kings rather than as regent for Peroz, her son by Sharbaraz. Before that, she was furious with him for overthrowing Sharbaraz just when she'd finally gained influence over the then-King of Kings by bearing a son. Before that, she was furious with Sharbaraz for not giving her the influence she reckoned her due as principal wife." The eunuch sipped wine and nodded first to Maniakes and then to the secretary who was taking down his words for further study.

"And what of Sharbaraz?" Maniakes asked. "How did he take it when he learned Abivard was moving against him?"

"He bellowed like a bull." Yeliif's lip curled in scorn. "And, like a bull, he raged this way and that, neither knowing nor caring how he might best meet the threat before him, so long as he could bellow and paw the ground."

With a faint *scrape-scrape*, the secretary's stylus raced over the waxed surface of his three-leaved wooden tablet. Maniakes slowly nodded. He hoped Yeliif would take that for agreement and understanding. Both were there, but so was something else, something that grew with every conversation he had with the beautiful eunuch: wariness. The next complimentary word Yeliif said about anyone at the Makuraner court would be the first. What was in a way worse was that the eunuch didn't seem to notice he was casually savaging everyone he mentioned. His view was so jaundiced, Maniakes had trouble deciding how much reliance he could place in it.

Experimentally, the Avtokrator said, "And what of Romezan? He's a noble of the Seven Clans. How does he feel about serving a sovereign born a mere *dihqan*?"

"It's no great difficulty." Yeliif's gesture was elegant, scornful, dismissive. "Give Romezan something to kill and he's happy. It could be Videssians, it could be wild asses, it could be those who followed Sharbaraz. So long as he welters in gore, he cares not what gore it is." *Scrape-scrape* went the stylus.

"He fights well," Maniakes observed.

"He should. He's had practice enough. He'd fight himself, I daresay, till the bruises got too painful even for him to bear." Somehow, malice was all the more malicious when expressed in that sweet, sexless voice. If Romezan had practice fighting, Yeliif had the same in backbiting—but he'd never wounded himself.

"And Abivard?" Maniakes said.

"I warned Sharbaraz of him long ago," the beautiful eunuch said. "I told him Abivard had his eye on the throne. Did he heed me? No. Did anyone heed me? No. Should he have heeded me? Majesty, I leave that to you."

"Suppose Sharbaraz had got rid of him," Maniakes said—actually, he said *Sarbaraz*; here in the city, he didn't care if his accent was imperfect. "Who would have led Makuran's armies against us this past spring?"

Yeliif returned a perfect shrug. "Romezan. Why not? He might have done better, and could hardly have done worse—worse for Makuran, I mean, as he made quite a good thing for himself out of failure."

Such cynicism took the breath away, even for an Avtokrator of the Videssians. Coughing a little, Maniakes said, "I begin to see why Abivard doesn't want you coming back to Mashiz."

"Oh, indeed," Yeliif agreed. "I remind him of the time when the world did not turn at his bidding, when he was small and weak and impotent."

For a eunuch to use that particular word, and to use it with such obvious deliberation, was breathtaking in its own way. Maniakes got the idea Yeliif had done it to throw him off balance. If so, he'd certainly succeeded. "Er—yes," the Avtokrator said, and dismissed the exiled ambassador from Makuran.

"I thought you'd want to go on longer, your Majesty," the secretary said after Yeliif had gone.

"So did I," Maniakes said, "but I'd had about as much spite as I could stomach of an afternoon, thank you very much."

"Ah." The scribe nodded understanding. "You listen to him for a while and it does kind of make you want to go home and slit your own wrists, doesn't it?"

"Either your own or your neighbor's, depending on whom he's been telling tales about," Maniakes answered. He glanced over to the scribe in some relief. "You thought so, too, did you? Good. I'm glad I'm not the only one."

"Oh, no, your Majesty. Any milk of human kindness that one ever had, it curdled a long time ago." The secretary sounded very sure. But then, in meditative tones, he added, "Of course, losing your stones, now, that's not the sort of thing to make you jolly and ready for a mug of wine after work with the rest of the lads, is it?"

"I shouldn't think so," Maniakes said. "Still, I haven't known any of the eunuchs here to be quite so—" At a loss for words to describe Yeliif's manner, he gestured. The secretary nodded once more. Having heard the beautiful eunuch, he did not need to hear him described.

Maybe his beauty had something to do with the way he was, Maniakes thought. He would surely have been pursued at the court of Mashiz, very likely by men and women both, his loveliness being of a sort to draw and hold the eye of either sex. What had being the object of desire while unable to know desire himself done to his soul?

When the Avtokrator wondered about that aloud, the scribe nodded yet again. But then he said, "The other chance is, your Majesty, you don't mind my saying so, he might be a right bastard even if he had his balls and a beard down to here and a voice deeper than your father's. Some people just are, you know."

"Yes, I had noticed that," the Avtokrator said sadly. He dismissed the scribe: "Go have yourself a cup of wine, or maybe even two." The man left with fresh spring in his step. Watching him go, Maniakes decided to have a cup of wine himself, or maybe even two.

When Kameas started to prostrate himself before Maniakes, the Avtokrator waved for him not to bother. To his surprise, the eunuch went through the full proskynesis anyhow. To his greater surprise, he saw a bruise on the side of Kameas' face when the vestiarios rose. "What happened?" Maniakes asked. "Did you walk into a door, esteemed sir?"

"Your Majesty," Kameas began, and then shook his head, dissatisfied with himself. He took a deep breath and tried again: "Your Majesty, may I speak frankly?"

"Why, yes. Of course, esteemed sir," Maniakes answered, thinking that might have been the most unusual request he'd ever had from a court eunuch. He wondered whether Kameas *could* speak frankly, however much he might wish to do so.

By all appearances, such unwonted effort wasn't easy for the vestiarios. But then, after touching his bruised cheek, Kameas seemed to steady on the purpose for which he had approached the Avtokrator. He drew in another deep breath and said, "No, your

Majesty, I did not walk into a door. I received this . . . gift at the hands of another of your prominent servitors."

At the hands of another eunuch, he meant, *prominent* being the next step below *esteemed* in their hierarchy of honorifics. Maniakes stared. Eunuchs' squabbles were commonly fought with slander, occasionally with poison, but . . . "Fisticuffs, esteemed sir? I'm astonished."

"So was I, your Majesty. I must say, though," Kameas added with a certain amount of pride, "I gave as good as I got."

"I'm glad to hear it," Maniakes said. "But by the good god, esteemed sir, what on earth set you and your colleagues to boxing one another's ears?" That sort of display of bad temper was a vice of normal men upon which eunuchs usually looked with amused contempt.

"Not *what*, your Majesty, *who*," Kameas replied, his voice going surprisingly grim. "The reason I have come before you, the reason I am violating propriety and decorum, is to request that you—no, to beg that you—find some way of removing this serpent of a Yeliif from the palaces, before it comes to knives rather than fists. There. I have said it." It couldn't have been easy for him, either; his breath came in little gasps, as if he'd forced his fat frame to run a long way.

"What on earth has he done, esteemed sir, to make you ask something like that only a couple of weeks after he got to the city?"

"Your Majesty, that Makuraner eunuch is a snake with a skin of honey, so that, his bite being at first sweet, one does not feel the venom till too late. He has, in the little space of time you named, set all who dealt with him in any way at odds with one another, playing with the imperial eunuchs as cat plays with mouse, making some hate the rest—" Kameas touched his cheek again. "—and every one of us suspect everyone else. Had Skotos risen from the eternal ice—" Kameas and Maniakes both spat. "—he could have worked no greater mischief among those who serve."

"What is he up to?" Maniakes asked. "Does he think that, by sowing discord, he'll make me want to supplant you as vestiarios? If he does, esteemed sir, believe me, he's mistaken."

"Your Majesty is gracious." Kameas bowed. "In point of fact, though, I would doubt that. As best I can see, Yeliif stirs up hatreds for no better reason than that he enjoys stirring up hatreds. It being winter, there are no flies whose wings he can pull off like a small, nasty boy, so he torments the servitors around him instead."

That was franker speech than Maniakes had ever imagined from Kameas. "We'll get to the bottom of this," he assured the vestiarios. "Summon the esteemed Yeliif. I will not condemn him without hearing what he says in his own behalf."

"Guard your ears well against his deceits, your Majesty," Kameas said, but he went off happier than he had approached the Avtokrator.

As they had been whenever Maniakes saw him, Yeliif's manners were impeccable. After prostrating himself with liquid grace, he inquired, "In what manner may I serve you, Majesty?"

"I am told," Maniakes said carefully, "you may have something to do with the recent discord among the palace eunuchs here."

Yeliif's large, dark eyes widened. He looked convincingly astonished. "I, Majesty? How could such a thing be possible? I am but the humblest of refugees at your court, beholden to you for all the many kindnesses you have been generous enough to show me. How can you imagine I would so repay that generosity?"

"Considering the way you talk about everyone you knew back in Mashiz, esteemed sir, I must tell you these reports don't altogether astonish me," Maniakes said. "The next good word you have for anybody will be the first."

The beautiful eunuch shook his head in vigorous disagreement. "Majesty, like so many others, you misunderstand me. I speak nothing but the truth, the plain, unvarnished truth. If this pains people, am I at fault?"

"Maybe," Maniakes said. "Probably, in fact. Have you ever known anyone who prides himself on what he calls frankness but only uses that frankness to tear down those around him, never to build them up?"

"Oh, yes," Yeliif replied. "I have suffered at the hands of such scorpions many times—and now, it would seem, again, or why would you have called me before you to tax me with these baseless calumnies?"

Had Maniakes been listening to Yeliif in isolation, he might well have been convinced the beautiful eunuch was telling the truth. He was convinced Yeliif thought he was telling the truth. Musingly, he said, "One measure of a man is the enemies he makes.

Among yours, esteemed sir, you seem to number both Abivard King of Kings and my vestiarios, the esteemed Kameas."

"They are prejudiced against me," Yeliif replied.

"It may be," Maniakes said. "It may be. Nevertheless . . ." Unlike Yeliif, he was not so frank as to declare that he trusted Abivard and Kameas' opinions further than those of the beautiful eunuch. Instead, still in musing tones, he went on, "Perhaps we would all be better served if you were to take a position somewhat removed from the contentious air of the palaces."

"I do not believe this to be in any way necessary," Yeliif said, more than a little asperity in that bell-like voice. After a moment, he realized he'd gone too far. "You are, of course, the sovereign, and what pleases you has the force of law."

"Yes." Maniakes drove that point home before turning conciliatory. "The post I have in mind is in no way dishonorable. I have received word that the city governor of Kastavala died of some illness this past summer. I think I shall send you there, complete with a suitable retinue, to take his place. Kastavala, you should know, is the capital of the province of Kalavria, where my father served as governor before I became Avtokrator."

"Ah." Yeliif bowed. "That is indeed a post of honor. I thank you, Majesty; I shall do everything in my power to ensure you have no cause to regret the trust you repose in me."

"I'm sure I won't," Maniakes answered. Being a Makuraner, Yeliif would not be overfamiliar with the geography of Videssos, especially that of the eastern portions of the Empire. Maniakes hadn't lied, not in any particular. He also had not mentioned that Kalavria was the easternmost island under Videssian rule: the easternmost island under anyone's rule, so far as anyone knew. No ship had ever sailed out of the east to Kalavria. No ship sailing east from Kalavria had ever came back. Once Yeliif went east to Kalavria, he was not likely to come back, either. Maniakes didn't think he would have any cause to regret that.

"Since this is a position of such importance, I do not think it should long remain vacant," the beautiful eunuch said. "If, Majesty, you are serious about entrusting it to me—" He made it sound as if he did not truly believe that. "—you will send me to it forthwith, permitting no delays whatever."

"You're right," Maniakes said, to Yeliif's evident surprise. "If you can be ready to depart from the imperial city tomorrow, I shall

ave an armed escort to convey you to Opsikion, from which
lace you can take ship to Kastavala."

"Take—ship?" Yeliif said, as if the words weren't any part of
he Videssian he'd learned.

"Certainly." Maniakes made his voice brisk. "It's too far to swim
rom Opsikion, and the water's much too cold for swimming this
ime of year, anyhow. I dismiss you now, esteemed sir; I know
you'll have considerable packing to do, and you'll need an early
start tomorrow, with the days so short now. Thanks again for your
willingness to fill the post on such short notice."

Yeliif started to say something. Maniakes turned away from
him, signifying that the audience was over. Trapped in the web of
court etiquette, the beautiful eunuch had no choice but to withdraw.
From the corner of his eyes Maniakes noted Yeliif's expression. It
was more eloquently venomous than any of his sweet-sounding
words.

Kameas came into the audience chamber a few minutes later.
"Is it true, your Majesty? The island of Kalavria?" Maniakes nodded. The eunuch sighed. His kind might not know physical ecstasy,
but this came close. "From the bottom of my heart, your Majesty, I
thank you."

"You *thank* me," Maniakes demanded, "for doing *that* to poor,
sleepy, innocent Kastavala?"

Avtokrator and vestiarios looked at each other for a moment.
Then, as if they were two mimes taking the same cue, they both
began to laugh.

Midwinter's Day dawned clear and cold. The cold had nothing
to do with why Maniakes would sooner have stayed in bed. "There
was a time," he said in wondering tones, "when I used to look forward to this holiday. I remember that, but I have trouble making
myself believe it."

"I know what you mean," Lysia said. "No help for it, though."

"No, not when you're the Avtokrator," Maniakes agreed. "One
of the things by which the city mob judges you is how well you
can take the flaying the mime troupes give out." That they had
extra reason to flay him because he was wed to Lysia went without
saying. His wife who was also his cousin understood that as well
as he did.

"As long as we're not in the Amphitheater, we can try to enjoy the day," she said, and Maniakes nodded.

"Well, yes," he admitted. "The only trouble with that is, we have to be in the Amphitheater a good part of the day."

"But not all of it." Lysia sounded determined to make the best of things. The past few years, that had been Maniakes' role, with her reluctant to go out in public. But now she tugged at his arm. "Come on," she said.

He came, then suddenly stopped. "I know what it is," he said. "You're so glad you can be up and about after you had Savellia anything but the inside of the imperial residence would look good to you."

"I suppose you're right," she said. Then she stuck out her tongue at him. "So what?" She pulled him again. This time, he let himself be dragged along.

When he and Lysia left the hypocaust-heated residence, breath puffed from their mouths and noses in great, soft-looking clouds of fog. Frost glittered on the dead, yellow-brown grass of the lawns between buildings. As if to fight the chill, a big bonfire blazed on the cobbles of the path leading east toward the plaza of Palamas.

A crowd of palace servants and grooms and gardeners, plus a leavening of ordinary city folk in holiday finery, stood around the fire. Some huddled close, spreading out their hands to warm them. Then a laundress dashed toward the flames, long skirts flapping about her ankles. As she leapt over the bonfire, she shouted, "Burn, ill-luck!" She staggered when she landed; a groom in a gaudy tunic caught her around the waist to steady her. She repaid him with a kiss. His arms tightened around her. The crowd whooped and cheered and offered bawdy advice.

Lysia's eyes sparkled. "Anything can happen on Midwinter's Day," she said.

"I know what that fellow hopes will happen," Maniakes answered. He tilted Lysia's face up to his for a brief kiss. Then he made his own run at the bonfire. People shouted and got out of his way. He leapt. He soared. "Burn, ill-luck!" he shouted. All over Videssos the city, all over the Empire of Videssos, people were leaping and shouting. Priests called it superstition and sometimes inveighed against it, but when Midwinter's Day came, they leapt and shouted, too.

The sound of determined running feet made Maniakes look back.

Here came Lysia, her shape shifting oddly when seen through the heat-ripples of the fire. "Burn, ill luck!" she shouted as she sprang. Making sure nobody beat him to it, Maniakes eased her landing. "Why, thank you, sir," she said, as if she'd never seen him before. The crowd whooped again when he gave her another kiss. The suggestions they called were no different from the ones they'd given the groom and laundress.

Arm in arm, Maniakes and Lysia strolled toward the plaza of Palamas. An enterprising fellow had set up a table with a big jar of wine and several earthenware cups. Maniakes glanced toward Lysia, who nodded. The wine was no better than he'd expected it to be. He gave the wineseller a goldpiece. The fellow's eyes went big. "I'm s-sorry, your Majesty," he said, "but I can't change this."

"Don't be foolish," Maniakes told him. "It's Midwinter's Day. Anything can happen on Midwinter's Day." He and Lysia strolled on.

"Phos bless you, your Majesty," the wineseller called after him. He smiled at Lysia. He hadn't heard that in the city, not often enough.

Lysia must have been thinking along with him, for she said, "After that, it seems a shame to have to go on to the Amphitheater."

"It does, doesn't it?" the Avtokrator said. "No help for it, though. If I don't sit up there on the spine and watch the mime troupes mocking me, half the city will think I've been overthrown and the other half will think I ought to be. I rule every day of the year but one, and I can't—or I'm not supposed to—complain about what goes on then. Anything can happen on Midwinter's Day." Now he gave the saying an ironic twist.

The plaza of Palamas, out beyond the palace quarter, was packed with revelers—and with winesellers, foodsellers, and harlots to help them enjoy themselves more . . . and, no doubt, with cutpurses and crooked gamblers to help them enjoy themselves less. Maniakes and Lysia leapt over several more fires. No one cursed them. Maniakes saw a couple of priests in the crowd, but one was falling-down drunk and the other had his arm around the waist of a woman who was probably not a lady. The Avtokrator shrugged and kept on toward the Amphitheater. He supposed even priests deserved a day off from holiness once a year.

People streamed into the Amphitheater, the enormous soup bowl of a building where horse races were held through most of the year. Just before Maniakes and Lysia got to the gate through which on most days, the horses entered, the Empress let out an indignant squeak. "Someone," she said darkly, "has hands that need a lesson in manners, but, in this crowd, to the ice with me if I know who." She sighed in something approaching resignation. "Midwinter's Day."

"Midwinter's Day," Maniakes echoed. Men had no shame during the festival. For that matter, neither did women. A fair number of babies born around the time of the autumnal equinox bore no great resemblance to their mothers' husbands. Everyone knew as much. Remarking on it was bad form.

Kameas, Rhegorios, the elder Maniakes, Symvatios, Agathios the patriarch, assorted courtiers and functionaries, a squad of Imperial Guards in gilded mail and scarlet cloaks, and the full twelve imperial parasol-bearers stood waiting by the gate. Rhegorios patted Kameas on the shoulder. "There. You see, esteemed sir? I told you they'd be here."

"They had no business wandering off on their own and leaving me to fret," the vestiarios said petulantly, giving Maniakes a severe look.

"Anything can happen on Midwinter's Day—even an escape from ceremonial," the Avtokrator said. Kameas shook his head, plainly disagreeing. He would have his way now; Maniakes was caught in the net once more. With a gesture more imperious than any to which the Avtokrator could aspire, Kameas ordered the procession into the Amphitheater.

The crowd in there fell silent for a moment, then burst into loud cheers, knowing the day's main entertainment was about to begin. Maniakes' father and Lysia's both drew prolonged applause; they'd made themselves popular in the city. So did Rhegorios, who was popular wherever he went. Marching along behind the parasol-bearers, Maniakes knew a moment's jealousy. Had Rhegorios wanted to usurp his place, he probably could have done it.

Then, Lysia beside him, the Avtokrator strode out into full view of the crowd. He was braced for the curses and jeers to come cascading down on the two of them, as they had on Midwinter's Days past. And there were curses and jeers. He heard them. But, to his delighted astonishment, a great torrent of cheers almost drowned them out.

Lysia reached out and squeezed his hand. "We've finally man-aged it, haven't we?" she said.

"Maybe we have," Maniakes answered. "By the good god, maybe we have."

Behind the parasol-bearers, they stepped up onto the spine of the Amphitheater. The Avtokrator's seat, set in the center, had a special property: a trick of acoustics let everyone in the enormous structure hear the words he spoke there. The converse was that he heard, or thought he heard, all the racket inside the Amphitheater, every bit of it seeming to be aimed straight at him. Sitting in that seat, he sometimes wondered if his head would explode.

When he held up his hand for quiet, he got . . . a little less noise. After a bit, he got still less, and decided that would have to do. "People of Videssos the city!" he called, and then, taking a chance, "My friends!" No great torrent of hisses and catcalls rained down on him, so he went on, "My friends, we've been through a lot together these past few years, and especially this past summer. The good god willing, the hard times are behind us for a while. In token of that, and in token of Phos' sun turning once more to the north after this day, let us rejoice and make merry. Anything can happen on Midwinter's Day!"

The applause almost took off the top of his head. He had to lean away from the exact focus of sound to save his ears. Then the first troupe of mimes swaggered out onto the race track. The frenzied cheers they got made what he'd received seem tepid by comparison. His grin was wry. That showed him where he stood in the hearts of the city—better than ever before, but still behind the entertainment.

He knew that would slip if he didn't at least look amused at every skit the mime troupes presented, regardless of whether it was aimed at him. The first one wasn't: it showed Etzilios fleeing up to Kubrat like a dog with its tail between its legs, and pausing to relieve himself as he went. It was crude, but Maniakes was glad enough to laugh at any portrayal of an old foe's discomfiture.

The next skit seemed to be about tavern robberies. The crowd ate it up, though it went past Maniakes. "That happened while you were in the westlands," his father said.

After that troupe came several men with shaved faces, one of whom set about poisoning the others and stabbing them in the back.

Kameas and the rest of the eunuchs on the spine of the Amphi theater laughed themselves silly over that one. Yeliif was already on the way to Opsikion. Maniakes doubted he would have been amused. The Avtokrator wondered how much the eunuchs had paid the mimes to get them to cut off their beards for their roles.

Another skit suggested that Sharbaraz, rather than thinking himself the God incarnate, thought he was the ecumenical patriarch, a dignity the mummers reckoned much more impressive. What he did when he discovered the patriarch had to be celibate made Agathios wince and giggle at the same time. Everyone was fair game on Midwinter's Day.

A new troupe came on and presented the spectacle of the Kubrati monoxyla being sunk and going up in flames. The mimes really did set one of their prop boats on fire, then leapt over it as if it were a good-luck blaze out on the plaza of Palamas.

Yet another troupe had a boiler boy obviously supposed to be Abivard trying to decide whether he should put on robes like those of the Videssian Avtokrator or the Makuraner King of Kings. When he decided on the latter, the mime who had been wearing the Videssian getup chased him around the track, to the loud delight of the crowd. Maniakes leaned over to Lysia and said, "I wish it had been that easy."

"Everything is easy—if you're a mime," she answered.

Maniakes thought he and Lysia would get away scot-free, but one mime troupe did lampoon them—and Agathios, too, for good measure. Glancing over at the patriarch, Maniakes saw him fume. That made it easier for the Avtokrator to sit and pretend he enjoyed the insults that made the city mob chortle.

But his good mood was quite restored when, in the next—and last—skit, he realized the nasty little man who kept getting kicked back and forth between mimes dressed as Videssians and others intended to be Makuraners, neither side wanting him, was Tzikas. The crowd laughed louder at that than they had at the lewd skit skewering him.

And then it was over. He got cheers when he dismissed the crowd: cheers, no doubt, from many of the people who'd jeered him during the mimes' mockery a few minutes before. He moved away from the seat at the acoustical heart of the Amphitheater and said, "That wasn't too bad—and now it's over for another year."

"Phos be praised!" Lysia said. "But you're right; it wasn't too

ad." As they were making their way out of the great arena behind
he parasol-bearers, she asked, "What do you want to do now?"—
heir ceremonial duties for the day were over.

He slipped his arm around her waist. "I know it's a *little* early
after Savellia was born, but it *is* Midwinter's Day. People will be
oo busy looking for their own good times even to think of bothering us," Maniakes said hopefully.

"Maybe." Lysia didn't sound as if she believed that, but her arm
went around his waist, too. Together, they walked through the
plaza of Palamas and the palace quarter, back toward the imperial
residence.

DEL REY® ONLINE!

The Del Rey Internet Newsletter...

A monthly electronic publication e-mailed to subscribers and posted on the rec.arts.sf.written Usenet newsgroup and on our Del Rey Books Web site (www.randomhouse.com/delrey/). It features hype-free descriptions of books that are new in the stores, a list of our upcoming books, special promotional programs and offers, announcements and news, a signing/reading/convention-attendance calendar for Del Rey authors and editors, "In Depth" essays in which professionals in the field (authors, artists, cover designers, salespeople, etc.) talk about their jobs in science fiction, a question-and-answer section, and more!

Subscribe to the DRIN: send a message reading "subscribe" in the subject or body to drin-dist@cruises.randomhouse.com

The Del Rey Books Web Site!

We make a lot of information available on our Web site at
www.randomhouse.com/delrey/

- all back issues and the current issue of the Del Rey Internet Newsletter
- sample chapters of almost every new book
- detailed interactive features of some of our books
- special features on various authors and SF/F worlds
- ordering information (and online ordering)
- reader reviews of upcoming books
- news and announcements
- our Works in Progress report, detailing the doings of our most popular authors
- bargain offers in our Del Rey Online Store
- manuscript transmission requirements
- and more!

If You're Not on the Web...

You can subscribe to the DRIN via e-mail (send a message reading "subscribe" in the subject or body to drin-dist@cruises.randomhouse.com), read it on the rec.arts.sf.written Usenet newsgroup the first few days of every month, or visit our gopher site (gopher.panix.com) for back issues of the DRIN and about a hundred sample chapters. We also have editors and other representatives who participate in America Online and CompuServe SF/F forums and rec.arts.sf.written, making contact and sharing information with SF/F readers.

Questions? E-mail us...

at delrey@randomhouse.com (though it sometimes takes us a little while to answer).

✎ FREE DRINKS ✎

Take the Del Rey® survey and get a free newsletter! Answer the questions below and we will send you complimentary copies of the DRINK (Del Rey® Ink) newsletter free for one year. Here's where you will find out all about upcoming books, read articles by top authors, artists, and editors, and get the inside scoop on your favorite books.

Age _____   Sex ❑ M ❑ F

Highest education level: ❑ high school ❑ college ❑ graduate degree

Annual income: ❑ $0-30,000 ❑ $30,001-60,000 ❑ over $60,000

Number of books you read per month: ❑ 0-2 ❑ 3-5 ❑ 6 or more

Preference: ❑ fantasy ❑ science fiction ❑ horror ❑ other fiction ❑ nonfiction

I buy books in hardcover: ❑ frequently ❑ sometimes ❑ rarely

I buy books at: ❑ superstores ❑ mall bookstores ❑ independent bookstores
   ❑ mail order

I read books by new authors: ❑ frequently ❑ sometimes ❑ rarely

I read comic books: ❑ frequently ❑ sometimes ❑ rarely

I watch the Sci-Fi cable TV channel: ❑ frequently ❑ sometimes ❑ rarely

I am interested in collector editions (signed by the author or illustrated):
   ❑ yes ❑ no ❑ maybe

I read Star Wars novels: ❑ frequently ❑ sometimes ❑ rarely

I read Star Trek novels: ❑ frequently ❑ sometimes ❑ rarely

I read the following newspapers and magazines:
❑ *Analog*	❑ *Locus*	❑ *Popular Science*
❑ *Asimov*	❑ *Wired*	❑ *USA Today*
❑ *SF Universe*	❑ *Realms of Fantasy*	❑ *The New York Times*

Check the box if you do not want your name and address shared with qualified vendors ❑

Name _____
Address _____
City/State/Zip _____
E-mail _____
                                        turtledove

PLEASE SEND TO: DEL REY®/The DRINK
201 EAST 50TH STREET NEW YORK NY 10022
OR FAX TO THE ATTENTION OF DEL REY PUBLICITY 212/572-2676

HOW FEW REMAIN

The dramatic new novel by
HARRY TURTLEDOVE
The Master of Alternate History

In 1862, key Confederate orders nearly fell into Union hands. But those orders were saved, the Rebels swept into Pennsylvania, smashed the Army of the Potomac, and assured Southern independence.

A generation later, America writhed once more in the throes of battle. Furious over the annexation of key Mexican territory, the U.S. again declared war on the Confederacy, and in 1881 the fragile peace was shattered.

This new war was fought on a lawless frontier where the blue and gray battled not only each other but the Apache, the outlaw, and even the redcoat. For along with France, England entered the fray on the side of the South.

Out of this tragic struggle emerged historic figures. A disgraced Abraham Lincoln crisscrossed the nation championing Socialist ideals. Cocky Theodore Roosevelt bickered with George Custer. Confederate General Stonewall Jackson again soared to the heights of military genius, while the North struggled to find a leader who could prove his equal.

Thanks to such journalists as Samuel Clemens, the nation witnessed the clash of human dreams and passions in this, a Second War Between the States.

Published by Del Rey Books.
Available at a bookstore near you.

THE GREAT WAR: AMERICAN FRONT

The stunning sequel to *How Few Remain*
by Harry Turtledove

1914. As Europe is engulfed in the fires of World War I, the United States and the Confederacy, bitter enemies for five decades, enter the fray on opposite sides. The USA, led by President Theodore Roosevelt, aligns with the newly powerful Germany, while the Confederates, under Woodrow Wilson, join forces with their longtime allies, Britain and France.

For both sides, this fight will be different from any other—a war fraught with global consequences, and waged with the chilling innovations brought about by the dawning modern age: the machine gun, the airplane, and poison gas. The terrible bloodshed will take place all across the North American continent.

The events of *How Few Remain*—the Confederate victory and the subsequent division of America—set the stage for this extraordinary epic of the first World War as it might have been. THE GREAT WAR: AMERICAN FRONT begins a chronicle in which Harry Turtledove will create a vast, vibrant canvas, blending actual events and players with a brilliantly reinvented history. This unforgettable, deeply moving, and superbly original novel is a masterpiece of imagination and another triumph for its acclaimed creator, the recognized Master of Alternate History.

Published by Del Rey® Books.
Available in bookstores everywhere.
Visit us at www.randomhouse.com/delrey/althist

HARRY
TURTLEDOVE

Published by Del Rey® Books.
Available in your local bookstore.